Most people know the story of the Mutiny on the *Bounty*: Fletcher Christian and his cohorts take over HMAV *Bounty* in the early morning hours of 28 April 1789, put the captain, Lieutenant William Bligh, into a boat with eighteen of his loyal officers and men, and sail the ship back to Tahiti to reunite with their island "wives" and friends. Leaving sixteen mutineers on the island by their own choice, Christian and nine British sailors, along with a handful of islanders, quickly depart Tahiti, feeling they would be too vulnerable to discovery because of the island's well-known location and its accessibility to ships sailing the Pacific. Those who had stayed behind in Tahiti lived happily, for a time, among their native friends. Even knowing they would most likely be discovered, they established families and strong ties to their native hosts.

When told of the mutiny by Captain Bligh, the shocked Admiralty would not, *could* not, let this heinous crime go unpunished. They sent HMS *Pandora*, an armed frigate, to the Pacific to capture the mutineers and return them to England for court-martial and hanging.

When Fortune Frowns is the story of that mission; the preparations, the outbound voyage, finding the mutineers, and another epic small boat voyage following the shipwreck on a reef. Carefully researched and well-told by noted maritime author William H. White, this little-known story closes the final chapter of one of the most infamous mutinies in maritime history.

BY THE SAME AUTHOR

The War of 1812 Trilogy:

A Press of Canvas (2000)

A Fine Tops'l Breeze (2001)

The Evening Gun (2001)

The Greater the Honor – A novel of the (1803) Barbary Wars (2003)

In Pursuit of Glory (2006)

All available from Tiller Publishing

www.tillerbooks.com

WHEN FORTUNE FROWNS

by William H. White

Cover art © Paul Garnett
Author photo © William H. White, Jr.
Artist photo © Paul Garnett

Graphic design and production by:
Scribe, Inc., 842 S. 2nd St., Philadelphia, PA 19147

Printed in the USA by:
Victor Graphics, 1211 Bernard Drive, Baltimore, MD 21223 USA

Questions regarding the content of this book should be addressed to:

TILLER Publishing
605 S. Talbot Street, Suite Two
St. Michaels, Maryland 21663
410-745-3750 • Fax: 410-745-9743
www.tillerbooks.com

ACKNOWLEDGMENTS

Few who write historical books, whether novels or non-fiction, stand alone. Others lend their time and expertise with research, knowledge, and helpful criticism. I would be quite remiss were I not to thank those kind souls who so willingly gave me time, knowledge, and help. They covered four countries on both sides of the world and were unstinting in responding to my queries, both in person and by email. I list them below, with my heartfelt thanks.

IN ENGLAND

National Maritime Museum Archives:

Liza Verity, Information Specialist, who provided almost every shred of information the National Maritime Museum held in its extensive library on the subject.

Royal Navy Museum Archives:

Allison Wareham, BA (Hons), FCLIP, Librarian & Head of Information Services at the Royal Navy Museum, HM Naval Base in Portsmouth. Ms. Wareham provided me the original log of *Pandora*, the "fine-hand" copies of the court-martial of Edward Edwards, his original sailing orders, and a myriad of original documents. She allowed me to photograph them which was an enormous time-saver.

IN AUSTRALIA

Peter Gesner, Sr. Curator Maritime Heritage, Museum of Tropical Queensland, Townsville, Queensland, Australia. For a behind the scenes look at recovered artifacts, allowing me to photograph them, information about the ship and her crew, and a tour of the *Pandora* section of the Museum. He was also the head diver/archaeologist in the recovery efforts of *Pandora* and spent some considerable time detailing the amazing accomplishments of his team.

IN FRENCH POLYNESIA (TAHITI)

There were too many people to mention specifically by name, but the local tour guides, monument attendants, and members of the general population were all most helpful in showing me Matavai Bay, Point Venus, and surrounds. Most of the local people were well aware of the story of the mutiny and quite knowledgeable about the local lore surrounding it.

IN THE UNITED STATES OF AMERICA

James Bourque, friend, gentleman, and man of letters for his help with the story layout and format of telling this tale.

Rob Holt and **Danny Adkins** for a read of the early manuscript and their encouragement, as well as their suggestions, which have undoubtedly improved the readability of the story, and, at least in Rob's case, because of a great deal of whining about why he hadn't made the acknowledgments in previous books where he provided similar courtesies.

Burt Logan, President of USS Constitution Museum in Boston, MA, used his extensive contacts in England to provide me access to the necessary museum staff in that country.

Joe Burns, friend and long-time supporter of my work, used the skills gained as a copy-writer to offer improvements and corrections to what I thought was a final draft of the manuscript.

William Martin, the New York Times best-selling author, for his encouragement to write the story of *Pandora* and the *Bounty* mutineers.

Paul Garnett, renowned maritime artist, friend, and authority on the *Bounty/Pandora* story, for his superb cover illustration of *Pandora* foundering off Australia. And for his vast knowledge and collection relative to the entire affair, from the conversion of *Bounty* from a collier to Bligh's command all the way to the trial and hanging of the mutineers.

James Nelson, noted author of maritime fiction and non-fiction, and **Louis Norton**, PhD, noted author of scholarly works in the field of maritime history, for their willingness to read the typescript and offer complimentary comments for the dust jacket, at some risk to their reputations!

I have to add to this list two men, long dead, who had the foresight to set down the story as it happened and immediately thereafter.

Bosun's Mate James Morrison and **Surgeon George Hamilton** both kept journals which were subsequently published and offered differing and often conflicting viewpoints (one a mutineer, and one in *Pandora*) of the events depicted here. Their efforts provided much of the detail which would not otherwise have been available. I owe them a debt of gratitude.

PROLOGUE

By the commissioners for
Executing the office of Lord High
Admiral of Great Britain & Ireland.

"Whereas, by an order from the late Board of Admiralty, dated the 16th of August 1787, Lieutenant William Bligh was appointed to command His Majesty's Armed vessel the Bounty, and by instructions from the said Board, dated the 20th of November following, was directed to proceed in that vessel to the Society Islands in the South Seas, in order to procure and transport from thence to some of the British Possessions in the West Indies, Bread Fruit Trees and other useful plants, the product of said islands.

"And whereas the said Lieutenant Bligh sailed from Spithead, on the 23rd of December following, in prosecution of his destined Voyage, and, by letter to our Secretary dated at Coupang (a Dutch settlement in the Island of Timor) on the 10th of August 1789, acquainted us that the said vessel, on her return from Otaheite with a large cargo of those plants in a very flourishing state, had been violently & forcibly taken from him on the 28th of April preceding, by Fletcher Christian, who was Mate of her and Officer of the Watch, assisted by others of the inferior officers and men, armed with muskets and bayonets; and that he (the said Lieutenant Bligh) together with the Master, Boatswain, Gunner, Carpenter, Acting Surgeon, and others of her crew (being nineteen in number, including himself) were forced into the Launch and cast adrift ten Leagues to the South West of Tofoa, the North Westernmost of the Friendly Islands, without firearms and with a very small quantity of Provisions and Water; and that having landed at Tofoa, and been beat off by the Natives with the loss of one of his Party, he bore away for New Holland and Timor, and on the 15th of June following, arrived at Coupang abovementioned, distant twelve hundred leagues from the place where the vessel was seized as aforesaid; from whence he and those who survived are now returned to England."

". . . On your arrival at Otaheite, and not finding the abovementioned armed vessel there, you are to endeavor to get the best information possible respecting her; carefully observing yourself, and strictly charging your officers and Crew, to avoid saying anything in regard to the cause of the Enquiry, until you shall have discovered whether the Inhabitants of the said Island have a knowledge of Lieutenant Bligh's having been dispossessed of her, as, abovementioned; where she is, and whether any of the Mutineers are on that Island.

"If you shall find that the Mutineers, or any of them, are on the Island of Otaheite, you are, the first moment it shall be in your power, to detain such Chiefs as you may be able to get hold of, and then, declaring the object of your voyage, and immediately appointing a strong Party, well armed, to go in quest of the Mutineers, require assistance, and Guides to direct the said party where to find them."

". . . Having so done, and not finding them at any of the abovementioned Islands, you are to proceed to Anamoka Road in the Friendly Islands (touching at Palmerstone's and the other Islands in the way) and pursue the like means for finding them; and, having succeeded or failed, in your endeavors for that purpose, proceed on your return to England, through Endeavor's Straits which separate New Guinea from New Holland; passing to the Southward of Java, into Princess Island in the Straits of Sunda, and as in this route the prevailing winds are to be attended to, it is necessary that you should remember that the Changes of the Monsoons, amongst the Islands to the Westward of Java and about Endeavor's Straits, are about May and November; there being no dependence (of which we have any certain knowledge) to passing the Straits after the month of September or beginning of October, altho' it may perhaps be accomplished in the month of November."

". . . In case you are so fortunate as to fall in with the abovementioned Armed Vessel and Mutineers, or any of them, you are to put on board such of your officers, Petty Officers and Foremastmen as you can best spare, [who] you shall judge best qualified and most to be depended upon, to navigate her to England, furnishing her with such stores and provisions, from the Ship you command, as may be necessary for that purpose; And you are to keep the Mutineers as closely confined as may preclude all possibility of their escaping, having however, proper regard to the preservation of their lives, that they may be brought home to undergo the Punishment due their Demerits."

". . . Given under our hands the 25th October, 1790

To
Edward Edwards Esq.
Captain of His Majesty's Ship
Pandora

At Spithead
By command of their Lordships."

****

Passages from the Sailing orders to Captain Edwards for the
voyage to the South Seas in pursuit of *Bounty*'s mutineers.

CHAPTER ONE

Whatley, England

*C*aptain Edwards! I had heard of him and, from the stories, thought him to be a hard man and known to have no tolerance for failure of any stripe! But it's an assignment, what you've been begging the Admiralty for these past three years. No matter that the vessel is only a sixth rate of twenty four guns. She's a frigate! Not the lumbering three-decker you served most of your midshipman years in during the late war with the Colonials in America. And surely not the mud and filth of the farm!

Those thoughts rattled through my mind in different order and sometimes in different words from the moment I received the letter from the Admiralty appointing me third lieutenant in His Majesty's Ship *Pandora*, a sixth rate frigate, which I would find in Portsmouth in a fortnight.

I had found a home in the Royal Navy during the War of Revolution in America, serving as a midshipman in *Egmont*, a seventy-four gun, lumbering, creaky, old bucket that sailed like a haystack, often making more leeway than headway. She had been embarrassed by a near mutiny the year before I joined her, but sailed off to the North American station in 1780, prepared to take on whatever showed above the horizon, assuming she might sail fast enough to catch them! For ten years—since just prior to my sixteenth birthday—I had served His Majesty, though not all at sea. Rather my sea service had spanned, so far, something a trifle beyond seven years. I had spent the past three years ashore and, in light of the paucity of my finances, I had, when I received the dreadful news of my exile from the sea, made straight away for my parents' small farm near the town of Exeter, struggling along on a bare subsistence and the meager offerings of my family as I wrote a steady stream of letters to the Admiralty requesting an assignment.

My sojourn ashore had nothing to do with my competence as a naval officer. Indeed, after serving my six years as midshipman, I stood for my examination for lieutenant in front of none other than Captains Collingwood, Jervis, and Smith, each of who congratulated me on my splendid performance. No, sadly, my almost three years ashore were occasioned by a lack of need and my lack of seniority in the Service. With the American War of Revolution over and done with and France and Spain not worrisome, there was no longer the need for our fleet to remain at the ready; any number of vessels, from three-deckers to bomb ketches, had been put in ordinary and their crews either reassigned to short-handed vessels destined to remain at sea, or sent ashore. I fell into the latter group.

I knew, in the spring of 1790 when Spain's monarch drew the attention of King George with a stance decidedly belligerent, that the fleet would rebuild in short order. I redoubled my efforts to find a berth suitable to a lieutenant who had received the notice of Collingwood and his associates. After some six months, the letter directing me to report to Post-Captain Edwards in HMS *Pandora* caused me no small amount of joy. The thoughts that the ship was a small one, would most likely see no action, and be ruled by a hard commander all fell by the wayside as I gave free rein to my relief and joy. There would be no boring blockade duty, watching the comings and goings of the Spanish fleet, for me! The very thought of what would be our assignment stirred my blood: the Admiralty had determined to send *Pandora* into the Pacific to recapture Lieutenant William Bligh's ill-starred command, HMAV *Bounty* and bring home to stout English gallows the piratical mutineers who had stolen the ship.

My parents, Rebecca and John Ballantyne, my older brother, Jason, and my little sister, Elizabeth, were all delighted at this grand turn of fortune. Many an evening they had endured my lamentations of neglect by the Admiralty and patiently sympathized with my frustration. I am quite sure their joy at my assignment stemmed not only from my own exhilaration, but also from the respite they would receive from my ceaseless ranting!

It was on the outskirts of Whatley, a farming hamlet near Exeter, that my parents had tended a small crop of grains and some sheep since before even my older brother was born. Hard work and some measure of luck provided a warm and loving home for their family, but most of the niceties were quite beyond their financial capabilities. And, while my initial departure for service meant one less hand to help with the chores, it also meant one less mouth to feed and body to clothe. I suspect that my current imminent departure held a similarly mixed sentiment.

Father and Jason helped me, as I hurried about, purchasing what minor articles I might need from the local shops. Mother and Elizabeth lovingly folded and stowed all my necessaries carefully in my sea chest, along with a few thoughtful parting gifts with which they hoped to surprise me. Then I was off, hasty good-byes after hugs and admonitions to "take good care" and "be strong, Son" filling the air and repeated as the cart, carrying my belongings, myself, and my father, creaked along behind their tired plow horse. Soon we were far enough in the offing to no longer be able to hear their good wishes, but, turning in my seat, I could still make out, highlighted before low-flying and threatening clouds, the three miniscule shapes with raised arms as they stood beside the muddy track which would turn into a more passable road only on the outskirts of Exeter.

The busy town, with shops, taverns, iron mongers, and every manner of convenience swallowed us up with nary a hiccup; there was every form of conveyance clogging the streets, together with people pushing their way through the throngs as they hurried along on one or another important errand. As the coach I would take for Portsmouth was already loading its passengers and their dunnage, we, my father and I, had little time for a lengthy good-bye; a brief hug, a smile from him, and a squeeze on my shoulder were followed by words much the same as those my sister, brother, and mother had offered only a few hours before.

"Edward," he said quietly as he helped me pull my sea chest from the cart, "do try to be careful. I worry about those pirates you're sent to fetch, what with them already having took over one ship."

"I will do my best, Father. And do not concern yourself with them taking over *Pandora*; I suspect Captain Edwards might have a thought or two about that." I smiled hopefully at him as I pushed the chest up to the coachman on the roof, where it would remain, protected to some degree from the elements by an oiled tarpaulin, while I rode in the cramped and jolting passenger compartment for the ride to Portsmouth.

From my seat in the coach, I watched as my father gave me a final wave and turned to mount the cart, whistling up the horse as he did so.

The journey and my uncomfortable seat quickly became even more trying and disagreeable; the cold rains that had fallen with distressing frequency for much of late October and into November had returned, no less diminished, and beat unmercifully on the roof and sides of our conveyance. The side curtains in the coach leaked badly, blowing out with the gusty wind, and with each blast of the cold breath of Aeolus, the unlucky soul sitting in the outboard seat received a baptism from the elements. After several of these soakings, the gentleman who had chosen that seat beseeched me to surrender my seat in the middle, claiming he suffered from the ague. To add credence to his claim, he offered a lusty round of hacking and wheezing, nose blowing and sniffling to which I ultimately succumbed and, with great jostling and "excuse-me's," we exchanged places. I draped my boat-cloak over me on the windward side, which kept most of the rain from becoming little more than an irritation, and tried to fall asleep, unsuccessfully.

"It's a naval officer ye are, lad?" My new friend, the one with whom I had exchanged seats, dug an elbow into my ribs just in case I had not heard his question.

I rallied myself from the near state of sleep I had attained to answer.

"Aye, I am that, sir." And closed my eyes in an attempt to forestall further conversation.

"Planning on pickin' up yer ship when we gets up to Portsmouth, I'd warrant, eh lad?"

"Aye, sir. I am that." I kept my eyes closed . . . to no avail.

"Well, that's a wonderful thing, it is. What ship would that be, lad? Or is it you're just hopin' to find one what might have a berth for a young chap of your stripe?"

"I'm assigned in HMS *Pandora*, sir."

"I am surprised to see you in officer's rig, lad. Seem a mite on the young side to me. Just promoted, then, are ye? Or p'rhaps a bit of interest in certain circles in London?"

"No, sir. I stood for lieutenant about four years ago. And I have no person in London or anywhere else looking after me, I assure you!" I looked at my inquisitor, somewhat miffed that he would think I must have political interest to advance my career and hopeful that he might leave me alone for a bit.

"Don't know of *Pandora*, Lieutenant. What kind of ship would she be? Mayhaps a small schooner or might she be tender to one of our fine ships of the line?" Apparently my look missed the mark or he had perfected persistence to an exquisite level.

"No, sir. She would be a frigate." I did not add "of the sixth rate." No sense in feeding his need to minimize my assignment.

"Oh my! A *frigate* she is. Of course! How lovely for you. A coveted and choice assignment, I'm sure. You must fancy yerself lucky indeed!" He smiled engagingly at me, suggesting that perhaps his words were not meant to be sarcastic.

"I am most pleased to be assigned in her. Thank you." *Now may I at least try to get some sleep?*

Again, I closed my eyes and let my head fall back against the hard cushion of the seat back. Perhaps I had satisfied his curiosity and need for chatter. Silence. I could sense my watch, hidden in my waistcoat pocket, counting off the seconds: tick, tick, ti . . .

"Reckon yer likely to be headin' down toward Spain and teach them Dons a thing or two. Heard only a bit ago that Lord Howe was outfittin' the fleet for a proper response to 'em. Aye, take yer *frigate* down there and let 'em know it ain't wise to get King George riled up. You teach 'em proper, lad." His enthusiasm, patriotism, and now, even some respect, offered a different tenor to his comments.

"No, sir. We'll be heading to the Pacific Ocean straight away with orders to recapture HMS *Bounty* and return to England the pirates that took her, for a speedy trial and hanging."

"Well now, there's a plum assignment, what? I recall readin' about that mutiny. Must have been last March or April. Something about the commander and a clutch of his sailors being set to sea in a ship's boat and sailing it all the way back to England. What a story, it was!"

"Yes, Captain Bligh returned to England in March of this year, but not in the open boat. He sailed that to Timor, an amazing journey in itself—it was nearly twelve hundred leagues he sailed—and found English ships to bring him and his men the rest of the way." I could not help but smile at his rendition of Bligh's epochal journey.

A particularly sharp gust of wind blew in the window, carrying the cold rain into our midst. I busied myself for a few minutes trying to adjust the curtain to avoid a recurrence and, when I turned back to my new companion, he appeared to be asleep, something to which I aspired.

As the coach moved farther and farther from the city and modern roads, our driver became unable to maintain his pace. The same rains, which had earlier upset my friend and then soaked me, had raised the devil with the roads. Those unpaved tracks over which we traveled had become mired and barely passable, as the rain, in various manifestations from desultory drizzle to thrashing downpour, continued with a perversity born only of a divine antagonist, for very nearly the entire journey to Portsmouth.

I began to fret, wondering that should I be sufficiently detained, Captain Edwards would surely sail without me. I checked my watch with increasing frequency and uttered a few well-chosen words, silently, to the Almighty, that He might get me into Portsmouth in a timely fashion. I need not have worried; I had two full days left before *Pandora* would sail and I knew well, from my wartime experience, that many details can conspire to delay even the most carefully organized departure.

With a burst of speed inspired, I am sure, by both the improved road and the close proximity of our destination, the coach, quite covered in mud, bounced into Portsmouth and pulled up to a public house, which served as both terminal and hostel. The stiff-jointed, weary, and disheartened passengers clambered down and, trying to avoid the larger of the puddles that surrounded us, dragged their baggage through the steady rain into the tavern. I followed.

The atmosphere within assaulted one's senses; smoke from the pipes and cigars of those already ensconced, the greasy, black emanations from the lanterns which gave off an anemic yellow light that extended barely six feet from the lantern itself, and the overpowering aroma of spilt spirits and ale all conspired to make my stomach churn and roil. Chairs, some on less than the full complement of legs, stood drunkenly at scuffed and scarred tables that likely had long been forsaken by the attention of a rag-wielding barman. A handful of patrons, obviously having sought shelter from the weather some time before, had used their idle time to the advantage of the publican, sampling his wares with abandon. They looked up when we entered, roused from their drunken stupors by the commotion of our arrival. Their bleary, half-closed eyes took in our forms, apparently without comprehension, and quickly returned to their previous endeavors: dozing or struggling to guide unsteady hands to half empty tankards.

My fellow travelers dragged their burdens to the more solid looking tables and settled themselves, apparently for the remainder of the night. My eyes, smarting from the noxious atmosphere, and my stomach continuing to churn, caused me to back out of the doorway to take stock of my immediate future. Clearly, the few rooms available in this establishment were already taken and I did not fancy sitting in the taproom in a rickety chair for the remainder of the night, as apparently my companions from the coach would do. After barely a moment's consideration, I made my choice: I would lug my sea chest out and seek lodging elsewhere, despite the lateness of the hour.

I hoisted my chest to my shoulder and, during a brief respite from the rain, staggered around a corner from the coach stop/hostel/public house. Half way down a narrow alley I espied a lantern, its light making strange reflections in the mists, which lit a sign proclaiming that rooms were available within. I stepped off the cobblestoned street, into the alley, and directly into a large puddle. I uttered a silent oath and struggled to maintain my balance. My boot made a sucking sound as I extracted it from the sticky mud beneath the several inches of water and pressed on toward my destination. My entry awakened a grizzled gent who had been dozing behind his desk and he groggily agreed to rent me quarters for the balance of the night. The room—more aptly a large wardrobe—cost me a pretty penny given the lateness of the hour, the inclement conditions without, and the greed of the innkeeper within. But take it I did and, inspired by my profound exhaustion, barely managed to undress myself before falling into a dead, dreamless sleep on the lumpy and well used bed.

After what seemed mere minutes, but was surely more sleep than I could expect at one time over the coming year, I awoke. Save for when at sea, I had always been slow to manage the swim from the depths of sleep to full wakefulness. My inner being must have heard the siren call, as this morning, I was instantly alert; one moment I was in dreamless sleep and the next, quite wide-awake. It could only have been my eager anticipation for what the day held that caused my slumber to end so abruptly and buoyed me to a joy I had not experienced for some three years! Had any soul been present to witness me fairly leaping from the bed, filled with exhilaration, he surely would have been hard put to attest to my sanity, especially on such a dismal day.

The rain of last night, now reduced to a mere drizzle, left tiny rivulets coursing down the panes of my window, further distorting the image beyond the glass. The view of the muddy street, running with rain and who-knew-what else, seemed less disheartening when viewed through the distortion of poorly crafted, and now wet, glass. Nor had the dawn, delayed by the low gray clouds, brightened the scene sufficiently to make out any detail, but having trod the same path only the night before, I knew well what was out there.

I turned away from the window to put a flame to the room's solitary candle and, as the wick caught and gradually filled my small quarters with a weak, flickering light, I took in the single chair and chest-of-drawers which, with my sea chest, filled that portion of the room not occupied by my bed. I shook my head silently as I recalled the princely sum I had paid for this lowly habitation, but at least, it had been dry!

Even the thought of trading these austere accommodations for the cramped and often shared living spaces, where I would reside for the next year and more, did little to dampen my excitement. I could scarcely contain my smile as I stripped off my nightclothes and made my morning ablutions.

I broke my fast with a bowl of tasteless porridge and coffee that left me gasping for breath. I barely noticed.

Stepping to the street where, mercifully, the heavens had wrung the final bit of moisture from the heavy clouds leaving mud and large puddles as testimony to the vigor of the storm, I found a ragged urchin eager to make a coin. After a brief negotiation, he agreed to fetch a barrow and haul my chest 'round to the quay in His Majesty's Dock Yard, where I hoped I would find *Pandora*. I stood in wait only a few minutes before he was back, barrow in hand, and off we went, the youngster leading the way with a sprightly step and me following behind, each of us doing our best to avoid the deepest of the puddles and the largest of the muddy deposits. In the cool air of the damp morning, steam rose in elegant, diaphanous wisps from the frequent piles of manure deposited by the dray horses that had recently passed this way. In spite of the lad's eager starting pace, our progress, once out of the alley, became slowed, hampered as we were by carts, horses, humanity, and the mud. I hoped the boy toting my chest was familiar with the streets and alleys he followed and we would eventually discover the Dock Yard and my new home.

"As I live and breathe! Edward Ballantyne, it is, and in the flesh!"

I stopped and turned around, halting my staggering porter with a word. The boy seemed to welcome a pause in his struggles with the barrow through the tracks and ruts made by heavily laden drays and at once, dropped into the barrow, seating himself in the scant space not occupied by my chest. As I studied the throngs to determine who might have called out my name, I noticed a large man, ample belly straining at the waistcoat buttons, unruly whiskers down each side of his ruddy face, lieutenant swab perched on his left shoulder, who was hurrying toward me, waving a meaty hand aloft. When he called out again, with a voice that would carry to weather in a full gale, I recognized one with whom I had shared the cockpit in the old *Egmont* and waved in greeting.

"Mister Corner! What a surprise to see you, sir. Are you assigned to a ship here? Or are you seeking employment?" I waited as he came right up to me and extended his hand in greeting.

"Aye, Edward. I have seen some of the poor souls casting about the waterfront with the hopes of finding a suitable berth. But not me, nor you, I'd warrant! Assigned as second, I am, in *Pandora* and under Edward Edwards, a commander tough as nails and mean as a cat. And it is my understanding that you as well are to be with us." He smiled as he spoke, perhaps belying his grim description and even his concern at being in the ship. Or perhaps it was the happy thought that we would again be shipmates.

"What a pleasant coincidence then, sir, to meet up with you. I am heading for the Dock Yard even now, hoping to find our worthy vessel with a berth close in, per chance, even in a slip. I would imagine she's loaded out and sailing shortly?" I was still concerned about the possibility that I might be late in reporting.

"Aye. Waiting on a few stores and our timepiece, but ready to sail on the tide within a day or so. And you may desist with the 'sir' nonsense. We shared more than two years of our midshipman days in that old bucket, *Egmont*, on the North American Station. Just because I was a wee bit senior and got to the gunroom afore ye does not warrant formality of that stripe. We'll just carry on as Robert and Edward then, as we'll be shipmates again, if it suits. No call for such formality among friends and former shipmates, especially ashore. Aboard, well . . . I needn't tell you. You've got enough time at sea to know the ropes, I'd warrant!" He stopped for a moment, the grin growing on his broad face. Then, grasping my arm in a vice-like grip, continued.

"Great it is to see you, again, Edward, and to know we'll be sailing together. I always thought you would do well and here you are!" He smiled broadly, his face becoming even redder with the effort.

A look of concern fleeted across his face. "I collect you've got the word on our assignment?"

"Aye, I am given to understand we are being sent out to recapture *Bounty* and those rascals that put Bligh and eighteen other hapless souls overboard."

Corner's expression returned to the broad smile that had earlier graced his corpulent visage. "That's it, precisely, and grand it is! South Seas, warm waters, and all those lovely islands—and ladies! I am told they are most scantily clad and show little concern for it!"

"Aye, sir . . . I mean, Robert. But I wonder how much time we might have to enjoy the wonders of 'all those lovely islands' and their citizens. Who knows where those scoundrels might have gotten to by now. And what of *Bounty*? How do you think Cap'n Edwards proposes to find the ship in the vastness of the entire Pacific Ocean? There is no telling where she might be." Without waiting for an answer, I rushed on, inquiring how much my former shipmate knew of the events that had caused us to, once again, become assigned in the same vessel.

"Have you seen the narrative Mister Bligh just published?" I suspected he had not as it was only recently out and I had only heard about it myself, but determined I was to lay hold of a copy.

I had read the newspaper accounts of Lieutenant Bligh's court martial and the terrible travail he and his men must have experienced. A miracle he had endured the experience, I thought!

Aloud, I offered, "And that wretch, Christian! What a scoundrel! Leading the crew like that in a mutiny! The shame for his family. That's one deserves to swing for his crime, I'll tell you!" I was well and truly horrified at the whole affair.

"Couldn't agree more, lad. And I ain't seen Mister Bligh's account, but did manage to read what the newspapers had to say. Most o' them agreed with you, as well." With that, he dismissed my youthful outrage, knowing, I am sure, that there would be ample time at sea to discuss and dissect every exciting and horrifying detail.

He stopped, sniffed the air, and looked around him. His next words brought us to more immediate matters.

"Since you mentioned you are headin' for the barky even now, I collect you might be glad to know one of our boats is in and waitin' alongside the pier. For me, in fact! A sixth rate like *Pandora* ain't likely to be assigned a mooring at the pier—not when all them three-deckers are fittin' out!"

I nodded and smiled. He went on, the perpetual smile still in place.

"I've a brief errand ashore here for Mister Larkan—he'll be our first lieutenant, you know—and then I'll be back on the quay quick as ever you please. Ye'll find the jolly boat 'bout halfway out the double dock in the slipway there on the larboard side. Past the mast pond, ropewalks, and the sail loft. Cox'n's name is Wisdom. Tell him who ye are, and that ye'll be joinin' me for the ride out. Long ride it is, and a wet one, I'll warn ye now, Edward. So have yerself a bit of a rest and I'll be back directly! Grand thing it is, to know ye'll be sailin' with us." He turned abruptly and strode off, his sword banging against his knee and his backside rolling like a crank ship in a seaway.

"Well, lad. Let us move along. Your rest is done. You heard the man: past the mast pond, rope walks, and sail loft, and halfway down the double dock on the larboard side. Off we go, then." I spoke to the boy who had spent the time while Corner and I talked unmoving in the barrow next to my sea chest.

He sighed mightily, but scrambled out, and picked up the handles with a grunt. Being familiar with the layout of the Royal Dock Yard, the boy seemed to have figured out that we had farther to go than I had thought. Off we went, dodging passersby, carts, some pulled by men, others by horses, and huge drays hauling great loads of supplies to feed the insatiable appetite of a navy that would swallow them up and not even a hiccup to show for it. I had overheard a conversation at my morning meal (if such could be called an actual meal) between two officers who debated the merits of sending the entire fleet Lord Howe had assembled to convince the Spanish of the error of their ways. France, apparently, had become an ally of Spain and, according to one of my unwitting informants, this was sufficient cause in itself to send the fleet to Biscay! In the short period I had been in Portsmouth, I had learned thirty ships of the line, nine frigates, and a plethora of smaller ships would make up Howe's fleet. But not *Pandora*!

Then it occurred to me that this armada would make it difficult indeed for our needs to be met and I wondered whether Captain Edwards had managed to organize the myriad of necessities, not only for our use, but also to refit *Bounty*, should it be required.

"Ye'll be wantin' to turn here, yer worship." The boy interrupted my thoughts of supplies.

He had set the barrow down and was pointing down a narrow alleyway. Following his outstretched arm, I saw, through the great wooden gates, which stood wide open, stone buildings lining both sides of a broad, cobbled, thoroughfare which appeared to be choked with carts, wagons, and the materials necessary to a great fleet. While I gaped, the boy set off, causing me to hurry along in his wake.

Down the alley we stepped, through the huge gates alongside a heavily laden wagon, and into the headquarters of the Royal Navy in Portsmouth. I paused, trying to get my bearings, locate the double dock where Corner had said I would find his waiting boat, and take in the awe inspiring sight of the huge yard. Between the stone buildings, which lined the boulevard immediately ahead, I could make out open-sided wooden sheds, holding great sections of masts on racks, and, well beyond them, the top-hampers of several first- or second-rate ships. A great bustle of activity seemed to be everywhere; not only was the entrance road jammed, but the narrow paths and alleys were even more clogged with heavy drays, carts, men, and equipments. It occurred to me, briefly, that the throngs of people I had seen earlier, both in Exeter and in Portsmouth proper, without the Dockyard gates, paled in comparison to the activities before me.

We made our way past a large mast pond to the right and a smaller one to the left, crossing between them on a stout wooden bridge. Three more stone buildings appeared ahead of us.

"What are those buildings, there, lad?"

"Why sir, those'd be warehouses where the Navy keeps its stores—ropes, spars, and like enough, them hogsheads o' fine Jamaica inta the bargain. Never been inside, but copped me a peek once or twice, I done, afore I got meself chased, that is. Yes, sir!" He laughed aloud at the recollection of his derring-do.

I smiled as well, amused that this child, this slip of a boy, had used the sailor's term for rum, but took care not to show it.

"Hmmm. I would imagine the docks might be over in that direction, then?" I pointed to our left where I had noticed the upper works of several vessels.

"Oh sir, yes. Right yonder there, yer worship might see topmasts showin' beyond that far building. There's a couple of three-deckers right there at the dock, there is, sir!" He smiled enthusiastically, hoping, I'm sure, that his information and guiding services would merit more than the pittance I had promised him for hauling my chest.

On we marched, the boy pushing his barrow with a bit more enthusiasm than he had earlier shown, and me trying to take in everything I saw, record it in my mind, and understand how it all worked together in spite of the apparent chaos which seemed manifest everywhere. We passed the ropewalk next to a line of smaller stone-constructed buildings in which I could see, through their open doors, neatly stacked coils of raw hemp waiting to be twisted into cables and lines for the fleet. A familiar smell assaulted my nostrils; after moment, I identified it as Stockholm tar, heating in great cauldrons for later application to the cables which would become shrouds and stays for the ships.

It's all coming back; the smells, the language, the hustle and bustle of a busy yard. Like coming home again!

We dodged midshipmen, each of whom dutifully saluted me as we passed, sailors, some of whom saluted, and draymen and 'longshoremen, all busily loading wagons, negotiating for stores, yelling at one another, or simply getting in the way, but mostly ignoring our passing or, should they have noticed us, shooting angry looks in our direction. As we passed, I could see inside the open door of one building; great coils of rope, big around as a man's thigh and destined, I was certain, to become anchor cables for some of Lord Howe's three deckers, spars of every description, all orderly and stacked like so much cord wood, and bulky piles of canvas which seemed, in the gloom within, to give off their own brightness, so white was the material. No hogsheads of "good Jamaica" though, in spite of my helper's earlier prognostication, were visible!

We eventually made our way through this teeming, chaotic hive of activity and emerged into a clearing of sorts on the left hand where I espied several slips, each containing warships in various stages of readiness: some had only their lowers up; others showed topmasts and some, appearing quite ready for sea, had yards crossed and sails bent onto the spars. Hopefully, I eased a bit to the left, but my guide and porter corrected my course.

"No, sir. Not down that way; likely to find yer boat yonder, near the boat pond, just there, sir." He pointed ahead to where I could make out a waterway cut into the very heart of the yard.

"Did not Lieutenant Corner mention something about a 'double dock', and a 'slipway', lad? I heard nary a mention of a 'boat pond'."

"Heard little of yer conversation, sir. But if'n I were seekin' a boat here in the Dock Yard, I'd have a look in the boat pond; that's where all the little boats're kept." He kept marching ahead, speaking over his shoulder to me.

"Well, my recollection is the slipway next to the double dock it was that he said. We will check there first, unless, of course, it is beyond the boat pond. Carry on."

"Already passed the double dock, yer worship. Boat pond's just there." Again he pointed. "But if it's back to the double dock you wish, then back it is." He had stopped, set down the barrow, and was clearly waiting for me to make up my mind.

I looked again at where he had pointed out the boat pond, then turned around and tried to guess where we might find the double dock Corner had mentioned.

"We will follow Lieutenant Corner's direction." I decided.

With an audible sigh, the boy picked up the handles and jockeyed the borrow about as I stepped off, heading back the way we had just come.

Aloft, I noticed patches of bright sky that could only signal a clearing and respite from the dreadful weather of the past several weeks. I took it as an omen, favoring our forthcoming departure with good fortune. Beyond the warehouses and lofts, I espied the great fleet, which would be sailing under Admiral Lord Howe. There seemed more ships than I could count, each bobbing and pulling at its moorings, seemingly eager in their own right to be off on suitable commissions.

Suddenly, I became aware that the boy, his barrow, and my chest had disappeared; I could no longer hear them behind me, bouncing over the cobblestones. My sightseeing was done for now, as I turned about, seeking a glimpse of the lad and my possessions.

Where could he have got to, the little rascal?

Then his diminutive form appeared beyond a throng, having turned off the broad road toward the water. Ahead of him, I could see the inboard end of what must be the double dock, immediately next to a slipway. He had slowed his pace, either sensing that I was still skylarking, awestruck by the organized chaos and enormity of the yard, or becoming weary of pushing his barrow and my chest. I hurried to catch up to him, remembering that, in spite of my three years of forced abstinence, I was still a naval officer and had better look like one instead of a visitor from some landlocked place, gawking at the sights!

The pier, between the dock and slipway grew wider as we moved down its length, until it seemed as far from one side to the other as it might be from the poop to the jib boom of a second- or third-rate ship. With the greater span, larboard to starboard, the people, wagons, and materiel seemed less dense and the boy and I made short work of the trip to where Robert Corner had told me I would find *Pandora*'s boat.

When I judged we were midway down the quay, I called a halt to our miniscule convoy and made my way to the larboard edge. With the tide at ebb, the water seemed a long way down, but I could espy no boat bobbing alongside. Nor, for that matter, any sign of steps leading down to the water, surely a requisite for disembarking from a small boat.

Perhaps it will be farther along towards the channel. All I have to do is find the stairs and there, I'd wager, will be the boat; Robert could surely not have gotten his bulk to the pier less he used the steps!

"No boat here, lad. We'll just work our way along the side here. Bound to be right along this way, as Mister Corner mentioned. Shouldn't be long now, and you'll be on your way a bit richer than when I found you." I didn't add, but thought, *and a good bit wearier!*

Fifty yards farther down the quay, I spotted a clutch of sailors sporting among themselves, apparently with little to occupy their time. A boat crew, perchance? As I approached them, whatever game they had been playing stopped and they studied the boy, the barrow, and me as we approached them.

"Are you seekin' *Pandora*'s boat, sir?" A lanky lad, his uniform awry— perhaps from their idle amusements?—stood to a casual attention and offered an equally casual salute.

"I am, indeed." I spoke as I returned his salute, doffing my hat. "Would you be Cox'n Wisdom?"

"How could you know my name, sir? I am he, without a question." His confederates, now also standing to attention, echoed the startled look he offered. I noticed the cox'n seemed to stand a bit straighter as well.

"No mystery, Cox'n, I assure you." I laughed in spite of myself. "I am assigned as third lieutenant in *Pandora*, Wisdom, and I happen to have crossed tacks with your boat officer, Mister Corner, a few moments ago, who suggested I might find you here and that, upon his return, we would ride out to the ship together. I am Lieutenant Ballantyne.

"Perhaps you might have a couple of your lads, here, relieve my young helper of his burden so he can be on his way." I pointed at the boy who had been watching the brief exchange with a dull expression.

As I produced the promised money for his assistance, his expression changed to one of interest and he stuck out a small hand, filthy, and calloused beyond his years, to receive it. The several coins that made up his compensation disappeared to his pocket in a flash and I smiled my acknowledgment of his profuse thanks while one of Wisdom's seamen picked up my chest. Pushing his now empty barrow with a sprightlier step than I would have thought he possessed, he disappeared up the pier almost as quickly as had my money from his hand.

With seemingly little effort, a strapping fellow with bulging forearms slung my chest onto his shoulder, climbed down the weed and slime covered stone stairs to the boat, missing not a step along the way, and gently deposited it in the bow. He rummaged about for a moment, then produced a piece of canvas with which he proceeded to cover the chest. I remembered Robert had mentioned it would be a wet ride, and long, out to the roadstead where *Pandora* was anchored, and was grateful for this small act of thoughtfulness.

"Thank you, sailor. I appreciate your covering the chest. I understand from Lieutenant Corner that the ride out might be a trifle wet."

"Aye, sir. A sure wager, that'll be! *Pandora's* well out yonder, and with the chop in the harbor, I'd warrant we'll all be some wet by the time we're hove alongside." Wisdom smiled ruefully, clearly not relishing the long pull out to the frigate.

As it would be inappropriate for a lieutenant in His Majesty's Navy to stand about skylarking with the boat crew (though, so glad I was at being back among seafaring men, I could easily have joined their frolic!), I wandered off, down the quay, studying the ships arrayed before me in the anchorage. A partially rigged three-decker occupied one side of the double dock to my starboard and, having taken its measure quickly, decided the fleet held much more interest. I stood at the end of the slipway, carefully gazing at the impressive show of England's might.

Which would be Pandora? *Surely a great number of frigates out there. A pity I can not determine which is to be my home!*

It was barely half an hour by my watch before one of the sailors in the boat crew cleared his throat behind me. When I turned, he saluted crisply.

"Lieutenant Ballantyne, sir. Lieutenant Corner has returned and requests that you attend him at the boat."

"Very well. I shall be right along."

As I walked back toward the land-side of the quay, I could clearly make out Corner's ample form in the midst of his sailors. He noticed my approach at the same moment, took a few steps in my direction, and in his booming voice, offered a greeting from a dozen and more paces.

"Well, Mister Ballantyne, I see you have successfully discovered where Wisdom hid our boat." He paused, his perpetual smile in place, and peered, through eyes squinting with an inner mirth, over the edge of the pier before resuming, "I would collect that one of these kind souls has had the bloody decency to stow your chest and cover it with some canvas. Right good, fellows. But of little avail, I fear. 'twill be likely only a trifle less damp than were we to swim to the barky and drag your chest along behind! Har Har!" He let forth with a booming laugh that, for a moment, caused all conversation near at hand to cease.

To Wisdom he said, "See if you might find a suitable place, safe and dry for this wee parcel, Cox'n. Wouldn't do to get the ship's timepiece drownded afore it even gets aboard."

After watching carefully as the lanky sailor stowed, with loving care, the canvas wrapped parcel, Corner looked about him and, seeing nothing that caught his interest, spoke to the crew. "Let's get us a move on, chaps. Can't stand around skylarkin' on the quay all day. Got an hour an' more just to get out to the ship—more if the tide's already turned. Cap'n and Mister Larkan will jolly well be unimpressed should we take longer than they think we ought to. And *that* would not a good way for Mister Ballantyne to start out at all!" This last, clearly an afterthought designed to hurry along our crew, caused me to glance sharply at my new messmate.

"How could they be upset by when I reported in to the ship, Robert? They don't even know when I'm supposed to be there. My orders say simply ' . . . before sailing'. Perhaps, I'm thinking, they might want a piece of your arse, but surely not mine. At least, not yet!" And I laughed with him when he realized his attempt to frighten me had fallen quite flat.

The cox'n and his crew were ready to get underway and, with a view toward protocol, I preceded my senior down the steps and into the stern sheets of the boat. As I still had on my boat cloak, even though the sky had brightened and brought a measure of warmth to the day, I took the precaution of drawing it around me, remembering the promised wet ride. As Corner lumbered into the boat and settled himself on the other side of the stern sheets from me, I noticed he did the same. And I also noticed that Wisdom shifted himself slightly to my side of the boat to offset Corner's ample displacement. And then the stalwart lads, their oars held aloft, pushed us away from the quay, lowered and, as one, dipped their oars into the gray, murky waters of Portsmouth Harbor. At the cox'n's command, each began to stroke, pulling us toward the entrance of the harbor. I thought their performance well done and smart and, feeling the boat's motion beneath me, suddenly felt quite at home, almost as though I had not been ashore for three long years.

"So, Edward; where have you been these last four years. I was tryin' mightily to recall when last I seen ye, and come up with right about the time old *Egmont* was headin' for the nacker's yard. As I remember it, you had just passed for lieutenant and moved out of the cockpit to the gunroom. Guess you didn't get much of a chance to enjoy that change, eh?" Corner's memory was spot on.

"Aye, Robert, you recall correctly. I managed a quick transfer to *Swallow*, a sloop, that lasted for barely six months before she, too, went into ordinary and, along with about half the gunroom and all of the mids, I found myself ashore on half rations. Been there, staying at my parents' farm in Whatley, since. You might imagine I was mightily pleased to get these orders to *Pandora*! Caring for a few cows and some sheep, putting up winter crops, mucking out barns, and acting the farmer is a far cry indeed from how I imagined I would be spending my life!" I smiled, in spite of my rueful memories. Then, as an afterthought, I asked him, "Is Cap'n Edwards as much of a tyrant as I have heard?"

"Can only tell ye what I've heard, my friend. Only been aboard my own self a bit more than a week and underway with the man while we brought her down from the yard at Chatham where she was refit." He pulled his boat cloak closer about him as a wave lapped over the boat's gunwale, leaving the depth of water in the bilge greater by an inch or more.

"Wasn't much of a cruise, as you might imagine. Paid our respects to old Admiral Dalrymple as we passed by Sheerness and to Sir Richard King at the Downs. Then we were here. We drew the short straw in crew though, I'll warrant." Corner paused, waiting for a reaction from me.

Of course, he got one, and immediately. "Whatever do you mean, 'the short straw in crew' Robert? Are not our lads fit to sail, or is it that we are short-handed?"

"Oh, we got the bodies. But they appear mostly to be the leavings of the press. Don't reckon the half of 'em know a brace from a lift and the other bunch might know, but wouldn't know what to do with either of 'em. Admiral Lord Howe got the prize picks for his own fleet—defending the Empire, and all that!" The disgust at our status—or lack thereof—was clear and I knew we would have our work cut out for us, to whip these men into a ship's company.

Hopefully, we had petty officers and ratings that had some seasoning. I asked.

"Well, there again, Howe beat us out. But we do have a few good ones and the sailing master, George Passmore, is a real prize. Knows his business and takes no malarkey from any. Cap'n Edwards seems to think well of him, to boot. Surgeon's not a bad sort, either, and, from the conversation I had with him a day or two back, seems to know his potions and knives!" Corner laughed at his little joke. "Right unlikely he'll need their use, save for accidents and the like, as we ain't headin' for action like them others. Course, if we get into a row with hostiles in the South Seas, he might have a bit of patchin' up to see to . . . less'n, o' course, the hostiles turn out to be *head hunters or cannibals* and then . . . well, guess there wouldn't be much to patch!" He laughed a great booming guffaw that caused Wisdom to start at its unexpectedness.

"What of you, Robert? Did you manage to stay employed during the bad time?" I used the expression I had heard others use and surely agreed with, at least from my own standpoint!

"Aye, that I did. And quite happily, I might mention. Spent most of it as third lieutenant in a fifth rate sailing the warm waters of the Caribbean, chasing the occasional pirate and Frog privateer. Right easy duty it was, and sad to be gone, I am. Spent a goodly amount of time working at the great guns and became quite adept at hitting what we aimed at. Cap'n was bloody fanatic about acquitting ourselves right when it came to firing and workin' the ship. But I reckon this might turn out to be just as pleasant. Save for the gunnery, I would imagine. Can't think we'll be needin' a deal of gunnery skills where we're headed, less'n we meet those hostile cannibals! And she ain't got much weight of metal, either. Fewer than two dozen wee six-pounders and a hatful of eighteen-pounder carronades. Four only, in fact. Course, with the pitiful excuse for a crew we got, might be better off not ever needin' 'em!" He laughed, though I think his heart was not in it. "But I 'spect the weather might be a trifle better than what our brethren headed for Biscay are likely to enjoy! And I would imagine our shore leave will be more pleasin' as well" His smile broadened, as he thought of the warm Pacific, tropical islands, and, as he put it, the 'lovely ladies.'

With the wind up and our boat out of the lee provided by the long quay, the chop in the harbor became bothersome and our oarsmen bent their backs and their oars to drive us farther from the near shore and out toward the entrance to the Solent.

Soon we were passing through Howe's fleet, dodging other boats plying to and fro on important missions with, I am sure, important personages within. The boats, mostly heading for the shore, made better time than did we, fighting the wind and seas. A few lighters, being towed out to the fleet, made slow progress—slower by half than us—lumbered as they were with stores, spare yards and cordage, canvas, and all of the sundry necessities required to keep a ship on station for an extended period.

As I took in the frigates of the fourth and fifth rates, the lumbering two-deckers and their attendant smaller tenders, the bomb and fire ketches, and the exciting activity evident on each, I envied, in a way, my comrades who would be peopling those mighty vessels. They would be heading off to, very likely, engage the Spanish fleet, doing what English ships had been doing for generations and garnering glory and honor for themselves and their vessels.

And getting themselves killed, in the bargain! I thought with a grimace. *Maybe a cruise to the South Seas might not be such a bad alternative. And surely, bringing those piratical rascals back to hang would be a lesson to any others who might consider rising up against their commanders. Yes, what* Pandora *would be doing might indeed bring glory to us, as well!*

"Well, Edward; there's our fair frigate!" Corner pointed over the oarsmen's heads.

About two cables ahead of us I could see a fine looking frigate, anchored by herself, and bowing and bobbing in the short seas rolling in from the Solent. She was tall, with topmasts and t'gallants rigged, and a long bowsprit and jib boom jutting perhaps seventy feet from her bluff bow. The forward spars described convoluted circles in the sky as the ship worked to her moorings. Three masts, the tallest of which rose some one hundred thirty feet from the deck, each had their yards across and I could plainly see canvas brailed to each with a harbor furl. At the stern, jutting quarter galleries with glass lights rounded the ship's transom, each with a lantern above. This would be the Great Cabin, home to our commander for the duration of the voyage. There seemed little in the way of ornamentation save for the name, *PANDORA*, carved into the transom.

Her topsides were black from the gun ports to the copper, with ochre above, stem to stern. Lower masts were varnished, while the mastheads and yards were well blackened. The standing rigging, obviously recently coated with fresh Stockholm tar, gleamed in the dull light filtering through the thinning clouds.

Well, she certainly is a sight smaller than old Egmont! I thought. *Rounding the Horn and sailing the far reaches of the Pacific might not be as pleasant as I had thought!*

"When was she laid down, Robert? Do you recall?"

Maybe were she not too old, it would not be so bad.

"Been in the Navy just a year longer than yourself, Edward. You two are about the same age, as far as the Navy's concerned!" Robert laughed.

Hmmm. I received my warrant in 1780, so she would have been built in 1779. Not too old, I'd reckon. Hopefully not falling apart yet!

I said as much, evoking a great guffaw from Corner which again caused Wisdom to start.

"I'd warrant she'll bring us back in one piece, Edward. Wouldn't you, Cox'n?"

"Aye, sir. A right fine ship, and well found she is. Got no worries about that one fallin' apart under our feet!" Wisdom opined without diverting his gaze from our course.

CHAPTER TWO

Portsmouth, England

My arrival on board had sparked little interest from any, save our first lieutenant, Mister Larkan, who greeted me with a terse, "Nice of you to join us, Mister Ballantyne. Thought you might have shown yourself a bit sooner, mayhaps even at Chatham. But, better late than never!"

"I had not any date to report, sir, save before sailing. I hope I have not inconvenienced you or Captain Edwards. Here are my orders, sir." And I handed him the envelope containing my written orders, the very same ones, not a month before, I had clutched to my breast like a long lost, and found, love. And the ones that directed me to report to the ship at Portsmouth!

"Quite so." Larkan's face gave no indication of his mood.

How could I possibly have made the ship at Chatham? I did not get my orders until barely a few days before she sailed for Spithead!

Larkan took the proffered envelope without a glance and turned to my escort, Robert. "You might show Mister Ballantyne to the Gun Room, Corner, and get him introduced to his messmates. I shall be with the captain. I expect we will be underway rather sooner than later!"

His word-play on my, perhaps, tardy arrival did not escape me and I could feel myself reddening a bit. He waited not a moment, but turned and made his way aft from the midships break, stepping over the multitude of unstowed necessaries still lumbering our spar deck, and, mercifully, missing my blush. Robert, however, did not.

"Don't concern yerself with Larkan's tone, Edward. He's been quite frustrated for a bit now, what with trying to get both hands and stores aboard and get the barky ready for sea. These landsmen we've shipped are a rum lot and most seem to have little idea of following orders. Petty officers and the warrants ain't faring much better with sortin' 'em out either, for that matter. I'd warrant it will be some interesting getting the ship to sea!" He spoke, turning his head over his shoulder, as we picked our own way through the maze of equipment, stores, spare cordage and spars, and all manner of casks and kegs, not yet struck below.

"Robert," I spoke as I made my way around a great coil of rope thick as a man's leg—a spare anchor cable, perhaps?—and hurried along in his wake. "Why are we loading all this extra cordage, spars, canvas, and whatever it is in these hogsheads? Surely the Admiralty doesn't expect us to be in such dire straits as to require their use?"

"As you will quickly discover, Edward, most of this," here he gestured about him, taking in all the piles of supplies lumbering our deck, "is not for our use. Should we find *Bounty*, we are to refit her as necessary and put sufficient crew and officers in her to see her safely home to England."

That would also explain the seemingly large number of sailors laboring under the starter of the bosun and the shouts and curses of the petty officers. They will become Bounty's *crew while those erstwhile rascals previously in the ship will languish in irons!*

Robert stepped down the aft hatch, disappearing from my view. I hastened to follow and, upon descending the ladder into the bowels of the ship, found myself on the gun deck. In the limited light filtering through the hatch gratings, I could see the small six-pounder carriage guns lining both sides of the space as well as the lower portions of the main and foremasts poking down from the spar deck to their point of ultimate termination, in the orlop, where I knew, without having to see it, they would be resting on top of the mighty beam of our oaken keel.

Once again, I queried my guide. "Why is our armament so light? I had thought even a sixth rate was entitled to twenty eight guns of at least nine-pounder caliber. It would appear that ours are but six-pounders, and scant in their count."

"Think about it, Edward." Corner continued his measured answers to my questioning as he stepped around a rail and put his foot on the top step of another descending ladder. "We are not going to war. Our commission is to find the mutineers and, if possible, *Bounty*. Highly unlikely we'd need to burden our wee vessel with the weight of nine-pounders, let alone twenty-eight of 'em! The Admiralty obviously seemed to think the extra room we gained by shorting our broadside would be well used to store the necessaries we might need to refit Bligh's late command, as well as quarter the men necessary to sail her home. Besides, we've also been fitted with four eighteen-pounder carronades!"

I thought about his answer as I followed him down the ladder. I reluctantly agreed, albeit silently, the choice made some sense. And it likely wouldn't be necessary to have a hostile engagement with *Bounty* to capture her. Especially as she herself carried a bare minimum of armament. And four carronades? Well, they're surely not likely to get us out of any trouble we might find either!

"Well, here we are, Edward. The Gun Room and our home for, perhaps, a couple of years." He stepped aside to allow me to pass into a narrow passageway lined, on both sides of the ship, with doors. Some stood open while others were closed. "You should be most comfortable in this one. Nice chap bunking here with you. Name's Hayward and, while he's a bit junior to you, seems personable enough. You should get along well, I hope." He smiled.

Hayward . . . name sounds familiar. Did I sail with him before I went ashore? Where do I know him from?

Then it struck me: Hayward, Thomas Hayward, was with Bligh in *Bounty* and made the now legendary voyage to Coupang in the open boat.

Why ever would one want to return to those same waters? He was but a midshipman, I recall, with Bligh. Did the Admiralty give him his commission based on his loyalty and that open boat voyage? I must remember to question him closely on his experiences; his tale will surely be the highlight of our trip out!

Corner knocked on the closed door, once, then, hearing no response, pushed it open, revealing a miniscule cabin containing two suspended cots, a writing desk, and tiny cupboard.

Certainly not Egmont! I thought as I stepped in to the room. There I had had a more spacious cabin, shared with two other lieutenants. But in my recollection, it was a good deal larger! *But then so was* Egmont! I thought ruefully.

"I'm straight across, doubled up with Larkan. In fact, we're all doubled up on account of the extra officers we'll be needin' should we be fortunate enough to find *Bounty*." He still stood in the passageway; a good thing as his bulk would have left little room for me in the cabin!

"You might find this a bit cramped," he continued. "Larkan said the other day that one would have to step out of the cabin just to change his mind!" Robert gave out with a brief but lusty chortle at his joke.

In a single glance, and almost without even shifting my eyes, I could take in the whole of the cabin. Hayward's sea chest poked out from under one of the suspended cots and I made the assumption that the other would be mine. As the weather topside had shown every indication of brightening, I shrugged out of my boat cloak and hung it on a peg, next to Hayward's. Several pair of shoes had been neatly placed near to his cot. His sword hung by the belt on another peg, next to his coat, his hat over top of it. Beyond those items and, of course, his chest, there was little evidence of my messmate's presence.

"This will do nicely, Robert." I smiled, more hopefully than optimistically, and turned about to leave.

Corner stepped aside and, as I gained the passageway, spoke. "Let's go to the wardroom and see if any of our mates are about. You'll need to meet them and now's as good a time as any."

Once again, he squeezed his bulk past me and led me farther aft. An open door at the end of the passage glowed with the flickering yellow light of oil lanterns and I could hear quiet conversation coming from within. He entered without ceremony and I followed.

Three men sat at the table, each with a stemmed glass holding, I presumed, wine. One was about my age, deeply tanned, and quite attractive in a manly way. To his left sat an older chap, his jacket off and his sleeves turned up to his elbows, in spite of the coolness of the room. Across the table sat the third officer, aged between his mates, but with a well-lined face and whiskers that extended from his ears very nearly to his chin. He had been speaking when we entered, but stopped immediately as Robert stepped into the room.

"Ah. Mister Passmore. So sorry to interrupt, but our third lieutenant has joined. Just here, he is. Thought you gentlemen ought to have the pleasure of meeting Lieutenant Ballantyne. He's already met Larkan.

"Edward, may I present our Sailing Master, George Passmore, our surgeon, Mister George Hamilton, and your cabin-mate, Lieutenant Hayward, late of His Majesty's Armed Vessel, *Bounty*. Gentlemen, Edward Ballantyne, late of the three-decker, *Egmont*."

I thought his reference to *Egmont* a bit out of date, but ignored it as each of the men before me rose and extended hands of welcome. The chap with his jacket off was Surgeon Hamilton, whose hand I took first. He smiled warmly and murmured some welcoming words, most of which I missed due to a loud crash, followed closely by a lively ruckus over our heads.

To a man, we all looked up, each, I think, expecting to see a body or piece of equipment come through the overhead! Of course, none did, but Passmore, our sailing master, uttered a curse, excused himself, and left the room. He stopped, just outside the door, and looked back in.

"Welcome aboard, Mister Ballantyne. I trust you will find our lively little ship and her crew of miscreants and malcontents to your liking!" He did smile, fleetingly, at his deprecating comment, and ran down the passageway toward the ladder which would take him up to the scene of the ructions, which from the sounds I could still hear above us, were still in full cry.

"Welcome aboard, Edward. George's sarcasm notwithstanding, I hope you'll find the ship as pleasant as your last. *Egmont*, was it? Don't recall her, but perhaps she might be a bit before my time." Hayward, only recently promoted to lieutenant, would most likely be three or four years my junior in both age and grade. He was well tanned, or perhaps just a bit swarthy, and his smile seemed genuine and welcoming.

"Thank you, George. I suspect she's long-since found her way to the nacker's yard, likely several years back. Lumbering old crate of seventy guns, she was, and sailed like a cathedral!" As I spoke, I realized I had called him by the wrong name and hastened to correct my error. "Please excuse me, *Thomas*. Distracted a bit by the excitement on the gun deck, I reckon. I look forward to hearing all about your travails in *Bounty* . . . and after!" Actually, I could scarcely wait to hear his tale, especially as I had not found a copy of Bligh's published narrative, and now, with sailing imminent, was unlikely to.

Thomas Hayward smiled and took my hand in a firm grip. "I would be happy to tell you of our ill-starred cruise, sir. Perhaps we will stand a watch or two together. It is a story to be told in more than one sitting, I assure you!" He sat down at the table again and picked up his glass.

Mister Hamilton, the surgeon, had also resumed his seat and again, smiled as he spoke. "Passmore's a fine sailing master and one of the few warrants aboard who can handle the rabble we have shipped as a crew. Don't let his brusque manner put you off, Edward; we can all learn quite a measure of skill from the man. And, generally, he is pleasant."

"Would you care to sit a moment, Edward, and join us in a glass. The good doctor was just sharing some of his thoughts about the South Seas with me and inquiring about some of the medical problems we experienced in *Bounty*." Thomas reached to the chair next to his own and pulled it away from the table for me. Robert took another while Hayward set out two more glasses and poured a measure of wine into each. "Besides, I don't imagine your chest will be down straight away so you've little to do right now."

"Thank you, sir. I will listen to you and Mister Hamilton as, having never been to the South Seas, I would have little to offer. I spent my time on the North American Station during the late war, where our most serious afflictions—at least in *Egmont*—were sailors who seemed plagued with misfortune, falling from the mainyard, driving a nail into a hand, and suffering the ill-effects of saved up rations of Jamaica!" I paused, as a further thought of those days occurred to me. "And of course, the scurvy. That was always there."

Hamilton was gracious enough to laugh at my attempt to amuse them; Corner smiled—he knew well I was not exaggerating the horribly routine nature of the ailments in our man of war—and Hayward simply looked at me, then back at Hamilton, ready to resume their conversation.

The fight, or whatever it was on the gun deck above our heads, had stopped, indicating that Mister Passmore had arrived on the scene, likely along with the bosun and mayhaps, the master at arms. The conversation about island maladies and difficult wounds held my interest only for a short while, being, as they were, somewhat melancholy; most of the problems either man mentioned ended in the death of the sufferer. At least the maladies we experienced, on *Egmont* rarely resulted in death. Save for our continual and usually losing battle with scurvy, of course. Surely, we lost more to that than to battle or injury!

"Gentlemen. Thank you for your hospitality. I believe I should pay my respects to Captain Edwards, so, with your permission, I will take my leave now. Thomas, I look forward to hearing about your voyage and . . . *experiences* . . . in *Bounty* and after. I am sure we will become great good friends! Robert, I will see you later, if you please." I stood, swallowed off the last bit of my wine, and turned to the door.

"You might want me to go with you to introduce you to the captain, Edward. He's no easy chap to deal with!" Robert made ready to stand, quite prepared to join me when I bearded the lion.

"I'd reckon to be able to manage it on my own, Robert. Remember Mister Johnson in *Egmont*? And I was only a midshipman then." I made reference to the terror of the North Atlantic Station who, frustrated with our complete lack of ability to engage any colonial vessel, made life quite miserable for everyone, most especially the midshipmen.

"How well I remember that miserable cove, Edward. But you have yet to meet our captain! A different story all together, I assure you!"

"Perhaps the first lieutenant is still with him and he will make the introduction. Should he not be, I think I can manage to report my presence in his ship without undue difficulty." I stepped out of the wardroom into the passageway, hearing the conversation resume in my wake.

I made my way up to the gundeck and aft to where a Marine sentry stood ramrod stiff outside the closed door to the Cabin. He saluted me and stepped to his left, effectively blocking the door to the captain's lair.

"Is Captain Edwards available, Marine? I should like to report my arrival in *Pandora*."

"I shall inquire for you. And your name, sir?"

"I am Lieutenant Ballantyne."

The sentry knocked sharply, once, on the lintel above the door and received a muffled, but to judge from the tone, less than welcoming response. He opened the door and poked his head in.

"Sorry to disturb you sir. Lieutenant Ballantyne would like to see you, should it be convenient."

I heard the response from an unseen voice which I took to belong to Captain Edwards.

"Aye, send him in." The voice was deep, the accent of a well-educated man and, in spite of his less than warm initial reaction to being disturbed, sounded at the least, neutral.

The Marine withdrew his head from the portal and stepped back to allow me entry.

"He'll see you, Lieutenant." His words were quite unnecessary as, obviously I had heard the exchange quite clearly.

"Thank you," I said, and stepped into the Cabin.

The first lieutenant sat in a round back chair opposite a small, curved writing table which was covered by a multitude of documents, papers, and notebooks, behind which sat a venerable, fine looking gentleman of about fifty years. A lined face, weathered, with a furrowed brow spoke of many years at sea and one well used to the responsibility of command. His whiskers were trimmed short, just below his ears, and he wore his dark hair long, tied in a queue which reached just below his collar in the style of an older generation; I could see streaks of gray along the both sides of his head. His face did not appear hard—weathered from long years at sea, yes, but not "hard" and his nose was perfectly straight above thin lips. He was in shirt-sleeves and his waistcoat hung opened, unbuttoned, though his stock was secured closely about his neck, and I noticed that his jacket, bearing the markings of post captain, was carefully hanging from a peg in the bulkhead. On a table near the curtained entry to his sleeping cabin stood a simple stand adorned by a curled, white, and powdered wig.

Upon my entry, he stood, smiled, and extended his hand. He was, I noticed immediately, a good bit taller than I. His hand, as I took it, was hard with calluses and large, making my own large hand seem miniscule in comparison.

"Mister Ballantyne. Nice of you to join us."

That was the second time I had been greeted that way, clearly making me think I had been tardy in reporting aboard.

"We will be making sail, I expect, with the tide on Sunday. You will have little time to familiarize yourself with *Pandora* so I recommend you use the time to your advantage. There are precious few in our crew who have experience and we will need knowledgeable officers to lead them. I presume, sir, you are aware of our commission?" The captain spoke in a deep voice, quietly, but the smile he had worn to greet me was gone, replaced by a much sterner expression, surely suitable to a commander.

Could this be the tyrant I have been warned of? Seems like a decent chap, though serious.

"Aye, sir. I am that. It is my understanding we are to fetch back the mutineers from Captain Bligh's late command and find his ship." I stood stiffly at attention in front of Edwards' desk, behind the first lieutenant.

Larkan turned around to study me as I answered the captain's query. His brow was furrowed, perhaps with thought, but he spoke not a word. The captain, for his part, resumed his seat behind the desk.

He looked up at me, again showing a pleasant expression, though not quite managing a smile. Was he pleased that I knew our assignment? "Aye, that is exactly our task. My sailing orders are quite specific to the importance of returning Christian and his pirates to England for trial and hanging as well as other tasks, including discovering the whereabouts of *Bounty* and, if possible, sailing her back with us. You will hear more on this subject tomorrow when Mister Larkan assembles the officers." Now, again, his face turned serious, his lips drawn into a thin line across his face as he paused in his recitation.

"For the present, Mister Ballantyne, I hope you have completed your errands ashore and are prepared to assume your duties as third lieutenant immediately. Sunday will be upon us before you know it!"

"Aye, sir. I look forward to being back at sea, and under your command. If there is nothing further, sir, I will begin straight away."

"You are dismissed, Lieutenant. As long as Mister Larkan has nothing to add?" Edwards, eyebrows raised expectantly, shot a glance at the first lieutenant, and rose from his seat.

To shake my hand again, I assumed, and started to extend my own in anticipation. Instead, Captain Edwards turned away, strode to the aft bulkhead where, for the first time, I noticed a brilliantly polished brass fireplace. Embers glowed in hues of red and orange in the firebox and a small bin of short logs sat near at hand. Edwards bent down and picked up a log, inspected it carefully, and placed it gently on the grate above the embers.

The fireplace was tall and narrow with an intricate design embossed on its face. A short pipe carried the smoke to a stack above, likely on the poop deck. I had never before seen such a magnificent and well-crafted fireplace, certainly on a ship, and was about to offer a compliment when the first lieutenant spoke.

"I will send the messenger for you when I have concluded my meeting here, Ballantyne. You may go about your duties." Larkan's voice was quiet, and he spoke, apparently watching the captain's actions, with his back still turned to me.

"Aye, sir." I turned about and stepped to the still open door.

When I gained the passageway, the sentry reached out and closed the door, muffling into obscurity the conversation which had resumed in the Cabin.

When I regained the weather deck, I noted that some further progress had been made in striking below the abundance of stores lumbering our weather deck, allowing me to walk quite unimpeded from bow to stern. However, the bleak weather had returned and a desultory, cold, drizzle fell from a leaden sky.

A great line of men, supervised by a crusty, weathered, looking warrant officer I took to be our bosun, passed small kegs hand to hand, along the deck and down a ladder where, I supposed, the purser or his assistant oversaw their stowage in the hold. I stopped to watch for a moment, as the bosun prodded a man with his starter, receiving a killing look, but also quicker movement of the keg he held. Down the line, one of the men in the line dropped his keg as he passed it along, receiving a shouted curse and a sharp blow from the bosun's starter.

"Good day to you, sir." I turned at the voice behind me to see a young man who couldn't have been more than fifteen or sixteen years of age. Close-set eyes fixed me with an earnest stare, but it seemed as though the young man's nose kept getting in the way of his vision; it was considerably larger than his narrow face could properly support. A mere suggestion of a chin softened what some might have thought a pointy face, and large feminine lips at once added to the softness as much as they overshadowed his lack of a chin. He doffed his hat in a salute, the water running off it and down his arm; to his credit, he held the salute until I responded which was a trifle longer than it should have been, captivated as I was by his unusual appearance.

"And to you, as well, sir. Who might you be?" I returned the salute.

"Sir. I am Midshipman David William Renouard—my friends mostly call me Willy, as me father's name is David and it avoids some confusion, I'd reckon." He added this last with a cautious smile. "If you are Lieutenant Ballantyne, I expect I will be under your direction during this cruise."

"Your surmise is spot on, Mister Renouard. I am indeed Ballantyne. You have been assigned to me, I collect?" I smiled, as much at the young man's enthusiasm as at his appearance.

"Oh, sir. I have indeed, and I look forward to learning from you. This is my first ship, sir. In fact, I have had my warrant only this past month! Mister Corner mentioned to me that you have seen action, during the revolt of the colonists in America." His expression was earnest to a fault, and he rushed on, breaking into a broad smile which, on his narrow face, seemed to take considerable effort.

"Is not our task the most exciting? I can only imagine that those cut-throat pirates we are charged with finding, were they to be aware of our assignment, must be quaking in their boots at the thought of being returned to England for hanging!" Young "Willy's" youthful enthusiasm would dwindle, I suspected, as our voyage became a reality rather than the romantic version he had envisioned.

If this is his first ship, he must have interest in high places to avoid the drudgery of beginning his career before the mast. I know I spent nearly two years as seaman before I won my own warrant. Who could be watching out for him? I must be careful how I handle this youngster!

"How long have you been aboard, Renouard?" I inquired, cutting off his rambling and zealous exclamations.

"Oh, sir. I sailed in *Pandora* from the dockyards at Chatham. And I was aboard as she finished her fitting out there. What a grand vessel she is, sir. Don't you think?"

"Well, she is that, Midshipman, she is that! You will discover, however, that she will become less grand, perhaps even quite small, as the commission proceeds! But for the present, I could use a guide around our 'grand vessel' should you not be occupied here."

"Oh yes, Mister Ballantyne. I would be most honored to show you through the ship, though I am not the most knowledgeable guide you might have! I have only been watching Bosun Cunningham here move our provisions and such downstairs as I have nothing to do more pressing."

"Renouard, you are aboard ship now and you must remember to use proper lingo when referring to such things as 'downstairs'; in a ship, we call it 'below' just as up there," I pointed to the maintop and beyond, "we call 'aloft'."

Had you done your time in the fo'c'sle, young man, you would already know these things as well as how to hand, reef, and steer!

The youngster colored visibly at my correction, but promised to remember in the future. And off we went on a tour of our 'grand vessel', spending the next hour wandering about the decks of the frigate, poking into every space from orlop to wet spardeck and from the butt of the bowsprit to the taffrail aft of the quarterdeck. Mercifully, the rain remained only an annoying drizzle. The midshipman chattered away with unbridled enthusiasm, most of his words quickly becoming as annoying as the wet. I allowed them to retreat to the back of my brain, becoming merely a buzz, little of which I actually heard, as I studied the layout of the frigate and wondered about my own assignment.

Goodness! Does he ever *run out of breath?*

My guide introduced me to any warrant, midshipman, or master's mate we encountered and, in the course of less than one hour, I had met our purser, Mister Gregory Bentham, two master's mates, William Oliver and Thomas Rickard, and the surgeon's mate, a Mister Innes. As we stepped back onto the spardeck, we discovered that the rain, for now at any rate, had stopped. But I noticed that the sky had not brightened, but only returned to its earlier gray pall as the scant daylight began to give way to the early November darkness. Low clouds raced across the heavens, driven by a mounting breeze.

More surly weather comin' on, I'd warrant.

"Mister Ballantyne, Mister Larkan would like you to attend him in the wardroom, if you please." A slovenly sailor stood listlessly before me, offering neither salute nor apology for his appearance.

One of our stalwart "Johnny Newcomes," were I to guess at the origins of the young man standing before me. A worthy representative of the effectiveness of our Impress Service! I surely do hope he's the exception and not the norm among them! I thought, as I took in the dirty canvas trousers, untrimmed hair, and dirty face. *Larkan could not have seen him in person when he sent him to fetch me. Must have simply told the quarterdeck watch to find me. Well, no time like the present!*

"Sailor, first off, you address an officer . . . or midshipman," I shot a glance at young Renouard who stood mutely to the side, "as 'sir.' And further, has no one mentioned to you your appearance? I think our first lieutenant might take some exception to the way you are turned out. I know I surely do. I will attend Mister Larkan. You will go and see to tidying up, and then you will report to your division officer or midshipman, telling him I so instructed you. And use 'sir' when you address him." He scowled at this, but said no more and left, I assumed to turn himself into a fitting representative of the Royal Navy.

Leaving the talkative Mister Renouard to his own devices, I started aft to 'attend' the first lieutenant. Larkan sat alone in the wardroom, facing the door, with his hands folded on the table in front of him. His expression, as I stepped into the room, gave me no hint as to his intentions. I simply assumed he had wanted to go over my assignment, quarters station, and the like. It was what any officer could expect upon reporting into a ship.

"Ah, yes. Mister Ballantyne. I collect the watch messenger was successful in his errand. Take a chair, if you please." Larkan neither stood nor smiled.

I said not a word, but did as he instructed and, pulling out the same chair I had earlier occupied, sat.

"This ship, as you may have already discovered, is filled with an assortment of *Johnny Newcomes*, trouble-makers, and the discards of the press. Few have easily adapted to life in a ship and the ones who have, seem to be malcontents from the merchant fleet. I do not expect my officers to treat them other than harshly should any presume to disobey or decline the opportunity to learn their new trade. Just because we are not sailing off to do battle with the French or Spanish is no excuse for slovenliness or less than proper performance from any."

I thought of the sailor who had fetched me to this interview. "Yes, sir. I would think not. In fact, I already suggested to one seaman that his appearance . . . and demeanor might benefit from proper cleaning, shaving, and a wash."

"One at a time simply will not answer, Mister Ballantyne; we must bring them around quickly. We sail with the tide on Sunday and woe be to any who do not toe the line. Regardless of our commission, this vessel is still a frigate of the Royal Navy and I know first hand that Captain Edwards has no tolerance whatever for commanding a sloppy ship. Even before we had slipped our lines in Chatham, he had cause to have three of our new recruits put to the lash, two for fighting and one for insubordination. To that end, all divisions will muster tomorrow for an inspection by the officers and myself. Any division showing poorly will suffer, as will the officer responsible for that division." He paused in his warning to study me closely.

Oh my! What have I gotten myself into?

In spite of the thoughts of a difficult year or two that swirled though my head at his words, I offered no change of expression or comment; the first lieutenant made the rules—or the captain did and the first lieutenant carried them out—and it was up to the officers to ensure they were followed to the letter.

What I did say, after a suitable pause, was this: "Sir, I have yet to see the watch bill or the quarters bill so I do not know what division will be mine." No point in waiting until one of the men committed some heinous act to find out that I was responsible for him!

"I have the bills in my cabin, Edward, and, should memory serve, you are assigned as signal officer, something which I doubt will tax you to any degree, as we will, for the most part, be sailing independently. In addition, you will oversee the activities of second division, ensuring that the larboard side long-guns are properly maintained and served and that when called to action, their crews can hit that to which they are directed. Mister Renouard will assist you in this endeavor and further will oversee, in an action, as many of the pieces in the larboard broadside as you feel he might handle without undue difficulty." At this point, Lieutenant Larkan actually smiled at me.

I was a bit taken aback by his use of my Christian name. Upon a bit of reflection, it occurred that he was, in reality, not a "hard" man, just one who, as first lieutenant, was carrying out his captain's orders, as he would for the duration of our commission. I smiled back.

"Yes, sir. I have already met Midshipman Renouard. Seems like an enthusiastic young chap and eager to learn. I shall do my best to teach him. Though I must say, his appointment to midshipman with no prior sea duty somewhat surprised me."

"Well, 'enthusiastic' might be *one* way of categorizing him; I expect that his youthful exuberance will be temporary. I would wager that he will be among the first to serve up his vittles to the fish once we clear the harbor! But that said, it would appear you have a clean slate upon which to write! I wish you good luck in that endeavor.

"And yes, I have been given to understand that Mister Renouard's uncle has a seat in Commons and, I am told, is on a quite friendly basis with the First Lord of the Admiralty. Something about his mother's relative being married to him."

I laughed and said that I would try to bring him along as quickly as possible, storing away the information regarding the youngster's apparently strong "interest" in London.

"The captain, Mister Ballantyne, is not one to suffer fools gladly, nor is he one to accept less than proper performance from any. He has been at sea from the age of eleven and seen action in any number of events. During the late war with the colonists in America, he is known, with the assistance of one other officer, to have put down a mutiny of forty six men in *Narcissus*, a brig mounting twenty guns. It is said that he turned the eight ring leaders over to the authorities in New York and dealt with the "followers" in the ship. The admiralty there saw fit to stretch the necks of five of them, not inclusive of the leader of the mutiny; he was hanged in chains. The other two who found themselves ashore were each given over two hundred strokes with the lash. Only one survived the beating. Those others he kept aboard suffered the lash as well, though with a less debilitating result." Larkan paused here, letting this information settle in my brain.

So much for the easy smile and warm handshake I'd earlier witnessed! I'd warrant then, that all the tales I'd heard of Edward Edwards being a "hard" commander were indeed true. Perhaps I should pass this bit of knowledge on to my sailors. It might help speed their acceptance of their lot!

"Have you any questions for me, Lieutenant?" Larkan looked at me, one eyebrow raised as if challenging me to make some foolhardy remark.

The words of my father, heard repeatedly during my formative years, bubbled through my brain. *"Better to say nothing, Edward, than to say something stupid!"* For a simple farmer, he enjoyed great wisdom and I kept my own council.

"No sir. I will see to my chores straight away." I stood, preparing to depart the wardroom.

"And Lieutenant: welcome aboard *Pandora*. I have every hope that we will enjoy a successful commission as well as a happy ship."

While I responded, "Yes, sir. I am sure both will prove true," I must admit, thoughts to the contrary rumbled through my brain like an over-loaded dray bumping across a cobblestone street.

"And one final item, Edward, if you please. I assume you have no servant to attend your needs as I saw none in your company when you reported." Lieutenant Larkan raised his eyebrows questioningly.

"You are quite correct in your surmise, sir; I have none." I had not enjoyed the use of a servant in *Egmont* either, being too new to the ward-room at the time. In point of fact, that I was entitled to the privilege had not occurred to me until Mister Larkan mentioned it.

I knew, as an officer in His Majesty's Navy that I was allowed a man-servant to wait upon me in the wardroom, see to my washing, brush my uniforms, blacken my boots, and the like. But this would be a new experience for me.

"Well then. You may as well select one of the denizens of second division to attend to your needs. Do try to choose one with a modicum of sense and not too rough around the edges, if you would. You may have him report to Spaulding, Corner's man. Show him the ropes, you know, so as not to embarrass you. He's likely hanging about the pantry, cadging food from the officers' stores!"

"Thank you, sir. I shall see to it when I muster my division." I turned and, without further ado, stepped into the passageway.

On my way forward, I stopped by the palatial quarters I would share with Lieutenant Hayward. My chest stood in the middle of the deck making it quite impossible to move more than one step into the cubby. I pushed it under the suspended cot I would occupy and, as I left, took my still damp boat cloak from the hook where I had earlier deposited it. The weather topside had been worsening before I was summoned to attend to Mister Larkan and, since I would have to chase down my midshipman, Renouard, to get started on our tasks, thought it prudent to have some protection from the rain.

The midshipman was still standing at the forehatch, quite fascinated with the continuing movement of goods and supplies being struck down to the hold. A halfhearted chantey had begun to establish a rhythm for the sailors and I watched, amused, as Renouard unconsciously tapped his foot to the beat of it.

I instructed the young gentleman as to what I wished done and sent him on his way. And then, while I waited for word that the second division had been mustered on the fo'c'sle, I went to find Robert, hoping to gain some further insight into our situation.

When I found him, my former shipmate was in the throes of sorting out the stores of powder and shot. I watched in the shot locker as he randomly selected diminutive six-pounder ball shot and passed it through a sizing ring designed to ensure its proper diameter. As most of the shot was new, it had not suffered greatly from the salt atmosphere and showed only rare spots of rust, which Mister Corner instructed the gunner to remove. Powder was a different story; the gunner had yet to make up more than a few cartridges for any of the guns save the carronades. This would have to be accomplished before sailing as, even though we not heading off to battle the Dons, Admiralty instructions required our battery to be ready at all times. The casks of powder would have to be checked more thoroughly than Robert could do, ensuring the proper mixture of nitrates and saltpeter, no moisture, and properly filled casks. Civilian purveyors of everything from powder to salt beef were not above shorting the measure and using stones or equally useless materials to round out the weight. There was so much to be done, and the ship would sail on the tide in barely over twenty-four hours!

As Mister Corner was occupied, I did not interrupt, but instead climbed up the ladder to the gundeck where I began to inspect the battery which was now my responsibility. While thus engaged, Renouard discovered me, accompanied by a master's mate who he introduced as Mister Reynolds.

More than a boy, this one! At least this *one's done his time as a midshipman and maybe even a year or two in the fo'c'sle!*

The young man—actually, he seemed closer to my own age than Renouard's—appeared to be well versed in the ways of a ship. That he was still a master's mate was simply an unhappy circumstance of a navy at peace with few ships in commission. After a few minutes of chat, Renouard mentioned that he had the second division assembled forward, on the fo'c'sle deck, awaiting my inspection.

Oh my! This is my merry band of Johnnies! I thought as I stood before them. Slovenly and sullen they appeared for the most part, dirty (which I could attribute to their recent labors), their hair unbraided, and, on the whole, most unseaman-like. The rain dripped onto their heads—many uncovered—unnoticed by most.

"I am Lieutenant Ballantyne. This division is assigned to me and I will be assisted in the task of turning you into seamen by Mister Renouard." I gestured at the mid who stood stiffly beside me. "I will brook no nonsense or improper behavior. You will do well to remember that." I hoped the last part of that fell on fertile soil in the midshipman's brain as well as the sailors'!

I noticed a few smiles in the ranks as I gestured to the midshipman, suspecting he had already demonstrated his limited abilities when he called the men to muster, and chose, for now, to ignore them.

How is Renouard going to turn these lubbers into sailors when he has not a clue as to what that even means? Nonetheless . . .

"How many of you have been to sea before?" I asked, my voice raised somewhat over the building breeze, which carried with it increasing rain. I was glad I had thought to collect my boat cloak before returning to the weather deck.

Of the seventy or so men who stood silently before me, barely a dozen raised a hand. One crusty-looking older chap stepped forward, pushing his way through the men in ranks in front of him, his hand still raised above his head.

"Sir, if you please. I am called Bill Steward. Gunner's mate in me last ship, the frigate *Doris;* of the fifth rate she were, sir. Disrated through a bit of a misunderstanding with one of our midshipmen there. But I know the guns, sir, and what it takes to work 'em proper-like. These chaps 'ere are strong backs and I reckon I might be a help to yer, sir, in shapin' some of 'em into right fine gun crews for those wee poppers we got below."

Steward was clean-shaven, wore his hair in a proper pigtail and his clothes, though clearly from the purser's slop chest, appeared reasonably clean and mended, as far as I could discern in the growing gloom. His face was lined and weathered and his eyes were squinted down, whether to avoid the now steady rain or from long days at sea I knew not. Aided by the touch of gray at his temples, I guessed his age at something approaching forty years which, should he have been at sea since a boy, would give him valuable experience I might make use of. He seemed to inspire confidence; I hoped it would inspire others as well!

"Thank you, Steward. You may step back. Who else among you has experience with great guns?"

A few hands appeared, tentatively, and disappeared before I might single out any. I took a step closer to the ranks, studying their faces and comportment as I tried another tack.

"Starting here, on my larboard hand, I want you to step forward, one after the other, and state your name and what you were doing when the press got you, or should you be a volunteer, why you are here and what your occupation was prior to now. Is that clear?"

A few nods, a few blank stares, and some muttering from the back ranks.

"Mister Renouard, you will write down the information these men provide, clearly, concisely, and accurately."

A panicked look crossed the youngster's face as he felt about his person for paper and a pencil. The look dissolved into a smile as he produced the required utensil and a folded envelope on which to write. It was clearly too small for the task at hand, but that seemed not to occur to the youngster. He poised his pencil at the ready and smiled at me.

Looking at the miserable collection of rascals and who knew what else who were assembled before me, I again wondered how ever I would make them into sailors! My glance fell upon a man of immense proportions, slouching in the front rank. He wore a stubble beard and his unbound, greasy hair fell wet and long to his shoulders. Under a worn tarpaulin jacket which showed no evidence of fastenings, he wore the shirt of a drayman, though most likely a none too successful drayman, and his trousers, clearly as unfit for duty as their owner, were of canvas tied to his waist by a length of line. But the feature that seemed most riveting, that held my glance for longer than it should have, was his eyes; hued a pale blue, they maintained a penetrating focus on whatever they saw, which at this point, was me. A bit off-putting, I felt.

Well, I thought as I shifted my gaze to his messmates, *got to begin somewhere!*

I pointed to the earlier focus of my scrutiny.

"You, there, the big fellow at the end, begin."

"Bully Rodgers is me name. From Newcastle, I am."

"Yes? And what were you doing prior to becoming a sailor?"

"Mindin' me own business, I was. Bloody rogues grabbed me right out of the ale-house where I was takin' me ease. Drug me right off to the piers and into a boat, they done." He paused, then added with a smile of some satisfaction, "But it took three of 'em, it did!" His pale eyes danced at the memory of what must have been a great row.

"Rodgers. Let us try again. What was your *employment* when the Impress Service found you in the ale house?"

"I had me own dray an' a tired ol' plug to haul her, I done. With the fleet fittin' out, I come down to Chatham Dockyards lookin' for work." A none-too-happy look, matched by his tone, spoke clearly of how much he enjoyed his new employment.

"I see. What has become of your horse and cart?" I asked, more out of curiosity than a sense of caring.

"Haven't a clue, have I? Reckon me partner musta got aholt of it now I ain't there no more. Mighta sold it and drunk up the money by now. Half mine, it was! Another bloody scoundrel, he is, on top of it. Bad as the Press Gang!" The eyes took on a whole new cast, penetrating and, I might add, a bit frightening.

I noticed Renouard writing furiously and glanced over his shoulder.

"Mister Renouard. You needn't write every word. Simply the man's name and his former occupation will answer nicely." I couldn't help myself; I smiled at his efforts and heard a few snickers and giggles from those near at hand.

"Step back, Rodgers. And it might be useful for you to remember the word 'sir' when addressing an officer. Next man."

A scarecrow, no doubt appearing even more emaciated by the bulk of Rodgers, stepped forward and wiped his mouth with the back of his hand. His shirt, likely once plaid, was torn in several places and hung on his frame like wash on a clothesline. Duck trousers, held up with a length of line, barely made it to his ankles, and showed patches at both knees. On his hip rested a sheath knife, which, I must admit, seemed a bit incongruous, given that he appeared not to be a sailor. His feet were bare.

"It's Bob Taylor, I am, sir. From right here in Portsmouth." He stepped back.

"Taylor. Step out again." He did and I addressed all of them.

"Try to recall that I don't particularly care where you are from. What I need to know is what your employment was, as I believe I might have mentioned a short while ago." Only two of them had thus far spoken and already, I was becoming frustrated with their apparent stupidity.

"Let us try again. Taylor, what was it you did prior to signing *Pandora's* Articles?"

His frightened look was partially obscured by the delicate hand he again dragged across his mouth. "I was . . . it were . . . seems . . . "

"Taylor: this is not a hard question, man. What was your employment?" I was fast approaching exasperation.

"Uh . . . didn't have none. Magistrate sent me here."

Oh my! A jailbird! Join the Navy or the work gang. Splendid!

I knew that many hapless souls found that the Navy was the better choice; at least they could count on regular food, some excitement over the day-to-day drudgery of prison life, and, in most ships, better company than they might enjoy in the county jail!

"And what was it got you into trouble, Taylor?"

"I . . . uh . . . got into a scrape with some worthless cove. Stuck 'im, I done, with me knife. Stupid sod found it conven . . . conv . . . "

"*Convenient?*" I offered.

"Aye. Conven . . . what you said. In the event, the stupid sod died on me. An' off I was to the lockup afore you could spit!"

Splendid! A murderer! What other delights am I to discover?

"And have you been to sea before, Taylor?"

"Aye, sir. Sailed in the merchants. One cruise, I done, to Africa and the West Indies, it were. In the brig *Elisa*."

Likely a blackbirder, on that run. But at least a sailor. And that would explain the knife.

"And during that cruise in the brig, Taylor, what were you employed at? Topman, quartermaster?"

"None of that, sir. Rated seaman I was. Stood me watches and heaved 'round when I was told. Helped with the guns too, from time to time."

An ordinary foremast Jack, then. Some experience with the guns might prove useful, though I would have to be mindful of his murderous ways!

"Next man."

A short, stocky chap stepped forward. He was dressed in reasonably clean canvas trousers—maybe not from the slop chest—a shirt that might have once been white, covered by a waistcoat of faded green. He wore leather shoes and a slouch hat was perched atop his head covering brown hair flecked with gray. Neatly trimmed side-whiskers and a smile completed the picture. He did not at once speak.

"Yes? And you would be?"

Renouard, you can help out here anytime you wish!

"Yes, sir. I am called Jonas Black. I was a house servant and when my patron fell on hard times, I was released to find my own way. That would have been three or four months past." He looked directly at me with a sure and confident stare. His accent was Midland and somewhat educated.

"I see, Black. You think you might be a gunner? Why is it that you chose the Navy?"

"Sir. I was down on me luck and had nary a farthing to me name after being turned out. Didn't fancy being a soldier and the signing bonus was better in the Navy."

An honest man! Well, perchance, here is my steward!

"You may step back in the ranks, Black." I turned to Renouard and in a quiet voice, added, "Make a mark next to his name, Midshipman. I may wish to speak further with him."

"What type of mark would you prefer, Mister Ballantyne?" The youngster looked questioningly at me, his pencil poised over the cramped writing on his now quite sodden envelope.

"Glory be, Renouard! Whatever you wish. It is your list." In my exasperation, I might have spoken a bit louder than was necessary for only the midshipman to hear, and again, drew a snicker or two from the front ranks. I quashed their merriment with a look.

And so it went. And for longer than it should have. It was nearly full dark and I knew supper and spirits up would soon be piped. There appeared to be a handful of sailors—and even a few who knew the guns—among the ragtag collection in the division, but the majority followed the pattern established by their brethren. They seemed generally to have been provided by the Impress Service and might easily have been rejected by other ships—the ones in Howe's fleet heading off to Spain. In spite of each of them having passed Mister Hamilton's none-too-thorough examination for robust health, it appeared as if our work was cut out for us!

And me stuck with this landsman, Renouard, who will be of no help whatever! But I must try to remember, he has interest in London.

I instructed the youngster, in a tone that gave away none of my distraction, to dismiss them just as spirits up sounded. None lingered when dismissed; even the landsmen had learned *that* call on the bosun's pipe!

"Black! You will remain for a moment, if you please."

The man who had earlier identified himself as a former "houseman" stopped and turned to face me. I studied him for a moment, considering my earlier thoughts on his abilities, before speaking. He twisted his canvas hat in front of him as he waited for me to address him further.

"You claim to have experience as a houseman. I am in need of a steward to assist with my uniforms, serve meals, and the like. It might prove more suitable to your talents than working in a gun crew.

"You would be an idler rather than a watch stander, and, should the ship go to quarters, you will likely be assigned to assist the surgeon, or should he not require your services, on hauley-pulley work on deck. You would have to be available throughout the day and night should you wish to take the job. And of course, I will tolerate no slacking, dishonesty, or slothfulness."

"Oh, Mister Ballantyne! That would be grand, for sure, sir. I would feel right at home serving you, sir. And I assure you, I will learn quickly the duties I must perform." The smile across his face seemed genuine enough. He actually rubbed his hands together, I assumed in anticipation of his new role.

"Very well, then. We'll give it a go. Find Mister Corner's steward—I recall his name to be Spaulding—and ask him to show you the ropes. You will begin at once and serve the evening meal later." I stepped away leaving the still beaming man to fathom his great good fortune.

The evening meal in the wardroom was a quiet affair, but attended by all the officers. I had by now met them all and a capable lot they appeared. I hoped I appeared the same to them!

Conversation centered on the ship, the captain (naturally), our commission, the mangy lot we had shipped as crew, and the people we all left ashore and would not see for a year and more. Across the table, I picked up on the conversation between Thomas Hayward and our surgeon, George Hamilton. They were discussing the incidence of that bane of a seaman's existence, scurvy.

"Had nary a trace in *Bounty*, sir." Responded Hayward to the doctor's pointed query. "The cap'n was quite adamant about using fresh vegetables and citrus fruits which he mentioned, on more than one occasion, were the way Cap'n Cook had done it. And Cook lost not a man to the scurvy in all his voyages."

"Hmmm. I have read Cook's reports as well as other treatises on the subject and I quite agree. But tell me, Lieutenant. How did you fare in the boat during your quite extraordinary journey to Timor?" Hamilton stared hard at the young man.

"Well, sir. That was a bit different, wasn't it? We had no fresh food save for some sea birds we were lucky enough to catch and the rare fish. Some of the lads were showing advanced signs of the disease well before we landed, but seemed to come around quick as ever you please once we got regular food, there in Coupang. Not more than six days of proper food saw most of them recovered. Only one failed to survive the effects of the disease, passing as he did some days after our arrival." Hayward's face clouded over as he recalled the arduous longboat journey. "And one got himself killed by some hostile natives early on when Cap'n Bligh had us land to take on some fresh water."

"Well, there's a spot of good news, what? Not, I mean, that one of your number expired from the disease, but that so many survived. I have recently read a new treatise on the matter by a chap named Gilbert Blane. Personal physician to Admiral Rodney he was and, with little else to occupy himself, began a study of the disease based on personal observation. Sent it to the Admiralty. Says in it that he has experimented with oranges and other citrus, especially lemons, while with the fleet in the West Indies and reduced the death rate from scurvy to virtually nil. Had been more than one in seven felled from the disease! Blane, I believe got his inspiration from the reduction, a rob, actually, of citrus used by Cook on his third voyage.

"Can't imagine why the Admiralty wouldn't sit up and take some notice of *that* for the life of me. Still making the ships load wort of malt as an antiscorbutic. Wort'less!" He snorted, his eyes crinkling in mirth as he saw that Hayward had noticed his humorous play on words, then went on. "But regardless, I aim to see our lads get as much fresh produce and citrus as we can find. You might have noticed that we have loaded several hogsheads of cabbage, as well." Hamilton sat back in his chair, signaled his steward for a glass of wine, and studied the young lieutenant from under a furrowed brow.

Hayward spoke, casting his eyes about the table, and saw that Hamilton's remarks had held all of us in thrall. "Mister Hamilton, I for one think that a splendid procedure. I had managed to lay hold of some orange rob from an acquaintance at Haslar Hospital, though sadly not enough to share out with my messmates. Happily, I shan't now have to feel any pangs of guilt about that!" He laughed, perhaps a bit nervously, then went on.

"When I noticed the barrels of McBride's wort of malt being struck below, I knew the Admiralty had yet to change its mind relative to dealing with scurvy . . . in spite of Cap'n Bligh's findings about fresh vegetables and fruits . . . and quite congratulated myself on my forethought. But you, sir, have taken care of the whole matter in one brilliant stroke! I thank you." Hayward laughed again, a trifle louder than necessary, I thought.

Hamilton nodded, a brief scowl crossing his face, perhaps at the young lieutenant's selfish admission. In spite of it, however, it appeared to all of us that our medico and Lieutenant Hayward's experience jibed and the benefits of their wisdom would devolve to all.

The balance of the meal, followed by several glasses of quite acceptable claret from Mister Larkan's private stock, passed with neither incident nor disagreement, as each of us talked to and took the measure of the others. My newly acquired steward, Black, seemed not only to have picked up quickly the needs of the wardroom from Spaulding, but managed to improve on them with several niceties, apparently brought from his previous employment.

With only three of us left at the table—the others had either retired or had gone topside to prowl the dark, rain-soaked decks—Robert turned to Larkan.

"What do you figure tomorrow holds for us, John? I would assume the captain will address the crew?"

"Aye. That is his plan. But before that, he will see all officers and midshipmen in his cabin immediately following breakfast. I would caution you both—and you might pass on this bit of intelligence to our messmates—that your watch, quarters, and station bills are complete and proper. Cap'n Edwards is not one to go to sea without first having tested his men . . . and officers! You may expect sail drills, exercising the great guns in dumb show, and an inspection of the hands. Woe to any who do not measure up!" The first lieutenant's look left no room for any doubt at his meaning.

"Thank you, sir. I can assure you we will take that advice to heart and be sure the others hear of it as well. If you will excuse us, I suspect both Mister Ballantyne and I have some work to do before we call the day quits!" Corner stood, buttoned his jacket about his ample girth, and moved toward the door. I followed, after first securing Mister Larkan's nod of permission.

CHAPTER THREE

Portsmouth

Saturday's dawn was dismal, the eastern sky barely showing the expected brightening: dark clouds promised more cold rain and the wind drove in from the Solent, whipping the waters of Portsmouth Harbor to a white-capped froth. Robert and I came on deck to discover that the sailing master and bosun had mustered the crew and detailed many to holystoning the weather deck. Hammocks had already been rolled tightly and secured in the netting atop the bulwark and the final items of our stores were just disappearing down the hatch to join the other necessaries stowed below already. Other of the sailors were coiling lines—halyards, sheets, braces, and lifts—securing them neatly on the pins surrounding the masts and lining the rails.

"The lads look a sight different from yesterday, Robert." I observed.

"Aye, they do that, Edward. Reckon the purser has already made a tidy profit on his slops!" He pointed at a few of the seamen nearby and added, "Shaved and pigtailed to boot! Guess the word has made the rounds about Edwards takin' a look at 'em later."

"Mister Larkan's compliments, sirs and yer presence'll be appreciated in the Great Cabin." A reasonably well turned-out seaman, likely the messenger of the watch, stood with hat doffed, awaiting our attention.

"Thank you, sailor. We'll be right along." Corner doffed his own hat, marginally, in response.

"Wonder who has the deck this morning, Edward. That chap was surely well coached. Maybe there's some hope for this collection of vagrants we've shipped! Let us not keep the cap'n waiting. I suspect he would suffer tardiness with the same measure of patience he holds for sloppiness and sloth!" Corner smiled as he turned to answer our summons.

As it turned out, we were not the last to arrive in the Cabin; Renouard, looking a bit worse for the wear, stepped in some minutes after we did, receiving a sharp look from Larkan as he closed the door and stood nervously to its side. Seeing Mister Larkan's expression, the youngster did have the good grace to color, glancing at his shoes to avoid the distasteful look. The first lieutenant also shot a look at me, thinking, I suspect, that I should have seen to the midshipman's promptness. I, too, colored briefly, an acknowledgment of my lack.

Around the Cabin stood or sat my messmates; Larkan, First Lieutenant, sat in a straight-backed chair to one side of Captain Edwards, who was seated behind his writing table. The captain had chosen not to don his jacket or waistcoat, nor was he bewigged; his dark hair, shot with gray, seemed more tightly pulled into the small queue than it had yesterday, but the powdered white wig still rested on the stand near the door to his sleeping quarters.

I noticed the surface of the table was quite covered with several charts as well as loose bits of foolscap. On the corner of his desk sat a sheaf of more papers, held down with a flint lock pistol. That gave me a moment's pause, just seeing it lying there in plain sight.

Robert Corner had stepped across the room and now balanced his ample frame on an upholstered bench below one of the quarter gallery lights. With his usual cheerful demeanor, he smiled and nodded at Larkan and Mister Harrison as well as the others in the Cabin. My other messmates had found chairs or stood, their hands held behind them. I had discovered an empty ladder back chair near the curtained entry to the sleeping quarters and close by the captain's wondrous brass fireplace. I carefully lowered myself into it and placed my hat in my lap. The fire had dwindled, now only ash and embers gave off a soft glow in the gloom of the Cabin.

Most all of the mids stood together except for a young man—Sival was his name, I recalled—with whom the late arriving Renouard had taken a position against the bulkhead by the door, as if to beat a hasty retreat should the opportunity present. While topside, the day was cold and gloomy, the Cabin, with all the bodies filling it, quickly became warm (I understood why the fire had been allowed to cool) and I noticed that a faint sheen of moisture had already covered the smooth upper lip of my privileged midshipman. He and Sival had their heads together, apparently whispering to one another.

Edwards, remaining seated with his hands folded atop the chart on his table, cleared his throat and addressed us.

"Gentlemen: now that you are all present and correct, there is any number of items requiring your attention. We are about to embark on a long and, quite possibly, perilous commission. Not only is the Admiralty unsure of where we might find the villains who set Mister Bligh and his fellows adrift, but they are equally unsure as to the whereabouts of *Bounty*. It is our task to find the mutineers and return them to England for trial."

Hmmm. He did not say "... trial and hanging. Perhaps there are innocents among them? Or is he simply being cautious?

Edwards continued. "We are quite prepared to take *Bounty*, should we be fortunate enough to discover where the rascals have sailed her, and we have the crew and officers to man her, along with the necessaries to refit whatever are her needs. She was, when she left Spithead in December of eighty-seven, lightly armed as there was no expectation of conflict. I am sure you have noticed that *Pandora* is not heavily armed either; it was the Admiralty's choice to reduce our weight of metal to allow us to carry the extra men and officers as well as the additional furnitures Bligh's late command may need.

"Having said that, I would caution any who might chose to forget the fact that we are, indeed, still a frigate in His Britannic Majesty's Navy and, regardless of being somewhat more lightly armed than normal for a sixth rate ship, we will be exercising the great guns, both in dumb show and in live firing. Our crew and officers," he stopped for moment, one eyebrow raised, and cast his eyes around the room, recognizing no doubt, that some of us had not recently been to sea. I thought his gaze lingered on me just a trifle longer than anyone else, except for my erstwhile midshipman.

He picked up where he had left off. "Our officers and crew will be competent in managing our battery as well as sailing the vessel. Midshipmen will be schooled in navigation by the sailing master and will, of course, maintain the journal required by the Service." He stared at the clutch of youngsters now.

"There will be no slackers or skylarkers tolerated, either in the ranks or in the wardroom. As you quite possibly have heard, I have little hesitancy in making an example of any who might need it." His eyes narrowed a trifle and, again, the eyebrow lifted in what I took to be a menacing look. There was nary a trace of mirth on his countenance.

I caught several glances exchanged among my new messmates and, more obviously, among the midshipmen. Some, Renouard especially, seemed quite put off by the captain's remark and seemed to pale at the captain's announcement. More than one set of eyes flicked to the pistol, still holding down the pile of papers. The captain's expression held a moment then became neutral again.

He went on. "Your men will be, in short order, I expect, as good as any in the Service. A credit to the profession. Any who seem incapable of measuring up to this standard will be broken and, should they still remain recalcitrant, will be put in irons. I know we have the dregs of the Impress Service aboard, but I have every confidence that you gentlemen, and the warrants and petty officers, will ensure they cast off the mantles and improprieties of their previous occupations and develop . . . quickly . . . into proper and capable seagoing professionals."

Captain Edwards now stopped his monologue and cast his eyes around the Cabin. This time, though, it was not just a glance that landed on each of us, but an intense gaze that seemed to bore into the recipient; it was almost as if he could stare into our souls take the measure of each of us. I noticed that more than one or two of our number seemed to squirm a trifle under those hard eyes. Myself included.

Across the room, Robert Corner caught my eye and with a small smile—more of a twitch in his mouth than a real smile—he winked at me. I took his meaning to be a repetition of what he had earlier told me about the captain being a hard man and offered what I hoped was a barely perceptible nod in acknowledgment.

Now it was the first lieutenant's turn. Unlike the captain, Larkan stood and while he spoke, turned about the room so as to address the entire group.

"I would hope there are no questions for the captain. I think he made his wishes quite clear for all of us and it is your task, gentlemen, to ensure those wishes are carried out *perfectly*.

"Since the frigate has been here in Portsmouth we have received many new . . . recruits, and with the need to prepare the vessel for a long voyage, there has been precious little time to train any beyond our immediate requirements. Now that we are very nearly ready to sail, it behooves us to hasten the process of turning all of them into sailors. To that end, following a muster and careful inspection of the crew by division, sail drills, line handling drills, and exercising the great guns in dumb show will be the order of the day." He stopped, turning quickly to face Renouard.

"Mister Renouard: have you something to offer us? Or is it simply you have enjoyed enough talk and are ready to execute your duties?"

The midshipman's face and neck turned scarlet. He set his eyes upon the deck, saying nothing. The youngster next to him, John Sival, took a half step back.

"Mister Renouard, I believe I asked you a question. Why is it now that you suddenly have nothing to say? I distinctly heard you chattering away like a bloody magpie with Mister Sival there. Perhaps you would care to enlighten us, hmmm?"

Again, silence reigned.

"MIDSHIPMAN RENOUARD!"

At this exclamation, the youngster snapped his head up almost as if he had been slapped; he wore a terrified expression and his voice quavered when he spoke.

"Sir! I was simply offering an opinion to John . . . I mean, Mister Sival, concerning our crew. I said, sir, that it would be a task more suitable to Hercules to turn them into sailors in one day."

"Well, Midshipman, I thank you for that insight. While your comments might indeed be spot on, you would do well to keep your quite useless thoughts to yourself and put your shoulder to the wheel with the rest of us. Are you up to the task, young man, or should I put you ashore? I am sure that one of Lord Howe's ships could use a bright, chatty midshipman. Hmmm?"

"Oh goodness no, sir. I mean . . . yes, sir. I am surely up to the task and might hope you would not put me off the ship. Please." The quaver was even more obvious now.

"Then I suggest you mind your tongue and learn to help your division officer, Mister Ballantyne, to run the second division. And tuck in your shirt tail, Mister Renouard. Hardly appropriate to have a midshipman looking slovenly, is it?"

Renouard hastily stuffed the errant shirt tail into his trousers, dropping his hat which had been tucked under his arm in the process. He bent to pick it up, to the amusement of his messmates, each more than likely glad it was Renouard whom the first lieutenant had singled out for attention. I noticed that his bending over to retrieve his hat caused his shirt tail to once again spring free from his waistband. He did not attempt to rectify it again.

"That will be all, gentlemen. You may return to your duties. Division officers, please see that I have your watch, quarters, and station assignments *post haste*." Larkan sat down and turned his attention to the captain. We all filed out of the Cabin in silence.

Corner and I, along with Tom Hayward, adjourned to the wardroom to discuss what we had just heard.

"I have the feeling that all we have heard concerning our illustrious captain will prove true," Tom offered as we took seats.

"Aye, seems he ain't likely one to suffer any shenanigans or fools. Perhaps Renouard might have been better off accepting Larkan's offer!" Corner laughed. "Edward, I presume your station bills are complete and correct?"

"Aye, Robert, they are. Spent half of the night guessing at which among my stalwarts might be capable and which not. I expect by now Mister Renouard has delivered them to Larkan. I have made Steward acting gunner's mate and instructed Gunner Packer to ensure he is up to snuff. With any luck at all, the two of them might whip the others into some semblance of form." I hoped it was not merely wishful thinking.

Mister Harrison and several other officers came in and took seats around the table, enlivening the conversation with their impressions of what lay in store for us. Precious little of what I heard from them, while offered perhaps, tongue in cheek, helped my newly developed misgivings nary a whit. I could not distract myself from the now bubbling worries I had earlier held concerning our captain and his reputation.

"Here now. There's the bloody Marine beating his bloody drum. That didn't take long. Guess we're at muster. Wouldn't do to be tardy for that, I imagine!" Corner's comment caused us all to stand, the scraping of chairs doing nothing to drown out the insistent beating of the drum.

On the quarterdeck, we joined the ranks of the other officers and warrant officers. Mister Larkan stood to the fore, close to the rail which separated the raised quarterdeck from the 'midships deck where the petty officers and midshipmen pushed and shoved the sailors, lining them up so the toes of their now mostly shod feet just touched a deck seam. I saw Renouard, still looking a bit disheveled, following Packer as he lined up my division. The other mids and masters mates seemed more willing to take an active role in their divisions, especially Reynolds, who was assigned to Robert's first division.

Perhaps Willy *will find some guidance from Packer . . . or his messmates. He seems not to be overly keen on his new employment right now. Mayhaps he's just a bit dispirited from the tongue lashing he got from Larkan.*

While I pondered these imponderables, the other officers had filled in our ranks—by seniority—and the men on deck had managed to align themselves in some sort of order. The midshipmen had joined the officers behind the railing on the quarterdeck, and our Master at Arms, John Grimwood approached Mister Larkan and doffed his hat.

"Sir. The men are correct and present."

"Very well, then, Mister Grimwood. Thank you." Larkan gave a halfhearted salute in return. "Mister Hayward, you may fetch the cap'n, if you please, with my compliments."

Lieutenant Hayward, the junior among us, stepped quickly to the hatch and disappeared, only to return a moment later in the wake of our commander.

Now in full uniform, including jacket, sword, hat, and his wig, Post Captain Edward Edwards cut an imposing figure as he stepped to the rail facing the crew. His left hand rested on the hilt of his ornate sword, while his right gripped the quarterdeck rail. He stood quite still for a long moment, his eyes roaming the ranks of seamen arrayed before him. He took in the unkempt (but surely improved over yesterday) appearance, the slouching attitudes, and sullen faces. It could have only been discouraging to think he was about to embark on a commission involving sailing to the other side of the world with this collection of street rubbish. Finally, he gave a barely perceptible shake of his head and spoke, his deep voice carrying quite clearly all the way to the butt of the bowsprit.

"Many of you have much to learn about being sailors in the Royal Navy. Your petty officers and my officers here," he removed the hand from his sword and gestured to us standing to his larboard side, "will teach you. Should you be unwilling . . . or unable to learn, you will suffer mightily as neither the Service nor I will tolerate slackers. Our commission will take us to the far reaches of the Pacific Ocean and where after that, we know not. But we will accomplish with alacrity that which the Admiralty has ordered us to do.

"I suspect you have heard many tales and yarns about me; they are most probably true. I am known neither for my patience nor my willingness to accept anything short of perfect performance. That you will not disappoint me, I have no doubt, and I . . . " He stopped, stepped to one side, and craned his neck to see something that had attracted his attention and interrupted his monologue.

Naturally, the officers and midshipmen also sought out the source of his distraction. So did the front ranks of the seamen, each turning his head, jabbering to his neighbor, and trying to make out just what was happening. Then I saw it.

In the second-to-last rank—I recognized none of the faces and so assumed they did not belong to me—two sailors, then three, and then the whole rank, seemed to be in dispute over something and, apparently were oblivious to where they were or who addressed them. A pair of burley petty officers, followed closely by the master at arms and the corporal of Marines—I noticed the bayonet was affixed to his musket—shoved with difficulty through the ranks to quiet the ruction. Words, disembodied and thus their source uncertain, drifted aft.

"Here you men. Belay that nonsense!"

"Seems like they ain't 'appy 'bout 'eadin' out, is they?"

"Watch yer tongue, Jenkins!"

"Mind the shovin' ye bloody bastard!"

"Here now. Make way. Let me through!"

"Watch it, there, lad. Ye'll get yerself strung up to the grating fer sure that way."

"Ow! Watch that bayonet, mate! Might get a body hurt with that pig sticker. Oooff!"

It seemed like a general, albeit somewhat subdued, melee had broken out, radiating aft from the original two or three antagonists to now include more of the ranks farthest from the quarterdeck.

And then a piercing scream, almost feminine in its pitch, rose above the general din. I struggled to see over the heads of the seamen nearest to hand, but could discern no source for the high-pitched wail. I shot a glance at Hayward, standing to my starboard hand and received a shrug in response to my unasked question. Leaning forward a bit, I took a look at Larkan, and next to him, Robert Corner. They were clearly horrified, but Larkan's entire countenance was so crimson as to be almost black. He leaned over the rail and spoke quietly to Bosun Cunningham; none among us could glean his words.

And then a shot rang out. The ensuing silence was exquisite, if brief. Only the creaks and groans of a ship working at her moorings, the cry of the occasional seabird, and the slap of the chop against our sides remained.

The respite was short-lived; the shot seemed not only to have quelled the disturbance, but rekindled it as well. Pandemonium, albeit of a lesser scale, returned. I heard several shouted comments and others that seemed merely exclamations of shock.

"Here, now. Who fired the shot?"

"You bloody scoundrel!"

Some of the men,—they appeared to be in the middle of the assembly—cried out, trying to determine the source of the shot.

Less confused—we knew the shot had been fired by one of us on the quarterdeck—the officers, myself included, looked about, trying to determine its source, looking this way and that, across the heads of the sailors and at each other. Hayward, it was, I believe, who gasped and uttered, "My gracious! It was the captain!"

Indeed it was. He stood at his place, one hand quite casually resting on the rail before him and the other held aloft, holding a still smoking pistol. Likely the same one I had noticed earlier holding down papers on his desk. His face was a mask of absolute fury.

"SILENCE! SILENCE FORE AND AFT!" The roar had come from the first lieutenant, closely following the stunning discharge of Edwards' pistol. After the sharp report of the flintlock, Larkan's command seemed a trifle redundant!

Encouraged by both the captain's no-nonsense response and that of the first lieutenant, the fracas was over almost as quickly as it had begun. The men returned to their positions and the petty officers and master at arms restored order, manhandling the sailors—both the ones near to the disturbance and as well as those who might have wished they had been—shouting and starting the sailors back into their ranks. The captain's pistol shot still rang in my ears, but the sounds of the ship, the slap of the water against the hull, the creaking of the rig as the ship worked at her mooring, and the groan of the wind quickly filled in, replacing it. And quietly, we all could hear with little effort the moan of what I took to be an injured man.

"Master-at-arms! Bring the ones responsible aft here, if you please." Larkan spoke only as loudly as necessary to be heard; no roaring this time. I would learn, as would we all, that the more quietly he spoke, the more likely it was that the outcome would be unpleasant for someone!

In short order, Mister Grimwood, assisted by one of my gunner's mates and the corporal, half dragged two reluctant seamen through the ranks of men and stood them before the rail of the quarterdeck. Larkan stepped closer to the rail and studied the two who slouched before him, each trying, I think, to look disinterested.

"Sir, there's one been stabbed back there. Might serve to have the surgeon take a look. Bleedin' like a stuck pig, he is, sir, and no mistake! Woulda brung 'im up, too, but seemed better to leave 'im where he was." Grimwood addressed the first lieutenant.

Larkan looked up, strained to see over the heads of the seamen, gave up, and shifted his gaze to George Hamilton, our surgeon.

"If you please, Mister Hamilton, would you have a look. Seems one of the lads has gone and gotten himself hurt." Then to the master at arms, "Have you anything to say about these two, Mister Grimwood, hmmm?"

"No sir. Just brawlin' they was, sir. Seems some disagreement over who owned a knife."

"Clearly, it would seem a knife mighta been involved if a man is indeed bleeding as badly as you say!" Larkan uttered under his breath, then shifted his gaze to the two slouching before him, their eyes uniformly set upon the deck as though something of rare interest had caught their attention.

"What have you to say for yourselves, lads? Can't have fighting and carrying on in the ranks, you know. Disrespectful to the captain, it is. Who . . . or what, started this . . . disagreement?"

Silence. Eyes still fixed to the spot on the deck, the one of such great interest.

"Men. You will answer me. I will not indulge this behavior." Larkan's voice grew a bit quieter.

Still no one said a word. One man did shift his glance from the interesting spot on the deck to Larkan's face, then moved his eyes across all of us on the quarterdeck. None of us said a word either. But Larkan saw this one might have something to say.

"You there. Speak up, lad. What was the problem back there?"

"I . . . uh . . . sir . . . I didn't have nothin' to do with it. 'Ceptin' I tried to keep Wickens, here, from stickin' Peters. Done it anyway."

At the mention of his name, Wickens (mercifully, not one of mine, as I had earlier prayed), looked up, stood a little straighter, and smiled. He actually smiled at our first lieutenant!

"Wickens, why did you feel it necessary to stab your shipmate? Peters, if I am to believe your mate here."

"'Ad me knife, he done, sir. Didn't mean to stick 'im. Just kinda happened." Wickens answered the question without looking directly at Larkan.

"Tell, me Wickens, if Peters had your knife, how was it you managed to stab him, instead of the other way 'round?"

"Took it from him, I done."

"Very well." Larkan now shifted his attention to the first man who had spoken.

"You there. What's your name and division."

The man, realizing his hopes of avoiding involvement, beyond that to which he had already committed himself, were dashed, snapped his eyes to Larkan's, waited a moment, then answered.

"Jefferies, it is, yer worship. Foremast jack, I am, and rated 'able'. Ain't got nothin' to do with these landsmen, now do I." I am sure he expected no answer.

"And you tried to stop the fight, Jefferies?"

"Sir, I tried, I done. But I reckon it was past stoppin'"

"Mister Grimwood, do you have anything to add from your observation?"

"Not a word, sir. When me men and I got there, one man—I reckon, Peters from what these two say—was down on the deck bleedin' from his side and Wickens, here, was standin' with a knife in his hand. Blood on it, I noticed right off. Jefferies had Wickens' other arm bent up astern o' his back in some kinda grip 'at seemed some painful to Wickens. Brung 'em both up here, I done, sir, straight away. Wasted not a minute."

As the master-at-arms finished his description, Surgeon Hamilton appeared from the ranks of sailors and made his way up the steps to the quarterdeck.

"Mister Hamilton?" Larkan asked.

"Dead, sir. Likely near to exsanguinated afore I got there. Told one o' Mister Cunningham's bosun's mates to sew him into his hammock."

Not even a full day aboard the frigate and one dead and likely one to be either lashed to within an inch of his life or strung up from the foreyard! What kind of mess am I into?

"Mister Larkan. I have heard quite enough. We have a ship to prepare for sea and a crew to train. We will handle this now. The crew is already mustered. They may as well witness punishment and a reading of the Articles of War. I have lost one man even before we sail; I can ill-afford to lose another. While he should more appropriately be sent ashore in irons, tried by a court-martial, and hanged, I have neither the luxury of time nor a sufficiency of seamen to indulge in such propriety. Having heard the case—or all of it I care to—I will sentence the offender to be lashed fifty strokes, to be carried at out once. He may be on the sick list for a time, but we will have his services thereafter.

"Following the punishment, you will inspect the men and then we will proceed to sail drills."

"Very well, Cap'n." Larkan doffed his hat in salute to Edwards, then raised his voice. "Attention to the Articles of War."

He then proceeded to read each of the thirty-six Articles, approved by Parliament and read frequently on His Majesty's ships of war; they dealt with the regulation and government of naval vessels and covered everything from blasphemy to mutiny (there were four of those), failure to perform one's duty, and, appropriately, murder. The Articles detailed those deeds deserving of the ultimate punishment, deeds which included murder, treason, theft, cowardice, desertion, sabotage, and sodomy, There was no interruption; the entire crew seemed rapt in attention. Perhaps it was more in anticipation to see what would happen to their mate.

"Bosun: bring the prisoner forward." Larkan spoke loudly enough to be heard by the entire crew even though Cunningham was barely ten feet away.

"Sir. Aye, sir. Which one would ye have, sir?"

"This one, here. Wickens, I recall to be his name. The one quick with his knife."

Cunningham took hold of Wickens' arms and propelled him a few steps aft, and directly in front of the captain and first lieutenant.

"Have you anything to say for yourself, Wickens?" Larkan asked quietly.

"Didn't mean to stick 'im, yer worship. Just musta happened, it done. Had me knife, though, he did, and no mistake there."

"Well, Wickens, he might have, indeed. But I am afraid the mistake was yours." Larkan's words caused Wickens to jerk his head up, looking squarely at the first lieutenant, as though he next expected Larkan to tell him the knife was Peters' all along.

"Your mistake was one of timing and extreme. There was little need to kill the man. We are about to sail on a long commission; it is likely that more of your mates—maybe even you, Wickens—will fall before we again set our anchor in Portsmouth Harbor. I expect we will need all hands to carry out the orders given us by the Admiralty.

"Captain Edwards has sentenced you to receive fifty strokes of the lash, sentence to be carried out at once."

Wickens' whole body went slack at this pronouncement; had not Bosun Cunningham a firm grip on his arm, he might have collapsed right there. An audible gasp came from a few in the front ranks of seamen—landsmen, I suspected, who knew little of the sea and the harsh realities of the Royal Navy.

Even some of our midshipmen gasped and two of them whispered to each other, clearly discussing the merits of so harsh a sentence. A sharp glance from Robert returned them to rigid attention and neutral expressions. Though his face held every indication of horror, I was pleased to note that Mister Renouard kept his own counsel.

Perhaps his experience in the Cabin . . .

"Bosun, you will rig the grating and trice up the prisoner."

Raising his voice to a quarterdeck command level, the first lieutenant now addressed the crew, still standing in the drizzle and cold.

"Hands to witness punishment. The Captain has refrained from hanging Seaman Wickens for murder; he will receive fifty strokes of the lash. Woe be to any among you who see this as a sign of weakness on the part of Captain Edwards; I assure you, it has only to do with manning the ship."

While we waited, two of Cunningham's petty officers manhandled a grating from the walkway over the gun deck to a vertical position against the bulwark and secured it to the quarterdeck railing. Having completed that task, at a nod from Cunningham, the two men stepped to where

Wickens still slumped in Cunningham's grasp, and took him by the arms, one on each side of the man.

As quickly as he was relieved of his burden, Cunningham, with a doff of his hat to the quarterdeck, turned about and, making his way through the ranks of seamen (which now seemed to open before him effortlessly), went down a scuttle forward of the mainmast. When he returned, he held a red baize bag, about two feet in length, but only a few inches in diameter.

Some of the seamen, the Johnny Newcomes again, whispered to one another, wondering what the long, narrow bag contained. Once they discovered its contents, they would never again take the appearance of the baize bag the same way!

Wickens' hands were securely tied to the top corners of the grating with small stuff, a light rope used throughout the ship; his head lolled to the side, making him appear for all the world unconscious. I could see his eyes were open wide, a combination of fright and anticipation of the pain he would shortly endure. The two bosun mates stood, quite oblivious to the continuing drizzle, one to either side of the grating, arms folded, feet splayed, and awaiting the orders they knew would be coming from Cunningham.

"Remove his shirt." Spoken clearly but not overly loud and quite without emotion.

One of the bosun mates shifted to a position behind Wickens and, seizing hold of Wickens shirt at the collar, gave a hearty pull on the fabric. The slop-chest shirt came away, leaving Wickens bare back exposed to the cold rain and, soon, the lash.

Even though I had witnessed punishment in the past—the first lieutenant on the old *Egmont* was a tyrant who did not hesitate to whip our seamen—it had been three years since I had seen a man triced up and lashed. As much as I tried to remain impassive, I could do little to control the revulsion I felt at seeing a man whipped like an animal. The rational side of me pointed out the necessity of maintaining discipline and making an example of one for the benefit of all . . . and after all, Wickens *had* killed a man. I supposed fifty strokes with the cat was better than hanging the man. Hanging offered no chance of redemption and perhaps Wickens—and his mates—might learn from the lashing that Captain Edwards would suffer no infraction aboard his ship.

My silent debate was interrupted by the roll of the Marine's drum, and Larkan's command: "Hats off! Master at Arms, carry out the sentence.

Fifty strokes, change at each count of ten." Then he addressed the bosun who would be overseeing the punishment and carried out by his mates.

"And Cunningham, should your man—either of them—hold back even a bit, he'll take the remainder of the strokes himself."

All hands removed their hats, officers and midshipmen held theirs aloft in salute. There was barely an eye in the vessel, from the officers on the quarterdeck to the lowest Johnny Newcome shivering in the rain, that was not focused on the tableau just off the quarterdeck. Only Captain Edwards held his eyes fixed straight ahead, seemingly focused on some distant object beyond the reach of the jib boom.

"Bosun: you may begin." Grimwood's tone was quite matter-of-fact.

Cunningham nodded to the larger of the two bosunmates. The man stepped forward and, while the bosun held the bag, he removed from it, the wooden handle of the cat. I noticed that the handle had been neatly decorated with leather and white line, and that neither was discolored from use. As he continued to pull it out of the red felt, the three foot knotted lines appeared and fell limply from the bag. Each of the nine strands had two knots tied, one near the end and one in the middle. The knots would ensure broken skin on the miscreant's back.

Wickens strained his neck to peer around behind him. As he saw the bosunmate take a firm hold on the wooden handle and comb his fingers through the strands to ensure they were untangled, he let out with a shrill cry, unintelligible, but clear in its anguish.

"Ten strokes, Moulter." Cunningham stepped back to allow his junior sufficient room to swing the cat.

Moulter turned sideways to the prisoner, drew back his right arm, and brought the nine strands of the lash whistling down on Wickens' bare back. The whistling sound ended abruptly in the slap of the knotted strands on flesh, followed closely by Wickens' tortured cry, "NOOOOOO," loud enough as to almost drown out Bosun Cunningham's count.

"ONE"

The procedure was repeated nine more times, the only difference being that Wickens' cry became less lusty with each stroke. Moulter seemed in no hurry, combing his fingers through the strands of the cat to ensure none were stuck together from the blood they drew with each stroke. Finally, ten had been completed and Cunningham stepped forward, touched Moulter on the shoulder, and took the cat from him. I noticed that the flesh on Wickens' back was striped in a pattern running from his right shoulder to his waist on the left side. Blood trickled down from each cut, staining the top of his trousers crimson.

The other bosunmate now stepped up and replaced Moulter. He took the cat from Cunningham, combed the strands through his fingers, set himself, and began the process, stopping when the count reached twenty. The second man used his left hand, causing the stripes he left on Wickens' back to criss-cross the previous set. Wickens had gone quiet by the time Cunningham's count reached seventeen, not even a groan escaped his lips; his head lolled to the side and he seemed to sag in his bonds. The flesh on his back was a mass of bloody stripes set in a surprisingly uniform crosshatch pattern, each dribbling blood to the top of his trousers where it created a spreading stain.

The drum continued its roll, the rain continued to fall disinterestedly, and the hands and officers stood bareheaded in respect, as the whistle and slap of the cat o' nine tails punctuated the sounds of the ship and the morning noises of Portsmouth Harbor.

Finally, it was done; Wickens' slack form was cut down from the grating where it had simply hung for at least the last fifteen strokes, motionless save for the involuntary flinches brought by each stroke of the cat cutting his flesh. Eventually, even those had stopped and, I am sure I was not the only one who wondered whether Wickens had succumbed. As his limp body hit the now stained deck, Wickens emitted a low groan. At least he was still alive and his mates, when so ordered, would carry him below and tend his wounds until he was able to return to his duties. We would be well to sea by then.

"Mister Harrison, you may tend to the prisoner. See that he is taken below." There was not a trace of emotion in Larkan's voice.

Harrison signaled one of the bosun's mates who unceremoniously threw a full bucket of salt water over the pulpy mess on Wickens' back, receiving from the broken sailor a lusty cry filled with the anguish of the ages. The screech quickly became a groan and the master at arms called out three of Wickens' mates to carry him below.

The men, officers, and midshipmen stood quietly during this ritual, some flinching only at the cry from Wickens, others, motionless, perhaps inured to the aftermath by the savagery of the whipping. With the grating and prisoner removed, we returned to the original purpose of mustering the crew: inspection, instruction, and a chance to hear our commission from Captain Edwards himself.

He now spoke quietly to his first lieutenant. "You may inspect the men, Mister Larkan."

"Aye, Cap'n." Larkan turned to Robert and me. "Gentlemen, you may accompany me, if you please."

I noticed, as I followed my superiors and the master at arms through the ranks, a different attitude among the sailors. There was no chatter or even movement among them. They each stood stock still as each of us scrutinized them. For my own part, and I suspect Corner's as well, I barely took note of Larkan's words as he offered his comments to us, comments which Grimwood took down. My head felt light and my stomach churned at the fresh memory of the flogging. Even through my fuzziness and distraction, I did take note that only a trifling handful of my sailors were criticized by the first lieutenant.

Throughout the inspection, Captain Edwards stood on the quarterdeck, watching the progress of the first lieutenant's party through the ranks. The surgeon and purser, our midshipmen and masters mates, and the captain's clerk, a man named Edmunds, interestingly enough, stood silently in the sporadic drizzle that did nothing to lift our spirits. Occasionally, Edmunds would mark on a piece of paper he held something the captain had told him.

Following Larkan's inspection of the men, we returned to the quarterdeck, Larkan reported his findings to the captain who simply nodded.

"You may dismiss the men, Mister Larkan. We will go to quarters and then sail handling stations shortly." Edwards spoke quietly, nodded to his clerk and the two warrant officers, and turned to leave.

The crew was dismissed with an admonition and the officers and midshipmen returned to their own duties; not a sound came from any. The slap of feet, bare and shod, on the wet deck mixed in uneven counterpoint to the low moan of the wind and the lapping of the waves on our sides. I suspected most of the Johnny Newcomes were stunned into speechlessness and the older hands simply realized the stories they had heard about our commander were true.

Captain Edwards, his thoughts perhaps betrayed by the thin line of his mouth, led the equally grim-faced officers to the aft hatch, each following him without a word. As we turned from the quarterdeck, I caught Robert's eye and raised an eyebrow in a silent observation. His expression, normally jovial and always ready with a smile, never changed; I might not have even been there.

Midshipmen and the masters mates, still shocked and silent, followed Mister Hayward, the junior of the officers, to the ladder below with heads down, hands hanging limply and none of the nervous and eager prattling that had so recently fitted about them like a cloak.

For my own part, my stomach still churned and roiled. It took an act of will not to heave my breakfast into the grey waters of Portsmouth Harbor.

Watching a man whipped to within an inch of his life was something I had not before witnessed, even on *Egmont*. The most our captain had ever sentenced was twenty-four strokes and most of those unlucky enough to receive them had, once cut away from the grating, walked away. One had even laughed as he put on his torn shirt. A scene not likely to be repeated in *Pandora*, at least not on this commission!

We were all in for a discomfiting cruise.

CHAPTER FOUR

The Solent

Late morning on Sunday, the seventh of November, seventeen hundred ninety, the second day following my arrival on board His Majesty's Frigate *Pandora*, saw us under reefed tops'ls, jib, and spanker, close-hauled, and heading into the rain-swept Solent.

Well, so much for the brightening weather! I thought ruefully. *I surely hope this is not a harbinger for the whole of our commission. Likely bodes ill, though. But at least I am where I belong: on a well found vessel heading to sea. And lucky I am to be here, rather than sailing blockade duty with Howe's fleet!*

The day had begun with a palpable sense of anticipation, surely throughout the wardroom and midshipmen's mess and, I suspect, in the gundeck and fo'c'sle as well. In spite of the rain, many of us, including John Larkan, Robert, my young midshipman, and Master's Mate George Reynolds, had been on deck since the barely perceptible dawn had lightened the eastern sky. While Bosun Cunningham's men had scrubbed the spardeck, even attempting to flog it dry in spite of the wet weather, the other officers had prowled about the deck, ensuring that all was in readiness for our imminent departure.

I had the watch and regularly glassed the signal tower at the Dock Yard, hoping to see the semaphore signal which would give us permission to heave up our anchor. Through the low fog and intermittent rain, trying to focus the glass on the spindly tower perched atop the administration building was difficult and I redoubled my efforts with each break in the rain.

Ragged patches of fog drifted with the wind like diaphanous bits of gossamer torn from a lady's dress, sometimes quite obscuring the whole of the shoreline, other times, flying away to reveal all that was there: the ships in the slipways, the buildings, and the small boats plying to and fro on sundry errands in the harbor. Finally, just as three bells were struck, indicating the time to be a half nine, the rain and fog both let up for a moment and there it was! The semaphore arms waving up and down, spelling out our number and instructions to make sail.

"Mister Larkan: I believe there is our signal." I called, handing the first lieutenant my glass.

"Yes, Edward. That is indeed the signal. You may so inform Cap'n Edwards."

"Mister Renouard, you will step below and send the captain my compliments and tell him the Dock Yard has given us permission to sail, if you please. Also tell him I am about to call the hands to sail handling positions." I retrieved my long glass from Larkan and held it to my eye as I spoke, confirming my understanding of the semaphore and instructing the quartermaster to acknowledge it with the appropriate flags.

It was not without confusion and many missteps that the men responded to the call for sail handling positions but eventually, all was in readiness. The effort of retrieving our best bower, complete with the shouts and curses of the bosun and Sailing Master George Passmore, was a clear indication of how inexperienced our hands were. Even some of the men walking the capstan bars around—a simple task if ever there was one—seemed to stumble and trip.

Setting sails—at least the part that took place on deck—was little different, and provoked angry shouts, swipes with Bosun Cunningham's starter, and utter frustration on the part of Mister Passmore. The topmen were, for the most part experienced hands who went about their duties skillfully, especially when compared to the confusion taking place on the deck below them. The sails dropped from their brails upon Passmore's command, but the men on deck, assigned to haul the sheets and braces, were slow to react to their orders, leaving the canvas to shake and flap in a noisy cacophony that threatened to drown out all but the most vigorous shouts. Even so, the men, on the whole, looked better than they had during sail handling drills only the day before.

Captain Edwards, the rain dripping from his hat and stoic in his silence, took the measure of those seamen he could see; the grim expression he wore spoke eloquently of his dismay at going to sea—indeed, around the globe—with this band of inept lubbers. From time to time, he would exchange a few words with Mister Larkan, no doubt commenting on the slovenly performance they were witnessing. He also maintained a watchful eye on his officers, noting, I am quite certain, those who functioned to his satisfaction in spite of the lubberly performance of the crew, as well as those who were less than sharp.

I have to admit to my own less-than-stunning performance, something I attributed to my three years of forced shore leave. But as we performed the evolutions necessary for getting the frigate under weigh, making sail, and setting our course to clear the shallow bar off Portsmouth Point, a good deal of my training returned to me and, by the time we were headed fair in the Solent, the waves smashing into our bow and sending showers of salty, cold water aboard, and the wind heeling the ship over, I had begun to feel quite at home in the vessel that, indeed, would be my home for the next year and more.

A year, mayhaps, even two! My goodness but that seems a long time. I have only been aboard for two days and I feel as if I had never been anywhere else!

As the ship pushed her way through the short, but steep, chop of the Solent, I watched the Isle of Wight pass down our larboard side and quickly vanish in the mists and rain. Unbidden, my mind began to re-live the previous days, before sailing, when we all got a glimpse of our captain's nature . . .

The two days, Friday and Saturday, had been a blur of frenetic activity, musters of crew and officers, and conjecture, in the wardroom, as well as, I am sure, in the fo'c'sle. We had learned a great deal about both the captain and the first lieutenant on Saturday, but what the future held for any of us remained a point of constant concern for each of us as well as a subject for discussion whenever the opportunity presented. Robert mentioned, only half in jest, that the midshipmen had surely been terrorized by Captain Edwards' quick justice. Hayward, likely recalling the heinous mutiny he had only recently experienced, added that he hoped the men were as well!

While all of us had been busy as beavers after the muster and inspection on Saturday, overseeing drills, checking powder and shot and seeing to the other stores and spare furnishings we might need before we saw Portsmouth again, I, for one, and I am sure most of my colleagues, found the time to contemplate the punishment meted out earlier that morning. It was that thought, I am sure, that caused the gun drills, firing in dumb show, to be less frustrating than they might have been for the men, and especially for Robert and me, as well as Gunner Packer.

Most of the men of second division had, for the most part, little more concept than did Midshipman Renouard of what was involved in preparing a carriage gun for firing and even less concept of where they should be during the evolution. Packer, Renouard, Corner, and I spent the first hour of the drill simply shoving and pushing the men into the positions they would occupy at various stages of the process. They made the effort and, after repeated "dry runs," at the least had understood most of their duties and where they should position themselves. By then we were ready to simulate firing the "wee" guns, as Acting Gunner's Mate Steward insisted on calling them.

"One of those "wee" guns rolls back over your leg in recoil, Steward, you'll find it less "wee" I suspect. Seen men lose most of a leg just by being in the way of one of these six-pounders in recoil, and that's for certain!" Packer had little patience for his new mate who, in spite of his somewhat carefree attitude, had proved early on not only his knowledge, but his ability to direct his men. For my part, I was glad I had appointed him to the position and suspected it would not be long before I made it permanent. Renouard was a different matter altogether, and I despaired of his ever learning to be an officer. He was surely not a "quick study," and seemed to spend much of the time staring into the distance, only involving himself should he catch me looking at him.

We finally arrived at the point where I felt the men could find their positions at quarters, recite the steps necessary in the firing of the guns, and knew what each of the various implements used in the process did. I so reported it to Lieutenant Larkan.

"I suspect live firing might be a horse of a different color, Lieutenant! Not much can go very wrong in dumb show. But at least they will know where to go and, hopefully, what to do when we give them powder and shot!" Larkan snorted, a bit disparagingly, I thought. As an afterthought, he added, "And how did our well-connected midshipman do, hmmm?"

I could only shake my head, preferring to say nothing than offer up the list of errors which I would discuss in some detail with the youngster when an opportunity presented.

Immediately we secured from quarters, Larkan ordered sail drills. This time, Bosun Cunningham and Sailing Master Passmore, under the direction of Robert and a clutch of master's mates and petty officers enjoyed the frustrations I had earlier experienced; the initial results were disheartening at best.

Landsmen had to be shown which line to lay hold of, where to stretch it out on deck, and how it all fit with what was happening aloft. A fight almost broke out over some disagreement and one of the antagonists grabbed a belaying pin from the mainmast pin rack and would have, most likely, broken the skull of one of his messmates, had not George Reynolds, Master's Mate, snatched the pin from him and, with the assistance of his dirk, encouraged the man to go about his business without further ado.

Midshipman "Willy" Renouard managed to step into the coil of the larboard main brace just as it was being released to run free. Only quick action by George Passmore kept the inept young man from being hoisted into the air by his ankle—likely to the delight of the sailors who would have witnessed it!

Through all of the drills, last minute stowing of materiel, and minor discipline issues, Larkan made his presence felt. The master-at-arms accompanied him, both men appearing to be in constant motion, showing up without prelude, and, with more patience than I thought the first lieutenant possessed, offering suggestions that would improve our performance, whether at gun drills, heaving around on a tops'l halyard, or walking the capstan around. Even he, though, occasionally reached a limit; at those times, he would simply nod to Grimwood, the Master-at-Arms, and they would walk away, Larkan shaking his head in resignation.

Finally we were done with the drills, the last of the casks and barrels were struck below to the satisfaction of Purser Bentham (who also seemed to be everywhere at once), spare anchor cables and other ropes faked out in the orlop deck, and the crew (the officers, as well) too exhausted to even complain.

And then it was Sunday and time to do what we had rehearsed, this time actually hoisting the anchor from the mud of Portsmouth Harbor and loosing sails from their brails. Quartermasters took the big double wheel and, after we made sail, followed the captain's quiet orders to steer the ship into the Solent. We were on our way!

Robert had the first watch once Captain Edwards was satisfied that his ship was managing the wind and waves. With a curt nod and comment to the first lieutenant, he stepped below.

Larkan picked up a speaking trumpet and shouted forward, into the wind, but well heard, I suspect, by all hands.

"Set the starboard watch! Idlers below. Bosun, pipe spirits up and dinner." Then, more quietly, "Mister Corner, you have the deck!"

Larkan stood to one side of the quarterdeck while his orders were carried out and Robert and Master's Mate Reynolds took over the duties of navigating *Pandora* down the Channel. Since I had no quarterdeck duties until I assumed the watch following the noon meal, I stepped forward from the quarterdeck and, ducking under a canvas spray shield, made my way down a ladder to the gundeck.

"You men! Lay ahold of those side tackles and secure that wee gun, afore she skitters across the deck. Look lively now!" Steward's voice was filled with an urgency born of an impending crisis and I stopped to determine the problem.

It took barely a second; the rumble of a twenty-four hundred weight carriage gun followed Steward's voice almost instantly, and I knew the rumble came not from it being hauled back into a stowed position against the closed gunport; the weapon was loose and rolling of its own accord toward the leeward side of the deck! I hurried forward.

A clutch of sailors stood in the middle of the deck, safely out of the way of the heavy carriage, but unsure of how to carry out Steward's orders; the side tackles had fallen from the blocks and now trailed along, stretched out in front of the gun, as though reaching back to the bulwark where they belonged. My acting gunner's mate grabbed several of the men and pushed them to one side of the cannon, directing in stentorian tones the remaining sailors.

"Lay hold of that rope, ye lubbers, and hang on. You there, grab up a capstan bar and shove it under the wheels. Lively, damn your eyes!"

As it turned out, it was I who picked up the capstan bar (I was closest and saw what it was he was trying to do), shoving it behind the rear wheels of the lumbering gun carriage as he had ordered. The bar wedged itself behind the wheels and arrested the rolling carriage.

"Oh, Mister Ballantyne. Didn't mean for you to be doin' that, sir. My . . . order . . . was fer that good-fer-nothin' lubber, yonder." Steward touched his forehead, saluting in apology.

"No need to apologize, Steward. I was closest and we got it done. Now, if you please, have your men drag it back into battery and secure it."

The men in question still stood, mouths agape, and unmoving. Perhaps seeing an officer act as I had was a novel experience for them. Steward quickly abused them of the notion and, with four men to a side, heaving on the side tackles while another four pushed from behind, they dragged the gun back into its position in the row of other six-pounders along the starboard side. The tackles were reeved through their blocks and properly secured back on the carriage.

"Steward," I said quietly to him after the task had been accomplished, averting a possible disaster, "how did that gun come loose? I checked those all side tackles myself yesterday following the gun drills."

"Haven't a clue, sir, now have I? Perhaps young Mister Renouard might be of help." The smile he offered told me he expected little help or knowledge from that quarter.

"Haven't seen Mister Renouard since before we cleared the harbor, Steward. Thought he might have been here on the gundeck. Reckon not, though." I looked about us, seeing no sign of the midshipman, only small knots of men gathered with their mess pails, eating the noon meal. "Regardless of how that gun got loose, it was quick thinking on your part that saved us from someone getting hurt or worse. Would have been a bit awkward, us not even an hour underway! Glad I don't have to explain it to Mister Larkan.

"Should you hear anything that might suggest the answer, do let Packer or me know, if you please."

"Aye sir. I'll nose about a bit and perhaps one of the lads might mention something about it. If that's all, sir?" Steward again touched his forehead and, when I nodded assent, turned and headed for his own mess.

I decided to have a look at the remaining carriages on the gun deck, hoping I might run across my missing midshipman. While all the carriages were properly fastened in place, I saw nothing of the errant Renouard.

After checking several other spots I thought a first-time mid might find exhilarating as we sailed down the English Channel in a fresh, albeit wet, breeze, I finally found him in the midshipmen's cockpit, curled into a ball, half in and half out of his diminutive sleeping quarters. He still wore his greatcoat and his hat lay on the deck beside him. The washbasin had fallen from its stand and lay in two pieces near at hand.

"Willy! Are you all right? Why are you laying on the deck, lad? Did you fall?"

As I knelt down beside the youngster, I received only a groan in response to my queries. Following close behind the groan was a retching noise accompanied by a small amount of vomit, which added to the small puddle already drying near to his shoulder.

"Oh my, Willy. I do believe you're seasick! Come along, now, and get up. You can't simply lay here and suffer. A turn around the deck and some fresh air will do wonders for you. Right, now, let's get you on your feet, then." Carefully avoiding the offensive pool, I clapped onto to Mister Renouard's arm and tried to pull him to a sitting position.

"Leave me be. Let me just die quietly. I have no interest in fresh air. Sick, I am, and desperately so. Go away!"

"Mister Renouard! Get to your feet! Now!

He opened his eyes, perhaps recognizing at last my voice. They were red-rimmed and shot through with redness as well. The boy had been quite obviously weeping in his misery. Perhaps my harsh tone—in an effort to help him—had been the wrong tactic.

"Willy, you must get up and get some air. Down here you will only continue to suffer and be miserable. Come now, I'll help you."

"No. I can't. This is wrong, Mister Ballantyne. I don't want to be here! Sick, I am. Feel dreadful. Should have let Larkan send me back. Can't possibly make a cruise in this ship. Don't fit and hate it! Howe's fleet, maybe a bigger ship, or staying ashore. Not cut out for this at all." His voice, broken with anguish and his current state of seasickness, brought out my sympathy for him and I redoubled my effort to bring him to his senses and get him topside.

"Don't be daft, lad. We've barely begun our adventure! Once we get to better weather, I know you'll be just fine and revel in your employment. Now let me help you up and we'll take some good clean air, fix you up right as rain."

Once again, I took hold of his arm. He remained limp, offering me no assistance whatever. His eyes closed again and he appeared for all the world to be comatose. Finally, I gave up and left him to wallow in his misery.

Outside the wardroom, I encountered George Hamilton, our surgeon and mentioned the seasick youngster to him. Perhaps he might send Mister Innes, his surgeon's mate, to have a look and offer some salubrious tonic to the boy. I did not mention his change of heart regarding being in the ship.

"Not sure the boy's suffering from the *mal de mer*, Edward. Seems like there's a passel of men down with some fever. Innes, when last I saw him, said it's been building a couple of days now and more falling ill every hour. Don't feel too splendid my own self, matter of fact. Just on the way to report it to the cap'n, but should I run into Innes, I shall surely mention Renouard to him."

"Can't be all that many getting seasick, George. What do you figure it is? Some malady picked up ashore?"

"No idea yet, lad. But I'll come up with something. And quickly, I hope! Can't just pop into the Cabin and say the men are sick without I tell him of what, now can I?" With that, our surgeon excused himself and made for the ladder to the gundeck and the Cabin.

I shook my head in disbelief. *Can this be anther harbinger of things to come? First a crew of landsman and miscreants, a flogging, dreadful weather, and now people falling ill before we're even out of the sight of the Lizard! Oh my! Oh my!*

When I regained the spardeck, I discovered the wind had increased some, now driving a cold, sharp rain before it. The rain managed to find its most uncomfortable way into every nook and cranny and, combined with the even colder spray, made life on deck, for any not under a shelter, miserable. I really couldn't blame poor Renouard for not wanting to be out in it! After ensuring the carronades were suitably lashed in place, I retreated to the wardroom, hoping that Black might produce some warming beverage before I took over the watch from Robert.

CHAPTER FIVE

At Sea: 32° 10' N, 14° 30' W

By the tenth day following our departure from Portsmouth, the weather had turned moderate, even occasionally pleasant. Unfortunately, the warming weather and clearing skies did little to ease the sufferings of our crew who had fallen to the mysterious malady which had shown itself even before we weighed from England. Renouard and young John Sival, messmates in the midshipmen's cockpit, were the only two among the officer cadre who fell prey to the disease. They were confined in an area of the orlop deck with the other men who were ill, but separated from the sailors by a curtain hung from the overhead beams. Mister Hamilton either recovered or refused to give in to it, performing his duties even without the services of his mate, Mister Innes, who had succumbed early on. In all, over thirty-five of the crew were laid low, a fact which created somewhat of a strain on those who stood their watches and the idlers who filled in at quarters for practice with the great guns.

Hamilton was convinced, and waxed eloquently and frequently on his thesis, that the cause of this sickness was the same as experienced in prisons ashore: gaol-fever, a result of the lumbered condition our ship was in, aloft and alow. Overcrowding in sleeping areas (the officers were surely sympathetic to *that* theory!), bad weather, lack of proper foods (it was nigh onto winter when we left and fresh produce virtually non-existent), and poor ventilation. He expected to put this aright in Tenerife.

Captain Edwards daily prowled the decks, watching the crew perform duties which, by now, had become routine for most of them. Larkan seemed to appear almost as if by some black magic art, often at times awkward for some of us.

At gun drill one day, when Steward stood shouting nose to nose with Bully Rodgers, one holding a rammer and the other holding a worm screw, each threateningly, suddenly there was Larkan, arms folded, scowl across his face, saying nothing, but observing.

Then, very quietly, threateningly, "Mister Ballantyne. Is there a problem here?"

"No, sir." I responded, equally quietly. "Just a small misunderstanding about Rodgers' task in the gun crew. I believe Gunner's Mate Steward has got it managed, sir."

"Very well. Carry on." And he disappeared just as quietly as he had arrived.

The argument, of course, had absolutely nothing to do with Rodgers' task in the gun crew. He was challenging Steward's authority and using his immense size as a threatening weapon, along with the worming screw he held. Steward, almost as large a man, was not intimidated and held his ground. Once I again, I applauded my foresight in appointing him to the position. And more that, I had managed to avoid having one of my sailors flogged.

The almost daily gun drills, first in dumb show, then in live firing, seemed to improve the skills of my men in second division. Some even began complaining about the repetitive nature, a sure sign they were comfortable with their duties. And when powder and shot had been issued, they frequently hit the empty barrels Larkan ordered towed out by a boat, causing great merriment and much backslapping among whichever crew had smashed the target. From time to time, there was a question about which gun had actually hit the barrel, but this issue was resolved by giving credit to several crews who had fired at the same instant. The thought of an extra tot of grog at spirits up perhaps contributed as much to the celebration as their success did! And the competitive spirit that manifested itself, quickly gave rise to increased accuracy with each firing drill.

Sails were set and handed, each time with fewer mishaps and shouted curses. By the time we had passed the latitude of Cape St. Vincent, our heavers on deck worked without difficulty—of course, the usual grumbling and curses directed at the topmen still existed, but spoken *sotto voce* if any officer or warrant was about—and the topmen could accomplish their tasks aloft in acceptable time.

I had stood my watches, feeling quite comfortable on the quarterdeck and tacitly in command, if only for four hours at a stretch. Thomas Hayward, my roommate and now friend, stood with me, awaiting the time when either Renouard was recovered from his illness or Mister Larkan allowed him to stand his own watches, perhaps with a master's mate as his junior officer. During quiet times, he responded to my never ending questions about Bligh, *Bounty*, Fletcher Christian, the mutiny, and, of course, what it was like in Otaheite. After all of Robert's salacious stories about the "dusky-skinned maidens," I sought the first hand experience of one who had been there.

Hayward occasionally held forth on the same subjects at meals in the wardroom, but for the most part, conversations in those quarters centered on who had taken ill (a few more each day), problems with our divisions (increasingly few with each passing day), and when we might see the peaks of Tenerife poke above the horizon. Naturally, the weather, which seemed some unsettled of late, was a topic we frequently dwelt on, each day as we made our southing, expecting it to improve.

It was shortly after we had sunk the island of Madeira astern, the weather squally but warm, and thus the hatches open, that we officers had just finished our midday meal and a cry rang out from the masthead, "Sail! Sail! Fine on the starboard bow!"

The first lieutenant sprang from his chair so fast as to knock it over backwards, unnoticed, and rushed out the door.

"We are close enough to Spain now, lads, that we might find opportunity has come a-knocking!" Corner, ever jocular, announced as he, too, stood (without mishap) and left the wardroom.

"I reckon now we'll find out if the lads are as comfortable with our battery when there's someone shootin' back at 'em!" The surgeon said to no one in particular. He looked around the room as we all seemed to await the beating of the drum calling the ship to quarters.

"Short handed and squally weather surely won't make for an easy time of it. Neither will those "wee guns" we carry, should that turn out to be a Don of any size." I remarked, also to no one in particular. I had unwittingly picked up on Steward's unkind reference to our diminutive battery of six-pounders.

I swallowed the last of a decent claret from my glass, stood, grabbed up my hat, and departed for the weather deck to see what was happening for my own self.

As I stepped out of the hatch, I was swept with a gout of rain. Thunder boomed in the distance, at first making me think it was cannon fire, but streaks of lightning, flashing ominously in the gloomy sky, at once put the theory of a fight to rest. Through the rain, I could make out Larkan and the Captain on the quarterdeck, each with a glass trained forward, and turned to see if I could see the object of their attention through the murk.

"Sir, I am quite sure, from the look I got of her, she's a warship and under a press of canvas." The voice from behind me startled me.

"Oh, Reynolds. Didn't see you standing there. I collect, then, you've caught a glimpse of her? From aloft, I would presume."

"Aye, sir." The master's mate responded. "I have. When we first caught sight of her tophamper. Trimmed neat and proper, set to t'gallants. No merchant would look like that! Couldn't make her hull though; too far by half, I'd warrant. But headed right for us, she is."

"Not likely to see much through this beastly squall, I'd imagine. Mister Hayward and you have the watch, I assume?"

"Indeed, sir. And just come down from the maintop, I have. Even with the weather, you can make her out from up there. Goin' to report to Mister Larkan . . . and the cap'n, as well . . . right now." He glanced at the quarterdeck where the first lieutenant and Edwards were still glassing the water ahead.

"Get along then, Reynolds. Won't do at all to keep those two waiting!" I encouraged the young man.

It was almost immediately he got to the quarterdeck that Larkan's voice rang out. "Beat to quarters, Mister Hayward, if you please. We shall see what this chap is about."

From out of nowhere, the Marine drummer appeared and began the insistent tap-tap-tapping of his drum which would send the men running to their action stations. Partitions on the gundeck were carefully removed and sent below, guns were cautiously released from their lashings (the ship was rolling in the stormy seas), and the boys scampered below to the magazine for powder charges. Sand was spread about the gun deck to ensure sound footing, and nets rigged above the spardeck to catch any falling spars, blocks, or rigging before it might hit the men working topside. The Spanish and the French navies were known for firing into the rig even though their intended target was generally their enemy's hull. Marines hurried to the ratlines and set themselves in the tops, hauling up the swivel guns with their ammunition of bags of nails, musket balls, and iron scraps, which would augment their muskets. Sail handlers were called out to clew up the courses to make the ship more manageable as well as preclude any chance of fire starting in the rig from flames reaching a sail close to the spardeck. And then we were ready.

As I went to my battery, I saw that Hayward was already well organized; Steward and Packer had the men in their positions with powder charges at hand, and the tompions had been withdrawn from the muzzles of the guns. Most of the men had their shirts off, and bits of rag tied about their heads to keep the sweat from running into their eyes when the action got hot. Fire buckets had been filled and sat near at hand. And of course, sand had been liberally sprinkled about the decks. There was little chatter and the men closest to the bulwarks peered out the open gunports, more often rewarded with a sea in the face than a view of our adversary, each trying to be the first to determine what or who it might be that we would be fighting.

I must admit to my own curiosity about that as well; I caught Hayward's attention and we stepped to the center of the deck, just before the mainmast.

"Reynolds seemed convinced she was a warship, Tom. You had the watch; you see her?"

"I did not. But Reynolds word is good enough for me. And apparently for Larkan and the cap'n as well. Hope she ain't too big. We are not exactly suited to take on a two-decker Don!"

"I can see her! She's standing right for us!" One of my sailors yelled, as he pulled back from the gunport, his face dripping with sea water. "Hull up, she is and cracking on!"

"Come along then, Mister Don! We'll give yer a taste of English iron!" Another of the lads clapped his hands together in eager anticipation.

Steward blew on his match, bringing the glowing end to a bright yellow flame.

"Easy, Steward. We have no order even to run out the guns yet. We don't even know what her flag might be. Mind your linstock near the powder." I touched Steward's arm to add some emphasis to my words.

I reflected for just a moment on the distance we had come; not just the distance from England—that was scant, in view of our ultimate destination—but the great distance this band of vagabonds and pressgang residue had come in learning their employment. Perhaps the flogging before leaving Portsmouth had provided some inspiration! I was proud of my lads and hoped they would fair well in the action we would soon see.

"On the gundeck: RUN 'em OUT! Larboard side. See to your powder and matches!" The cry came down to us, well heard, and immediately, the men ceased their excited chattering.

But only for a moment. As the heavers clapped on to the side tackles and hauled each of the guns into battery, a lusty "huzzah"—it may have begun by one of the after crews who had not been able to see our intended target—went up and was joined enthusiastically by all hands, both in my second division as well as in Robert's first division on what would be, should we maintain our current course, our disengaged side, once the fighting began.

One of my lads, peering through the now occupied gun port of number two gun, withdrew his head and cried out, "She's fired a gun! Saw the smoke from it, I done."

This sent up another cheer from all quarters as the men knew certain that we would fight. Their cheer must have drowned out the report of the gun.

"SILENCE! SILENCE FORE AND AFT!" Robert's booming voice cut through the noise easily and at once, the men fell quiet.

"Easy fellows. Remember what you've been trained to do. Listen to Mister Ballantyne's orders." Packer spoke to the hands as he walked up and down between the rows of guns, patting the occasional sailor on the shoulder as he passed.

"Blow on your matches, lads. Make ready." I turned aft and raised my voice to a sufficient level to ensure the aftermost of my crews heard.

In the gloom of the gundeck, I could see, illuminated in the flaring lengths of slowmatch, the gun captains crouching behind their pieces, holding the flame well away from the powder-filled touch holes. Their crews, shadowy forms making grotesque phantoms in the flickering light, stood to each side of their respective guns; some held worm screws and rammers, while others held their wet sponges, ready to leap to their duties the moment their gun had fired and finished its recoil.

The tension was palpable. The men—all of us, in fact—were about to be tested. Had the crews learned enough to be efficient and quick when the time came to engage? Would they remain that way when the first enemy shot smashed into our hull, or rig? When their mates fell, mauled by a splinter or round shot, would they stand there dumbfounded, or do their jobs? All these thoughts and others tried my own ability to focus on the job at hand. How would I stand up to the test?

Yes, to be sure, I had experienced similar situations in the late war with America, but that was many years ago and I was merely a midshipman with little responsibility. These men were *my* sailors, my responsibility, and were they to fail, it could only be that I had failed them. I muttered a short prayer for our success. Surely, in our continuing and long-term struggle with the Spanish and French, God would not, *could not*, abandon Britain!

"Stand easy, on the gundeck! We'll see no action this day. She's one of our own!" The voice, not the first lieutenant this time, rang out through the ship.

"Here, lad. Move away from that port and let me have a look." I spoke to the sailor who, after he announced she had fired, had resumed his position watching the approaching ship.

"On the gundeck. Number two gun, half charge of powder only. Fire on command." This time it was the first lieutenant's voice.

Number two gun, the first in my battery, was on the leeward side of the ship. This was an acknowledgment of the other's shot, apparently also a leeward gun. It meant either surrender, or they wanted to speak.

The gun, at Steward's order, was hauled away from the side of the ship, the shot and powder withdrawn, and reloaded with a short cartridge. He nodded to me, as the men once again hauled the twenty-four hundred-weight gun and carriage into battery.

"Ready on number two," I shouted aft.

"Fire, if you please, Mister Ballantyne!" Larkan must had either come below or was standing on the grating above our heads.

In any case, I did as he ordered.

Steward jammed his linstock into the touch-hole. The powder there caught the flame and sparkled and flared. A second later, the flame had reached the flannel bag of the cartridge; it ignited and the gun discharged with a modest roar and a short whip of flame that shot out of the muzzle. Due to the light powder charge, it only jumped part way back in recoil; the men again had to haul it back the rest of the way in order to swab the barrel for any flaming bits of cartridge, and reload it.

I could feel the ship bearing up and slowing down.

Reckon we're going to have a bit of a talk. Wonder who it might be?

As if to confirm my thoughts, the cry went out for topmen to man the yards and clew up our tops'ls.

The ship slowed and, with the sea running as it was, began to wallow as we ranged alongside the other vessel. We secured from quarters. And while there was some grumbling from the men that they had not been able to test their gunnery skills, I suspect that most were relieved. I wondered myself how we might have fared, had the unknown ship turned out to be hostile and well practiced in the art of naval warfare.

When I gained the spardeck, I could see quite plainly a smallish brig hove to about a cable's length from our leeward side, also wallowing in the long sea. The white Cross of St. George whipped in the breeze from her spanker gaff. The thunderstorm had passed and the rain stopped. A brightness in the western sky gave hope the sun would soon reappear.

Captain Edwards stood on the lee bulwark, gripping with one hand the mizzen shroud, while his other held a speaking trumpet to his mouth. Across the water, I could see another figure in the same pose.

"Ahoy, *Pandora*! What news on the Dons? Has Howe left Portsmouth to your knowledge?" The voice floated across the waves from the brig.

"As of our departure a fortnight ago, he had not. Likely to have by now. What news from you?" Edwards shouted back.

"Heard from a merchant just yesterday St. James settled matters amicably with Madrid! Reckon there's not to be a war with the Dons—at least not right away. Sure they'll find something else to get riled up about. Or the Frogs will!"

The captain of the brig bore good news. I am sure that when the Court of St. James, the seat of the British government, offered some opportunity to Spain to avoid an armed conflict, the Dons leaped at it, no doubt as sure as we were they would fare poorly in any contest between us.

"We've been chasing Admiral Cornish for a week and more. Bound for the Indies, he was. Caught him up just two days back and turned him around. Where're you bound?"

Edwards raised his trumpet again. "Otaheite to collect the *Bounty* pirates and find the ship."

"Well! Best of luck to you, sir. And good hunting!"

"Thank you, sir. And a safe passage home to you as well!"

Edwards jumped down from the bulwark with more agility than I might have expected from a man of his seasoning and nodded to Larkan. "You may make sail, if you please, Mister Larkan. We'll be pressing on."

As the topmen were still at their posts on the tops'l yards and most of the crew, now secured from quarters and with little to do, were ranging about the spardeck, the task of making sail went quickly and smoothly. *Pandora* bore off, settled to the motion of the sea, and headed for Santa Cruz on the island of Tenerife.

Many of the men were still suffering the mysterious illness that had plagued us from the outset of the cruise, Renouard and Sival included. Several others of us had experienced brief bouts with the sickness, but nary a one of the officers had yet to succumb to its evils. Hamilton mentioned, regularly, that arrival in Tenerife would provide an instant cure as he planned on loading a quantity of fresh fruits and vegetables available there. While he would not go so far as to call the malady scurvy, I suspect he thought some of the men were showing early signs of the dread disease in spite of his preparations to the contrary.

At supper that night, we listened, with less than enthusiastic attention, to our surgeon, as he once again waxed eloquent on the enormous variety of antiscorbutics as well as the fine wines of Tenerife. I think many of us paid closer attention to his discourse on the wines available than to his oft-repeated eloquence on scurvy and its prevention.

"One must hope that the word of peace between Britain and Spain has reached them. Were it not to have, we might have to fight our way in!" Robert, his usual good humor a-bubble, mentioned something that none among us had thought of!

"Surely, with the proximity of those islands to Spain, they must have been told by now!" George Passmore, our sailing master, offered. He seemed a bit easier these days, with a crew now of seamen, rather than the blundering malcontents we had left Portsmouth with!

"Hayward, what of that rascal Christian? Is all that I've heard of him true?" John Larkan, one who rarely spoke at meals save on ship's business, changed the subject quite abruptly, perhaps tiring of the doctor's monologue.

Thomas paused before he spoke, taking a swallow of his wine while, perhaps, contemplating his response.

"Mister Christian was . . . or should I say, is . . . a Manxman and, while Bligh befriended him and taught him, he held no great fondness for any Englishman. But I could not label him as a 'rascal.' Opportunist, perhaps, even quite distracted by his liaisons in Otaheite, but he only became a rascal—a scoundrel, if you will—after he took the ship.

"I found him a quite competent sea officer, a fact for which I credit Captain Bligh. Of course, Christian was an officer only because the captain named him such. He started out with us as a master's mate. The captain was the only true officer aboard, a fact which might have contributed to the unrest in the ranks."

Hayward paused again, realizing he now held the attention of each of us, completely. He looked around the table, swallowed another draught of wine and continued.

"I heard from Edward Young, my messmate in the cockpit, that Christian had intended to leave the ship by himself that morning in a raft he had secretly built from some spare spars. The man desperately wished to return to Otaheite, to his young woman that he claimed to have married in the local custom. But when he came on deck to assume the watch and found the officers on deck to be asleep, he organized a few of his colleagues who were equally desirous of returning, but had not been included in Christian's original plan.

"Mister Young, of course, stayed in the ship. I recall him pining for the life he led while we harvested the breadfruit plants and mentioning more than once that he would not be averse to returning to the island at some point." Tom laughed ruefully. "Reckon he's done that!"

"To be sure, I'd rather have a well-found ship under me than a few spars lashed together! You were, what, a week at sea at that point?" The first lieutenant inquired.

"Oh no, sir. It was three weeks, to the day, that we had sunk Otaheite astern. To be sure, there were many islands near at hand though. We had stopped at one only days before the mutiny to refill our water. Nomuka, it was, if I recall correctly. In fact, many said the incident following that stop had inspired Christian to his dastardly act."

"Well, Mister Hayward, pray tell us. You can't keep us in suspense after a remark like that!" Corner spoke, raising his glass in a silent toast to our narrator.

"Well, in a manner of speaking, it was Christian who sparked it. Bligh had put Mister Christian in charge of the watering party, but ordered him to leave the weapons in the boats and remain unconnected with the natives, should they encounter any. When Fletcher refused the order, Bligh accused him of being afraid of the islanders.

"Now, no man takes kindly to being called a coward, which was what Bligh had essentially done. When Christian took the party ashore, in a highly exercised state, they did, in the event, make contact with the islanders who proceeded to steal tools from the unattended boat. Bligh was hysterical about it and sent the master, John Fryer, ashore to take control of the party and stop the thefts. Which, of course, he quite failed to do.

"When the master returned and reported further thefts, it was Fryer who faced the captain's rage. Bligh then took control himself, invited the natives aboard to trade and seized five chiefs whom he held as hostage against the return of the tools. He then mustered all hands on deck and ranted at them for quite some time. I recall he referred to the crew as a 'parcel of lubberly rascals' and, when he noticed one of the men not paying attention, threatened to shoot him!"

A general gasp issued from around the table.

"So it was Bligh who brought this whole mess on himself, then?" Robert asked.

"In a manner of speaking he did, but Mister Christian seemed to go out of his way to provoke the captain. In the cockpit we thought it a bit odd that Fletcher would treat the man, who had shown him special interest, in such a rude way, but I don't recall any of us ever asking him about it.

"After some coconuts disappeared from the gundeck where they had been stowed, the captain berated Christian. I don't believe he thought Fletcher had personally stolen them, but held him responsible for their disappearance. Christian was, after all, first lieutenant. But even though at times he seemed awfully set on provoking the captain, there were other times when he defended him and corrected, quite sharply, I thought, those who would speak out against Bligh. And it was not as though he was the sole recipient of Bligh's wrath; indeed, at times Bligh could be remarkably antagonistic towards others in the crew. And then sometimes, our captain would be positively charming, benevolent, in fact. Christian, as well, could be pleasant, willing to share his knowledge, and of good humor from time to time. But both men could act the churl quite without warning, to the detriment of any within their range!

"The night before the mutiny—I told this to Edward just the other day when we were on watch—I was invited to the Cabin for the evening meal with the commander." Tom looked at me.

I nodded in agreement. "But did you not say that Mister Christian had been first invited and declined?"

"Aye, I did and he did. But I mentioned it only to keep you from thinking that Bligh was an intolerant man with Christian constantly under the gun. The captain dealt with problems as they arose and then forgot about them. But it was only natural that Mister Christian, as first lieutenant, would have the most contact with the captain, and thus likely receive the brunt of the captain's rage when it appeared."

A murmur of agreement made its way 'round the table. Larkan, our own first lieutenant, stood, apparently ready to go topside. He paused, after pushing in his chair, and looked at Hayward.

"I read Bligh's pamphlet, which I got hold of just before we left Portsmouth, in which he mentioned his utter astonishment at such a well-concealed plot against him. He specifically mentioned that he was most attentive to any grievances from the men and made special effort to discover any symptoms of their discontent. I recall he only flogged one man during the trip out. Could that be correct, Thomas?"

"I can recall only the one, sir. At the Horn it was, and we were all stretched to the breaking point, having at the time—it was something approaching three weeks of perfectly dreadful weather—the devil's own luck in rounding the Cape. Snow, ice in the rigging and on deck, frostbit hands and feet, steady gales that forced us well south, only to beat us back to the Atlantic side before we could make the turn. We were all exhausted and one man refused to go aloft. Bligh had him beaten right then and there. But that was all that I remember. Even in Otaheite, when the troubles were beginning to boil, there were precious few given stripes.

"But as to his surprise at the 'well-concealed plot' against him, I can only offer that until that fateful morning, there was no plot; only Christian seemed to have a desire to take his leave."

"Hmmm. Would have thought a man like Bligh would have made regular use of the cat, what with that viper's nest of scoundrels he commanded." Larkan did not wait for a counter to his thesis, nor did comment on Tom's retort about the mutinous plot. Instead, he nodded goodnight to the group and left.

"Well, who would have thought Bligh would be so reluctant to order a flogging. There's a surprise!" Robert smiled, rose, and followed Mister Larkan out the door.

The next morning, I happened to have the watch when the lookout cried from the foretop, "Land! Land off the larboard bow!"

The peak of Tenerife had popped above the horizon, poking up through the morning clouds. A lovely and welcome sight it was to all of us! But with the breeze now failing, it would be another two days before our best bower came to rest in the roadstead of Santa Cruz.

CHAPTER SIX

With the mutineers in Otaheite

The small schooner the mutineers had months before begun building was ready to be rigged by early November of 1790, just about when *Pandora* sailed from Portsmouth and almost fourteen months since the men had resettled in Otaheite. The sixteen mutineers remaining on the island felt they needed a small vessel capable of traveling between the neighboring islands both for their own amusement as well as to evade capture, should a vessel flying the Cross of St. George appear in Matavai Bay. The men had built the handy little ship under the direction of Bosun James Morrison, late of His Majesty's Armed Vessel, *Bounty*.

Morrison had confided in his friend, former Midshipman Peter Heywood, also of *Bounty*, that he had another plan for the newly constructed schooner: he, with those who wished to, would sail her to Batavia and find a ship there to take him home to England. By necessity, he included in his plan, mutineers Charles Norman, Carpenter's Mate, Josiah Coleman, Armorer, and Thomas McIntosh, also a carpenter.

"I am convinced that no court-martial would ever convict us, Peter, as we had no hand in Christian's dealings. Unwilling participants, we were, and victims as much as Bligh and his lot." Morrison had repeated the mantra both to himself and others since the sixth of June, 1789, when *Bounty*, now under the command of Fletcher Christian, had again set her anchor in Matavai Bay.

Without question, the sailors' girlfriends and wives, not to mention most of the islanders, were overjoyed to see the ship return. Reunions and celebrations included all from the Matavai area and many others from neighboring districts. But when the reveling died away some ten days later, Christian ordered *Bounty's* anchor hove up and the ship got underway; he and his tightly knit band of supporters had determined Otaheite and particularly, Matavai, were too vulnerable to discovery. It was with mixed emotions that they left their newly won paradise, seeking a more secure refuge.

After a three month sojourn to several other islands—the men had been unable to reach accord on where to settle—Christian returned *Bounty* to Otaheite on the twentieth of September, 1789, some six months before Captain Bligh would reach England. Still unable to agree with his fellow mutineers on a suitable location, Christian and eight others, along with a collection of islanders, both men and women, left the following day for a small island he had heard of but never seen: Pitcairn. He left sixteen in Otaheite by their own wish.

The Sixteen had separated themselves into small groups, each choosing a native girl or family with whom to live. Morrison, along with another mutineer, John Millward, was "invited" by Poeno, a lower chief of the Matavai area, to set up his residence in the chief's compound. Many of the others also found lesser chiefs who would welcome them. And following a period of acclimation to their new homes and settling in with their new "mates", the men had needed a project with which to occupy themselves. Morrison's schooner provided the perfect solution.

The little ship represented a great feat of naval architecture; she was thirty feet on the keel (thirty-five feet overall), nine and a half feet at the beam, and had a depth of hold of five feet. She was fastened with iron fittings, created in an improvised forge by Josiah Coleman, the Armorer in *Bounty*. Most of the other men, along with a score of natives, helped the construction process by cutting logs and dragging them to the construction site. The vessel took a bit over five months to build.

Launching their ship from the building site, over a half mile from the water, was the next problem to surmount. An army of four hundred people from the Matavai surrounds solved this by dragging the eighteen- ton ship down to the water.

Selecting tall, straight trees, Morrison supervised turning them into masts for his schooner and fitting them to the vessel. With no cordage or canvas suitable for rigging and sails, the bosun asked for his host's assistance yet again. The women of Poeno's village wove cordage from palm fronds and vines, and sewed native mats together to create sails. A brief maiden voyage to the neighboring island of Moorea showed Morrison that his vessel was sound and, even with makeshift sails, showed a good turn of speed. It also showed them that the native mat sails and palm frond rigging would not answer for the trip to Batavia; proper canvas sails and hempen rigging were going to be necessary should the plan come to fruition.

While Morrison and his fellow mutineers pondered this turn of events, they laid the ship up under a roofed structure to protect the hull from the rain and sun, the wet season being upon them. They returned to their idyllic lives, in peaceful co-existence with their native hosts.

"George, did not Christian teach you some navigation?" Morrison asked of his former shipmate and midshipman, George Stewart, one day as the two strolled along the beach, oblivious to the gentle rain that fell almost daily.

"Aye, James, he did that. Made me a watch captain on top of it. Why do you ask?"

"Still trying to figure a way to escape this tropical prison, I am. *Resolution* (the men had named their creation thus) will surely make the trip to Batavia with proper sails and rigging, but we've no one to navigate us on that long a trip. Without a talented navigator in our company, the voyage would likely end in disaster. It occurred to me that you might handle that chore. What say you?" Morrison smiled and raised his eyebrows questioningly.

"James," Stewart replied, halting his steps to turn and face the sea, "even a bosun must know that to navigate one requires tools and instruments, not to mention a chart of some kind. Have you any secreted away, to be brought forth in contemplation of such a journey?"

"I have not, George. I reckon I was hopin' you might!"

"You are out of luck, my friend. Christian took the instruments and charts—those he didn't give to Bligh—with him in *Bounty*. I am quite without any of the necessaries for such a voyage." Stewart shook his head and smiled. "Besides," he went on, "I have no desire to leave this place . . . as you seem to. It does not appear a 'prison' to me; quite the reverse—it is my home now. I am quite blissful here with Peggy and my dear little girl. Have a fine garden and a father-in-law who is a chief."

"Should we be able to make the voyage, you might bring 'em with you . . . your wife and daughter, that is. I doubt your father-in-law would give up the benefits of being a chief." Morrison chuckled as he tried another tactic.

"I wouldn't subject my family to the rigors of the open sea in such a small vessel, and navigatin' her to Batavia would likely be beyond my ken. I must decline your offer, James; I intend to stay right here until I die!"

"I understand that, George. I had intended to take my own wife, Tarreredooa, with me, should we embark on such a voyage; don't think I would much fancy life without her!" Morrison pressed, to no avail.

"You might ask Peter Heywood. He knows near as much as me about navigatin' . . . though I doubt he has any of the instruments or charts he would need either." The midshipman paused, studied the sea for a moment, then added, "He's a bookish one and, should he be willing to tear himself away from his dictionary efforts, might be willing to take on such a chore. But maybe not." Stewart referred to another midshipmen, late of *Bounty*, who like Christian and others aboard, was a Manxman with little love for the English, and well educated.

Realizing his quest of a navigator would come to naught, Morrison turned inland, followed by George Stewart. As they entered the path through the forest, they caught the muted sound of footsteps, slapping the undergrowth and wet leaves, apparently running. With the dense foliage and rain, neither man could not determine the source or direction of the sound.

Suddenly, a native, followed closely by a mutineer gasping for his breath, burst out of the jungle.

"James! You must come at once. Churchill's been shot. Dead, he is, and not a doubt about it." The white man panted as he gained his wind.

"Muspratt, what's this nonsense? I just saw Churchill not two hours ago. He was fit as a fiddle and more 'n likely, cookin' up some mischief with his chum Thompson. I recall seein' a jug o' something in his paw." Morrison laughed as he addressed the messenger, William Muspratt, a close confederate of Charles Churchill, master-at-arms in *Bounty*, and an abettor to Fletcher Christian in the infamous mutiny. Morrison still had not figured out why Churchill and Churchill's other close friend, Matthew Thompson, had not sailed with Christian when he left the Sixteen in Otaheite.

"It's a fact, James. Shot dead he is, and by none other than his friend, Thompson. Natives are quite riled up about it. You better come straightaway." Muspratt's breathing had returned to normal, allowing him to speak without gasping, but the sense of urgency in his mission to find Morrison still rang through his words.

"Thompson? Why those two were thick as thieves! What would possess Thompson to shoot his friend?"

"Don't know, James. Only got there myself after he'd done it. Come now." Muspratt turned and raced back through the jungle, Stewart and Morrison close on his heels.

By the time they arrived at the scene, Morrison saw at once that Muspratt's description of "riled up" islanders was spot on; the men were chanting and brandishing war clubs capable of crushing a man's skull. The women wailed and all were dashing about in a frenzy. One of the men held aloft a human head, waving it about by its hair.

"Oh dear God! What has happened here." Stewart grabbed Morrison's arm and stopped him from running headlong into the melee. "Better see if we can find out what has got them so worked up afore we march in there. They don't seem all that likely to answer questions right now, James."

Recognizing the wisdom of the former midshipman's advice, the bosun stopped and watched the display for a moment. John Millward, another of the Sixteen, stepped up behind him, touched him on the shoulder, and spoke quietly.

"Thompson's dead too, James. Saw the whole bloody thing with me own eyes, I did."

"Damn all, John. Don't come up behind a man like that. Scared the wits right outta me, you done!" Morrison collected himself with a deep breath and added, "You said Thompson's dead too? How'd that happen? Muspratt said Thompson shot Churchill."

Millward looked over Morrison's shoulder at the islanders, now moving toward a hut at the far edge of the clearing. "Aye. That he done, James, and then the natives—I think that chap yonder was the one what started it—killed Thompson." The young man pointed out one islander, the one still waving the crushed skull about his head, to the newcomers.

"Where was Matte during all this?" Morrison referred to his *Tayo* or chief, head of the Matavai district and Morrison's friend.

"Didn't see him meself, but I'd warrant he's not far off now. You think he can settle this down? They look to me like they's ready for more blood."

"Millward, go and find him, and while you're about it, find Peter Heywood as well. Bring 'em both here."

The sailor trotted off as instructed to find the two, Morrison turned to George Stewart who had remained mute, mesmerized by the spectacle.

"Heywood oughta be able to help us in talking with Matte. That book of words he's writin' has got him a pretty fair command of their language and Matte's English ain't so grand, in spite of my teachin' him. I reckon Millward should find Heywood right in his house writin' away in that bloody book. Might prove useful now!"

By the time the chief lumbered into the clearing, the islanders had calmed somewhat and his appearance silenced them completely. Heywood showed up shortly after, standing with Morrison and Stewart, who whispered a description of the scene when they arrived.

"Mister Heywood, would you ask Matte to tell us what's actin' here. I reckon he's getting' the tale right now from them over there who's waving their arms and shoutin'."

The former *Bounty* midshipman stepped a few paces into the clearing and called to the chief in the language of the islanders. At first, Matte (Morrison's name for the man; his actual name was Tynah) ignored the young man, but when he had finished listening to his people and calming them to a great degree, he waddled to where Heywood stood, exchanged a few words in the language of Otaheite, and together, the two approached Morrison and Stewart. Muspratt and Millward stepped aside to let the ponderous chief stand directly in front of the bosun.

"Why did your subject kill my man, Matte?" Morrison asked simply enough as to not need translation by Heywood.

Tynah studied the bosun for a moment and launched into a rapid-fire answer to his question. Heywood concentrated on the words, knowing that Morrison's command of the island tongue was minimal. When Tynah finished, Heywood explained.

"Apparently, Churchill and Thompson had got drunk, along with Brown—that chap from *Mercury* who jumped ship here some months back—and thought to have their way with the young daughter of that fellow yonder." He pointed at a tall, middle-aged native, comforting a woman, presumably his wife. "According to Tynah (Heywood, having learned the language, would not refer to the chief by any name other than the proper one), only Thompson committed the act. The girl's brother, in a fit of rage, swung his club at Thompson, knocking him down.

"When Thompson regained his senses, he seems to have gone crazy and grabbed up his musket. He fired it, wildly, it appears, killing a father and his child, and wounding the face of another, a woman, according to what the chief learned. Tynah says none of those people had anything to do with the family of the girl. Thompson apparently was just firing in a drunken rage. When Churchill, who had disappeared, found Thompson with the gun and saw the killed natives lying about, an argument between the two arose. Tynah mentioned it seemed some hot and bitter, according to the ones who witnessed it. Without warning, Thompson turned the gun on Churchill and shot him dead.

"The islander named Patirre confessed that he had killed Thompson in revenge. Seems Churchill was Patirre's friend and, quick as ever you please, got enraged after Thompson shot him; he gathered up a small group of five or six natives and went to Thompson's house. Patirre saluted Thompson and managed to get himself between Thompson and his guns whereupon he knocked him down. The others held Thompson down with a board across his chest and Patirre dashed in his skull with a large rock.

The head, what was left of it, that the fellow was waving about, belonged to Thompson.

"Others are out even now burying the body, along with those of the man and his child Thompson shot."

Morrison listened to Heywood's translation of the chief's explanation without uttering a word. He shot a look at the islanders across the way and noticed that most of them were gone; a few remained to see what, if any, action Morrison and his fellow mutineers might take.

"Ask Matte if this is over. Are they calmed down now?"

A brief exchange followed and Heywood translated. "Tynah says revenge has been exacted and his people are satisfied. I'd reckon that means we go about our business and try not to kill any more of them!"

Tynah waved and walked away, nodding to his people as he passed them. The remaining islanders dispersed, and Morrison, followed by Heywood, Stewart, Muspratt, and Millward, returned to their own houses. The Sixteen were now Fourteen.

CHAPTER SEVEN

In Pandora: *26º 32' N, 28º 50' W*

"That is surely a fine tasting Madeira, John. I always knew Tenerife had grand wines, but this tops even the ones I purchased! Well done!" Our surgeon, George Hamilton began to pour himself another glass of Larkan's dinner offering and smiled at the first lieutenant.

"Thank you George. I must say, the one of yours we enjoyed last evening is surely comparable. I trust you managed to secure more than a few bottles of it. Sadly, this lovely Madeira was only available in limited quantities and I was allowed only a few paltry jugs. Hope to save a bit for the Pacific."

Hamilton stopped pouring, taking the first lieutenant's meaning quite clearly.

We were sailing broad only a week out of Santa Cruz, headed for Rio De Janeiro, our last stop before Cape Horn. The weather had greatly improved; easy breezes from the Northeast, and long swells from astern had moved us along quite nicely. With only a single flogging two days out to mar an otherwise comfortable sail—one of our people had managed to secrete enough ardent spirit aboard to turn him into a staggering drunk—we had enjoyed all the benefits deriving from a mostly content and trained crew, fine weather, and the resultant pleased wardroom. And more importantly, a pleased commander.

"I must say, gentlemen, I think the fresh produce I managed to acquire in Santa Cruz has had a most salubrious effect on the men. I can't say it was only the fruits I found; could easily have been the result of the tea and sugar I have been administering quite without ceasing since we won our anchor. Most of them are now up and about, even young Mister Renouard! I trust, Edward, you are glad of his assistance now that he has mended?" Hamilton looked at me and smiled, almost as if he were daring me to comment on the further misadventures of my inexperienced midshipman.

"Oh, indeed, George. He is quite up to snuff—at least as regards his health. I thank you for restoring the lad. However, I am more pleased to have some of my seamen back, Bully Rogers, to name but one. Renouard is quite useless, save for the most mundane of tasks. Rogers, in spite of his inexperience and early difficulties, has come along quite nicely. Strong as one of his dray horses, he is, and seems to get along with the other men as well."

My steward, Black, cleared away the remains of my dinner while Spaulding, Robert's man, placed a figgy-dowdy in front of Larkan along with plates for each of us. With our having only just come from a land of plenty, it was made with fresh fruits instead of the dried figs and raisins we might expect later in the cruise. When Hamilton muttered a few words to his steward, a lanky Welshman named Whitten, a fresh jug from the surgeon's private stock appeared and was duly passed from man to man around the table. Obviously, Larkan's comment about his short supply of the Madeira had taken root!

While the bottle made its way around the table and the first lieutenant dished out the dessert, Robert brought up our visit to Tenerife.

"Have you gentlemen ever seen a place as pretty as Santa Cruz? I can tell you, I have sailed the Caribbean stem to stern and can recall little that might compare with the beauty of the place. And the bay, with its surrounding mountains topped by the Peak of Tenerife, my goodness, what a sight! Surely tops Antigua, for my shilling.

"I managed to secure a horse one day and ride up into those hills as they rose majestically up from the waters of the bay. The farther up I got, the more glorious was the sight. Made me wish I had even a modicum of talent as an artist! It fairly screams for someone to paint it!"

"Did you manage to get into one of their little forts up there, Robert? I know I did and, while I was not overly impressed with the batteries they mounted—merely little six-pounders, they appeared to be—there were quite a great number of them. Forts, I mean, not their guns! I suspect that had the Courts of St. James and Madrid not come to terms, it might have been a bit of a challenge to remain in the harbor!" Nods around the table offered silent agreement with Tom Hayward's observation.

"I wandered about the city a bit, in search of citrus and drink," Hamilton added. "Lovely little houses, they had, all white, of course, each set on rising land with each street built just above the one below it. Gave the place a terraced look, I thought. And the Governor's garden! What a joy. I wandered quite happily there for well longer than I should have. Couldn't seem to tear myself away. I say, I could have stayed in that island for certainly more than the paltry five days Edwards allowed!"

Not wanting to be left out of their waxing eloquent about the city we had visited, I added, "I thought the large fountain, playing in the center of the town, provided a definite coolness to the air. You could feel the difference when you moved away from it—even a single street. The poor sods living there must suffer dreadfully from that heat!

"Mayhaps that's why they all seemed so dreary and downtrodden. Shuffling along, dragging jugs and packages here and there, or driving little wagons pulled by donkeys. And their soldiers! Goodness me. Did you see how miserably they were clothed? Most of 'em looked more like vagrants than soldiers of the Crown, by George."

"They weren't George's soldiers, Edward. They belonged to Carlos!" Robert made us all laugh with his play on my words.

"I did learn something interesting about young Renouard from his own lips after he'd become sufficiently lucid to chat with me the other day." I changed the subject, as we had all been to Santa Cruz, and thought sharing some news about my youngster might be of more interest. It was. I continued, noticing the surprised looks my preamble had received.

"Seems he began his career in the Navy as a captain's servant. Spent some six months as such before, in his words, he became disenchanted with the life. Found it unsuitable for a gentleman of his background. Appealed to the captain, following his departure from servitude, for a midshipman's warrant. And got it!" I smiled at the recollection of "Willy" telling me early on he had only just received his warrant.

"Well, Mister Ballantyne, here's a tidbit you didn't glean from him. I would lay a wager you can not imagine who might the cooperative captain have been." Larkan, a wolfish smile pasted on his lips, shifted his glance around the table.

It was Robert Corner who guessed the answer. "Surely not our own Captain Edwards? My word!"

"Yes, indeed it was he. And it had been Renouard's good fortune to have been assigned as Edwards' servant. Seems Captain Edwards did a favor for an acquaintance in the Admiralty, and up springs a newly warranted midshipman for the Crown! Only logical he would be assigned in *Pandora*, given those circumstances.

"Edward, I would tread carefully, as I may have suggested earlier, with your young gentleman; not only interest in the Admiralty, but within our own vessel, as well!" Larkan broadened his smile at the look of dismay that must have crossed my face.

"Well, Ballantyne, there goes your chance at having Renouard 'kiss the gunner's daughter'!" Robert laughed as he brought up the age old punishment of bending a recalcitrant midshipman over a carriage gun for what amounted to a spanking.

"Well, you might consider mastheading him if he doesn't come around. I have found that to be a most convincing opportunity for reflection on one's sins. In fact, Captain Bligh threatened me with it more than once and did, in fact, send my friend John Hallett to the cap of the maintop on two occasions I can recall. Spent two complete watches up there the first time. Less the second, if memory serves." Tom Hayward laughed at the recollection. Others around the table smiled, recalling their own days as midshipmen and the travails of life in the cockpit.

"As I expect we'll be crossing the line soon, it would be my guess that Mister Renouard will take his indoctrination with some degree of resistance. Might be an opportunity to suggest—after the fact, of course—that he 'lean into it' and make himself into a proper mid." Hamilton sounded as though he were only partially jesting. "That would, of course, be only my *medical* opinion!"

"I say, John. Has the captain approved the ceremony for that auspicious event?" Robert queried.

"Can't say I mentioned it. Had a few other things on my mind of late. But I will surely bring it up at the first opportunity. Can't imagine a ship of the Royal Navy crossing the line without the proper observance!" Larkan responded.

Then, with a smile, he looked about the table. "Who among you has experienced crossing the equator? Robert, I assume you have, and of course, I have. Hayward, you too, I'd expect, given your recent experiences in *Bounty*. What about you, Ballantyne? Are you going to be suffering whatever indignities our bosun might come up with, alongside your midshipman? George, How about it? You surely must have crossed at least once."

Hamilton was the first to respond. "Indeed, John, and not once but twice. I can surely be included in the ranks of 'shellbacks" right along with you and Hayward."

I had quite forgotten about the ignominy of the crossing ceremony; and, of course, I had seen duty only in the North Atlantic. So, as Larkan mentioned, I would be 'suffering the indignities' right alongside Renouard! I made a mental note to figure out how far in the future that day might be. The recollection of light-hearted bantering among previous shipmates about the discomfiting travails flooded into my brain; surely, I thought, they must be exaggerated—tales of shaving one's face with a rusty barrel hoop and then smearing the poor sod's body with evil-smelling brews of God-knows-what. Well, I thought, I would take it like a man!

The figgy-dowdy gone, the wine decanters offering only dregs, and the distant chiming of seven bells signaled the meal done, and the first lieutenant rose from his chair. We all followed suit, leaving the detritus of the meal to our stewards to clear away.

And young David 'Willy' Renouard was once, albeit briefly, doing the same work! Imagine! Small wonder he thought he'd be more suited to the role of an officer.

When I gained the quarterdeck, I was surprised to find the midshipman waiting there for me to begin the formal relief ritual. Aside from having lost a fair bit of weight from his recent illness and looking a bit pale compared to the rest of us who had been out in the sun, Renouard looked fit. He smiled and doffed his hat in salute when he spied me emerge from the hatch and broke off his conversation with the junior officer of the watch.

George Reynolds, Masters Mate, and John Sival, Renouard's friend, had held the quarterdeck for the past four hours while the rest of us enjoyed our leisurely dinner. We would take control of the ship while they enjoyed a late dinner and some rest.

Reynolds supplied me with the information relative to our course, winds, and contacts on the horizon (there were none; we were quite alone in this stretch of ocean), doffed his hat in salute and stepped aside. Out of the corner of my eye, I saw Willy perform the same rite with Sival. Now we had the watch.

"Well, Mister Renouard, it is surely nice to see you up and about. Are you fit?" I asked as I checked the course the two quartermasters on the wheel were maintaining. Spot on.

"Aye, sir. I am that. Feeling much improved and glad of it. Did Mister Hamilton determine what the malady was that laid so many of us low?"

"Not that I know of, but he did mention that the tea and sugar along with the fresh citrus he provided you all seemed to be the restorative he sought. I am sure you will regain your strength quickly now you are once again healthy and the past weeks will be just a distant memory." I smiled at the young man and added, "It will be convenient and pleasant to have you, once again, assisting me with the men. More than one of them inquired about your circumstances while you were under the weather."

"Is it true, sir, we are heading to Rio de Janeiro? I heard mention of that in the cockpit from some of the other mids. I do hope it is true."

"Quite so, Willy. We are indeed heading for Rio for more provisions as it will be our last opportunity before rounding the Horn. We will, I understand, head directly for Otaheite once clear of the Cape." I glanced aloft, saw the foretops'l shiver along its edge and instructed the helmsmen to ease her half a point.

"You may take a turn about the spardeck, if you please, Mister Renouard, and make certain the watch section is up and about and looking to their duties. It will be coming on dark shortly and better to do it now than after the night settles upon us."

He left, starting forward up the windward side. I watched as he stopped to speak to a clutch of sailors gathered by the foot of the mainmast. I could hear no part of their conversation, but it did not seem contentious.

My goodness, but it's getting warm. Even as the day wanes, the sun is still strong! I can only imagine what it will be like in a week or so when we are on the "line".

That thought, of course, brought to mind the comments made earlier in the wardroom about the traditional ceremony attendant to the crossing.

Oh my! The Line! I will surely be subject to the same rites of passage as any other who has not yet made the crossing. I hope I will not embarrass myself or my colleagues in the wardroom! Come now, Edward. How bad can it be? They are common sailors and I am an officer. They will dare not antagonize me or any other officer. Should they get out of hand, I am sure the first lieutenant will quickly bring them to check. Besides, once it's done, they will again be answering to me and the other officers, and will run the risk of retribution! No, I am sure it will be quite all right.

I hoped.

Did not Larkan mention he had crossed the equator . . . and Robert, as well? Will they take roles in the ritual? They would surely be more likely to give their attention to the officers and midshipmen? Oh dear! I shall have to discover what Robert knows about this!

And so my thoughts rambled as *Pandora* plowed through the rolling swells, south south west, a bone in her teeth, her sails straining under the strong trade winds, heading for Rio. But before we would gain port, the Equator. I wondered if Renouard was aware of what the future might hold for him as well.

I noticed as one of the quartermasters, not on the wheel, turned the sand glass, and checked my own watch, surprised to discover that half our watch had passed and it soon would be full dark. I instructed the same man to see to the lantern in the binnacle and cast the log while we still had some daylight. Almost as I spoke, darkness descended upon us.

The night hit hard—there is little twilight in these latitudes—and the heavens quickly filled with myriad stars, too numerous by half for one to count. Their reflections in the sea were eerie, little points of light that bobbed on the surface, coming and going as the surge permitted. Astern, small sea creatures emitted a glowing testament to their presence in our foamy wake. Except for the wind groaning in the rigging and the occasional creaks and moans of the ship as she worked through the swells, the night seemed also to bring silence. I could hear no seabirds crying overhead nor any other natural sounds. It was as if there existed nothing in the world but our ship, tiny in the vast ocean; not a vessel, not a human, not a creature. Of course, other than those in our ship, there *was* nothing else about, at least that we might perceive.

"Mister Ballantyne?" Renouard was back, reappearing on the quarterdeck silently. The spill from the binnacle lantern cast a yellow glow on his face recalling his appearance when first he took ill some weeks ago.

"Yes, Mister Renouard. I assume all is quiet about the deck? No problems? The watch at their proper stations?"

"Oh, yes sir. Indeed. I saw nothing out of the ordinary. The men are simply standing about, talking among themselves and smoking. Several asked me where our next port would be. I told them Rio. I hope that was all right?"

"I am sure it is not a secret. Since none were allowed ashore in Santa Cruz, perhaps they are hoping the captain will give them a run in Rio. I doubt it."

We lapsed into silence again, each thinking our own thoughts. Mine centered on things both professional and mundane: how was the ship moving, were the sails full, were we on the proper course? Occasionally, errant notions appeared: King Neptune torturing those who had yet to cross the Line, storms at the Horn, and the like. But for the most part, I remained focused on my job at hand. What Renouard was thinking remained a mystery. Then he spoke and I discovered where *his* thoughts were centered.

"Mister Ballantyne, when you were ashore in Tenerife, did you see any canaries? I would think they must be rife there, what with the islands being called the Canary Islands."

"Actually, Willy," I responded, jerking my thoughts away from the ship. We stepped away from the wheel and binnacle, out of the light and out of earshot of the watch on the quarterdeck. "The Canary Islands are not named for the birds; it's the other way 'round. The birds are named for the islands, as that is where they were first found. Those islands were named by the Romans, presumably their discoverers, who found large and, I am led to believe, quite fierce dogs roaming wild about the hills. I have never heard how the dogs got there, but one must assume that someone beat the Romans to the islands and left some dogs."

"Uh, dogs? Not birds?" His tone was witness to his complete bewilderment at my revelation.

"I would assume that somewhere in your education, Willy, you studied Latin?" Without waiting for an acknowledgment, I continued. "*Canis* is Latin for dog. They were originally called *Insula Canaria*, or Islands of the Dogs. Hence *Canary Islands*. For the dogs, not the birds. Have you not read the sailing directions? I am quite certain that is where I discovered that information. I would have thought that the sailing master would have seen to it that all the mids had read the navigational tracts for our course." I paused, raised my eyebrows and then realized that he could not see my expression in the dark. A wasted gesture!

"Uh, yes sir. I did read them. Guess I missed the part about the history of the islands. Sorry, sir. I . . . " He stopped, perhaps realizing that excuses would not answer.

"Very well, then. Now that you are mended, you might consider paying closer attention to such things as learning to be an officer and the topics— navigation, seamanship, gunnery, and the like—people are trying to teach you and your comrades in the cockpit. I would submit that that is why you are here." I knew full well that he was here because of interest in the Admiralty and the action of Captain Edwards, but for those same reasons, I would be unlikely to mention them!

In an effort to end the conversation, I stepped back to the wheel and peered into the binnacle. The quartermasters were spot on course, and while I could not see the sails in the gloom of the moonless night, I listened carefully for the telltale slap of shivering canvas, a sign the wind had veered slightly. Nothing. All was well. *Pandora* pressed on to the southwest. And then Robert's booming and cheery voice sounded in the dark as he hauled his ample girth from the hatchway.

"Ready for your relief, Edward?" Must be bloody boring up here!"

I started, surprised that the watch had passed so quickly and it was already eight o'clock. I said as much.

"Aye. Wouldn't you know. Time passes quickly when one is enjoying oneself! And I am sure the quiet and restful atmosphere of the quarterdeck at this time of night lent themselves to your enjoyment! And of course, scintillating conversation with young Renouard!" Even though I could barely make out his face, I knew from his tone that he was smiling broadly at his own sarcastic wit.

I did not share the thoughts that had been running through my mind about the line crossing ceremony, saving them for another time when we would have a bit of privacy.

Hayward showed up moments later, ready to relieve Renouard and then it was done. A quiet and orderly transfer of command—or should I say, *temporary* command! I headed forward to stretch my legs a bit, speaking or nodding to the sailors as I passed. Then I retired below to read, write a long put-off letter to my family, and go to bed.

CHAPTER EIGHT

Otaheite, Late November 1790

With *Resolution* deemed seaworthy, at least for short inter island sails, some of the mutineers took the little ship a-visiting. After their maiden voyage, Morrison realized the sails he had for the vessel, made of woven mats with twisted vines for rope, would not answer in any kind of weather nor would they last for an extended voyage. But, as he lamented to William Muspratt, "They's what we got, lad. We'll just have to make do with 'em."

And so, with little else to occupy their time, five men, Muspratt, Morrison, Coleman, Millward, and McIntosh, loaded some provisions aboard, and pushed out of the shallows of Matavai Bay. Morrison had deemed the weather fair and, with high spirits, the men steered their little ship for the opening in the reef. A native canoe followed them out, to just inside the reef, but returned to shore before entering the open sea. They had originally told the sailors they would accompany *Resolution* to Tettooroa, a small island to the north of Otaheite and only a day's sail or paddle away.

"Thought they was goin' with us, Bosun. Why d'you suppose they went back." Muspratt queried Morrison as they watched the native canoe reach the beach again.

"No idea, lad. Mayhaps the seas'r too big for 'em. *Resolution* seems to handle 'em easily, just like she did when we tried her out couple of months back."

"Mayhaps they think there's some weather comin' in. What about that? Them local chaps seem to have a good idea of what's in the offing hereabouts." Muspratt pressed.

"Seems like a fine day, to me, Bill. And we surely ain't goin' terrible far. Not even any clouds up there, to speak of. Just them ones low on the horizon. Shouldn't be a problem, even if they's got some weather in 'em. We'll be eatin' a roast hog with our friends at Tettooroa and tastin' their fine spirits by the time it gets here. Now, if you would be so kind, clap a hand on that vine we use as a sheet and give 'er a bit o' slack."

Morrison was wrong. The easy east-southeast breeze they had enjoyed soon turned to a gale. The little ship struggled to stay upright as the men struggled to empty the seawater from her. All the while, Muspratt and several of the others who had heard the earlier exchange, shot threatening looks at James Morrison, struggling himself with the tiller, as he fought the waves and the vessel's inclination to bring her head to wind.

"You lads, see about shortening her down. This wind's tearin' hell outta our sails. Hand the mains'l down to a scrap and I'll try to get her to heave to. Mayhaps, she'll ride easier that way." Morrison shouted to his crew.

As darkness approached and the rains began, *Resolution* lay hove to, wallowing in the huge rollers, as the wind screamed through her rig. Twice the men had been forced to further shorten the mains'l as the wind shredded the exposed parts of the matting that constituted the sail. The woven fronds, separating from the mats, had sharp edges that cut any hand attempting to control them, even the calloused and horny hands of life-long sailors. And all five men spent at least forty-five minutes out of each hour bailing. The rain now came in torrents, adding more to the bilge than the seas.

"It'd be a welcome sight, would a Royal Navy frigate appear over the horizon, I'd warrant! Not that we'd be likely to see 'er in this weather and blackness." Millward offered during one of their infrequent breaks in bailing. "I can tell you, lads, I'd offer meself up for whatever they gave me, just to get out of this wee bucket Morrison's built. Gonna kill us all 'fore this night's done."

"You'd likely get yourself hung, Millward. And half the reason I built this 'wee bucket,' as you call her, was to get us off to a place where we might find employment without any bein' the wiser. I ain't so confident as you boys are that the Admiralty is just going to forget about us. If Cap'n Bligh made it in someplace and has got hisself back to England, I'd warrant they'll be a ship sent out to have a look for us . . . and Christian and his fellows. God help us all if they find us! I'd wager it won't go well for any!" Even over the fearful noise of the wind and the seas pounding the little vessel, Morrison's voice conveyed quite clearly his absolute belief— and the concern that his belief brought to the fore—that sooner or later, the Navy would come a'visitin'.

Dawn came, and with it, a respite from the rain. Even though the sun did not immediately show itself, the brightening skies gave the men some hope that their ordeal might be drawing to a close. And daylight made even their untoward circumstances more palatable. The wind, however, continued to blow a gale, and the seas threatened constantly to overpower and upset the boat. Morrison shared out some sodden food and a fine tot of the ardent native brew they had all become quite fond of. They bailed now only slightly more than half of each hour, allowing for some rest and a chance for each to partake of the restorative qualities of the food and drink. Not a soul complained about the soggy biscuit and pork; they were too busy wolfing it down, chased by the alcohol brewed by the Otaheitians from palm leaves. His men were exhausted, bedraggled, and, while angry at the bosun, grateful to be still alive. And Morrison was angry that none of their natives friends had warned them of the likelihood of this nasty bit of weather.

"Why do you suppose Matte didn't mention to me we was gonna get a blow? Seems like he mighta said something. Or any one of them. It's a year and more we been their friends and lived with 'em. You'da thought one of 'em mighta said something. Wasn't no secret we was headin over to Tettooroa." Morrison posed his question to no one in particular.

And no one in particular, or, in fact, at all, answered him. Two of his crew, Coleman and McIntosh, were engaged in bailing, lethargically scooping their buckets through the sloshing water between their feet and then turning to dump much of it overboard. Either they did not hear Morrison's questions or they simply chose to ignore them. The other two, Muspratt and Millward appeared to be asleep, one draped over the gunwale, while the other, Muspratt, was simply curled up on the bottom of the boat, oblivious to the water washing around him. Morrison continued to curse their friends for not warning the mutineers of the potential for bad weather, especially his host and chief, Matte—Tynah, as Peter Heywood called him.

"Well, I reckon their pulling back to the beach and not following us like they said they would might be took as a warning. But, damn all, they cudda shouted to us. Seems only right. Course, Matte wasn't in the canoe so I reckon I can't throw too much of the blame on his shoulders. But, damn his eyes, he musta known, too! Knew where I was goin, for sure.

"Mayhaps they's lookin' to be rid of us. That trouble with Churchill and Thompson a few months back . . . but that's over and done with a while now and ain't been mentioned since.

"Millward! Wake up, you lout! Peona make any mention of this weather comin' in?"

Millward, a guest of a sub-chief of the Matavai area and resident of his compound when ashore, but now just a wet, exhausted, sailor, stirred, but deigned not to respond. An eye, bloodshot and underscored with dark circles, cracked open a slit, and glared at the bosun before it closed again.

Morrison, for his part, slipped back into silence, keeping his own council, while he attempted to figure a way out of the mess they had gotten themselves into.

By late morning, the wind began to ease and, in the character of those waters, the seas laid down quickly. When the sun finally broke through the clouds, to shine with, at first, warming and welcome rays, the men cheered, rousing themselves to a small celebration. Within an hour, though, and the sun almost directly overhead, that same warmth turned to scorching heat. Ironically, the men found it useful to dip their now dried shirts into the sea before draping them over their heads and shoulders. The wet provided a false feeling of comfort and shelter.

"Where do you reckon we got to, Jim?" Coleman demanded as they attempted to sort out their stock of provisions and determine a course to sail with what was left of their sails.

"I'd wager that blow took us closer to that island west of Tettooroa—what's it called? Tettahah, I recollect. Think we might head a bit west of north and we should see it. Anybody got a better idea?" Morrison's tone was challenging and, clearly, he was not soliciting a debate. Save for William Muspratt, none of those with him had any inkling at all of where the neighboring islands lay in relation to Otaheite. Of course, the midshipmen from *Bounty* all had a pretty fair idea of these islands and how to navigate, but then they weren't aboard. And Morrison knew, they mostly had remained aloof from the foremast Jacks who made up the rest of the mutineers on Otaheite.

As Morrison expected, there was no discussion about his plan; he was the captain of the vessel and the men had all served too long in the Royal Navy to ever question their commander. Tettahah it would be, for better or for worse. But Morrison himself was unsure of their position or the exact location of Tettahah, especially as they had spent the better part of the previous afternoon and night simply drifting in the trackless sea, blown about by the gale and turbulent seas.

So, while the men turned their attention to repairing what they could of the tattered sails and getting the little ship moving in the direction Morrison indicated they should sail, the bosun's mind reeled with questions, inner arguments, and silent debate over his announced decision.

It was well into the afternoon watch, by Muspratt's calculation, when Coleman stood up, walked forward, and squinted into the sun, getting lower in the western sky.

"You chaps think that might be a boat, a canoe of some kind, out yonder?" He asked.

The other three stood, craning their necks and straining their salt rimmed eyes to see what Coleman saw . . . or thought he saw.

Then Morrison stood. "Take the tiller, Bill. I'll go up there with Joe and have a look my own self." He did not wait for a response from Muspratt, but simply let go of the tiller and started forward, knowing that Muspratt would take up steering the boat.

His mind was leaping for joy. He hoped beyond hope that Coleman had indeed seen a boat. Even should they not be near land, at least the natives in it could tell them where to find land. He tried to keep the eagerness out of his voice as he approached the foredeck.

"Where away, Joe?" He spoke softly, struggling with the excited hope he felt.

"Right yonder, Jim. 'Bout a point off the larboard bow, there. I'd wager a fair piece 'at's one o' them canoes with the outrigger set to one side." Coleman pointed.

Morrison squinted into the sun. Yes, by George, there *was* indeed something out there. And it did look like an outrigger canoe. It appeared to be under sail. He studied it for a moment.

"I'd bet you're spot on. Joe. And I think it's closer than it looks on account of it ain't real big. So if I am right about the size, they can't be real far from home. Mayhaps their island, whatever it might be, is just over the horizon."

To himself, Morrison added, "And if I am lucky, it will be Tettahah! Don't know what else it could be, but you can't be certain out here. Lot o' these islands look alike."

He turned to face aft. "Bill, ease her down a point. Looks like Coleman is right. We'll go have a look for our own selves. Start your sheets, lads, and see if ol' *Resolution* can catch 'em up!"

Had not the natives in the outrigger seen the mutineers' boat, its tattered mains'l and sadly torn jib filled, but at the same time, flapping the frayed pieces of mat like ribbons in a young girl's hair, it is unlikely *Resolution* would have caught them. But they rounded up, dropped their own sail and began to paddle toward the British sailors.

They neared the native craft, and Morrison ordered the men to "hand the sails, lads. These men'll show us the way in."

As the outrigger came alongside, excited chatter filled the air. Clearly, the natives asked questions about the vessel, its condition, and the obvious poor condition of its crew, but the words came so fast, spoken by all ten of them in the canoe at once, that neither Muspratt nor Morrison, with their limited command of the language, could decipher much. And of course, the British sailors, eager to find out where the storm had blown them, interrogated the natives as eagerly, but in English. Finally the jabber quieted and Morrison and Muspratt, exchanged looks, and tried to converse with the man they took as the group's leader.

The two men struggled to explain what had happened to them; when one ran out of words, the other filled in. Eventually, the natives, who indeed were from Tettahah, understood and made the Englishmen understand they would lead them to their island, distant only a few hours sailing. And they hoisted their lateen sail, made of the same woven mats as were *Resolution*'s, and headed home. The British hoisted their own sorry sails and followed, keeping up as best they might with the faster, more agile, outrigger canoe.

After more than a few hours—the western sky was glowing red as the sun dropped into the sea—the tired and hungry mutineers followed their native guide through the break in the reef surrounding the island of Tettahah, and dropped their anchor into the clear, and mercifully quiet, waters of a pristine lagoon.

A handful of natives had gathered on the beach to welcome, not only their own men back, but to see who these strangers might be. Hospitable to a fault, they launched a few canoes and paddled out with gifts of food and flowers, singing as they stroked through the darkening lagoon. The mutineers went on shore where they spent the evening and into the night eating, singing, and telling the story of their survival of the storm. The women provided new mats which they quickly sewed into replacement sails for *Resolution*. The islanders seemed incredulous that they had ever left Otaheite, knowing that the storm was coming, and even more incredulous that the mutineers claimed not to have known.

The following morning, heads ringing from the surfeit of potent island drink the men had consumed, they weighed for Taboona, a short ten mile sail to the south with the intent of moving on to Mo'orea from there. Tettooroa, their original destination, was forgotten.

At Taboona, the local chief, Pohooataya, came aboard with two roasted hogs, some breadfruit, yams, and taro, and wished them well on their further journey to Mo'orea, requesting that they pass on his greetings to his cousin, the chief there.

The sail to Mo'orea, now only about as long as their original voyage to Tettooroa would have been, passed without incident save for the tattering of their replacement sail. Again Morrison exclaimed for a piece of canvas, knowing they could never leave the islands without proper sails. But without a "civilized ship" as he put it, canvas would remain only a dream. And more than likely, were they to come across a "civilized ship," it would be British, making the need for canvas moot, as the men would likely be taken prisoner once their status as the mutineers from *Bounty* was determined.

The bosun lamented his conundrum as he visited with Fatowwa, wife of the chief of the district. The other four mutineers found other entertainments with the locals for a few days, until Morrison received a message from Mottooarro, a district chief on the other side of Mo'orea, asking the men to come there, to Cook's Harbor, for a visit. The messenger had been instructed to provide piloting services as the reefs around the island were dangerous to the uninitiated.

Accompanied by Fatowwa in her own canoe, *Resolution* made the short trip with no mishap in fine weather, dropping their anchor in a small cove just to the west of Cook's Harbor. Mottooarro and his wife, Tarreredooa, paddled out with great fanfare and came aboard with several others known to the mutineers. The men saluted the chief and his wife with six muskets. After a brief visit on the ship, the men went ashore with the natives, explaining their visit was purely social.

Mattooarro gave orders to his people that their friends should want for nothing. Hearing this, Morrison explained he needed new mats to repair, once again, his sails, but the chief told him they were in short supply.

"You offer your hospitality and say we 'should want for nothing' and yet, you claim to be unable to fulfill this simple request." Morrison struggled to contain his temper.

"I can not give you what I have not in my possession." Mattooarro retorted. "But you shall have food, drink, and other entertainment while we try to get that which you need. In meantime, you will come and see Bligh's cattle."

While Bligh and *Bounty* had visited in Mo'orea, the captain had presented the islanders with a dozen and more cattle, both cows and bulls. He explained that if the natives took good care of them, they would reproduce and English ships visiting in the future would pay for fresh beef with iron fittings, something the natives held in high esteem.

When Morrison and the chief got to the western part of the island where the cattle were being tended, Morrison was surprised to find only a single bull, five cows, and a cow calf. One of the cows was great with calf and the bull had, somehow, broken his left hip which, untreated, caused it to wither.

"Even with three legs, the bull is strong, Morrison. He made two calves already!" Mattooarro announced proudly.

"Well, you should keep him with the cows, then. Their offspring will be most welcome by ships that call here and they will pay handsomely for your beef."

"As long as I am chief in Mo'orea, it shall be done as you say, Morrison. But after I am gone, who can say what will happen." The chief smiled, apparently expecting to remain in authority for some time.

It was nearly a fortnight, during which the men reveled with their hosts, before some freshly made mats appeared and, with great ceremony, were presented to Morrison. The new "sails" were immediately bent on to the spars in *Resolution* and within the space of a few days, the ship weighed amid fanfare and canoes filled with singing Mo'oreans. Musket salutes from the mutineers answered the natives' farewell.

Returning to Otaheite by going round the other side of the islands, they stopped at Vyeere for a brief visit. The locals there offered to provide a few hogs and some root vegetables should the men pay them with iron nails. Coleman, as the armorer and in charge of the firearms aboard, went ashore to fetch some sand to clean their muskets as he had no emory or pumice.

While there, he was seized by a small group of natives who brandished large stones and threatened to kill him, saying he had grabbed one of their wives and hid her aboard *Resolution*, using her ill. It was Coleman's good fortune that another group of natives, friendly to the English sailors, appeared, negotiated for Coleman's freedom by explaining, Coleman gathered from what he could glean from the rapid-fire conversation, that it was impossible for the sailor to have the man's wife as *Resolution* had only arrived that day. Coleman, for his part, promised to return with a gift of some iron nails for all involved.

Following the armorer's return to his mates, Morrison, angry at the offensive behavior, ordered an armed party, consisting of Coleman, Millward, and McIntosh, to go ashore and seek out the natives who had caused the initial problem. The next morning, led by Coleman, they did just that.

As they approached the house belonging to the man whose wife had disappeared, he fled, having been warned of their arrival. Coleman, seeing several natives running through the bush, ordered the men to fire at them, which resulted in two natives being wounded, though not severely. The wounded natives begged for quarter, which was granted. Nonetheless, the party of mutineers plundered the man's house, carrying off all manner of possessions.

When they returned aboard, Morrison, angry that his armed party had only wounded and not killed the man, demanded and received from the natives, a peace offering of a large piece of cloth, but sadly, not of sufficient strength to use for sails. The following day, the men weighed for Otaheite, arriving to a warm welcome late in the afternoon.

CHAPTER NINE

In Pandora: *3º 27' N, 28º 15' W*

"Deck there! Ho! Deck!" The cry from the lookout in the tops of the foremast caused me to take a step forward from where I was amusing myself watching the quartermasters anticipate and correct little deviations in the ship's course.

I looked aloft and saw the sailor stationed on the foremast alternately waving his arms and pointing to weather. "Make your report, lookout! Calling to the deck is no way to report a sighting!" I shouted up to him.

He continued to point while he shouted back, "Don't know what to say, sir. Ain't seen nothing like that afore."

I shifted my gaze to the windward side of us and, in the distance, saw huge vertical clouds shaped like thin funnels that seemed to stretch right to the water. There must have been four or five of them and, while I could not make out the lower portion of any, they appeared to be moving. I grabbed my long glass and scrambled into the mizzen ratlines. When I reached the fighting top, I steadied my balance against the even roll and heel of the ship, braced the glass against the shroud, and peered at the strange phenomenon.

"What have you, Mister Ballantyne?" I heard Larkan's voice drift up to me.

"Not a clue, sir. Clouds of some kind, I'd warrant. But I've never seen anything like it before. Seem to be moving towards us, though." I shouted back and climbed down.

The first lieutenant took my glass and studied the shapes from the windward rail of the quarterdeck.

"Messenger. Step to the Cabin and offer the captain my respects. Tell him we have several waterspouts heading for the ship. I plan to go to quarters directly. You have that, young man?" Larkan apparently had experienced these before, though why he planned on sending the men to quarters for clouds was beyond my ken.

The messenger hurried to the scuttle. Larkan turned to Renouard and said, "Pass the word for the bosun and the marine drummer, if you please, Mister Renouard. Quickly."

Renouard ran off as quickly as had the messenger, shouting for both men as instructed.

"Sir, if I may be so bold as to inquire, why are we going to quarters?"

"Those are waterspouts, Edward. Quite common in these latitudes, but a bit unusual to see so many that close together. Were one of them to pass over us, we would be ruined in an instant. Rip the rig right out of her, I'd warrant. Very powerful winds in a circular movement that suck up everything in their path, including a ship, should one happen to be in the way. Leave us a perfect wreck, I would warrant.

"We will go to quarters, man the guns and shoot the spouts. With luck, we can interrupt the suction they have and cause them to collapse. When you get to your guns, double shot every other one; the remainder, load with canister. Pass my instructions on to Mister Corner as well, if you please."

I was stunned! Shoot a waterspout? While it did seem reasonable in theory, it also seemed equally preposterous to waste powder and shot at what was essentially a cloud. When the bosun appeared moments later, still hitching up his trousers (he had been found at the head), he stopped just short of the quarterdeck, doffed his hat to Larkan and me, and stood silently.

Larkan gave the order. "Mister Cunningham: pipe the ship to quarters. Ensure the marine drummer moves throughout the lower decks as well. We will be having some practice with the great guns shortly."

Cunningham raised his pipe even as he turned about and blew lustily the call to quarters. I could hear the drum start the beat of "Heart of Oak" almost immediately after the pipe finished.

Tum dada tum tee tum

Men poured out of hatches and scuttles, wondering, I am sure, why they were being called to quarters in the middle of the afternoon when no gunnery practice had been scheduled. Topmen headed aloft as they had been trained to do, awaiting the order to shorten sail, idlers gathered on the spar deck to heave and haul on sheets and braces as ordered, and the majority of the sailors, after rushing topside to see what was going on, hastened back to the gundeck to man their assigned guns. Including me.

"Mister Corner. Mister Larkan wants the weather side guns double shotted with every other one loaded with canister, if you please. We're going to be shooting at waterspouts!"

"Aye. Waterspouts." Corner said nothing further at once, save to give the crews their orders, send the boys scampering for the powder magazine and advise the gun captains what we were about. I was doing the same.

I could hear orders being shouted topside and the running of bare feet over our heads. Then the ship heeled a bit more, straightened up, and, over the noise of our battery being dragged back from its stowed position, heard the distinctive cacophony of luffing sails, shouted commands and curses, and then the rhythmic slap of feet as the men walked away with the sheets. The ship had tacked. Now which side would be engaged with the "enemy" I wondered? I stepped to the ladder.

"Mister Larkan," I called aft. "Will the larboard side still be engaged?" I could see Captain Edwards standing at the rail, a glass at his eye, studying the spouts.

"Larboard for now, Mister Ballantyne. Have your starboard side ready as we will tack again immediately we have fired, should our shot not have the desired effect."

I waved an acknowledgment, but could not help recalling his earlier comment about the waterspouts picking up a ship of our size and tearing it apart.

Wouldn't we be better off just to tack away and remain clear? I asked myself, and then posed the same question to Robert.

"Unpredictable, those buggers are, Edward. Don't know what they're likely to do. Better to try and 'kill' 'em with shot than guess where they're headed. Seen it done couple of times when I was in the tropics a year and more back. Sometimes it works brilliantly, others, not so well." He stopped, looking around the gundeck and, seeing that everything was ready, called to our young midshipman.

"Mister Renouard. Report to the quarterdeck my compliments and tell the first lieutenant that we are ready and loaded as instructed, if you please."

I could not resist. "What happened the times it didn't 'work so well', Robert?"

"Oh well, you know. There was this one spout came right at us. We fired mightily at it—only had wee six-pounders, you know—and the bloody spout just swallowed up our shot like a chicken pickin' up corn. Came right at us, it did." He stopped again.

I waited until I could no longer bear it. "Robert, *we* have only six-pounders. What *happened?*"

"Edward," he started again with a twinkle in his eye, "I shouldn't be tellin' you this. Spout came right over the ship, sucked it right up into its great maw, spun it around like a toy, and spit us out two or three miles away, rig gone, ship capsized, and not a man-jack on board who was alive! Killed us all, it did!"

I had thought the twinkle in his eye had been provoked by my obvious nervousness at our small weight of metal and the approaching spouts. Obviously, he was preparing to give me a yarn of Herculean proportions.

"Really," I retorted. "You surely seem to have recovered well from your early demise!"

Corner laughed aloud, clapped me on the back and said through his guffaws, "Well, lad, let's see if we can't avoid the same fate in *Pandora*. There'll be time enough for yarnin' when this is done." He turned to peer out the gunport, checking the progress of the nearest of the spouts.

"On the gundeck! Stand by. Your target will be the one on the larboard hand, larboard battery engaged. Stand by!" Larkan's voice resonated through the gundeck.

The men took their positions; rammers, spongers, loaders, side tackles all ready. The chatter was gone; serious faces glanced around and out the port trying to see how close the waterspout had gotten to us.

"Blow on your matches, boys!" I shouted to the gun captains. "Larboard spout's your target. Check your aim. Fire in sequence on my command."

I bent and peered through the gunport of the nearest gun. The spout was coming now, and seemed to be about at the full range of the guns. The gout of water it threw up around the base swirled upwards, being drawn into the funnel and spun around as the whole thing moved forward, then sideways, then forward again. All the while, the base of it, where it actually touched the water, was obscured in spray as thick as rich Yorkshire cream, white and frothy, as it was sucked upwards.

My God! That thing is huge! Robert was right; there's no way to tell where it's going! Oh my! I surely hope this works.

I stepped away from the gun so as not to be in the way and waited for the order from the quarterdeck to open fire.

Each of the gun captains stood with a smoldering length of slow match clipped in a linstock. They held them away from the touch holes so as not to have an ember set off the powder there prematurely and, when had I shouted to them, each had blown on his match, causing it to burst into a small yellow flame. On the order to fire, the first, or forward-most, would jam the flame into the pan of powder on top of his gun, igniting the train of powder through the breach and into the flannel cartridge bag in the bore of the gun. Less than a second later, the gun would roar, spew out a six foot tongue of flame and smoke, and jump back in its tackles, having sent two six pound iron balls or a load of canister on the way to the target. Then the next gun captain would do the same thing and so on until all the guns in the larboard battery had fired.

Immediately on firing, the gun would be swabbed with a wet sponge to remove any burning embers from the powder charge or the flannel bag, and a new cartridge would be shoved home followed by wadding, two iron shots or canister, and another wad. When the gun was hauled back into battery, that is with its muzzle poking out the gunport, the gun captain would spill a dram of black powder from his horn into the pan and wait for the next order to fire.

"Stand by your matches . . . FIRE!" Larkan's voice came down to us from the scuttle.

"FIRE!" I yelled to my crews.

KABOOM! KABOOM! Each gun fired as the gun captains had been instructed, kicking back in their breachings like something alive. As quick as they came to rest at the extent of the side tackles, the crews, trained by almost daily practice since leaving Portsmouth, jumped into position to swab and reload their pieces.

I saw Robert poke his head out one of the gunports and moved to follow suit. The nearest waterspout, one of three now which seemed to be standing still, was a rifle-shot distant and, as I watched, five or six shots, iron ball and canister, ones from the after-most guns, struck the base of the whirling funnel.

At first, nothing seemed to happen; the shot appeared to have gone right through it. Then, as I continued to watch, the froth at the bottom seemed to grow less thick and fall back into the sea.

"It worked, by God, it worked! It's breaking apart." The excitement in Corner's voice was contagious and the men let out with a cheer at their success.

Looking again, I saw the spout simply disintegrate, the water it held falling back to the sea. And then it was gone. But the others were not.

"Save your cheering, lads, and stand by your guns. We're not done yet! There's another pair of 'em need the same treatment." Corner shouted over the cheering.

I felt the ship tacking as Captain Edwards and Mister Larkan brought her about to expose the starboard battery for another shot. The maneuver would also take us out of the path of the remaining spouts, assuming they continued as before. This time, I surmised, we would be shooting for the entertainment of the men.

When she settled on the new course, the gun crews, on command, shifted to the other battery and primed and aimed the guns.

"Stand by! Wait for my command." I instructed, noting the enthusiasm of the men and fearing they might let it run away with them.

I watched through the gunport as the two moved on an almost parallel course with us, about one thousand yards distant. I wondered briefly if Larkan would select a target or not.

Robert acted instead. "Take the forward one, you lads. You others, go for the after one. On my command!" He had divided the battery, fore and aft, so as to hit both spouts at about the same time.

He was going to try and "kill" them with one broadside. They weren't as enormous as the first one which we had successfully destroyed, but by using the whole larboard battery so perhaps, he thought five guns on each would be sufficient.

"FIRE! And make 'em count!" Before the last word was out of his mouth, the forward-most gun spoke, followed closely by the next and the next.

In the ringing silence, I peered again out the port. One of the spouts seemed unaffected by our efforts, but the other one, the forward-most, was collapsing on itself.

How about that! I would never have thought that would work. Reckon I still have more to learn about this employment! And I thought Robert was simply teasing me.

"Well, Mister Corner, I'd warrant we can claim a victory. Two out of three came down! Better than having one of them pick up the ship and kill us all like happened to you!" I laughed, partly at turning his joke around on him and partly out of relief that we had not been hit by the spout!

"Aye. Often as not it does, but there are times . . . "

The ship tacked back to our original course and shortly thereafter, I heard the bosun pipe us down from quarters followed closely by the call for spirits up and drum rolling out the "Nancy Dawson."

I had quite lost track of the time and a glance at my watch told me the call to spirits up was not a reward for the excellent shooting, more it was simply time for the evening ration of grog, the crew's evening meal, and the change of the watch. I was now officially off watch and, anticipating some interesting conversation, made my way to the wardroom.

" . . . for that to work, my friend. Surprised, I am, and not a little." Mister Hamilton, our surgeon, was holding forth as I entered.

"Not something I've experienced before, I can say in truth. But I am mightily pleased it did. Don't know if you saw that big one, George, but

I fear, had it struck us, we would not have fared well. Not a bit!" Mister Bentham, our pinchpenny, was obviously impressed with our prowess at gunnery.

"I wouldn't expect a purser, Gregory, to have experienced much of that stripe, especially one who has only made one cruise, and that in a line of battle ship. Blockade duty off France, was it not? Not too many tropical phenomena in Biscay, I'd warrant!" Hamilton seemed never to miss a chance to mock our purser and he often managed to make his voice even sound like Bentham.

"Robert seemed to think it would work. At least, that's what he said to me just before we fired." I spoke to the two men as I took a chair at the table.

"Well, I would expect nothing less. He's not going to say 'we're doomed if that strikes us,' now is he?" Hamilton looked at me and, had he not smiled, I would have taken his words as a taunt.

"Actually, he did. Not in so many words, but he did make it known that we might perish if our attempt was unsuccessful." I recalled clearly the yarn Corner had told as we waited to fire.

"Ah, Mister Larkan. Brilliant move, sir, and well executed, if I may say so. Never doubted your tactic for a moment!" Hamilton stood as the first lieutenant stepped into the room, poured himself a tumbler of whatever wine was decanted on the sideboard, and took a seat.

"Thank you Doctor. Only seen it done once before, but it worked then. The cap'n thought it might work as well, though I am not sure he was quite as convinced as I was. Never said a word, though. When that first spout came down, he merely looked at me and nodded. Had it not happened as I had expected, I might have been at the grating myself!"

"I am sure that not even *our* captain would have his first lieutenant flogged, John. Maybe mastheaded with a mid, but flogging would never answer!" Hamilton laughed.

"Speaking of midshipmen, how is young Renouard doing these days, Edward. I only see him when he's got the watch or on some errand or another for, I presume, you. Seems to keep to himself when he's not on watch or working." Larkan turned to me.

"He's making scant progress, sir. I have been working around him on the gundeck and he has the sense to simply stay out of the way. On our watches together, he does precious little save run errands or take up space on the quarterdeck. I despair of him ever standing for lieutenant. Wouldn't wager a great deal on him as master's mate, either, for that matter." I responded soberly. "Claims navigation is quite beyond his ken and, while he seems to understand the rigging and sail handling, he can not hold a course to save his bloody neck.

"I had him on the wheel for a bit yesterday. You will recall we had a fine breeze and were sailing large in the forenoon watch. He was chasing the compass all about the sea. Drove the watch on deck to distraction, trimming sails to follow his errant course."

"Well, had he spent some time as a foremast Jack before winning his Warrant, he would have learned to hand, reef, and steer. Have you had him aloft, yet? Maybe a spell with Mister Passmore might be helpful." Larkan had taken a quite serious tone.

"Oh yes, sir. Indeed, he's been aloft. Agile as a monkey, he is, and not a bit afraid. He helped reef the mizzen tops'l just the other day. Put him up there with the mizzen cap'n—Dedworth, I believe his name to be—to keep an eye on him. I was thinking myself that maybe assigning him to Passmore would allow him to do something he seems comfortable with, rather than having him on the battery, which still appears to startle him at every discharge."

"Then let us do exactly that, sir. And no more about it. I shall so inform the captain. I am sure he will have an interest in the young man's progress." Larkan had made a small joke about the captain's "interest" in Renouard as the young man had "interest" at the Admiralty.

"I am about to make some changes to the watch, quarter, and station bill in any case. Corner tells me we ought to give young Oliver and his colleague, Reynolds, some time on the quarterdeck. Thought I'd put Reynolds with you and Oliver with Corner. I guess Sival will stand with Hayward. Any objections?"

Larkan referred to George Reynolds, a master's mate, and from what I had observed in the past month, quite handy. William Oliver, also a master's mate, I barely knew. And John Sival, a youngster and Renouard's close friend, had gained the reputation of being a bright young man, quickly absorbing all the information he could. In fact, Passmore mentioned to me that Sival had become quite adept at all phases of navigation, being already familiar with the mathematics necessary to successfully determine a position.

"Nary a one, sir. I look forward to helping Mister Reynolds move his career along. And thank you."

"Thank you? For what? Relieving you of Renouard? I suspect you'll get another shot at the boy before this cruise is done. Don't thank me yet!"

Corner stepped into the room at that moment, his constant smile and ruddy cheeks giving him an air of joviality that we all enjoyed.

"Another shot at who, might I inquire?" He went immediately to the sideboard and helped himself to a glass.

"We were just discussing some changes to the watch bill, Robert. Any objections to taking young William Oliver under your wing? I recall you had told me Hayward could manage his own watch so I thought I would give it a go. At least 'til we make Rio."

"Not a bit, John. Seems just right to me. And Oliver, I'm told is a bright young chap."

"When do you imagine we'll raise Rio, John? Thought we were fairly flying along from what I've been told. Half expected to hear a cry from the masthead of 'land ho!' anytime over the past few days." Bentham's tone belied his eagerness to set his feet again on *terra firma*.

"Well, we should cross the line in another two or three days and then, if the trades hold as they have been, shouldn't be more than a fortnight will see us in."

"Well, jolly, that. Perchance by the new year, then? Lovely news, I'd say!" The purser's enthusiasm grew as he digested this bit of news.

For my part, my mind, unbidden, turned again to crossing the line, now an imminent and looming event.

Two or three days! Oh my!

Recalling yet again the stories I had heard from former shipmates, I could see only ugliness, not the humor I had thought would accompany the ceremony.

Well, I surely won't be alone in this endeavor! I'd wager Bentham's not crossed before and of course, the mids and master's mates. Time will tell, I reckon, how any of us will manage.

Black, my steward, and Spaulding, Corner's man, came in with the table cloth and utensils for our evening meal, and we all stood to make room for them. A knock caused us to turn to the door where a Marine stood, rigidly at attention.

I could not recall the man's name, but recognized him as one of the sentries who kept the vigil outside Captain Edwards' Cabin.

"Sirs. Beggin' your pardons. Cap'n's compliments and would Mister Larkan, Mister Ballantyne, and Mister Hayward join the cap'n in the Cabin for the evening meal?" The man's posture never changed a whit, nor did his expression. In fact, I could barely discern that his mouth moved when he uttered the words.

"Supper? With Cap'n Edwards? Why isn't that delightful! I am sure both Mister Hayward and Mister Ballantyne would be delighted to sup in the Cabin. As for me, my regrets, but I have any number of chores which require my attention. Please so inform Cap'n Edwards." Larkan never even looked at me when he committed me to dine with Edwards. And Hayward wasn't even in the room; won't he be surprised!

It was the first time, to my knowledge, that any, save the first lieutenant, from the wardroom had been so invited. I knew several of the midshipmen had been invited, and of course, Larkan's duties had him in the Cabin frequently, not just for a meal. But that was business, not of a social nature. Though I could scarce believe that there would be much of a social nature in the Cabin tonight! As if to confirm my own thoughts, Robert caught my eye, winked and made a wry face. This would be an evening of note!

At the appointed hour, Lieutenants Thomas Hayward and Edward Ballantyne, dressed in their finest with jackets brushed and boots gleaming, presented themselves to the Marine at his post outside the Cabin door which was closed as usual. As it was the same Marine on watch as who had been sent with the summons (note, I did not say *invitation*!), he did not wait for us to state our business. When he saw us approach, he turned and rapped his knuckle on the door jamb, opened the door, and spoke quietly, presumably announcing our arrival. A muttered, but unintelligible, response filtered out to our waiting ears.

"You may go in, sirs. Cap'n Edwards is expecting you." Having spoken, he pushed open the door the rest of the way, we did as he told us, and the door closed behind us.

"Lieutenants Ballantyne and Hayward reporting, sir." I spoke, as the senior of us.

"Yes, of course it is. And I do know who you are, as well." Edwards did not look up from his desk, but continued to scratch his quill across an almost-full page of foolscap.

Tom looked at me as if to say, "Now what?"

I simply continued to stand at attention just inside the door; he took my lead and remained stationary.

Within a minute or so, which seemed quite a bit longer, Edwards looked up, took our measure, and decided we were acceptably turned out.

"Gentlemen, please excuse me for keeping you waiting. Just wanted to finish a note while the thoughts were fresh in my mind.

"Please, take a seat." He gestured to some chairs, one near his desk and several others near the beautiful and still shining brass and copper fireplace. Given our latitude, the fireplace was cold, and I took one of the chairs by it. Hayward took another opposite me. I noticed a trickle of sweat coursing down his cheek.

"This is a real pleasure, Cap'n. Thank you for inviting us to join you for supper." I offered by way of starting a conversation.

"Hmmm. Yes, well, I thought it time to have some of you come 'round. Sorry Larkan was too busy, but ship's business must come before socializing, what?"

"I know the first lieutenant was sorry not to be available, but he did mention he was changing the watch bill, which I imagine was his plan for this evening." I could scarcely believe I was making excuses for the first lieutenant!

"I trust you gentlemen are satisfied with your employment? I know *Pandora* isn't some fancy line of battle ship with all the pomp and circumstance attendant, but we have, with some exceptions, a reasonably decent group of people in the fo'c'sle, despite their origins, and a fair collection of officers. And baring an unforeseen encounter with hostiles, a good likelihood of seeing Portsmouth intact when our assignment is done."

I had heard from Robert that the captain always referred to the crew as "his people." That he was pleased with their performance so far reflected positively on our "fair collection of officers." We both nodded and answered in the affirmative with some enthusiasm.

After a bit of small talk, the captain's steward entered. He was a diminutive soul, quite bald, and, as if to further minimize his small stature, seemed incapable of standing straight. He mumbled something that sounded like "supper" and "table" which I took to mean he was ready to serve us. A decanter of wine appeared on the sideboard adjacent to where I had earlier noticed glasses had been set out. But since the captain had said nothing about it, neither Hayward nor I made any move to help ourselves.

Without warning, Edwards stood and motioned us to the table, now set with a white cloth, cutlery, and more glasses.

"Mister Hayward, sit here, to my left, if you please, and Mister Ballantyne, you may take the chair to my right." Captain Edwards stood momentarily at his place at the head of the table while we moved to our assigned seats, then sat himself down. We followed suit.

"Witherwax, you may serve out the wine, if you please." Edwards spoke in a neutral tone without turning toward his steward.

Nonetheless, Witherwax (more than likely a pensioner from the Naval Hospital) clutched the decanter with two hands and poured liberal measures into, first the captain's glass, then mine, then Hayward's. The man was obviously sensitive to seniority issues.

"A good man, Witherwax. Took a piece of grape in his back which damaged his spine. During that bit of discord with the colonies in North

America, it was. Laid him up permanent, got his pension, and now assigned in *Pandora* as my man. Remembers the old days like yesterday, he does. Ain't that right, Witherwax?" Edwards may have smiled at the man. It was so fleeting I couldn't be sure.

But Witherwax bobbed his head in agreement and, for a moment, his rheumy eyes twinkled, perhaps remembering the "old days."

We sipped our wine—a very nice one which I guessed Edwards had obtained in Tenerife—in silence for a moment or two. Neither Hayward nor I felt easy in our surrounds and waited for the captain, our host, to speak. Finally, he pierced Tom with a flinty stare and cleared his throat.

"Ahem, Mister Hayward. Would you care to tell us some tales of Bligh and his troubles in *Bounty*? I would be most interested in hearing your assessment of those wretched pirates he sailed with."

Tom shot a glance at me, took a breath and turned to Captain Edwards. "Yes, sir. Anything specific you might be interested in? Or would you like just my opinion of the cruise?"

"I believe I mentioned something about your assessment of the mutineers, did I not?" Edwards was not smiling.

"You did, sir. I shared the cockpit with several of the midshipmen who preferred to stay with Christian in *Bounty* after the . . . um . . . mutiny, sir. Edward Young for one. Seemed right pleased, he did, to join forces with that rascal and held both a cutlass and a pistol during the bad time. In point of fact, he waved his cutlass in my face more than once while we were embarking into the boat. He had frequently mentioned that the cap'n thought him a 'worthless wretch,' words we assumed he heard directly from Bligh.

"Peter Heywood was another, though I think he would rather have taken his chances in the boat than remain in the ship. Cap'n Bligh, however, declared there was room for no more as we were already showing precious little freeboard. So Heywood was forced to sail with Christian to where ever he decided to take them. John Hallet, one of the mids, went with us in the boat, though I don't think the cap'n favored him much.

"Christian, of course, seemed a bit strange to some of us from time to time. He would often and intentionally try to provoke the captain and I recall an instance where, in front of the entire company, the two argued in high tones, seemingly without regard for their surrounds. At other times, Mister Christian was as even-tempered as you please. And, in my opinion, a fine sailorman. Taught me and Heywood much of the navigation we learned. Convinced the captain we were able to stand a watch on our own.

In fact, we were about to be relieved from the watch when the trouble began." Tom paused in his recitation to taste his wine.

"And the common sailors? Can you tell me which of them I should expect trouble from, should we be fortunate enough to find the scoundrels?" Edwards pressed Tom. I might as well not have even been at the table.

"Well, Cap'n. I knew most of them. We had been in close quarters for quite some time and it would be impossible not to have crossed tacks with most of the men." Hayward paused, looking into the air over my head.

"I would have to say Churchill would be one and quite possibly his associate, Thompson; thick as thieves they were, and lined up behind Christian quite quickly. Of the others, I can not say, but would offer Muspratt, Burkitt, and Millward as likely confederates of the first lieutenant, as well. And perhaps a chap called Thomas Ellison, a boy, actually, though quite a hard one, that."

"You mean, by first lieutenant, Christian, I presume?"

"Well, yes, sir. I do."

"It is my understanding the Bligh made him *acting* first lieutenant through some prior connection they had. Hmmm?"

"Umm. Yes sir. We just took him as first lieutenant. We had no officers, save Cap'n Bligh in the ship, sir. Just the four midshipmen and a couple of master's mates. Fletcher signed aboard as master's mate. He told us he had sailed before with Bligh and knew him to be a fine seaman. We quite thought he liked the captain . . . until we had been in Otaheite for several weeks. It was then we noticed a change. In both men."

I never uttered a word. Witherwax had served a large tureen with melted cheese in it, which Edwards served out with biscuits as Hayward told his tale. I noticed that Tom had barely touched his serving, while I had nearly finished my own. Comes from keeping silent, I reckon.

"While I never sailed with William Bligh, I knew him to be a generous man, a fine seaman, and generally patient with his people. Would that agree with your assessment?"

Tom paused, finally having taken a spoonful of his cooling cheese dish into his mouth. I suspect he weighed carefully his words while he chewed.

"Uh . . . yes, sir. There was many an opportunity for him to act otherwise, but he seemed unwilling to be provoked. I can recall only one flogging during the entire cruise out." Hayward suddenly stopped, perhaps realizing who his audience was.

"Oh? Just one? Seems unlikely with that pack of rascals he shipped." Edwards raised his eyebrows.

My friend and messmate pressed on, albeit more carefully.

"Mmmm, yes, sir. Only one can I recall. It was after we had been savagely beaten by Cape Horn. Dreadful weather, it was, with ice and snow everywhere. Gales of wind and mountainous seas. Thirty days we spent trying to gain the Pacific, sailing as far south as the ice and then back to South America, only to be blown back into the Atlantic each time.

"When the cap'n decided we had had enough, he ordered us to wear ship and head off toward the Cape of Good Hope. One of the topmen refused to go aloft, saying the rig was unstable and covered in ice. The cap'n said nothing at the time, but after we wore and were headed fair to make our easting, he order the man seized up and whipped. After that, there was no further problem with the men, sir. At least, nothing that would merit the use of the lash."

"Hmm." Edwards said nothing further. He offered us both another serving of the melted cheese and a biscuit. Tom declined, having not yet had an opportunity to finish his first. I accepted.

Suddenly, Edwards stopped chewing, looked at Hayward and asked, "You said there was only one man flogged during *the trip out*. Are you implying that he had others flogged once in Otaheite?"

"Well, yes, sir. He did. And one of the natives as well."

"And what crimes had these miscreants undertaken to commit?"

"Four of the men deserted, sir. I recall it was Churchill, Muspratt, and Millward, along with one other whose name escapes me, who ran off. And the native had stolen an azimuth compass. His chief, a man called Tynah, found him and brought him and the compass to the ship, suggesting Bligh should kill him.

"Bligh would not risk further damage to our relationship with the natives and ordered the man to be given one hundred strokes."

"That might be a death sentence for some." Edwards remarked, softly, almost to himself.

I thought of the tale of his experience with a mutiny during the War for American Independence and wondered briefly how many of the men he had punished with one hundred strokes succumbed.

"Indeed, sir, I was there with the ship's company and many of the natives. I am sure Bosun's Mate Morrison laid them on with gusto, but it was only the last two or three that even broke the skin. The man, when he was cut down, walked to the rail, jumped into the sea, and swam ashore. We were astounded! Tynah began to carry on something dreadful, ordering his people to fetch him back. But the cap'n simply said that justice had been served and leave him go."

"I would imagine, then, from the incidents you have related, that the trouble began while the ship was in Otaheite?" Edwards continued to press.

Tom merely nodded, his mouth full of—by now—cool, melted cheese and a soggy biscuit.

I had listened to this entire conversation, offering nary a word of my own. As I mentioned, it was as if I was not even there, but I found it fascinating to be simply an observer. While I had heard some of these tales during my time with Tom, the captain had obviously not. Watching his reactions was quite instructional!

With each revelation that Tom uttered, the captain become more focused and more determined to discover the "real" story of Bligh's troubles, as well as, I thought, settle upon a course of action for finding and catching the "mutinous scoundrels" that brought such dishonor to their ship and the service.

"I trust, that should I find these rascals, you would be able to identify each of them?" Edwards' eyes bored into Tom.

So that was it! He wanted to be certain that our fourth lieutenant, unusual in a sixth rate, would earn his keep once we arrived in Otaheite.

Tom bobbed his head enthusiastically and answered in the affirmative, which seemed to satisfy our host for the moment. Edwards fell silent, stared at his plate, and, one must presume, contemplated what he had learned from Hayward.

Then, quite without warning, Captain Edwards turned his chair, scraping it on the painted canvas deck covering that adorned his Cabin, and faced me.

Now I reckon it's my turn. Glad I've finished my supper!

I felt a trickle of sweat run down my back and wrote it off to the hot climate and lack of any moving air in the Cabin. Or perhaps not.

"Mister Ballantyne. I am given to understand from Mister Larkan that Midshipman Renouard is under your care." He simply held his gaze on me; nothing in his face suggested the statement was anything but that. Surely, it was not a question.

Well, I thought, *he was until a short while ago. Now he's someone else's problem. I hope Sailing Master Passmore enjoys his company!*

Aloud, I stuttered, "Uh . . . well . . . yes, sir. That is, sir, he was until this afternoon."

"Oh? And what, may I ask, transpired to change his assignment?" Edwards' voice remained even, just a trifle louder.

Just tell him it was Larkan's decision. Broaden his education and all that.

"Uh . . . Mister Larkan thought the youngster might benefit from spending some time with the sailing master, sir. He—Mister Larkan, that is—changed several assignments. I recall him saying he was working on the watch, quarter, and station bills this very evening. He reassigned several of the midshipmen and masters mates, I believe, sir." I hoped I hadn't said too much and that Larkan would not mind my taking his wind on the subject.

"I don't care a fig for those others; Larkan can reassign them to the cook, for all I care. I do, however, have an interest in young Renouard and had mentioned to Larkan I wanted him assigned to a lieutenant who might be able to teach him something. That was your assignment, Mister Ballantyne."

I was speechless. I stared at the captain. Obviously all the rumors of his interest, and perhaps that of the Admiralty, as well, must be spot on!

"Sir . . . " I stammered, unsure of how to respond. "Mister Renouard has been assigned to me since we sailed. I have tried to teach him about the great guns, the mathematics of trajectory, mixing powder, and handling the m . . . people. Sir. I think it possible that some of it might be beyond his grasp." I paused, watching his expression.

He seemed not pleased. I added, "Or perhaps it is beyond my ability to teach him." I studied his eyes, and added, "But he is very talented aloft, sir, and understands the rig quite well, it appears." I smiled, hopefully.

"So, you decide to put him in an employment where he is comfortable, is that it?"

"Uh . . . well . . . sir, it was not I who shifted his assignment. Mister Larkan . . . "

"I don't care a fig for Mister Larkan, Ballantyne. The boy was assigned to you. See that you continue that assignment and teach him. He will never stand for lieutenant unless he understands gunnery and navigation, as well as the rig. Just on account of his *comfort* aloft, there would be even more reason to maintain his employment below, with the guns. I am holding you responsible for his education. The boy was a *steward*, for heaven's sake! Make him an officer!" Edwards' voice had gained volume throughout the conversation and, while he was not yet shouting at me, I felt it was not far off.

"Yes sir. I will speak to Mister Larkan directly." I spoke up, not quite as loudly as he had been speaking but loud enough to credit my manly acceptance of this unfortunate turn of affairs.

I stole a look at Tom; he was at once incredulous and, I reckon, grateful it was me under the gun and not him. His jaw was slack, some unchewed food showed in his partially open mouth, and his eyes sparkled with mirth at my predicament. I scowled at him. And Witherwax chose that moment to arrive bearing our dessert, a platter of duff.

The steward placed the platter in front of the captain who seemed to barely notice it. He then stepped to the sideboard, his back to us, and replaced the barely-touched decanter of wine there—perhaps with a claret or something for after dinner. Briefly, I wondered if we would be at table long enough to sample the latest offering.

Edwards continued to stare at the duff in front of him, most likely without seeing it. Finally, Witherwax shuffled quietly to the captain's elbow and muttered, "Would you like me to see to the duff, sir?"

"Hmm? Duff? Oh, my yes. No, Witherwax, quite all right. I'll take care of it. Pour out some of that claret you just brought in, if you please. I expect my guests will have a glass as well."

What had so distracted the captain, I had no idea. Was it our conversation about his protégé, or was it that he was still contemplating the heinous crime of mutiny and the scoundrels who committed it?

The remainder of the meal passed with inconsequential chat about the ship, the hot weather (how hot it was in the Cabin was not mentioned!), and that we would be making only one more port call before our arrival in Otaheite. While the captain offered little in the way of charm or *bonhomie*, we had no more inquisitions or tirades. Hayward and I left, with permission, after only one glass of claret, as grateful to have escaped as, I suspect, Captain Edwards was to be rid of us.

CHAPTER TEN

Otaheite, December, 1790

William Muspratt lay on his back, shifting his gaze from Morrison to the native who delicately tap-tap-tapped the sharpened hog's teeth into Muspratt's chest, creating a geometric design on the skin. Each of the teeth had been dipped into a mixture of soot, made from burning the Candle Nut, and water. The result was a bluish-black ink that, when injected under the skin, left a permanent mark.

From time to time, the native would glance at Morrison's tattoo, also on the chest, to ensure he had got it right. Most of the mutineers were, by this time, tattooed much in the same fashion as their island hosts; geometric designs encircling their arms and legs, and some form of personal design inked onto their chests or backs. Many had, in imitation of their native friends, also had offered their posteriors for decoration as well. The process was quite painful, but, as Peter Heywood had explained to them, would ensure acceptance into the native culture. Anticipating a long stay in Otaheite, none had been reluctant to adopt this form of personal adornment.

Muspratt was currently enduring the creation of a star on his chest. From time to time, each of the men visited the tattoo artist to have their personal designs augmented with further geometric lines and shapes. To a passerby, the procedure must seem as though the recipient of the native art was undergoing a form of torture contrary to his will. But each man followed the example of the natives, refusing to cry out through their clenched teeth, during the process.

Even the women had themselves tattooed, though in more austere patterns, and rarely are their legs marked above the ankles. The women's hands were sometimes marked with small spots, and, of course, like the men, their posteriors were heavily marked with the blue-black ink.

The artist paused in his labors, rocking back on his haunches to admire his handiwork. Muspratt allowed a great sigh to escape from between his still clenched teeth; it seemed to him as if he had not drawn a breath since the process had begun nearly an hour before.

"Is he done? I am not sure how much more of this I can take, Jim." Muspratt looked from his former shipmate, to the native, to his chest. The design was unrecognizable due to the blood that covered most of it as well as the upper part of his chest.

"Stop your complaining, Bill. He's got a bit more to go. You don't want him to tell his chums what a milksop you are. Even their women don't make a sound.

"When Tarreredooa had more marking put on her backside, she never even flinched. Didn't whimper or moan or nothin'. I was there and, knowing how it must have hurt, could barely believe it. But there you are: nary a peep from her!"

"Aye, my rump's been done too, but it wasn't near as hurtful as this is! Your wife musta quaffed a taste or two of that local grog to ease the pain, I'd wager. Only way I can think to stay still and quiet! Wish I'd taken a pint or so my own self!"

The native artist pushed forward onto his knees again, pressing his subject back down on his back. He dipped two of the sharp teeth into his ink, positioned the paddle holding them (and several more) over Muspratt's chest, and picked up little mallet. Muspratt groaned, closed his eyes, and drew a breath.

When Josiah Coleman found them sometime later, Muspratt's artwork was finished and he and Morrison were sharing a bit of tobacco in a pipe. Some blood still ran down Muspratt's chest but much of it had congealed, leaving a discolored mess where, in a few days, the newly drawn five-pointed star would emerge over his left nipple. Coleman wore the short sash-like garment that went 'round his waist and between his legs, forming a kind of diaper. He had adopted the native dress early on and advocated its use to his mates as being more comfortable than the tattered tarpaulin trousers many, including Morrison and Muspratt, still preferred. Morrison had yet to get used to it, though all of them, with their tattoos and suntanned bodies, looked as much like the natives as white men could.

"Tynah's been looking for you, Jim. Looks like there might be a dust up 'tween his people and some others—said it was Tyarrabboo's crew over yonder." Coleman pointed with his chin at a neighboring island.

"Oh hell, Coleman. You didn't believe him, did you? Ol' Matte's ready to fight at the drop of a hat and probably trying to stir something up. What could they have to fight about now?"

"He didn't say, Jim. Just asked if I had seen you. He was heading for Heywood's hut to talk with him about it. You likely ought to find him. You know he don't take kindly to bein' kept waitin', especially by any of us."

Morrison, realizing that the mutineers were accepted largely due to Tynah's sufferance of them and his influence over his subjects, agreed with Coleman's wisdom and stood.

"All righty-oh, then, young Josiah Coleman; let us go and seek out King Tynah and discover how we might serve him." The former bosun's mate put on the exaggerated accent of an educated man.

Morrison's sarcasm was not lost on Coleman who guffawed lustily. Even Muspratt, feeling better now that he was no longer having holes tapped into his chest, smiled and rose to follow the two.

They found the king deep in conversation with Midshipman Peter Heywood. Both men squatted outside Heywood's hut and spoke in the native dialect, still largely unintelligible to many of the mutineers. If one looked only at the tattoos both the king and the eighteen year-old sported about their bodies, it would have been difficult to distinguish native from white man.

"I'm told Matte wanted me to attend him. Something about a problem with natives from Tettooroa. You find out anything?" Morrison had long abandoned any use of "sir" or even the pretense of respect.

Heywood looked up, said something to the king, and stood.

"It would appear that Tyarrabboo's gone and got his back up about some woman one of Tynah's men is claimed to have stolen. He wants us to join them in an expedition to sort them out. With our muskets, of course."

"You try to talk him out of it? You know these people give no quarter nor seek it; bound to be a good deal of killin', they get into a scrap like that. Not that I care, but I've little interest in getting' caught up in the middle o' something that oughta stay 'tween them."

"He seems quite adamant that this is the only solution. Told me that Tyarrabboo sent a messenger across with a war club, signaling that they wanted to fight. He says he can't ignore the challenge without being thought less than a man and then . . . well, he said one of his own might challenge him as ruler."

"Hmmm . . . that would surely not help our needs a whit! Reckon we better have a look." Morrison looked at Tynah, who had remained sitting.

"Matte: when you planning to attack them?"

The native spewed forth a lengthy stream of words which Peter Heywood loosely translated as "in the next moon." The midshipman explained, though it was unnecessary, "He means when next the moon is full. By my reckoning, that would be in about three or four days.

"I don't know about this woman his man is said to have stolen. Nor have I learned which of the men might be the culprit. Tynah seems some reluctant to share that with me."

"See if you can find out any more about this. Schooner's put up for the rains so we'll have to use canoes to get there. He planning a big war party?"

"Aye, it would appear, based on what he tells me, that there will be four or five war canoes, in addition to us."

"Hmmm." Morrison scratched his armpit thoughtfully. "So he's got somewhere in the range of seven hundred to a thousand men? Sounds like he's bloody serious about this nonsense. And all over some damned female!"

"Well," relied the midshipman, "I would reckon it has more to do with taking over another kingdom than the slight he mentioned. Tynah's been agitating to add Tettooroa to his holdings almost since we arrived here. This 'nonsense,' as you put it, is simply a convenient excuse.

"Of course, there's always the chance that Tyarrabboo will launch an attack here before Tynah can rally his people and attack there. But when I questioned him about that possibility, he merely shook his head, saying Tyarrabboo made the challenge. I would imagine that must mean we have to go to him." Heywood shifted his glance between Morrison and the still-sitting king.

Morrison thought about this for a moment, then turned and strode away. Over his shoulder he said, again to Heywood, "Sounds more than likely to me. Matte's a stubborn old cove, and not one to be trifled with. His idea of what's right sets the rule. Just like ol' bloody Bligh!"

Two days later, as the darkness descended over the island, nearly one thousand natives, men and women, gathered in the vast clearing where ceremonial events were carried out. On the inland side, the mountains rose precipitously, covered in lush trees and almost impenetrable jungle. But now, there was little green to be seen. With the sun almost below the horizon beyond the mountains, the near side grew darker and darker, but the crimson sky to the west set off the craggy peaks in stark relief.

On the eastern side of the island, the blue of the Pacific Ocean had changed from its sunlit turquoise to the deep royal blue occasioned by the growing darkness. The darkness of the sea, east to west, was cut by a brilliant path of yellow luminescence as the full moon rose out of the sea and highlighted the tops of the gentle swells.

But none of the assembly noticed the beauty and grandeur of the scene; their collective gaze was focused on the huge bonfire that had been built at the center of the clearing, casting dancing shadows almost to the edge. A smaller fire, some distance apart, was tended by a clutch of women, preparing a feast to be consumed a bit later. Knots of men, large and small, discussed, in animated voices, a variety of subjects, surely all important, but generally unintelligible to the Englishmen. Each of the islanders carried their war clubs or spears, casually resting them on their shoulders or on the ground. All of the weapons were carved with intricate patterns, each reflecting the geometric tattoos sported by their owners. Lying near at hand were shields, painted in gaudy colors and woven from tightly interlaced palm fronds. The warriors were dressed in traditional battle and ceremonial kilts of palm instead of the short sash, called a *marro*, that they wore regularly.

"You gotten a look at Tynah? I'd rather expect him to be at the center of all this ruckus." Richard Skinner, as tattooed as any of the islanders, but one of the mutineers, asked no one in particular. He carried over his shoulder a musket, one of several dozen the men had kept when Christian sailed off from Otaheite.

"He'll show up right smartly, I'd reckon. It's his party, after all. Likely waitin' on the right moment to make his appearance." Millward answered as he took the measure of the goings-on.

"Sounds like they's quite a number here. What are they doin'?" Michael Byrne, the blind fiddler from Bligh's crew, moved his head as though he were looking about the clearing, but the men knew he could see little more than shadows.

"Right now, Mike, they ain't doin' nothing but standing about. Must be nigh on to a thousand of 'em, though. They . . . hold on a moment. What's that about?" George Stewart, former midshipman and frequent complainer, especially about their former commander, pointed to a group of men marching into the clearing, singing a war chant.

Each of the dozen and more natives in the van of the procession was a perfectly formed specimen; tall, muscular, and handsome of countenance, each wore a tall headdress of bright feathers which added to his already considerable stature. Short kilts covered their loins to mid-thigh, and their skin, tattooed and lavishly coated in cocoanut oil, gleamed in the firelight.

The British mutineers turned to look where their former shipmate pointed and saw, following the leaders, six equally handsome men carrying a pallet. The bearers were even more statuesque than the king's guard,

143

similarly turned out save for the feathered headdresses. They stood straight and tall, even under the considerable weight of the ceremonial pallet bearing the bulk of King Tynah.

"Well, I would reckon that'll be Tynah on the pallet. Making quite a remarkable entrance, I'd say!" Stewart exclaimed.

"Bugger was always fond of showing off his strength. Things oughta start hoppin' right quick, now." Morrison leaned on his musket, shaking his head at the ostentatious display.

The procession approached the center of the clearing, where the bonfire cast its dancing shadows and the reflections of the yellow, orange, and red flames on the oiled skin of the participants. Those who had been standing idly by stepped closer and, wanting to curry favor with the king, fawned over the man, some even casting themselves prostrate on the ground. His bearers lowered the pallet carefully and Tynah alighted to stand regally before his people.

He wore a garland of brilliant black and red feathers wrapped about his shoulders and reaching to the ground, a long cloak made solely of scarlet feathers, and a headdress of palm leaves woven with multi-hued flowers. Around his loins, he wore the woven kilt that reached to mid-thigh. He stood for a moment, surveying the pressing crowd, then began swaying to one side, then the other, as if to a rhythm only he could hear.

"Ain't seen him in that rig, afore. Reckon he needs to look like a king to get his people riled up for battle!" Morrison shifted his musket to his shoulder as he waited with his men to see what Tynah would do next. He did not have to wait long.

Tynah, without warning, stopped his swaying and raised his arms aloft, letting forth with a bellowed oath, which Heywood translated for his companions.

"He says, 'Let the heavens and the gods send us forth to take our enemies and bear our wounds like men. Those who die will do so in glory, serving their king.' Sounds a bit high and mighty to me!"

A great cry went up from the assemblage, cacophonous and lyrical at the same time. The women sent up their own cry, higher pitched and pleasantly complementary to the deeper more resonant tones the men offered.

"Well, they must not think so. Sounds like they're buyin' it lock, stock, and barrel!" Byrne, his head cocked as he listened for some familiar sound in the uproar, shouted, so as to be heard above the still raucous cheering.

The chanting began again, slowly overriding the general din until all the voices were as one, an enormous voice of supplication that would reach to the heavens. It was quite unintelligible to the British sailors, even Heywood.

"What on earth are they shouting, Peter? Can't make out a single word of it." Stewart shouted into his fellow midshipman's ear.

"Nor can I, George. Must be adulation to Tynah or some type of war chant."

Tynah now moved closer to the huge fire, the crowd parting in front of him. The scene put the men watching in mind of the Red Sea parting before Moses. The orange and yellow tongues of flame that shot skyward reflected in his feathered costume, altering the colors and adding dancing shadows that exaggerated the king's movements; the spectacle made him seem larger than life. Again, he raised his hands to the now darkened heavens. Almost as one, the voices of his people were silenced. Not even the birds that typically called out during the twilight dared make a sound.

He began another incantation in a deep voice, his arms still raised aloft. After several minutes his stentorian tones ceased, and unlike the previous time he had shouted to the gods, this time, the crowd remained silent. He lowered his arms and stooped over, disappearing from the view of the mutineers, standing many ranks away from the center of attention.

When he straightened up and again raised his arms skyward, he held a young goat, struggling to escape from the king's strong grasp.

"My stars, Peter, he's going to throw that poor creature into the fire alive!" Stewart was at once repulsed and captivated by the spectacle.

But George Stewart was mistaken; Tynah shifted his grasp on the still struggling goat and, taking a long blade from an attendant, deftly slashed the animal's throat while he held it above his head.

The goat's cries were silenced as torrents of its life blood spurted out of its neck, washing down over the king's arms and shoulders. The black feathers now took on the same hues as the red ones, covered in blood and glistening in the firelight. When the animal had bled out, Tynah, with a lusty roar, heaved the lifeless body into the flames. The crowd screamed its approval and shortly the chanting began again as the smell of roasting flesh, now mingling with the smells of whatever the women were cooking, permeated the air.

"Well, ain't that something! Glad he didn't throw in some young maiden like I heard they done in the old times." Morrison spoke to Josiah Coleman, who, with the other men, had pressed forward, the better to see the goings on.

"Aye, that would surely be a waste of a female! Ain't gonna do no good anyway, be it a goat or girl. He should be havin' practice and such with their weapons. Like in the Navy."

"They do that pretty regular, Coleman. You seen 'em at it. This is just to get they's blood up. Makes 'em believe they can't lose to their enemies in battle. Oughta be some grog starting to flow right quick, I'd warrant." Morrison spoke without taking his eyes off the fire and his host, Matte.

And shortly, as the bosun's mate had predicted, casks and huge jars of the potent liquor, distilled from palm and different fruits, began to appear, causing each of the islanders to cluster about them, dipping hearty rations from within. It was not long before many were quite intoxicated, with more joining their ranks with each passing hour. The Englishmen were not about to abstain. The way Muspratt put it, "They expect us to fight for 'em, they'll be wantin' to share their grog with us!"

By the time the moon had dipped below the mountains, the dim star-light and flickering embers of the fires lit a scene of debauchery—or its aftermath. Bodies sprawled about the clearing, native and English alike, most unconscious, others simply in a stupor, and still others, entwined in soporific coupling. The women were as quick as the men to pour a liberal tot for themselves and equally quick to enter temporary liaisons with whomever was handy. It took only a short while for the liquor to work its magic, first creating chaos, and then, ending it with stuporous collapse.

CHAPTER ELEVEN

In Pandora*: 1º 10' N, 25º 40' W*

"Run a gauntlet? Whatever does that mean? I've heard of *throwing down the gauntlet*, but running one? And what on earth for?" Renouard was quite perplexed.

He sat, as he had been for the past hour and more, well within my earshot, on the carriage of one of our spardeck carronades. With him was Thomas Rickard, a master's mate, who had been assigned to teach the recalcitrant midshipman the elusive art of navigation. I had, after consulting with Larkan, made the assignment in the hopes that Rickard might succeed where others, including George Passmore, our Sailing Master, myself, and one of Renouard's messmates, had failed. Apparently the lesson was over for the moment and the two were embarking on a discussion of the punishment only this morning meted out by the captain to, sadly, one of my own for helping himself to the possessions of his shipmate.

Stealing is one of the most heinous of crimes on a ship of war and generally dealt with quickly and harshly. Usually somewhere from a dozen to eighteen strokes with the cat answers nicely. Apparently not with Captain Edwards; he awarded Bully Rodgers the opportunity to face his shipmates despite his protestations of innocence. Robert Corner had confided his surprise in the severity of the punishment to me as I took over the watch from him at noon. While I was not unduly surprised at the punishment—after all, Edward Edwards was in command—I was surprised at the culprit; I had thought Rodgers, while surely not the tallest mast in the harbor, at least honorable in his dealings with his messmates, and well-tolerated by them. His performance in the second division had been, for the most part, quite acceptable, and his great physical size and strength more often than not, a boon. Except, of course, when provoked beyond his tolerance.

I hoped that, when he was forced to walk between the lines of his shipmates, each armed with anything from a barrel stave to rope-ends, he would control his temper, make the requisite two passes through the gauntlet, and get on with it. His strength, when provoked, would allow him easily to heave most of the others, bodily, a notable distance, including over the side. Should that happen during his punishment, God alone knew what might befall my sailor. As the punishment was to be imposed shortly before spirits up, we would not have to wait long to discover how Rodgers would react.

Meanwhile, *Pandora* plowed happily through the sea, nearing the line with each passing hour. We made a respectable six knots in the light airs prevalent in these latitudes and were just now—or rather at the noon fix of our position—only slightly over a day's sailing from King Neptune's appearance. I pondered, for the thousandth time, what the crossing ceremony would be like.

Of course, my imagination, having nothing save the yarns and tales of messmates past and present to go on, ran rampant, conjuring up all manner of wickedness and frightful denigration of all, especially the officers and midshipmen. I was quite sure the crew, those who wore the distinction of "shellbacks", would not miss the opportunity to repay some of the kindnesses we had shown them during the almost two months we had been at sea.

Robert, of course, sensing my trepidation, fed on it like a hungry shark, telling yarns in the wardroom equally as tall as the one he told me of the waterspouts. In his devious way, he never, or rarely, directed them at me, but merely shared his stories with one or another of our messmates, while I was nearby, perhaps chatting idly with another.

"You might consider bracing the yards a trifle, Edward. Seems the wind has veered slightly." John Larkan, his hands on his hips, stood to one side of the quarterdeck, a bit to my rear.

How long he had been there or how he had gotten there without my seeing him spoke eloquently of just how far my poor bedeviled mind had wandered! I snapped myself to the present and gave the necessary orders. As the yards were hauled around to more efficiently catch the wind, *Pandora* dug her shoulder in the sea and heeled a bit more. She seemed happy to respond to proper management and rewarded us with an additional knot of speed.

"Sorry sir. Guess I must have been daydreaming. Won't happen again." I stammered, embarrassed to be caught out like some landsman midshipman.

"Oh, I am sure it will. Happens to all of us, now and again. Now might be a good time to muster the crew for your man's punishment. Have the master at arms line them up at least fifteen to the side down the larboard side. The balance, those not on watch, will form ranks and observe, hopefully to learn a lesson for the future. Let me know when the hands are right and proper. I shall be below."

"Aye, sir." I doffed my hat, using the opportunity to wipe the beaded sweat from my brow.

I was sure the heat of the day had produced the moisture, but embarrassment might have played a small role.

"Pass the word for Mister Grimwood, if you please, Sival." I knew my junior watch officer has heard every word of the conversation with the first lieutenant (and likely delighted in my embarrassment) and knew also, almost for a certainty, by supper time, it would be a cause for revelry in the cockpit.

The hint of a smirk I noticed on his face, as he stepped forward to do my bidding, confirmed my guess.

Grimwood showed up within moments, responding to Sival's cries down each hatch and scuttle. With him were two Marine corporals.

"Muster the men, Mister Grimwood. Form the gauntlet down the larboard side, fifteen to the row, six feet apart. The others, put in ranks to observe. And, Grimwood, I want no slackers in the gauntlet; see to it that they are all fit and put Calligan in the center of one row."

Timothy Calligan was the man whose possessions Rodgers had purloined. In light of the articles taken, I still thought the punishment might be a bit severe, but consoled myself with the thought that it would serve as an example of what another, should temptation find them, might also expect.

Cunningham's pipe and the Marine's drum began their syncopated tunes and the men, knowing full well what was to happen, began to appear on the spardeck. Each of them, I noticed, carried some form of implement. Some had short lengths of rope while others chose an idle belaying pin. Still others preferred barrel staves and one, I saw, had the hoop from a barrel opened into a straight line, potentially deadly. Many more than the thirty who would participate had come prepared to inflict bodily harm on their shipmate. Calligan, when I spotted him, had shouldered his way to the front of the assembly, and carried an axe handle. Oh my!

Perhaps Rodgers isn't as well-liked as I had thought! Seems as though they're all ready to give him some punishment. I thought, watching those eager faces and hearing their excited chatter.

While the men were forming up, the officers, warrants and midshipmen was assembling on the quarterdeck in ranks, as was usual, by seniority. The surgeon, George Hamilton, stood prominently in the front rank as it was likely his services would be required at some point in the proceedings.

Since I still had the watch, I was exempted from the officers' muster and took the time to watch them, making eye contact with Robert, still hastily drawing the front of his straining waistcoat closed with one hand whilst struggling to insert the gold buttons into the proper buttonholes with the other. It seemed a losing effort and I smiled in spite of the somberness of the occasion. Corner noticed my observance and smiled ruefully back. He finally gave a shrug of his shoulders, grinned at me more broadly, and pulled his uniform coat around him to hide the unwilling waistcoat. Tom Hayward was the last of the commissioned officers to fall into line; with the exception of Sival, who still held the watch with me, the mids and warrants were in ranks behind the officers. I turned forward again to see how Grimwood and the bosun were progressing with our people.

As I watched this preparation from the sanctity of the quarterdeck, I was struck with how little any of us, officers or midshipmen, knew of our men. To be sure, I knew most of the men by sight (as did most of my colleagues, possibly excepting the captain), obviously my second division lads better, and decided they were a rum lot, most of them. Even though we lived in the close surroundings of a small ship, those of us in the ward-room and cockpit were insulated from the tars who lived forward and, for the most part, on whom our lives and the security of the ship depended.

Certainly, we thought we could identify potential trouble-makers, but perhaps not, as Rodgers had proven. Who among them would panic in a perilous situation? Who would run, given the opportunity ashore? Which of the men might think to foment a mutiny, as had Fletcher Christian, who at the start of *Bounty*'s voyage, was the protégé of the captain, only to become his undoing?

"Mister Ballantyne? Cap'n's comin' up." Sival started me from my reflections.

I quickly checked that all that I could see was in order, at least within the confines of the quarterdeck, and stood attentively by the binnacle. The scuttle to the Cabin was behind me. In front of me, John Larkan stepped up from the spar deck, nodded in response to my doffed hat, and stood facing aft, and the officers, warrants, and midshipmen assembled there.

"Good afternoon, Cap'n. The men are present and proper and ready to administer punishment." To the captain, he doffed his hat.

"Very well, Mister Larkan. You may proceed." Captain Edwards reso-nant voice seemed somber, as if he regretted what was to take place. But he himself had sentenced Bully Rodgers to run the gauntlet instead of twenty or thirty strokes of the cat. He stood, properly turned out in full uniform despite the heat of the day, his sword hanging at his side, and rested his gloved hands on the rail separating the quarterdeck from the rest of the ship. I could not see his face, but from the past occurrences of all hands witnessing punishment, suspected he wore no expression whatever, his eyes staring straight ahead, perhaps at our bowsprit. I wondered idly if he would watch Rodgers being beaten by his shipmates.

"Silence! Silence fore and aft!" Larkan's voice rang out.

The chattering, bantering, and general skylarking stopped at once, the men forming again into the ranks they had been assigned. They all stood at attention, those forming the gauntlet holding their cudgels at their sides, the others in neat ranks running fore and aft behind their shipmates. They all swayed in unison with the gentle motion of the ship, making them appear to be linked together by some invisible harness.

"Mister Grimwood: You may bring up the prisoner and proceed."

Grimwood saluted smartly and nodded to the two Marines who flanked him. They turned about and marched forward, disappearing down a hatch amidships.

When they returned, Bully Rodgers marched between them, fury discoloring his face. I could see the muscles in his bare shoulders bunching like coiled serpents and he alternately clenched and unclenched his fists, causing the muscles and tendons in his arms to leap about like ropes whipped by a savage wind. He walked stiffly between the two Marines, each with a hand lightly on Bully's elbow. Their outboard hands held muskets, bayonets fixed, pointing to the sky. When they reached the spot in front of the quarterdeck where the punishment would begin, the little entourage stopped and the Marines, at least, stood to attention, saluting the quarterdeck and the master at arms.

"Tucker Rodgers, you have been sentenced to run a gauntlet of your messmates in execution of the sentence imposed upon you for thievery by Cap'n Edwards.

"You will walk, mind you, I say *walk*, between the ranks of your mates to face the punishment they might wish to mete out to you. Should you falter or stop, one of these Marines, who will be behind you, will encourage you with a bayonet. When you have reached the end of the gauntlet, you will turn about and retrace your steps to your starting point. Are you clear on this?" Grimwood's voice was loud enough to be heard by all assembled.

Addressing the men forming the gauntlet, Grimwood advised that any shirking their duty would follow Rodgers through the lines.

In a quieter voice, presumably only for Rodgers' ears, he said, "Keep moving, lad, and take your punishment like a man. These boys here ain't your enemies, they're your shipmates. You're a big chap and, I suspect, you can stand the punishment."

The Marines turned Rodgers about and walked him to the start of the double line of men. Cudgels were raised, barrel staves waved about, and I noticed that Calligan smacked the axe handle into his palm in a most threatening manner.

"Stand ready in the gauntlet!" Grimwood called out, quite unnecessarily I thought, as Rodgers, with his now single escort, took his place. The other Marine had gone to the far end of the line to receive the prisoner and turn him about.

"Start him moving." His voice was flat, without passion or feeling, and loud enough to be heard by the Marine with Rodgers only a few feet away.

The Marine shifted his grip on his musket, now carrying it in two hands with the butt under his right arm. The bayonet was a bare foot from Rodgers' posterior. The sailor was shirtless, wearing only a pair of -ragged canvas trousers that came to mid-calf, and he, like most of his messmates, was barefoot. A quiet word behind him started him into the ranks of the men; instinctively, he put up his arms to ward off the blows that began to rain down on him. It was quite apparent that each of the men took Grimwood's admonition seriously and held nothing back.

There was no drum beating, as was the case with a flogging, and the only sound, save those of the ship moving the water and the groaning of blocks and lines, was that of the cudgels, staves, and rope ends landing on Bully's unprotected body. But he kept moving, stoically, eyes straight forward, and except for the first few steps, his arms at his sides.

His stride faltered a few times as blows landed on his head and one particularly creative sailor swung his barrel stave low, hitting the big man behind both knees. Before he had made it halfway down the line, blood flowed freely down his back, and I am certain, his face and chest. But still he stayed the course, uttering nary a sound save for the occasional grunt when a particularly savage blow landed.

I watched for Calligan and picked him out in his original spot, but now leaning forward, watching Rodgers' progress, obviously eager to add his personal punishment to that of his shipmates. After all, the slender landsman was the victim of Rodgers' supposed larceny and should contribute to the best of his ability. He held his axe handle in two hands, ready to swing a mighty blow. The prisoner maintained his steady pace, seemingly oblivious to the blows raining down on him. Watching his progress, wishing for the brutality of it to be over, I saw the big man turn his head slightly to look his accuser in the eyes. Then, seemingly to invite the little fellow to hit him harder, he actually moved a bit toward Calligan's side of the line. Calligan raised his weapon higher, a look of concentration and revenge distorting his face.

As Rodgers' drew abreast of his accuser, the axe handle started down, aimed in an arcing blow directly towards his face. Without breaking stride, Rodgers raised his blood-smeared arms, and grabbed the wood, wrenching out it out of Calligan's hands. He threw it disdainfully down on deck and, while his stunned shipmates looked on, grabbed up Calligan by the neck and the crotch and raised him over his head.

Turning, he took a staggering step and pitched the struggling landsman over the heads of the outboard line of the gauntlet and over the rail into the sea. The silence, in the wake of this outrageous and stunning act, was exquisite.

"MAN OVERBOARD!" Someone cried out, followed by the stentorian voice of our captain: "SHOOT THAT MAN. SHOOT HIM! NOW!"

Pandemonium broke out; officers shouting, the sailors shouting as they rushed to the rail to see their shipmate floundering in the sea, and Bosun Cunningham, ever calm, calling for assistance in getting the cutter launched. Someone, I think it was a midshipman on the quarterdeck, had the presence of mind to heave a line over the leeward quarter for Calligan to catch hold of.

Over the bedlam and confusion, I watched as Rodgers, seemingly forgotten in light of the more urgent needs of the man overboard, turned to face aft. It appeared that he looked directly at me, blood obscuring any expression on his face, and shrugged his broken and bleeding shoulders. The orderly lines of the gauntlet had dissolved into pandemonium, the sailors who had manned it crowding the rail, yelling, and pointing. Rodgers remained in place, unmoving while the men had rushed to the rail, and now stood alone, seemingly disinterested in the activity at the bulwark or, for that matter, in the sea.

The Marine who had been at his back urging him forward had, over the noise, apparently heard Edwards' order, raised his musket and fired at point blank range. Rodgers crumpled in a heap on the deck, the ball having taken him in the forehead. Once again, following the discharge of the musket, all hands, including those at the rail, fell silent, gaping at their fallen shipmate. Several of Rodgers' messmates rushed to his side, kneeling in the growing puddle of gore staining the snowy deck. Forgetting my duties for the moment, I too reacted and leaped to the deck, pushing sailors out of my way as I struggled to gain the side of my fallen sailor.

Grimwood was wading into the sea of men; Bosun Cunningham had, with the help of several sailors, made the cutter ready to swing out, and punishment forgotten now, officers quickly gained control and issued orders to wear the ship, sending topmen aloft and heavers to their sheets and braces. I realized that I could do no good for Rodgers and returned to my responsibilities on the quarterdeck where Sival was shouting to the man in the mizzen top to keep his eyes on Calligan and his arm pointing at the still flailing, splashing sailor. In the three steps it took me to reach the wheel, I passed the surgeon heading for the melee, presumably to determine that Rodgers was indeed dead.

Larkan had taken over maneuvering *Pandora* to heave the ship to and Cunningham had the boat hoisted and ready to set in the sea alongside as soon as our forward motion slowed. Calligan was still floundering in the waves, but had quite missed the line thrown out to him. It would be up to the boat to rescue him. At least the lookout in the mizzen top still had him in sight, pointing at his barely visible form as Sival had instructed him. The ship slowed, foretops'l backed, others shivering, and the bosun set the boat alongside with barely a splash.

His crew pulled willingly, following directions from the ship; they, from their water's edge vantage point, could not see more than a few yards in the heaving seas and so, amid much shouting of "Bear to larboard," "Bear more to starboard," from the ship, they did not make a notably fast trip to where Calligan was hoarse from shouting, fatigued from waving his arms to attract their attention, and scared beyond words.

Captain Edwards, his face a mask of grim anger, was agitated; he paced the sanctity of the windward side of his quarterdeck, occasionally craning his neck to see what progress Cunningham was making toward the floundering landsman. He smacked his fist into the palm of his other hand repeatedly and more than once, cried out, "Make haste there, in the boat. I can ill-afford to lose yet another man. Make haste, you lubbers!"

Make haste they did and, within less than an hour from when the late Bully Rodgers heaved the unfortunate sailor into the sea, he was back aboard, and the ship back on her course for Rio. The bosun oversaw some of Bully's messmates as they holystoned the stained deck.

"Never in my considerable years at sea have I ever witnessed anything quite so alarming! Shocking, it was." Our surgeon was holding forth on the recent events as, later, I stepped into the wardroom, still stunned.

I sat, said nothing, and listened as some of my more vocal messmates held forth on the lightning-fast delivery of justice by Captain Edwards.

"I can hardly believe the man is a monster of that stripe. Had I not witnessed it with my own eyes, I would have been hard pressed to take a retelling of the event as fact. Why on earth would he order the man shot? Having him run the gauntlet was even a bit extreme, though I have seen it ordered before." Corner offered, his usual good humor evaporated in the face of the discussion.

"Gentlemen: Cap'n Edwards is our commander and as such is obliged to do whatever *he* sees fit to do to maintain discipline and order on *his* ship. If that calls for, in his mind, having a thief run the gauntlet, or having a drunk or insubordinate seaman flogged, or even hanging a man, then so be it. Consider that Rodgers literally *threw* the man overboard, with, I am certain, the intent of killing him. In the captain's mind, there was no question about what the punishment would be for Rodgers; it was simply the quickly settled issue of *when* to carry out the sentence. I am sure the example set for the other men will serve long and well to maintain order in the ship." Larkan, second in command to Edwards offered, executing his role of support to a fault.

With the grumbling coming from the fo'c'sle already, I shouldn't wonder if the 'example' the cap'n made of Rodgers might not serve some other purpose sooner. If it could happen to Bligh, who was a tolerant commander, why not . . . Before I could even run out the rest of my thought, Corner opened his mouth and almost echoed it.

"Wonder if we might see a few run, should they be given shore leave in Rio." He suggested. "There might be a few of our people who could take ordering a man shot down like some rabid animal as a bit extreme."

"I would be quite surprised were Cap'n Edwards to approve shore leave for any beyond officers, mids, and the warrants. I suspect he wants to get in, pay his respects to the head man, and get the necessaries for our passage out. You gentlemen might recall that from Rio, we will turn Cape Horn and head straight for Otaheite. As long a trip from Rio as we have had just to get this far. Farther, in fact.

"You might wish to offer some guidance to your people." Larkan spoke softly, his tone echoing the still stunned mood of the wardroom. "And Mister Corner, you might consider your words a bit more carefully in the future. I am not sure Cap'n Edwards would appreciate you questioning his decisiveness."

I was glad I had kept my own thoughts to myself.

Robert simply raised his ample eyebrows at the first lieutenant, accepting the admonition without comment. None was needed.

"You know, the cap'n might have done Rodgers a kindness, having him shot like that." Hamilton turned to face us. He had been staring out a gunport, opened for ventilation in the easy weather we enjoyed in these latitudes.

"A *kindness*? Good heavens, man. Whatever do you mean? Surely killing someone would not be considered as kind by any!" Corner responded, half rising from his chair, the warning offered only moments ago quite forgotten,

"Calm yourself, Robert. Think about it. Rodgers had been beaten to a bloody pulp and he was only half way down his first trip through the gauntlet. He still had to finish that one, then turn about and do it yet again. I doubt, given the severity of the wounds he had already received, he would have survived the second run through. I examined him quite thoroughly while you were all consumed with rescuing the poor chap he tossed overboard. Those lads took their work to heart. Likely remembered what Grimwood told 'em at the outset about not slacking off. The poor sod's wounds, even at that point, were some severe!"

Corner muttered, less under his breath than he might have wanted, "Aye, especially the small round wound in his head!"

I continued to hold my tongue throughout this discussion, content to listen to my more experienced brethren. I agreed with Robert that both the gauntlet and the shooting were something a bit extreme, but I also understood Larkan's point of view regarding Edwards' fixation on discipline and order. Hamilton, I thought, made some sense as well, though I could not myself tell the extent of Rodgers injuries, I was sure Hamilton's assessment was likely on the mark. But Rodgers was a big, strong chap and might have indeed survived the beating. Of course, we would never know. Maybe Hamilton was just trying to make us feel better about the unfortunate incident. But the thought that had passed through my brain earlier still flitted about the edges of my consciousness, causing me some disquiet.

My unease stemmed more from a question I could not answer than the likelihood of the heinous event itself: which side would I be on? The conversation around me continued in desultory tones as I worked on my own puzzle. But neither the conversation or any solution came to a satisfactory conclusion.

With no warning whatever, Robert changed the subject, his elfin grin returning, undiminished. "Our position is less than one degree north of the line, John. Reckon we'll be getting' a wee visit from old King Neptune sometime tomorrow?"

"I suspect you're quite right, Robert. Should cross sometime during the morning watch, if this breeze holds."

My mind, eager to be rid of the unanswerable question with which it had been wrestling, started at Larkan's words.

I have the morning watch! Perchance I will be unable to leave my post for the ceremony! And while I might not participate in the humiliation of it all, I will most surely have crossed the line!

"I would assume the cap'n will have no problem with our crossing plans? Have you had a word with the man on the subject?" Corner pressed the first lieutenant.

"Indeed, and more than a few, Robert, and, after today's events, I hope they were not wasted! I shall ensure he will give us his blessing. In fact, perhaps I should see him now, before we have to bury Rodgers." Larkan rose from his chair.

As his hand reached for the knob, the door opened, seemingly of its own volition, and revealed a young sailor, a boy actually, standing, hat in hand, his fist raised as though he were about to knock. His expression mirrored Larkan's temporary confusion, but without the mirth that the lieutenant enjoyed almost at once. It was the quarterdeck messenger.

"Uhh . . . oh . . . sorry sirs. I meant to knock. The door uh . . . opened quite on its own." The young man, was obviously stunned by all of us staring at him, enjoying his obvious discomfort.

"Well, what would you have for us, sailor? A message perhaps from Mister Hayward?"

"Aye, sir. A message."

"Well, don't just stand there. What words has Mister Hayward entrusted to your care?" Corner seemed to enjoy the boy's apparent distress.

"Oh, yes, sir. The message, sir." He looked in wide-eyed terror around the room at the four of us sitting there, waiting. "I mean, sirs.

"Mister Hayward's compliments and I'm to tell you the corpse of the man Cap'n Edwards shot is ready to be sent to the deeps . . . sir."

"Is that how Mister Hayward told you to say it, sailor?" Larkan's tone told us he could scarce believe it was.

"Pretty much, sir." The messenger had paled and stiffened his posture a bit in the face of the question.

"Oh, come now. Really, he told you 'the man Cap'n Edwards shot'? Or did he say 'Rodgers' body had been prepared for burial'?"

"Uh . . . something like that sir. Couldn't 'member all of it." The boy was squirming uncomfortably now, twisting his hat with both hands.

"Very well. You may tell Mister Hayward to muster the crew for burial and have him tell the captain . . . no. Belay that last. *I* will tell the captain. I can only imagine how *that* message might come out!" Larkan pushed past the messenger and headed aft to the Cabin.

"Maybe he'll remind our commander that we cross the line tomorrow. Perhaps he'll be in a good mood, now he's about to watch the results of his efforts get slipped over the side!" Corner's anger, pushed just beneath the surface, now bubbled up with renewed vigor.

"I'd mind my tongue more closely, were I you, Robert. Never know who might be at the door." Surgeons sometimes offer advice as well as poultices.

After several minutes of seemingly mindless conversation, platitudes, and a few short sea stories about crossing the line (mostly for my benefit, I suspected), we heard the Marine's drum and the bosun's whistle calling all hands to muster. Silently and, with sufficiently somber faces, we ascended the ladder to the spar deck and thence to the quarterdeck.

The crew was appearing, shuffled into proper ranks by Grimwood's people and the bosun's mates. I noticed half a dozen of our Marines standing to, near the spar rack, dazzling in their red jackets and freshly whitened trousers. Their muskets, with bayonets fixed, shot bright reflections of the late-day sun across the deck. The mood was sober and reserved; there was none of the banter, chattering, and skylarking which generally occurred when the people were assembled—at least before Captain Edwards took his place on the quarterdeck.

The midshipmen and warrants, including George Hamilton and Mister Passmore, our Sailing Master, the bosun, gunner, and carpenter all took their places behind the officers. The spots closest to the railing and in front of the officers' ranks were reserved for the captain and first lieutenant. The formation was the same each and every time we assembled, whether to hear the Articles of War read (every Sunday), witness punishment, or witness some poor sod being sent to his eternal resting place, somewhere in the darkest, coldest recesses of Neptune's domain. With the death (dare I say "execution?") of Bully Rodgers so dramatic, visible to all, and recent, I expected some *soto voce* comments, mutterings, or grumbling. There was not a sound.

"Cap'n's on deck!" Cried young Lieutenant Hayward.

"Attention on deck!" Cried Mister Grimwood.

The shuffling of bare feet, stamping of boots, and the slap of musket butts all gave indication that Grimwood's order had been heeded with alacrity. Few eyes wandered from the straight ahead stare.

Edwards, followed by Mister Larkan, made his way around the end of the officers' ranks and the two of them took their places at the railing of the quarterdeck. Against his chest, the captain held a leather-bound Bible in the manner of a country parson, his finger tucked within, apparently marking the passage he would use. He did not have on his hanger (nor did any others of us), and, with his jacket buttoned across his stomach, I could not discern if his pistol was tucked into the top of his trousers. I hoped it was not.

Rodgers' bulky form lay under a shroud and rested on a plank, one end of which was balanced on the bulwark. The inboard end of the plank rested on a make-shift support. I could see the outline, at his feet, of the two eighteen-pound shot which would ensure a fast trip to the bottom and no chance of returning to the surface.

The captain stood quite still for a long moment, surveying his people, his ship, and the sea. His eyes were squinted against the glare and his side whiskers fluttered gently in the easy breeze. His lips mimicked his eyes, a thin line perfectly straight across his face. His feet were splayed to balance him against the slow roll of the ship and his free hand rested on the rail in front of him. He nodded at Larkan.

"Attention to burial at sea. Doff hats!" Larkan called out.

Everyone, including the officers and the captain, removed their hats and held them at their sides.

And then, his voice raised to be heard, Edwards began reading from the "Rite of Christian Burial At Sea."

At the appointed time, along with the words, "We commit his body to the deeps," Larkan nodded at Grimwood who, in turn, motioned to two Marines standing at the inboard end of the makeshift bier. Still at attention, each lifted a corner, raising it to chest height. The corpse of our shipmate, Tucker "Bully" Rodgers, wrapped in his weighted shroud slipped off the plank. A quiet scuffing sound, canvas on rough wood, accompanied the sight of the form as it slid over the bulwark. Silence for a short moment, then a splash as it hit the sea, throwing up a small wave, momentarily confusing the easy swell. Within a second or two, the sea returned to its timeless motion, leaving nary a trace of Rodgers' entry into its domain. The weighted shroud disappeared into the darkening, untold depths, where it would rest for eternity, while *Pandora* and her uneasy crew sailed on.

There were no final words from the captain save, "Mister Larkan, you may dismiss the people."

CHAPTER TWELVE

At the Equator

"Mister Ballantyne! I can scarce believe it, but there's a voice calling out from under the bowsprit. Something about 'coming aboard.' What should I do?"

John Sival, still my junior watch officer, some startled by the event, was rushing aft to the quarterdeck. I had earlier sent him to check on a sailor who appeared drunk and was standing on the pinrail at the mainmast.

"What exactly did the voice say, John?" I used my most sincere voice, trying to calm his fears. After all, one did not hear a human voice emanating from *before* the bow of a ship on a daily basis and it must have rattled the young man.

"I didn't catch all of it, Mister Ballantyne. What I did hear, though, spoke of coming on board us and rallying to him 'shell' something or other." There seemed to be still a slight tremor in his voice.

"Mister Ballantyne, as you are the officer of the deck, I think you should inform the captain that King Neptune wishes to come onto the ship and judge—and initiate—those who have not yet crossed the line!" Larkan, again appearing like a sprite from nowhere, suggested in a quiet voice. He held his octant at his side.

Oh my! This is the start of it, then. We must be at the Equator. Nothing for it, I reckon, save to inform Edwards as he said, and, hopefully, keep my station on the quarterdeck. I glanced at my watch, slipping it from my waistcoat pocket unseen. *I still have another three hours before I am relieved.*

"Mister Sival. My compliments to Cap'n Edwards and we are at the Line with King Neptune requesting permission to board. Smartly now, lad, and return here immediately you have delivered the message." I was pleased to hear no hint of tremor in my voice!

Within a moment or two, he was back, wreathed in smiles which I thought a bit odd, considering where I had sent him.

"What did he say, Mister Sival?"

"He actually *smiled*, sir and said we should invite Mister Neptune into the ship. He also mentioned he would be on deck shortly and that the first lieutenant might handle things until he arrived." The young man was so relieved that he was bobbing his whole body, like some strange bird.

I glanced at Larkan, standing at the bulwark of the quarterdeck, a smile on his lips. He nodded and said, "Well, Mister Ballantyne, you *are* the watch officer. Go and welcome Neptune into *Pandora*. Mister Sival and I will keep an eye on things here for you."

I doffed my hat and stepped to the short ladder leading to the spardeck and forward. As I gained the mainmast, I heard the voice that Sival must have heard earlier.

"Ho! Ship ahoy! I shall come on board of you!"

It came from under the bows, just as young Sival had said, and sounded a bit hollow, as if from the bottom of a barrel.

"Aye, sir, and welcome you are to *Pandora*! Please come aboard." I cupped my hands and shouted forward, still moving in that direction.

As I passed the foremast, I saw three large sailors at the hammock netting about over where the anchor was catted. Two, it appeared, had recently climbed over the rail, using a Jacob's ladder, which the third had secured for their use. One of the figures recently aboard stepped toward me, followed by a smaller—though not by much—compatriot.

The first was a sight! Barechested and wearing both a hideous mask on his face and a large swab on his head, he held aloft a boarding pike which someone had modified to create a trident, Neptune's scepter, as it were. His exposed arms, legs below his shortened pantaloons, and chest had been colored green, presumably to make him appear fish-like. The other figure, slightly smaller in stature but greater in girth, wore a similar get-up, but was naked save for a gargantuan loincloth which encircled his great belly and was tucked between his meaty thighs. He, too, had been daubed with the same green coloring.

I stopped my forward progress as they approached, not knowing quite what to expect. They both marched straight up to me and stopped a scant two feet from where I stood rooted to the deck.

In a booming voice, the first shouted, "It's King Neptune, I am. And here to call forward all Shellbacks to sit in judgment of your Johnny Raws." He turned to the other seaman, the one dressed only in the diaper, and gestured. "My child, my sweet little infant here, will assist us!" And with that, the "baby" took a seat on a six-pounder carriage, let out a wail, and stuck his thumb into his mouth.

As one might imagine, I was dumbstruck! I noticed a few of the watch section standing near at hand, amused beyond words, elbowing each other and pointing at the grotesque characters before me. Likely had a few thoughts and comments about my own self, as well!

"Aye, King Neptune. I am Lieutenant Ballantyne, at present the watch officer on the quarterdeck. I shall see to rallying your subjects, sir. Perhaps you'd enjoy a chair to rest in after your long swim?" I was trying to get into the spirit of the occasion.

I grabbed one of the gawking sailors and sent him to fetch Bosun Cunningham straight away. When the bosun appeared, grinning ear to ear, I suggested he muster our shellbacks on deck and the remaining, the uninitiated as it were, should be paraded aft of the mainmast.

"Moulter, you look a sight! Your own Ma wouldn't recognize you in that rig!" Cunningham laughed, speaking to "King Neptune."

And quite right he was! I had not recognized the bosun's mate myself. A tattoo, a bare-breasted maiden, graced his bicep. I had missed it, being partially covered by the green coloring. Now I stared at the "baby" to see if I might determine who this diapered figure might be. After a moment, realization struck.

Steward! It has to be Steward, my own gunner's mate! Must have been the green color and the swab on his head that threw me off!

Cunningham, his laugh with his mate done, knuckled his forehead in acknowledgment of my order to muster the men and stepped quickly aft, raising his voice for the Marine drummer. And then his pipe sounded the call for "all hands" shrilly and down each scuttle. For my own self, determining to remain out of the line of fire, I returned to my duties on the quarterdeck.

The men, wise to what was afoot, mustered quickly and almost eagerly, the more experienced among them anxious to see what would befall their shipmates who had yet to cross the line. Even the landsmen seemed unconcerned about the initiation they would soon receive. More than likely, they welcomed the break from the daily routine and monotony of a ship at sea in fine weather.

With the people mustered, Neptune picked several brawny sailors from the group of shellbacks—there were but a couple of dozen of them—and formed his "court." His "throne" was a hogshead, brought up from the hold, and placed next to the foremast pin rail. His "baby" sat on an empty powder keg (looking ridiculous as he dwarfed the diminutive keg with his bulk!) to one side. Their half-dozen hand-picked shellbacks, the "court," were arrayed to either side, grinning and chattering in anticipation of what would be coming.

"My royal court and minions of the sea tell me there are many aboard this fine ship uninitiated in the mysteries of the salt. Where is the captain?" Neptune boomed out.

"I am here, King Neptune." Edwards voice rang out as he descended the ladder from the quarterdeck.

I really hadn't expected the captain to take any part in the crossing ceremony, but perhaps he thought it best, in light of the past day's happenings, to show a bit of humanity. He marched forward, in full uniform, sword and all. When he stood in front of the "king," Edwards saluted him and asked his business.

Neptune repeated that he was in the ship to bring into the fold those unfamiliar with the mysteries of the salt. It was all very respectful.

"Well, Neptune, that's quite fine. Do your business, but try not to create too much of a disturbance in my ship. And move it along. I can't wait, hove to, here all day. Must get back on course quickly." Edwards, ever the commander, responded with more good will than I would have thought possible.

He stood for a moment, surveying the assembly, nodded to Neptune, and turned about to head aft. Neptune, for his part, made a sweeping and likely disrespectful bow to the captain's back and roared out, "Where is the shaving gear I requested? We must have some of these landsmen scraped clean so when they kiss the baby, they will not scratch his delicate skin!"

This, of course, was greeted with ribald laughter and great guffaws, and quickly some hands produced a large bucket, (what it was filled with, I could not discern from my position on the quarterdeck) and several well rusted barrel hoops.

With a frown, I recalled the use of barrel hoops and staves yesterday in another "ceremony" and wondered if I would see something similar today.

"Baby Neptune" had his belly smeared with some noxious mixture—it looked like mast slush—and the shellbacks each picked up a barrel hoop.

"Bring forward those to be welcomed to the great mysteries of the deeps!" Neptune cried out.

I noticed one of the other warrant officers whisper in Neptune's ear, but of course, had no idea of what was said. I found out quick enough!

"I am told we have officers and midshipmen as well as sailors in the ship who are "Johnny Raws". It is only fitting that those of loftier position be welcomed first. Who is the senior among them?"

My heart skipped a beat when I heard this and I noticed that a trickle of perspiration was making its way down my neck, and not just from the warm temperature. When I saw hands pointing aft, I gulped.

"Mister Ballantyne! As third lieutenant, you would be the senior among the exalted officers who has yet to join our group. Please step forward and be initiated!" Neptune called out, his voice clearly reaching me on the quarterdeck.

"I am most sincerely sorry, King Neptune. I have the watch and can not leave the quarterdeck. Should you still be here when I am relieved in three hours, I shall be most delighted to pay you a visit!" I shouted this in my best command voice.

To no avail. "Quite all right, Mister Ballantyne. I shall assume the watch for you. Go right ahead forward and become a shellback." Larkan smiled, flapping his hand dismissively.

Bloody helpful Larkan!

With manly stride, I marched myself down the ladder and up the spar-deck to stand in front of Moulter/Neptune. I hoped my status as an officer would help me.

"Please, sir. Have a seat right here and, if you would be so kind, remove your jacket and waistcoat. Wouldn't want to get lather on them!" Neptune grinned and pointed to a chest situated on the larboard side.

I did as I was told, trying to hold a smile on my face. As soon as I was seated, two hands, obviously from the ranks of the "court," took position in front of me. One held a shockingly rusty hoop while the other dragged the bucket—the one I had noticed earlier—across the deck to my feet. He reached a great paw into it and, grabbing up a handful of the noxious mixture within, slathered it, none too gently, on my face.

The lather proved to be lard from the galley, slush for the rig, and bilge water. A lovely and malodorous concoction, it was! I tried, with some success, not to gag as the "lather" was spread across both my nose and mouth. The other, the one with the "razor," began to scrape away the lather with great delight. I could hear the laughs and hoots of the watching crew. Even my fellow officers—*especially* my fellow officers! Corner, his huge belly heaving with the guffaws he enjoyed at my expense, was laughing so hard his eyes were mere slits in his head and tears streamed down his cheeks.

When I was pronounced shaven, Neptune motioned me to him.

"You must now kiss my child's belly, and ask permission to join our fraternity." He boomed out at me, pointing to Steward, his "infant."

Accompanied by more joviality, catcalls, and laughter, along with words of advice from my shipmates, I stepped bravely over to where the "baby" was perched on his powder keg. I noticed his belly had been smeared with something even more unpleasant than the shaving "lather." I knelt before him, sought the permission as instructed, and made to kiss his ample girth. As my head reluctantly approached the target—I was hoping a close pass at the disgusting mixture coating his belly would answer—the "baby" grabbed the back of it and pressed it into the mess on his stomach. This time, I did gag. He held my face to his ample girth until I thought to suffocate!

When he released me, I stood, my shirt ruined, my face covered in the noxious slop that had coated his belly, and my pride trampled upon. Steward made a small motion with his hand and suddenly a great gout of sea water poured over my head and shoulders, completely soaking me.

"Now that you are cleaned up a bit, Mister Ballantyne, we welcome you to our order of shellbacks." The "baby" smiled broadly and extended his hand in welcome. Again, laughter and, this time, cries of "Well, done, Mister Ballantyne," greeted me.

I laughed along with them, whether from the joy of becoming a shellback or surviving the indignities of the initiation intact, I knew not. But I had done it! I now could enjoy the ritual as others suffered it.

The midshipmen and master's mates came next, going through the indoctrination by twos—I reckon I was honored as an officer to receive special treatment—and all took it in good stride. No tears, no crying out, no untimely comment. All except David "Willie" Renouard.

Mister Renouard had watched my trials and those of his messmates; the ordeal seemed, in his mind, to be degrading, which of course, it was intended to be. He mentioned that he preferred not to participate in it.

"Moulter, it is disrespectful to treat an officer of the Crown in this manner. I will not be participating in your debasement. Obviously, my messmates seem not to mind, but, I assure you, I do. Very much." Having spoken, Willy turned and began to walk away.

With a nod to two of his court, Neptune ordered him returned. The two grinning men stepped forward, one to each side of the reluctant mid, and, each taking an arm, lifted him bodily from the deck, turned him about, and set him again facing his judge. I could not help but notice the smiles wreathing most of the faces around us, Shellbacks or not. And me included. Obviously, my midshipman had done little to ingratiate himself with the men.

"Mister Midshipman: I know not who this Moulter is. I am King Neptune and you are in my domain. No one can cross the line without proper initiation; it is the ruling of my court that you, like your messmates, be properly instructed in the mysteries of the deeps. You will be shaved and you will be supplicant to my child." Neptune spoke loudly enough for all around him to hear quite clearly his words. There was no laughter now, only an expectant silence to see what might happen next.

Young Willy squirmed in the grasp of the two sailors. "I will NOT be humiliated thus. I wanted no part of this voyage and surely I want no part of your nonsense . . . you and your 'court,'" he screeched and increased his struggles to escape.

"Shave him!" Neptune shouted to his henchmen. Handclapping and laughter now from most all of us.

Again, the youngster was bodily lifted to the "shaving bench" and, while the two men "steadied" him, another slathered his face with the noxious brew. When he opened his mouth to further complain, the man with the shaving soap was quick enough to get a large dollop of it inside. Sputtering and choking, Renouard quickly closed it, now struggling and squirming less. Even his fellow mids, their ordeal over, were laughing at him as the fellow with the rusty barrel hoop "shaved" him.

As the mess came off his face, I noticed tears streaming unabated down his cheeks and, for a moment, felt sorry for the lad. I shot a glance at Moulter and shook my head. The "king" just smiled at me and motioned to his henchmen to bring the midshipman to "Baby Neptune" for the obligatory "kiss." Again, cheers and laughter from the men.

Renouard got the same treatment as I and his fellows had, except that while they were waiting, some of the "court" had applied a fresh coating of sludge to "baby's" ample belly. Few of the men gathered around, both the initiated and those still waiting, watched any others get "shaved." All eyes were on Willy as he knelt before Steward.

He said nary a word during this part, figuring, I am sure, that it would do no good. His face was dutifully pushed into the baby's belly, held, and then released. As soon as Renouard felt that no one was holding him, he stood erect and staggered away from the laughing men. Through his tears, barely visible over the mess coating his face, he glared at all concerned and shouted, "I will see you flogged to within an inch of your useless lives, you bastards!" The laughter had stopped, mid-stride.

Never, to my knowledge, had Willy used such language. Always well spoken, even in his frustration over trying to learn his employment, he had remained the gentleman. I knew he would not succeed in having anyone flogged, but I wondered if he would find some trumped up charge later in the commission to use against these men.

"Mister Renouard. I would suggest you retire to the cockpit and clean yourself up. And you might calm down at the same time." I spoke quietly to him, hoping he would take my advice.

The young gentleman stared at me as though he had no idea of who I was. Then, still trembling, either with rage or frustration, he stalked away aft, amid guffaws and catcalls from the hands.

The ceremony went on with no further mishap. As the last of the men was being introduced to the mysteries of the deeps, Captain Edwards appeared to the cry "Cap'n's on deck!"

"I think we have wasted enough time with your nonsense, Moutler. You will return to your duties, as will all of you. This will stop now." Edwards spoke for all to hear.

The gaiety stopped with a gasp. The old hands in the ship had never experienced a captain interrupting a crossing ceremony and seemed appalled that this captain had.

"Cap'n, we've about done with our duties here, sir. I am pleased to report that all hands have come forward and joined the order of Shellbacks. Seen to it with my own hand. I will be taking my leave of your ship straightaway." King Neptune stood, knuckled his forehead, and made for the bow from whence he had come. "Baby" Steward and several of his "court" followed behind.

"Mister Ballantyne. I believe you still have the watch and Mister Larkan would have a word with you at your convenience." Edwards, no trace of a smile on his face, took in my badly soiled and wet clothes, turned and made his way aft. The silence he left in his wake spoke volumes. The men, initiates and old hands both, silently drifted off to clean up, see to their duties, or find a patch of shade in which to wait for the change of the watch and spirits up.

As he had made no mention of me cleaning up prior to resuming my watch, I went straight to the quarterdeck without stopping at my cabin for even a dry shirt. With the equatorial sun beaming down, it was nearly dry anyway, but still liberally coated with the slop that had been smeared, none too carefully, on my face earlier. I took the steps on the ladder two at a time and was some relived to see our first lieutenant watching me and smiling at my appearance.

"Well, Mister Ballantyne. I see you have successfully negotiated the rocks and shoals of becoming a Shellback. As your watch is very nearly done, I shall retain the deck while you go and change into a more proper uniform. I am sure Mister Hayward will be up straightaway to assume the watch. I will see you in the wardroom for dinner when I come down." He stopped and I turned to leave, but then he spoke again.

"I understand from the cap'n that young Renouard might be indisposed for a while. Perhaps you would be good enough to organize one of his messmates to fill in for him until such time as he feels fit."

"Aye, sir. I will see to it directly. And thank you, sir. This mess is beginning to smell a bit untoward." I knuckled my forehead in the manner of a seaman as I had not returned my hat to its proper place since my initiation. No sense in ruining that as well as my shirt.

As I passed the door to the Cabin, the Marine stationed there was just closing it. And Willy Renouard was making for the ladder to the cockpit. He did not see me and I did not call out to him. Black, my steward, was waiting for me outside my cabin. He smiled at my appearance but said nothing.

"You went through the same thing, Black. How is it that you're not as much of a mess as me?"

"Oh, sir. I was, indeed I was." He wrinkled his nose. "And about as foul smelling as well. But being a steward has a few advantages aside from being rated as idler and eating well. My clothes are soaking right now in a tub where I suspect your shirt and trousers will be most welcome. I have laid out for you fresh ones as well as finding you a bit of hot fresh water from the galley you might use to clean up a trifle. Sir." He held out his hand for the offending articles of clothing, which I peeled off quickly.

Hayward chose that moment to leave our cramped quarters. He sniffed the air as he went by me. "Oh my goodness, Edward. I see there has been little change to the recipe used in shaving or kissing the baby. I have found that a bit of lard works quite well at removing what remains on your face. Then, of course, some strong soap! Well, there you are and I shall leave you to it; I have to take the watch." Smiling broadly, he made for the ladder.

CHAPTER THIRTEEN

Otaheiti, Late December 1790

"Tynah really expects us to fight in his bloody scrap? Seems like his warriors ain't nothin' but sufferin' from the hot copper—them's what ain't still drunk!

"Hope them others on Tettooroa was celebrating last night like we was. If those lads be hale and hearty, it won't be much of a contest!" James Morrison, spoke to Midshipman Peter Heywood.

Morrison held the unofficial post of leader even though he was only a bosun in the Navy. Heywood, Edward Young, and George Stewart, all former midshipmen before they became willing—or unwilling—mutineers, were young; Heywood was seventeen at the time of the mutiny, while the other two were twenty-two and twenty-three respectively. Without the authority of the Royal Navy, their respect had to be earned; it would not derive from a uniform.

Morrison, the oldest of these mutineers, was a natural leader and, eschewing the midshipmen, the others looked to him for guidance. But he often sought the wisdom and education of the one midshipman who had learned quickly the ways and language of the natives.

"Seems to me we'd be some foolish to make an enemy of Tynah over this, Morrison. We agreed to help them out and I suspect our welcome here would be a bit less warm were we to back out at this point.

"I can't imagine the battle, should there actually be one, will be terribly long . . . or terribly bloody. These lads don't seem to have the taste· anymore for a fight; they got their blood up last night due mostly to the spirits that flowed. Likely in the harsh light of morning, paddling all the way across to Tettooroa and then getting knocked senseless, or worse, by a war club would not be high on their list. But they'll go and so will we."

Morrison studied Heywood through red-rimmed and blood-shot eyes. He put a hand to his forehead, trying in vain to silence the war drum someone inside his head was beating. The early sun, streaming across the sea in blinding effulgence, had each of the men seeking a shadow to ease their sufferings. There were precious few shadows to be found on the beach. One man, Tom Ellison, floated face down in the sea, occasionally lifting his head for a breath. The war canoes had been dragged to the water's edge before sunup and the Otaheitians, about seven hundred of them, were sitting or standing at the tree line while they ate what, for some, could easily be their last meal. Wives and girlfriends stood with them, still decorated in the flowers they had worn last night. From the mutineers perspective, the natives appeared to feel no better than did the Englishmen.

Then Tynah appeared from the trees accompanied by his high priest, raised his enormous war club and gave a mighty bellow. His men, food and women forgotten, took up his cry and followed him to the canoes. They assembled on the beach, squinting and shading their eyes from the early sun. Their ranks filled the beach, swallowing up the mutineers, who, with their sun browned skin and native tattoos, were nearly indistinguishable from their hosts.

But, of course, not to Tynah. He pushed his way through until he faced Morrison and Heywood, whom he addressed in the native language. Then he pushed back through the throng of his warriors and nodded to the priest. During the silence, Morrison nudged Peter for a translation.

"He says we are to get loaded in the first canoe and make sure we have our muskets, powder, and ball." Heywood mumbled.

"Looks pretty hale his own self, considering what went on last night," offered Stewart to no one in particular.

"Memory's a bit foggy, but I did not see him after things got really stirred up. Likely he retired to his wives and spent the night in the arms of one or another of them." Morrison said, perhaps with some envy.

And then the priest, standing on the raised stern of the nearest canoe, raised a scepter in one hand, lifting it over his head. He was a small man with bowed legs and a fringe of hair surrounding his nearly bald pate. His arms were wiry and strong and, in spite of the bowed legs, moved with agility and grace. A narrow face with wide-set eyes gave him a look at once severe and dull. As with the other men, his body was heavily tattooed, geometric designs covering most of his legs and arms, while his posterior was colored almost black from the artist's efforts.

He stood for a moment, watching the throng of warriors, his scepter still raised aloft. Then, when he judged the moment right, he brought a large conch shell to his lips and blew, closing his eyes and puffing out his cheeks with the effort. After a long blast on it, he spoke out to the now silent warriors. Peter Heywood translated for the benefit of the English.

"Fight manfully and there is no fear of defeat. They have come to us in anger, and we shall go to them with our weapons of war. We can not be humbled as you are Tynah's warriors and enjoy the favor of our gods."

Heywood had to shout the last part, as the assembled natives greeted the priest's words with lusty cries and cheers of encouragement for each other. Then Tynah signaled on his own conch shell, and quickly the men and the mutineers climbed into the canoes and, those who were not to paddle, settled themselves for the journey to their victory. Some of the English allowed their heads to drop to their chests and dozed on and off for a part of the crossing.

The ride across the fifteen miles of open ocean to Tettooroa seemed like nothing at all. Each canoe had over a hundred paddlers and made swift work of the distance over the still-calm sea. As the neighboring island broke the horizon, Tynah blew on his conch shell and let forth with a mighty war cry, echoed at once by his minions and accompanied by the beating of clubs and spears on shields or the sides of the canoes. The paddlers seemed to gain strength from the bellicosity of their mates and redoubled their efforts. The final few miles passed under them in short order. And then they were there, a glistening, black sand beach welcoming them. A hundred yards back from the water, trees, plants, and vines were all swaying gently in the easy breeze, making a quiet sound like the luffing of canvas sails.

There was nary a soul on the beach; no war party, no lookouts (that they saw), no canoes pulled up, nothing. The men followed Tynah as he leaped from the canoe in the shallows and followed him at a run up the beach, the English mutineers lagged a bit, hoping to keep as many natives to their fore as possible. Their muskets, however, were dry, charged, primed, and at the ready. The priest stood on the bow of one of the canoes, shouting prayers of victory and encouragement to the men. He would be the last of Tynah's men to cross the beach.

Had the advance moved more silently, the men would have heard a distant conch shell being blown inland a bit. But they did not, and quite without warning, a stone, perfectly round and fired from a native sling, sang through the air, missing Tynah by mere inches. The chief, if he even noticed it, paid it no mind and, followed by his men and the Englishmen, galloped toward the tree line.

As the van of the group broke into the trees, more *whoops* and blasting conch shells, accompanied by shouts of encouragement and invocation of their own gods, greeted the Otaheitians. In seconds, their "hosts" appeared as if by magic, swinging war clubs and whipping their slings about their heads, each containing a deadly projectile the size of a single grape shot. The men from Tettooroa were big, strong, and seemingly fearless; they heaved spears with startling accuracy and brandished weapons that looked to the English like boarding pikes. There were hundreds and hundreds of them. Quickly the battle was joined, hot coppers forgotten, kill or be killed the only thought in each head. The singing of leather slings as they whirled about their owners' heads, the *whoosh* of spears flying through the air, and the thump of war clubs smashing human bodies filled the air, accompanied by the counterpoint of occasional musket fire.

Heywood lifted his musket, selected a huge warrior about to launch a spear in his direction, and fired. The man staggered, dropped his spear harmlessly at his feet, and crumpled to the ground, a surprised look on his dying face, and a large red hole in the left side of his chest. The other mutineers followed suit, selecting enemy warriors as targets and covering for each other as they reloaded their muskets. All around them, the battle swirled, war cries, grunts, shrieks of the wounded or dying, and the thump of club on shield or head, filling the air.

"Stewart! DUCK!" Heywood shouted to his friend, some three steps astern.

A spear, thrown with deadly force and equal accuracy, missed Heywood's head and headed towards the form of Midshipman George Stewart who at that moment was kneeling in the brush, reloading his weapon. He looked up at Peter's cry, saw the spear, and rolled to his right. Heywood's cry and his quick response saved his life, as had he not rolled to the side, the spear would have surely taken him dead center in the chest. As it was, the razor-sharp head of it clipped his left arm, opening a sizeable gash in his bicep. For a moment, nothing happened; Stewart looked at his arm, saw he had been cut badly, and seemed puzzled as to why he was not bleeding. Then suddenly, blood gushed forth, staining the foliage around him, his side, and his leg. Dropping his musket, the young midshipman clutched his arm, trying to staunch the flow.

"Damn! That hurts like sin!" He said, almost to himself.

Heywood jumped back to help his bleeding friend.

"George! Are you badly wounded? Here, let me help you." He grabbed his friend's arm below the wound, steadied him, and ripped the sleeve out of his own shirt. Fashioning a crude but effective bandage from the dirty linen, Heywood removed his friend's hand from over the wound, and looked at the damage. He could see the bone in Stewart's upper arm quite plainly, glistening white in contrast to the gore around it. Heywood shook his head as he wrapped the linen around the arm, pulled it tight, and tied it.

"I'm afraid that star you had added to your decorations a while ago may be unrecognizable, George. That spear wound seems to have removed most of it quite effectively." Peter tried to give his friend something to think about besides the pain in his arm.

"Go on with you, Pete. We can't be stayin' here or some other bugger with a spear or tomahawk will finish what his mate couldn't. You've tied it up fine. I doubt I'll drop from a scratch on my arm! And I can get the tattoo repaired once this heals." Stewart spoke strongly, but his small black eyes darted here and there, while his almost swarthy complexion paled.

He had to be wondering, as was Heywood, if these natives dipped their spears into some poisonous brew when they went into battle. Time would tell.

With Peter helping steady him, the two ran farther into the jungle, pausing only for Stewart to finish reloading his musket while Heywood kept his at the ready. They could hear the shouts of Tynah's men as the rear guard plunged pell mell into the undergrowth, dodging sling-fired missiles and spears. Whenever they came across an enemy warrior, it was war clubs and long knives. Grunts, cries of anguish, and the lusty whoops of both sides' warriors were complemented by the cracks and thumps of clubs and the mushy *thwack* of spears finding a target in someone's flesh. Over all of this, the sporadic fire of muskets from the English sailors made a cacophony that, while not deafening, surely added immeasurably to the confusion.

A scant twenty yards to the east, Morrison and several of his men were busy, using dropped clubs, musket butts, spears, or whatever was handy to press whatever advantage they had. The whole battle seemed to be moving deeper into the jungle and while the Englishmen had their hands full, Tynah's men were even busier, each often taking on two of the enemy warriors at a time. They kept pressing forward, plunging into the jungle, fighting for every step they took, but driving the Tettoorroans before them. Showing no signs of fatigue, the Otaheitians swung their huge clubs, retrieving spears from the dead or dying to throw them again and again.

The killing ground covered now nearly a mile from where Tynah's men and the mutineers had first leaped from their canoes. From time to time, Tynah could be heard letting out a frightening roar, either of encouragement to his men or outrage at his enemy. The battle field was littered with the dead and dying from both sides; there would be a host of grieving wives and families this night.

"Reckon that'll be their village there." Morrison, panting with the exertion of his efforts, gasped out to Heywood and Stewart. "Have you seen the others? Got Coleman, Muspratt, and Skinner with me. Thought the others was with you."

He noticed the blood decorating Stewart's arm, chest, and trousers. "What happened to you? Not quick enough to dodge one of these coves?" but Morrison held little regard for the midshipmen and only dealt with Heywood because of his knowledge of the natives' language and his friendship with Matte.

Peter looked at the bosun; blood streamed from a cut on his leg and he held his left arm in a peculiar fashion. It might have been broken, the midshipman thought. "Likely the same woes that befell you, Morrison. Stewart here was quick enough, however, to avoid taking the spear in his chest." He went on to answer Morrison's original question.

"Saw Sumner and Burkitt just a moment ago. Heading for the village after a couple of locals. Haven't seen the others."

Morrison looked toward the village, saw only a sea of mostly naked humanity, and shifted his gaze back to Stewart and Heywood.

"Got tangled up with a big cove who seemed intent on doing me dirt. Got in a good lick with something looked like a pike and then his mate come up and was about to brain me with his club. I blocked it with my arm, but I think he mighta busted it. Leastaways, I was grappling with the murderous bastards!" His implication was clear.

"Well, better your arm than your head, Morrison!" Stewart offered, preferring to ignore the insult.

"Aye, but my head's likely harder. Probably wouldn't a busted like this useless wing!"

"I think it a bad idea to stand here and jabber like a flock of parrots, lads. Let's press on. Battle's passin' us by!" Heywood, ever the diligent one, directed.

As if to add emphasis to his statement, a stone, fired from a sling, thumped into the tree a foot away. Heywood looked around for the source, found it, and raised his musket. When he pulled the trigger, the hammer dropped, made a spark, but then nothing more. The weapon would not discharge. The native who had thrown the stone ran towards the three men, waving a war club above his head. It was clear his intent would not be salubrious to the Englishmen's health. Peter had reversed his musket, now holding the useless firearm like a club.

Morrison snatched Stewart's musket from his hand, raised it up one-handed, and fired at point blank range into the native's chest. The war club dropped, but his momentum carried the man forward and he took two more steps before he went down.

With a difficulty he was reluctant to admit, Morrison reloaded the musket, handed it back to Stewart. As he stepped over the fallen native, he picked up the dropped club and headed farther into the jungle where sounds of the continuing fight could be heard.

Another hour saw the fighting wind down to a few isolated pockets of conflict. Tynah, his arms and chest colored with the blood of those he had dispatched, stood tall and unscathed in the center of the clearing that had been the village; all the houses and lean-tos had been destroyed completely and lay in heaps of thatch, logs, and cloth on the gore-tinged earth. They would soon be put to the torch.

"What did they do with the women and kids, Heywood? Kill 'em all?" Stewart asked his friend.

"Likely not, George. I would imagine the men sent 'em all up to the mountains long before we even landed. These folks think fighting is just for the menfolk." Heywood shifted his glance around the ruined village; Tynah's men were busily removing heads from the fallen Tettoorroans and, after hoisting them aloft in triumph, piling them up in the center of the clearing.

His thoughts about the brutality of the event and his conversation with George Stewart were interrupted by a blast on a conch shell. Tynah's priest had signaled the end of the conflict, declaring his men the victors. The Englishmen stood together, away from the gore-covered natives, discussing the battle, sharing stories of their own prowess (which undoubtedly would grow with time!), and badgering Peter Heywood about what would happen next. Several of the mutineers were without their muskets, but had provided themselves with native weapons in their stead.

"Well, their practice is to drive these poor sods off their land and Tynah will put one of his people in charge as a chief subordinate to him. The vanquished ones are obligated to pay obedience to Tynah's man and, as long as they do, they can use their lands. According to Tynah, however, it is most unusual for those they overcome to remain, preferring instead to go with their former chief and partake of his disgrace." There was much nodding by the mutineers in response to Peter's explanation.

"Those chaps gave no quarter. I saw it my own self: one of Tynah's warriors had had his leg broke so the bone was sticking out. He laid there on the ground just staring at the fellow who bested him. Had to have been in some considerable pain, I'd warrant. The other gent stepped up close, said something in their heathenish language which our chap answered, and then he swung his war club up over his head and smashed it right down on the poor bloke on the ground. Don't reckon he ever knew what hit him. Dead quicker 'en hell—and on his way there just as fast, I'd imagine." Muspratt spoke knowingly.

"Aye. He would have done that. Great dishonor in being taken prisoner or going home with broken bones, missing limbs, or what-have-you." Heywood agreed, shooting a glance at Morrison as he did so.

"Ain't no disgrace in this, lad." He tried to lift his broken arm, but grimaced at the effort and nodded to it instead. "This here's a sight better than some of those coves with busted heads. Coulda been me as easy as them, but I was too quick for 'em."

Work on the destroyed village continued apace, while the priest applied a poultice and palm leaf dressings to some of the more serious wounds his warriors bore. Tynah was everywhere, like a good commander, congratulating his men, building up the fighting prowess of their enemies (to make his own men appear even stronger), and discussing with his sub-chiefs who he would place in command of the vanquished district.

The priest made his way to the English and said words to Heywood, which Heywood answered, pointing to several of his former shipmates including Morrison and Stewart.

The priest carefully picked up Stewart's injured arm and, with a grunt of contempt, removed, none too gently, the filthy, blood-soaked bandage the Peter had earlier applied. He stuck two fingers into the gaping wound, prying it open, and made another short sound as he studied the cut muscle, visible bone, and still flowing blood. George gasped and went pale. Then he released Stewart's arm and walked away.

The men were puzzled, especially George, who's arm now hurt even more than it had, after the priest-cum-medicine man had poked his long, narrow fingers into it. Beneath his sun-burned complexion, his face remained pale.

"What was that all about, Peter? Am I supposed to just stand here and bleed?"

"He'll be back and with medicines for it and you others who got hurt. He might even set your arm, Morrison." Heywood responded, a bit absently.

And, quick as ever you please, back he came, followed by an acolyte carrying a variety of items in his arms. He motioned to George to sit and then squatted in front of him. While the men watched, the priest spread a large leaf on the ground, using it as a mixing board. He poured several liquids and some bright red powder into it, mixed it up into a paste and using another leaf, scooped it liberally into the wound in Stewart's arm.

"Oh my God! Holy Mother, but that hurts!" Stewart flinched and cried out.

The priest had a firm hold on his arm and simply looked at the young midshipman. Then he scooped a bit more into the opening, spread some of the remaining mixture on yet another broad leaf and wrapped it around the wound. He secured it with a plaited vine and stood up.

"Well, there you are, George. Good as new and fit as a fiddle." Heywood laughed. "The pain will likely ease up in a while; some of what he put into that poultice was a narcotic that these folks use for pain. You should be fine in jig-time!"

The priest was now ministering to Bosun Morrison. He had bound up the wound in his leg using the same poultice that he had put on Stewart's arm. Morrison, his pride to the fore, made not a sound. Until it was time to fix his arm.

The priest now lifted the limb from the front of Morrison's trousers where the bosun had put it, and began to straighten it out. Morrison let out with a roar that rivaled Tynah's battle cry. Tears streamed down his weathered face as the priest continued to pull the arm straight.

Heywood was unable to resist. "You know, Morrison, these people consider it a sign of weakness to cry out."

Morrison glared at him and grunted something that sounded like "bugger" through clenched teeth.

Now Morrison's arm was straight, the priest felt around his elbow, probing with his fingers. With a satisfied grunt, he began to bend the arm back. Morrison's eyes got wide with the pain, but this time, he remained mute.

Suddenly, the priest jerked the bosun's arm straight out forward, then put it across his chest. It was too much for Morrison to stand. He let out with another bellow that caused many of the natives to notice him and smile. The priest took a plaited vine and secured the arm across Morrison's chest, tying the vines behind his neck. He said something which Heywood translated as "Don't move it until the next moon."

The other mutineers who had been wounded were treated as were the natives and Tynah called his council together. After they had met briefly, a new chief was installed in Tettooroa, a man named Eatooa, who would remain there as Tynah's sub-chief. His family would be sent over to join him.

The warriors and the mutineers walked wearily back to the canoes, climbed in, and as the moon rose from the eastern sky, they paddled down the golden path it provided toward Otaheite. In one of the canoes were the bodies of some hundred or so of Tynah's fallen warriors; they would be prepared, prayed over, and burned on a pyre before the moon rose again.

CHAPTER FOURTEEN

In Pandora: *57º 27' S, 64º 11' W*

"Well, Edward. There she is!" Hayward pointed through the morning haze at the uniquely shaped rock at the bottom of South America: Cape Horn. He looked about, taking in the calm seas, non-threatening sky, and the few huge sea birds floating aloft on the breeze, and smiled broadly.

"What a difference from the way this place looked when last I saw it! My goodness, but that was dreadful. I hope never to experience weather like that again!" Tom shook his head at the horrific memory of his attempted rounding of the Cape in *Bounty*.

"You had a spell of nasty weather, I recall you mentioning. But *Bounty* never made it into the Pacific from here, did she?" I asked, struggling to remember the tale Tom had told at supper one night several months ago in the wardroom.

"Oh my stars. It was awful! For thirty days we battled gales and mountainous seas. Bligh took us all the way to the ice and back to the Cape more than twice, and each time, we'd be beaten back, unable to turn to the North. Shortened down we were, and ice everywhere. Never were we able to put more than a scrap of canvas on the yards; every time we tried to force a bit of weatherliness out of that old collier, the yards split or the sails blew themselves to shreds before we could hand them. Awful, just awful it was!

"Finally, Cap'n Bligh just gave up trying to weather that bloody rock and ran off back to the East for Africa. Only choice he had, I'd warrant, unless he wanted to kill all of us and sink his ship! By comparison, this weather is wonderful! Not too cold, winds fresh, and the seas—for here—almost flat!

"We had to keep sending the topmen aloft to chop ice out of the rig; Bligh and Christian were afraid we'd be top-heavy and capsize in the enormous seas. What a job of work that was! Nearly lost a few over the side, slipping in the rig. Had any actually fallen, they would have been doomed;

there was not a chance of turning the ship, or even heaving to, to collect them. And the water was so cold, they'd likely have been frozen in minutes anyway." Hayward shook his head at the memory. "I expect some of the men might have welcomed death in those freezing seas to what they endured aboard!"

I shot a look at my friend, trying to determine what he meant by his last comment. His eyes were unfocused, simply staring at the approaching island called Cape Horn.

"You mean Bligh was being tyrannical? Did he whip many during those days, Tom? I would think the men might have thought about taking over the ship then!"

"No, Edward. I told you and the others long ago that Bligh was patient and a fine commander. He understood that the men were at the end of their rope; that's why he turned about. And as to thinking about mutiny at that point—I doubt there was a man in the ship who thought any but Bligh would have sunk us long before then! He was a fine seaman."

I looked around us. It was hard to imagine the dreadful conditions Hayward described, especially when seeing the seas as they were today. And I thought there was little chance of ice forming in the rig or on deck; had not the surgeon mentioned at breakfast that the temperature was forty-eight degrees? Tom and I were standing on the starboard side, about even with the foremast. A number of off-watch seamen stood in small clusters around the deck, watching as the infamous Cape Horn got closer.

The seas were long swells, lifting us gently as each rolled to the East, following the incessant westerlies that blow uninterrupted in this part of the globe. *Pandora* was under full tops'ls, reefed courses, spanker, and stays'ls. We made, according to the chip log, nearly ten knots through the water. I looked aft toward the quarterdeck.

Robert, his boat cloak billowing behind him, stood by the two quartermasters at the wheel. He caught my look and waved, his usual grin plastered across his face. Next to him, Captain Edwards and First Lieutenant Larkan watched our progress toward the diamond-shaped rock of the Horn. They kept a wary eye on some craggy islands, close enough aboard for us to see they were a haven for sea birds; white guano covered the black rocks, and above them, albatrosses and frigate birds rode the air currents effortlessly, occasionally diving into the frigid sea to collect a fish.

It was the last day of January, seventeen ninety one. We were nearly three full months out of Portsmouth and Larkan felt we had, with some good weather, about two months ahead of us to Otaheite. It was hard to believe that only a bit over a month back, the temperature stood daily in the nineties and now there was a chance we would see an ice island floating in the sea!

We had spent Christmas at sea, little noted save for the greetings we shared and a nice plum duff in the wardroom, but three days later, sailed into Rio de Janeiro. We saluted the fort there and, fortunately, our salute was returned instantly. Equally as quickly—in fact, almost before our anchor had set—an officer from the fort was climbing up our side to welcome us and speak to Captain Edwards.

Naturally, only Edwards and Larkan met with the man, but the first lieutenant shared with the rest of us his outrage—as well as the captain's—over the man's declaring that a troop of soldiers would be put aboard to "ensure there were no untoward events." According to Larkan, the captain exploded like a volcano, letting off a thundering tirade at the poor sod who, after all, was only the messenger! Quaking in his boots, he tried to explain that this was the custom in Rio. Edwards was adamant; it was beneath dignity of the British flag to allow foreign soldiers aboard in any capacity, and until this issue was resolved to our satisfaction, the captain would not go ashore to pay his respects to the viceroy.

As it turned out, no troop of soldiers appeared and, not only did the captain pay his respects to the viceroy, almost all of his officers did as well. I was most gratified to be included as I was keen to see this foreign land! There was a suite of carriages awaiting us at the quay, each accompanied by an officer on a fine charger. The surgeon general of the city spoke clear English and served as translator for all of us, save when our own surgeon "general" was badgering the poor man with an incessant barrage of questions concerning everything from local diseases to flora and fauna, customs, and habits of the locals. Our entourage passed through every principal street, and visited the public gardens which had been laid out with great care and expense by the current viceroy's predecessor.

Every imaginable species of flowering plant is grown and lovingly tended and, at one end of this quite spectacular garden is a grand mall, frequented by those of higher station. The finery of Europe is well represented as the citizenry stroll about.

At the end of this mall, there is a building, octagonal in shape and larger than any other I have ever seen. It is wonderfully furnished, and from time to time, afternoon entertainments are put on by local and traveling troupes. Painted panels around the room and on the ceiling are representative of the commerce of the area, mining, the whale fishery, and the indigo trade. On other panels are depicted (so I was told) every animal native to Brazil, scenes of the country, and on one, birds native to the area, but done with their feathers rather than with paint!

We also discovered the reason why soldiers accompanied us as we traveled about the city; when the French circumnavigator, Bougainville, stopped in Rio, his chaplain was assassinated as he strolled the streets by himself. Since that time, orders have stood that all officers of a foreign nation will be accompanied by a commissioned officer and all others, presumably seamen, will be escorted by a soldier. Of course, that had little bearing on us; none of our seamen, save in work parties, would be given any shore leave.

Robert noticed, and pointed out to me and Hayward, that the public works of the country was performed by convicts or slaves, all chained together. They sang a mournful dirge as they worked which was accompanied by the clanking of their chains as they moved about. A truly melancholy picture they made. Obviously, this country, like others, had its seamy underbelly, but its occupants, and presumably those living on the more comfortable side, took it quite in stride.

The ship spent one week here, provisioning for the long journey ahead with fresh produce, citrus, as well as beeves, chickens, and pigs. Tom and I were assigned the job of finding plants and gewgaws that might be useful in securing the cooperation of the natives of Otaheite when we needed their help in locating the mutineers. Corner, shortly before we won our anchor, went on shore to make astronomical observations, set our timekeeper, and adjust the other navigational instruments.

Then it was time to say good-bye to our new friends (both Tom and Robert had managed liaisons while ashore and were quite forlorn at the prospect of leaving them) and make our way to the lower tip of the continent where we would then set our course for Otaheite. We were remarkably fortunate with the weather, we had a fair breeze all the way down the coast and, as the temperatures dropped the farther south we went, we all were quite comfortable. And even my reluctant midshipman, Mister Renouard had come around.

Several days following his disastrous meeting with King Neptune, I sent for him. The denizens of the wardroom had agreed to remain distant while I interviewed the youngster in spite of eagerness on the part of both Larkan and Corner to witness it.

"You sent for me, Mister Ballantyne?" He stood outside the open door awaiting an invitation to enter.

"I did, Renouard. Come in."

He stepped in and began to take a seat opposite me. "I did not invite you to sit. You may stand at ease." I was taking a page from Edwards' book.

He stood, swaying easily with the motion of the ship, and waited until I "finished" examining some important papers. I could feel his stare all the while, but let him stew for several minutes.

"Are you ready to resume your role as a midshipman in the Royal Navy? Or do you prefer that your messmates continue to carry your load, do your work, and cover your obvious short-comings?" I asked, when I looked up at his worried expression.

Silence.

Finally, "Yes, sir."

" 'Yes, sir.' What? You wish to return to your duties or you wish to have your fellows assume your responsibilities?"

"I . . . uh . . . that is, sir, Cap'n Edwards told me . . . "

"Renouard," I interrupted, "do you see the captain in this room? You have run the course with the captain and he has turned you back over to me to make you into a competent sea officer." That wasn't entirely true, but Edwards *had* told Larkan to do whatever was necessary.

I went on. "You can not run to the captain every time something happens that you do not like. And yes, before you protest too loudly, I do know your history with the captain. But as I mentioned, Cap'n Edwards wishes you to become a contributing member of his ship, not some whining, sniveling boy who expects his commander to protect him." I studied the youngster's face as I laid it on, watching his expression become more and more gloomy with each sentence. Each word seemed to strike him like a cat o' nine tails. He actually flinched at some.

For a moment after I finished, Renouard said nothing. Just stared at the wall behind me. I could see his eyes darting here and there as if looking for a way to escape . . . or disappear like in some conjurer's trick. Then he shifted his gaze to me. And seemed to stand a little straighter. Was he mustering up his courage?

"Sir. Mister Ballantyne. I did not want to join this ship, I did not want to sail to Otaheite, and I did not want to serve under Cap'n Edwards. My mother's relatives, with interest in Whitehall, prevailed upon the captain to take me aboard after they had secured my warrant." He stopped. I nodded, aware, as I mentioned, of his history.

"But here I was and, at the outset, I truly did try to make the best of it. My complete lack of experience, save as a steward, was readily apparent to all hands—officers, mids, masters' mates, and especially, the sailors.

They—the foremast hands, I mean—made it clear from the outset, that they had little respect for me and would not do my bidding unless you or another officer was about. When Mister Larkan, before we set out, asked me if I wanted to be set ashore or join Howe's squadron, it was all I could do not to cry out 'yes' in a loud and clear voice. But I didn't, because Mother's relatives and the cap'n would have likely flayed me alive!"

"I doubt they would have gone to those extremes, Willy. But they would surely have been disappointed in you."

"Yes, sir. I even tried to delay our sailing, thinking I might, somehow, do better, given more time before we weighed. Or at least try to figure out what I was to do."

"Delay our sailing? Whatever do you mean, Renouard?"

All of a sudden, the memory of the unsecured cannon flashed into my mind. I did not give him the opportunity to respond.

"Willy. Was it you who removed the lashings from one of our battery as we left Portsmouth?"

Silence. I noticed a tear begin to form in the corner of his eye. His shoulders slumped.

"Yes, sir. I did."

"Why, for heaven's sake did you think that would delay us? We were already in the Channel. Someone could have gotten hurt or even killed with that gun rolling around the gundeck. What on earth were you thinking?"

"Only that should it roll across the deck and make a hole in the side of the ship we would have to go back and get it fixed. I admit I did not consider that someone might have been hurt or killed. Sir."

I simply looked at him. This was quite beyond anything I had expected. Until he mentioned it, I had quite forgotten the loose cannon that Steward and I managed to catch before it did any damage. I recalled looking for the midshipman after that and finding him sick in the cockpit, the start of a widespread malady in *Pandora*.

"But you were sick when that gun carriage got loose; you could barely stand, as I recall. You couldn't have . . . "

"Sir." He cut me off before I could finish. "I loosened the train tackles before I took ill, sir. Didn't make a difference until we got into the waves in the Channel. But by then, I was hoping to die and didn't even think of it. I'm deeply sorry for my actions, Mister Ballantyne." The tears were rolling quite freely down the youngster's smooth cheeks by now, but he again straightened his back and looked at me with an unwavering eye. "I am ready to stand any punishment you or Cap'n Edwards see fit to bestow on me, sir."

I was stunned! I had thought this boy, this ill-begotten midshipman, was never going to amount to anything and I would be bedeviled by him throughout the entire commission. Now here he was, admitting to a serious crime, albeit two months after its commission, and willing to stand his punishment like a man. His treacherous behavior had obviously weighed heavily on his mind all that time.

The crime was tantamount to sabotage or, I suppose, treason, and one could make a reasonable case for death. Had the perpetrator been a foremast Jack and the captain making the decision, I had little doubt as to what the outcome would be. But this was different entirely; we were not at war or on a war footing and the young man before me was not only under the direct care of Captain Edwards, but had significant interest in Whitehall. I put the thought of *that* punishment out of my head, reconciling it with the realization that the crime was far astern in the wake and no one had been hurt, including *Pandora*. But, I reasoned, there *has* to be *something*. I had to think.

"Mister Renouard, you will resume your duties and watches. You will spend any off-hours catching up on your studies so that you do not lag your fellow midshipmen. Should you need help with your subjects, ask your messmates first; should they be unable or unwilling to satisfy your needs, you let me know. I expect by the time we get to the Cape at the bottom of South America, you will be as knowledgeable as any mid in the ship regarding navigation, maneuvering, sail handling, and steering.

"After I have thought further on your crime, I will determine a proper punishment for you. And may I add, sir, your progress with your studies will have a direct bearing on my thoughts. You are dismissed."

Just before he turned to leave, I detected a small upturn at the corners of his mouth. The tears had stopped and, after saying a proper thank-you to me, he left.

Well, Edward, you certainly handled that *with great insight and brilliance! Well*, I argued with myself, *maybe I did. He admitted to the deed which was, as it turned out, of little consequence, and perhaps, I might have saved a career, turning a spoiled child into a productive officer. Time will tell.*

Now his deadline was upon us. I had heard no bad reports or complaints from any since our "conversation," and I had witnessed more than once, the youngster standing on deck alongside the sailing master, shooting the sun with his sextant. Robert had told me on several occasions that Renouard had come to the quarterdeck when Robert had the watch (with one or another of the master's mates) and requested that he be allowed to steer the ship—of course, with proper supervision. I knew also, when he stood with Hayward, that he peppered my colleague with questions and, according to Tom, seemed to absorb the answers. But had he changed?

Yes, it appeared that he had. And I had not come up with a suitable punishment for his Portsmouth "folly" nor, might I add, had Mister Larkan. In fact, the first lieutenant complimented my judgment in handling the situation.

"Sir. The captain's compliments and he would have you attend him on the quarterdeck, if you please." The watch messenger had been sent by Corner to fetch me.

"Thank you, Webber. I shall be there straightaway."

"Reckon Edwards wants my opinion about rounding the Cape, Tom. We'll continue this conversation later, if you don't mind. I would enjoy hearing more of your yarn." I laughed as Hayward smiled at my silly assertion.

"Mister Ballantyne. I was just telling Cap'n Edwards how you thought young Renouard had progressed over the past month and more. He'd like to hear it from you, I think." Larkan cut me off as I made for the ladder to the quarterdeck.

"Aye, sir. Is he pleased?" I thought being prepared might be helpful.

"Oh, I think he is, indeed. I am sure he did not fancy going home and telling Mama Renouard that her little boy was an abject failure. You, it might appear, may have saved him that chore. So yes, I would say he does seem pleased."

So, it was with a light step and a light heart that I hopped up the three steps onto the quarterdeck and headed for the "captain's walk" on the leeward side.

"Cap'n, you wished to see me?"

"Oh, right . . . Ballantyne. Yes, I had Mister Corner send for you. I trust it caused you no inconvenience?" Edwards turned from watching the sea rush by our side as I spoke to him. He did not look angry . . . nor did he look pleased.

Did Larkan misread his mindset? Am I detecting a bit of joviality or even kindness in his voice? Well, we shall see!

"None at all, sir. I was watching us approach Cape Horn. Never been this far south, have I. Quite exciting, I must say!"

"Very well, then. We shall get you back to sightseeing, should you have nothing better or more productive to occupy yourself, quick as ever we can! Wanted a word with you on my young charge, David Renouard."

I blanched a bit at the "sightseeing" comment, but tried to maintain a neutral expression.

"Yes, sir? How can I be of help?"

"Oh, I think you already have been some considerable help. Larkan tells me the youngster is finally beginning to show some promise. Seems to have taken to mathematics and navigation and is eager to learn about all the elements of being an officer. I have barely clapped an eye on him since . . . well, I think it was before we called in Rio . . . yes, I recall now. The last time the youngster paid me a visit was to complain about his treatment in the Crossing the Line ceremony. Mister Larkan tells me you are, at least in part, responsible for the change." His deep-set eyes locked on to mine for a reaction to the compliment. When I did not react, his eyebrows went up, perhaps in surprise, and he continued.

"Tell me, Ballantyne, what did you do? How did you bring the boy about? I had about given up on him."

I flushed. I could feel the color rising up my neck both at the compliment and at the thought of telling one of the hardest commanders in the Royal Navy that I had "gone easy" on a lad who had tried to sabotage his ship.

"Thank you sir. I had a few words with him several days after the Crossing the Line ceremony. I knew he had . . . had a word with you shortly after that affair." I watched Edwards as he had just, a moment ago, watched me and was rewarded with a nod. "But I was unaware he had not visited you since.

"After that, I simply told him we expected more of him and that it was time to pick himself up and become a proper midshipman. Or I'd see him put ashore in Rio. Naturally, Cap'n, I would not have done that, but he didn't know that I wouldn't. Seemed to shake him a bit and he promised to give it a go. Appears that he has done so!" I smiled, hoping the answer would satisfy.

It did. Edwards actually started to *smile* back at me and then, almost as if he had caught himself, "harrumphed" and followed it with a scowl and, "Well done, lad. Perhaps it's the approach I should have taken early on with him. Pampered him too much, I did. Listened to his nonsense and carrying on. For his mother's sake."

I had trouble picturing our commander *pampering* anyone in his ship and thought there might be another reason than 'his mother's sake' involved.

And for your own sake, with whoever is his 'interest' in Whitehall. I added, but kept it to myself. And made my escape.

"Oh, my goodness! Is it time for you to relieve me already. I must have missed spirits up and dinner piped down." Robert stopped my hasty departure from the quarterdeck with his booming voice and a wide grin. "Quite a sight, that. Eh what?" He added, pointing at the looming diamond-shaped island off our starboard bow.

"It certainly is. Never supposed I'd see it—or least this soon! And no, it is not close to the time for your relief. And furthermore, it's not to be me, but Hayward." His infectious laugh caused me to join him, and laugh I did, albeit quietly. This was still the quarterdeck, after all!

CHAPTER FIFTEEN

In Pandora*: 38º 30' S, 105º 20' W*

"G entlemen: I expect we are on the order of two weeks, maybe a trifle
more, from our destination. As our Sailing Orders are extraordinarily
specific as to the task ahead, I would suggest that each of you and your
mids read them carefully, even should you already have done so. I have
had my clerk make three additional copies for your use to that end.

"To refresh your minds, we are to find and secure the mutineers and find
and sail home *Bounty*. And we have not a moment to waste in accomplishing this. We must be through the Endeavor Straits, using the vague charts
Captain Cook left for us, before the summer monsoon arrives. Should we
miss the opportunity, we will proceed back around the Horn; I suspect we
might not be as lucky there as we were a month or so ago.

"We have had, for the most part, a trouble-free passage. Aside from the
usual disciplinary issues, there have been few problems to contend with.
Our rounding Cape Horn was surely one of the fastest I have ever heard
of; barely two weeks of calm seas, generally fair breezes, and no ice to
speak of. And so far, we have enjoyed remarkably fine weather here in the
broad expanse of the Pacific. We have been blessed."

Having spoken, Captain Edwards sat down again at his desk. We
remained standing. His gallery lights were open and the warm breeze that
had, for nearly three weeks in the Pacific, pushed us toward Otaheite,
rustled the papers on his desk and caused his side whiskers to tremble, a
fact that Hayward found most amusing.

"I assume none of you gentlemen have any questions for the captain?
I think he was quite plain in his remarks." Larkan asked the group. I am
sure he did not expect an answer as he immediately said, "Very well, then.
You are dismissed."

Corner and Larkan headed forward to their cabin, while Hayward,
Passmore, Hamilton, and I made our way to the deck. I would be taking
over the watch shortly from Master's Mate George Reynolds. And Renouard

was again assigned as my junior officer, an occurrence that mostly pleased me, given his new demeanor and attitude.

"Tom," I spoke as we left the earshot of the Marine sentry and the sanctified area of the Cabin and started up the ladder, "do you think we'll find those rascals in Otaheite? It's been . . . what . . . nearly two years since they put you and Bligh and the others into the boat. They might have gone anywhere!"

"I have no idea, save that Bligh, when he returned to England, seemed quite convinced that Otaheite was where we would find them. For myself, I truly hope we do; I can scarce wait to get my hands on Christian, not to mention a few of the others. But Christian, should he be there, will make the trip worthwhile—for me at any rate!"

"Were there not some of your mates from the cockpit that went off with the scoundrels? What of them?" I asked, knowing Tom had mentioned his friend Peter Heywood and George Stewart, both late of the *Bounty's* cockpit, many times in his tales of life on the ship and during their first stay in Otaheite.

"I have no interest in them. Heywood was a great good friend, but he chose to remain in the ship with Christian and the others. Same for bloody George Stewart. Always complaining about one thing or another, he was, but mostly Cap'n Bligh. Those are no different than Morrison or Coleman, or that strong friend of Christian's, Churchill. A real scoundrel, he is!" Tom shook his head at the memory of his shipmates.

I felt sorry for him, in a way. He had turned his back on messmates and friends who, as I had learned from his tales during our passage, had little choice but to remain in *Bounty*; there simply was no more room in the cutter. The boat was nearly swamped as it was and one or two more would have surely put them gunwales down. But as the boat with Bligh and eighteen men separated from his late command, the captain cried out to those who had begged to come with him, "Never fear, my lads! I'll do you justice if I ever reach England!"

He had, of course, reached England. And justice was about to be done. While once some of those remaining in *Bounty* had been his friends and messmates, my friend now had lumped those youngsters into the same pot with the mutineers; in his mind, there was now only one category for those who did not make the open boat passage with Bligh: mutineers. They were no longer worthy of his affection or even a kind thought. I spent some considerable time pondering this change in my messmate. Finally, I pressed him.

"Tom. If those chaps were your messmates and chums when you left the ship, why should they not be now? You have not seen them in two years, nor do you have any idea of what they have been through with Christian and his cronies. You said yourself they had asked to come in the boat, but there was no more room. It could have been you and Hallet left aboard while your friend Heywood and . . . what was his name . . . the other mid? Oh yes. George Stewart . . . while those two went in the boat with Cap'n Bligh. Would you not expect that they would still be your friends when . . . and if, you saw them again? Why should their having stayed in *Bounty* cause you to lose your affection for them?" I studied Hayward carefully, watching for some crack in his determined expression.

There was none; the man was adamant that, should he ever see his former messmates again, they would be no better than the mutineers with whom they had been living for two years, regardless of whether or not they actually participated in the mutiny. As he mentioned, more than once to many of us, their participation would be determined by a court-martial when we brought them back to England in chains.

Having had enough of my persistence, Tom went forward on some imagined errand while I made the three steps up the ladder to the quarterdeck to relieve the watch. Renouard, still eager and finding joy in his employment, was already there, relieving his counterpart. Pleasantries and necessary information exchanged with Reynolds, as well as a brief synopsis of the meeting in the Cabin, I assumed the watch, prepared to be bored beyond words until spirits up was piped before suppertime. A ship in fine weather, sailing alone in deep water, with a constant breeze of wind and a decently trained crew, does not provide much in the way of excitement. The joy and exuberance of the experience had long since faded for me and most of my messmates. Renouard, through his new-found enthusiasm, still seemed to revel in our passage through the water and, at half the normal intervals, was causing the chip log to be heaved and marking our course and speed on the chalk board.

"Oh, my goodness, Mister Ballantyne. Is this not just splendid? How well she sails even though I suspect her bottom is some fouled. Do you think Cap'n Edwards will careen her when we get to Otaheite? Then think of how well she'll swim! I'll warrant our passage home will be even faster than the voyage out!" If Willy had said most of that once during the watch, he likely had said it a half dozen times!

What had I created! I began to think I almost preferred the sullen, inept, and unwilling Renouard of old! Of course, I did not, but this enthusiasm and glee should have worn off by Tenerife; instead, here it was just show-ing itself in the past few weeks.

Some of the boredom was broken when Hamilton, the surgeon, appeared at the foot of the ladder.

"May I come into the quarterdeck, Mister Ballantyne?" He asked.

"Of course you may, Doctor, and welcome!" I responded instantly, hoping for some kind of news, something that might occupy my mind for the next few hours.

"All is well, I presume? Not a large sick-call, I noticed."

"Oh my, yes. Things could scarcely be better! The fruits and vegetables I procured in Rio, along with the salubrious weather we have been enjoy-ing since then, have done miracles for the men's health. Our only hospital residents are those two topmen, one with a crushed hand and the other, Cobb, I think it is, with a touch of ague. While Jenkins' hand may not mend to perfection, I expect him to be back on deck in a day or two. Cobb, likely tomorrow. So yes, Mister Ballantyne, things are better than well!" Hamilton fairly gushed with joy at our good fortune.

And on we sailed. *Pandora* making a fine turn of speed (as my midship-men reminded me every half hour), the surgeon happy with the general health of the people, some of us getting tired of the passage, and perhaps, one of us dreading our arrival in Otaheite.

It seemed that with each passing day, my friend Tom Hayward became more morose. I wondered if perhaps he might be experiencing a pang of guilt about his earlier expressed hard feelings toward his former mess-mates. I had struggled with his attitude for quite a while, but could make no headway in understanding it or his unwillingness to at least withhold judgment until he spoke with Heywood and Stewart.

About a week before our anticipated arrival in Otaheite, the carpenter, Mister Montgomery, and two of his mates began constructing a small house on the poopdeck.

"What's that to be?" I inquired one day after I could discern a shape and size.

It seemed too small and too low for any person so I presumed it must be for additional provisions acquired locally in Otaheite.

"Reckon it's to be a prison, of sorts, Mister Ballantyne. For the muti-neers, when we find 'em."

"But there are *twenty-five* of them, if they're all alive still. How on earth would they fit in there?"

"You'll have to ask the cap'n that one, lad. I've no idea, myself. Just seein' to what he and Larkan wanted built."

When it was finished, still incredulous at the supposed use for it, I paced off the sides and front of the . . . box. That's all it could be called; it was but eleven feet front to back, eighteen feet athwartships, and was not as high as my chest. Two small openings, neither as long as my forearm, had been cut into each side, and there was a hatch, less than two feet square, built into the top. Clearly, Montgomery had been mistaken; this would have to be for stores that would not benefit from being held in the dark and damps of the orlop. Mayhaps fresh fruits or possibly livestock. That had to be it; yes, I was sure of it!

We had passed by Easter Island during the first week of March and, as our sojourn continued through the vast reaches of the Pacific, we passed several islands; none were on our charts so, while we did not stop at them, we did assume the honor of naming them. Of course, our sailing master, George Passmore, as well as the captain, ensured that they were properly marked on the charts and Passmore even drew silhouettes of them in the margins, a certain help to future sailors passing through these waters. One of these islands we christened Lord Hood's Island, in honor of First Viscount Samuel Hood, one of the heroes of the Empire, while another was named for Lord Carrisfort.

And on twenty-three March, seventeen hundred ninety one, we sailed into Matavai Bay, Otaheite. Hardly had we backed our tops'ls and dropped our best bower into the crystal turquoise water when a native canoe came alongside and a dark-skinned young man clambered up our side, agile as a monkey.

A fine looking young man, he welcomed us effusively with great expressions of joy. To our inquiry regarding the whereabouts of *Bounty*, he smiled broadly and told us, in rudimentary English, that Mister Christian and eight Englishmen had sailed off in *Bounty*, along with a clutch of native men and women, long since. He also told us Christian had told them Bligh had settled in Whytutakee where Captain Cook was living, and had given *Bounty* to him as a reward for his great service.

Great service indeed! I thought, as I am sure did my messmates when they heard this utterance. *Wonder if this chap remembers Tom Hayward, late of* Bounty?

We had purposely kept Tom out of the young man's sight until Larkan indicated he should be brought forward. I could not begin to express the surprise the young native showed upon seeing our shipmate. Obviously, he remembered (then) Midshipman Hayward very well! Pleasantries were exchanged and then the native was questioned concerning the whereabouts of the Englishmen. He, of course, would not know them as mutineers or even that they had done anything wrong!

Barely had he begun to tell us about his white friends than another native canoe arrived alongside, also carrying a dark-skinned, tattooed man who climbed up our main chains with no difficulty. Imagine our surprise when, instead of a few words of English mixed with the local dialect (which Tom spoke, to some degree), the new arrival began speaking clear, though common, English! He announced himself as Josiah Coleman, Armorer, late of HMAV *Bounty*.

Coleman wore the same decorations on his arms and legs as our first visitor and was very nearly as dark-skinned. He also wore, not a pair of canvas trousers as one might expect a sailor to wear, but a long strip of cloth wound about his middle and passed between his legs, in the manner of a diaper for a baby.

"I am turning myself in to the Royal Navy. I had nothing to do with the mutiny and would wish most sincerely to clear my name. The worry of it has weighed heavily on me for nearly two years and I can not express my relief at seeing one of His Majesty's frigates here in Matavai Bay! Yours is the first to appear since we have been living here." Coleman spoke quickly and convincingly of his innocence.

I, for one, was reasonably convinced from his tale, but as Tom reminded us, the matter of his innocence was for a court martial in England to decide, not us. Larkan shouted for the master at arms, Mister Grimwood, and, when he appeared, instructed him to bring manacles and leg irons for our first "captured" mutineer.

But before they were even produced, another canoe was alongside, this one carrying two dark-skinned and tattooed men. They followed their predecessors up the main chains and, unlike Coleman, stood on the bulwark requesting permission to come aboard in perfect English. So, more mutineers, I presumed.

I happened to notice Tom, who was still engaged in conversation with the young native, when he espied the two newcomers. His jaw dropped, his eyes grew large, and he stared in speechless awe at the sight.

As soon as the two were given permission to board, I understood. They introduced themselves to those of us gathered in the waist.

"Sir," the eldest said. "I am George Stewart, late midshipman of His Majesty's Vessel *Bounty*. This is midshipman Peter Heywood, also of *Bounty*. We are relieved to see a vessel of the Royal Navy and hope that you will take us back to England to clear our names of any attachment to the heinous crime that occurred in *Bounty*."

They were both heavily tattooed, bare-chested, and burned dark by the sun. One, Heywood, it was, wore the remnants of knee britches, while the other, Stewart, wore a cloth not unlike Coleman and the native. He also had the scar from what appeared to be a recently healed wound in his upper arm with a tattoo of some sort visible at the edges.

"Mister Grimwood: more leg irons and manacles, if you please. It seems we have some additional volunteers." Larkan's joy at this turn of events was unmistakable.

"You need not concern yourself with irons, sir. We came aboard quite on our own and have no intention of causing any trouble to any aboard. I would have expected, perhaps, to find a berth in the cockpit." Heywood, assuming Larkan to be the captain, addressed him in a most earnest manner. To no avail.

"Not only will you be ironed, Mister Heywood, you will be confined with the rest of your rascals until such time as we reach England. Do not concern yourself with mess bills in the cockpit; I assure you, it will not be necessary!" Larkan smiled at the two midshipmen.

Heywood looked at each of us, seemingly hopeful of discovering an advocate in our midst. He shook his head sadly.

"Well, you will do, sir, what you will. I can not worry about that which is beyond my control; I have suffered the frowns of fortune before and, I am sure, will again. But I can only restate my innocence of that of which you accuse me." As he spoke, he continued to search our faces. Suddenly, he espied Tom; he eyes grew wide.

"Tom! Tom Hayward! Is that not you? You made it in the boat with Bligh! I am most relieved. We feared Christian had given you all a death sentence, sending you off in a small boat, so heavily overloaded. Did all of you survive? Where did you make shore? How did you get back to England?" Heywood stepped forward, toward his former messmate, as stunned to see him as Tom had been moments before, to lay eyes on Peter.

"I am *Lieutenant* Hayward, Midshipman. Though I know not why I should call you by that title any longer. You are a disgrace to the Service and I find it quite untoward that you even recognize me." Tom took a step back; his words were an angry snarl.

I was shocked at the venom from my friend. I knew he had held his former messmate in low esteem, but this was quite beyond the pale!

"Excuse me, *Lieutenant* Hayward. I am sorry my presence causes you discomfort. But as you well know, I had nothing at all to do with the mutiny or Fletcher Christian's actions. If you will recall, I begged Bligh to take me in the boat, but as you, no doubt, also recall, it was overloaded then and Stewart and I were left to our own devices with the mutineers.

"Frankly, *Lieutenant*, I was a bit surprised that Bligh took you and Hallet with him. After all, had you two not been asleep on your watch when Christian came on deck, the mutiny might never have happened! And that, sir, is straight from Fletcher Christian himself. I wonder if *that* subject came up during your voyage with the cap'n." The silence following this monumental accusation was deafening!

I was slack-jawed and stunned into speechless shock. Larkan, Corner, and Grimwood were equally horrified. Tom glared at his former friend, his color rising either from embarrassment or anger I could not tell. He finally managed to sputter, "Where did *that* interesting bit of bilge come from? Is that how you have sustained yourself all this time? Hallet and I were most certainly *not* asleep when Christian came on deck nor at any other time during our watches. You could not be more wrong. But you are the mutineer and I am here, a free man, an officer of the Royal Navy, to see you brought back to England to stand trial at a court-martial for your crime."

Perhaps that would go a distance toward explaining why my friend had earlier disavowed his former messmate. I thought. *Tom's denial sounded a trifle weak to me.*

"Gentlemen, that's quite enough of that. Peter Heywood, you are accused of mutiny and will be confined with the rest of your fellows, in irons, until we reach Portsmouth, where you will be turned over to the Admiralty for court-martial. That is when a finding of your guilt or innocence will be made. Not before. Cap'n Edwards' orders are to ensure there is no chance of any of you escaping and to keep you alive until he gets you home. And that is precisely what we intend to do.

"Mister Grimwood, you may put the manacles on this man and the other, if you please." Larkan had heard enough and took charge.

Captain Edwards appeared and strode purposefully into our midst. He was resplendent in full uniform including his jacket and sword in spite of the sweltering heat.

"So, Mister Larkan. I appears we have apprehended some of our mutineers already?" He looked carefully at the three men now wearing wrist manacles. "And who might you villains be?"

Before our captives could respond, Larkan answered. "We have two midshipmen—or should I say *former* midshipmen—and the armorer of Bligh's late command, sir. This is Peter Heywood, George Stewart, and Coleman."

"Very well, then. Put them in the box." Edwards threw a thumb over his shoulder, gesturing at the recently completed structure on the poop.

My God! The carpenter was right! It is *to be used as a prison! How in heaven's name will we fit them all in? Even with Christian and eight of his scoundrels gone, there will still be sixteen of them to squeeze in.*

As the men were led aft to their new accommodations, more canoes began to come alongside. These carried men and women, all natives, it appeared, and all seemed most joyful and happy to see us. One of them came to under the main chains and several men climbed out and scrambled to the deck. One of them was not a native as we had originally thought, but another of the mutineers.

"Sir. I am Richard Skinner, late of *Bounty*. Filled with remorse, I am, and wish to turn myself in." He was as dark as the others, equally as tattooed, and wore the native cloth about his midsection.

"Welcome aboard, Skinner. You may join your mates. Take him aft." Edwards wasted no time in pleasantries. Of course, he likely would not have with any of his own people either.

"Mister Corner. You and Hayward will take a boat ashore and see if you might turn up the other rascals who seem unwilling to join us on their own. Take half a dozen Marines with you and be sure you are all armed." Larkan studied the shoreline and the trees beyond with his glass. "Perhaps one of these locals might share some insight as to the whereabouts of our remaining villains."

"Aye sir. Might take us more than a short while, should they not wish to be found. We will take some provisions in case we are obligated to remain ashore for any length of time." Corner acknowledged and called for the boat to be made ready.

While the boat was prepared, more natives had come aboard. Hayward questioned them in a mixture of their dialect and English as to what had become of the other Englishmen. They seemed either unwilling or unable to answer his queries, looking from one to another in apparent confusion.

"They are unwilling to give up their "friends" and can not understand why we are confining those who have come aboard. We will most likely have to seek the assistance of one of the chiefs. I will try to turn up one of them ashore." Tom had determined that none of our native visitors was a headman.

"Perhaps it might answer were you to take some gifts along, Lieutenant. From what I am given to understand, these simple folks seem to respond to them." Edwards suggested.

"Sir. With all respect, it is not the time for gifts yet. Once we have found one of their chiefs, gifts will not only be in order, but expected, if we are to secure their cooperation." Hayward drew on his experience of having spent considerable time on the island when he sailed with Bligh.

In short order, the cutter was splashed and, with Corner, Hayward, and six Marines aboard, cast off and pulled toward the shore. Several of the canoes followed it in. With little to do now but wait, I made my way aft and peered into the box where the four mutineers were now confined.

Each was seated on the deck, legs outstretched before them. Their ankles were fixed into a long bar that ran down the center of the box and was fitted with shackles so that they could not stand. Their wrists still wore the manacle chains Grimwood had applied on deck. I was horrified! Surely this would not be their lot for the entire remainder of our commission! Already the heat was building inside and I could see them sweating profusely as no breeze found its way into the prison. I also noticed two wooden buckets standing in the corners which would likely see use as the "necessaries." They would surely become unpleasant in the extreme in the heat. I resolved to have a word with John Larkan about their treatment.

By the time the evening meal was piped, there was no sign of Tom and Robert who, it seemed, had found it prudent to go inland in their quest. The wardroom was empty for supper, being only Larkan, myself, and George Hamilton in attendance. Mister Passmore, our Sailing Master, maintained the watch on deck, to be relieved later by one of the masters' mates.

"Surely Cap'n Edwards will not keep those men confined as they are for the duration? It would be inhuman!" George directed his question to the first lieutenant, beating out my own query on the subject. "They will suffer greatly if they are not allowed to walk about and get some fresh air from time to time. I fear for their survival in this heat."

"Cap'n Edwards has determined that the mutineers should have no contact with our people. They have already fomented one mutiny and, in his opinion, are expert in their employment. As we are instructed to bring them back to hang, they would have little to lose should they incite another mutiny." Larkan said around a mouthful of melted cheese and bread. "They will be kept in irons and in the box until we turn them over to the Admiralty. However, the cap'n was most adamant that they be given the same rations as our people, even though they are entitled only to two-thirds as prisoners. Of course, spirits are quite out of the question."

"I shall speak to the captain about this. It would be my considered opinion that some will die en route should they not get exercise and fresh air. And that would be contrary to our orders. The captain was quite clear that his instructions are to *keep them alive*." Hamilton was irate at what he perceived as inhuman treatment of the prisoners.

"You do as you will, George. I fear your entreaty will fall on deaf ears however." And so ended the conversation on our current contingent of captives.

After a brief stroll about the deck following supper, I retired to my cabin, still thinking about our commission, the mutineers, and my friends ashore in what could develop into an ugly, and perhaps, hostile situation, should they find the remaining English.

CHAPTER SIXTEEN

Aboard Pandora: *Otaheite*

Dawn, when it came, was as sudden as could be; one moment it was night, the next, the sun breached the horizon, first, as the sliver of a fingernail which nonetheless, filled the eastern sky with oranges, yellows, and reds. The colors merged with the blackness of the night sky, creating purple tinges streaking upwards as the dark gave way to the dawn. With each passing moment, the orange orb climbed farther into the sky and the warm light spread over the sea, turning the white-tipped waves into sparkling gemstones and casting a warm glow as it brightened the black sand beach lining the calm waters of Matavai Bay. As the mountains farther inland received the warming light, their blackness, which only moments before, had quite frustrated any chance of definition, became a wondrous palette of greens, browns, and yellows. Birds announced the new day in raucous cacophony.

I had slept poorly, suffering the torments of the concerns I took with me from the wardroom the night before, and so was prowling about the deck as the day dawned. In spite of my awe at the beauty of the place—I had not really had the opportunity to appreciate it yesterday with all that was happening—I was spell-bound by the exquisite smells that drifted off the land. Too many to identify, I eventually stopped trying and simply savored the sweetness of the air, breathing deeply of flowers, rich volcanic soil, and the wonderful smells of morning cook fires. I immediately resolved to suggest to our first lieutenant that the ship be opened up at every available place to let the pungent, stale, odors of a long passage escape and be replaced with the aromatic delights of this tropical paradise.

Along with the dawn came the canoes; more than a dozen, filled with both men and women, who seemed, but for a few, joyful and friendly. On closer examination, they were as handsome as our native visitors of yesterday, both men and women wearing bright flowers in their hair and chanting a rhythmic song as they paddled. Neither the men nor the women wore any garment beyond the swaddling we had observed yesterday on both the natives and the mutineers, and ranged, in the tones of their skin, from a dark coffee color to a fine bright color that is almost white. Their features were closer to European than Negro with small mouths surrounded by thin red lips and dark eyes. It appeared that most wore brunette hair, but the style of it ranged from short to shoulder-length. But even in the soft morning breeze, each of them displayed hair that was neat and carefully trimmed.

Captain Edwards had ordered armed guards to patrol the ship during the night as he had been warned that the local people are famous for slipping stealthily aboard and stealing anything that catches their eye. Now our Marines, those remaining aboard, and several of the bosun's mates, were gathered in a knot, staring in awe of the attractive natives in their canoes. The sailors shouted out to them, suggestively and rudely, especially to the women, but the Marines stood silently, hands fondling muskets which they held at the ready. For now, the natives seemed quite content to lay on their paddles alongside, singing what now had the sound of a doleful lament.

Larkan appeared, studied the canoes and their occupants, and determined they posed no threat. He repeated the captain's orders that the natives were not to be permitted aboard until he so ordered, but at the moment, that appeared not to be a concern. It seemed likely to me that, having had our forge working for nigh on to two weeks before our arrival, making iron nails, knives, and trinkets to trade for or, if necessary buy, information, the locals would soon be standing on our decks!

It was shortly after breakfast was piped and we repaired to the wardroom to partake of some sustenance, that the messenger appeared at the open door, fist poised to knock and momentarily confused that he found no door upon which to knock.

"What is it, Wells? Has the watch officer sent you?" Larkan, sitting facing the door, saw the man first.

"Aye, sir. Mister Reynolds said to tell you our cutter's made off from the beach and is coming back."

"Very well. I shall be up directly." Larkan said.

"Also, sir. There's likely more'n a dozen more native craft millin' about the ship. They ain't doin' anything, just paddling around and singin' their songs." Wells smiled with just part of his face as he recalled watching the young maidens in the boats.

"Fine, Wells. Please inform Mister Reynolds I shall be on deck straightaway and ask him to inform Cap'n Edwards of Mister Corner's return. That will be all."

"Well, John. What's your wager on Robert? Do you think he discovered the whereabouts of the other rascals from Bligh's unfortunate ship?" Hamilton grinned at the first lieutenant, still sure that we would be unsuccessful in rounding up all the mutineers.

To some extent, he was already right; Christian and eight mutineers had, "a long time ago," sailed off in *Bounty* to parts unknown. But I suspected that Edwards would spend whatever time he could tracking them, as well as those still in Otaheite, to fulfill his commission.

We watched Corner and Hayward approach, parting the native canoes as they neared our side. Lines snaked down to the bowman followed by the man ropes and, with an agility one would not expect in one with such a large girth, Corner scrambled up the side followed immediately by Tom. Larkan was there to greet them.

"Well! I certainly hope you two enjoyed your bit of shore leave! I trust you found none of the villains, or they would be trussed up like pigs in your boat."

"We discovered they have built a boat, a schooner, in fact, and, upon learning of our arrival, set sail for a neighboring island—that one, there, it was." He pointed to an island, perhaps fifteen miles distant, with mountains nearly as high as those on Otaheite. "Said it was called Mo'orea, or some such." Tom nodded, acknowledging Robert's accurate pronunciation. "We heard different numbers, but I reckon there must be about seven or eight of them on the boat.

"I had our sail rigged and set off after them, but realized we would never make a landfall before darkness settled in. And, of course, I could not be certain which island would be their destination, despite the rumor I had heard. After several hours of futile pursuit, I returned to Matavai Bay, up there a bit," Robert pointed to a headland several miles from where we now were at anchor, "and went ashore. We discovered their houses and, if Tom, here, understood right, some of their wives and families. Seems nearly all of 'em have taken native wives and some have produced offspring." Here Robert smiled in his telling. "Couldn't say I blamed 'em a bit. Bloody handsome, the women are here!

"We did enjoy one great stroke of luck, though. We came upon a chief who will likely be of some help in locating our missing mutineers. I have heard him called 'Otoo', but Tom seems to recall his name being 'Tynah' from his previous visit here. Nonetheless, whatever his name, he is apparently the headman for the district along the bay."

I watched Tom nod again in agreement and add, "Doesn't matter much about his name; all these chaps here have several names. Should they beat someone in a battle, as often as not they will take his name . . . and his family. Seems a trifle off to me, but there you have it. At the end of the day, they will generally answer to any of them, especially if there are gifts involved!"

"Aye," Corner took over the conversation again. "This Tynah . . . or Otoo chap gave us to understand that the English still on the island took to the hills. Seems there's a different district up there with a different headman. The local fellow, this Otoo chap, seems less than friendly toward the other one. We might use that to enlist his assistance in finding the villains. And, he mentioned he would send a messenger should the schooner return to Matavai."

Robert thought for a moment, trying to recollect if he had left anything useful out of his narrative. "I suspect we shall have to go inland, to the high ground there, and fetch them." Corner's voice gave away his frustration of an unsuccessful mission and perhaps, an uncomfortable night ashore. Likely the thought of marching his lumbering person up the mountain in tropical heat did little to improve his outlook, either!

Hayward added, "We shall most certainly be expected to provide gifts for this chief, Tynah, in order to secure his assistance. Knowing these people to some degree, I would suggest we start with a small gift, something to get his attention, and then let nature take its course. As Mister Corner mentioned, I know Tynah. A decent chap by all measure, but not one I would trifle with. Has a bit of a temper as I recall. Many of 'em do, come to think about it!"

Larkan nodded seriously. "I shall so inform the captain. I am sure he will be pleased that we have made some progress . . . small, by any lights, but nonetheless, progress." He shifted his glance to Robert and then Tom. "You two go below and find some breakfast. I would warrant you might be a trifle sharpset!"

The two officers smiled their thanks, doffed their hats, and made for the scuttle amidships. Larkan headed aft to the Cabin with his report, and after a moment, I followed my friends below to ask questions that Larkan had either not cared about, or not thought of.

"Tom." I found him shirtless in our cabin, bent over a freshly filled basin with a towel pressed to his face. "What about the people over there? Are they as handsome as what we've seen alongside the ship? And the women, Tom, how are they? Do they always dress so immodestly? I remember you told me a long time ago that the men freely gave visitors the gift of their wives' favors sometimes; did you find any 'favors' in your return here last night?"

Hayward straightened up, wrung out the sodden towel, and pressed it again to his face. Then he turned to face me. "Do you really presume I would tell you had I been so fortunate? And yes, the people here are very handsome indeed. And they do not consider themselves immodest in the slightest. That is how they dress and behave. You must try to control yourself Edward . . . and your baser instincts! Quite unbecoming to an officer, I must say."

I bristled at being chastised by my junior in both age and seniority, even if he was my friend. "I would be surprised, Tom, had you not been titillated beyond words when first you sighted these people from the deck of *Bounty* even though you were only a mere slip of a boy. Barely old enough to act on your adolescent desires, was how I recall you putting it your own self! I see no harm in admiring them and, should the opportunity to sample their favors arise at some point, I suspect I will succumb. I am only human, after all!"

"Indeed," Hayward sighed, a bit wistfully, I thought. "Aren't we all! Now I must see if Black can muster up some vittles. I am, as Larkan put it, 'some sharpset.' "

Later that same day, Tom took the pinnace and a crew ashore, including a small coterie of Marines, to present King Tynah with the present of a bottle of fine Jamaica. While he initially encountered, by his later telling, a bit of resistance from Tynah, it was mostly for show and the rum quickly dispelled it. Tom was welcomed to the king's house, where he lived with his two wives, for a meal which included some of the local drink made from coconut milk well fermented. The rum Tom had brought was not offered, likely put aside for the chief's private consumption.

Having begun the process, the local custom dictated that now the king would be expected to pay us a visit. Tom explained we should expect Tynah and others—he rarely traveled on official visits without a retinue—to carry out his obligation within a day or so.

And sure enough, the very next day, and with some notable fanfare, two huge, double canoes bearing the chief and his entourage, made their way—it was easier for them to get through the phalanx of canoes still encircling the ship than it had been for Robert and Tom—to our side, and with some ceremony, the group, all of them, clambered up the boarding slats.

Captain Edwards, in his full uniform, was there with Larkan and the officers to greet these important natives. He smiled a great deal and returned the warm greetings of our guests with a level of enthusiasm I had not before seen.

Hayward had explained to all of us, including the captain, that Otoo, or Tynah, as most knew him, would not personally accept gifts on this visit. But by introducing the large retinue that had accompanied him, the chief neatly circumvented this minor inconvenience. In his place, and to avoid any embarrassment to the chief, each member of his party would accept gifts, cheerfully, on behalf of their leader. And of course, should the Englishmen and their king wish to offer additional gifts for wives, lackeys, and other men in the group, they would only be too welcome!

Each of us, in turn, were presented to Tynah and his wives and dependents. Tom handled most of the introductions using a mixture of the local language and English, of which Tynah had a limited command.

I, for one, was very impressed with my friend's ability to speak what sounded like a most difficult tongue. To me, the sounds, while almost musical, bore no semblance to any language I had ever heard spoken. Pleasantries were exchanged, Tom translated, and I studied the natives. They were not unlike those we had already seen, but were considerably more statuesque. Especially Tynah.

The chief stood over six feet in height—closer, I'd say to six and a half feet—with a suitably large girth. In spite of his ample belly and heavy legs, he appeared very fit. His features were pleasant with a narrow nose, dark eyes, and thin lips. His hair was not black, but a dark brown in color, and he wore it wild and bushy, recalling a dark cloud encircling his head. An elegant mustache graced his upper lip and, perhaps in a gesture observed from previous visitors, he seemed wont to stroke it with great frequency. His disposition seemed good-natured and pleasant and a broad and frequent smile showed off startlingly white teeth. Geometric designs were tattooed upon on his legs, arms, and back. His chest was decorated with what appeared to be a large fish. About his loins, he wore the traditional length of cloth which served only to cover his nakedness. A short cape of what I took to be feathers, all of a most brilliant scarlet in color, covered his shoulders, and a small wreath of greenery adorned his head.

Since he was chief of the Matavai District, where almost all the ships visiting Otaheite called, the English captains had dubbed him "king," assuming he was king of the entire island. And Tynah reveled in it, considering himself the equal of his "great, good friend, George," *our* George III of England!

With Tynah, were, among others, his wife, a large, coarse-looking woman of perhaps thirty years, and a young girl, who I took to be his daughter. I was mistaken; Tom explained she was his concubine and went by the name of Alredy. The large woman, functionally, the queen, was called Edea. Both women were practically naked, wearing short kilt-like skirts and smaller versions of the cape worn by Tynah. Instead of the garland of greens, they wore crowns of brightly colored flowers about their heads. I found that I was unable to take my eyes from the youthful and gentle beauty of the lovely Alredy, a fact which Tom noticed and quietly suggested I desist from.

To hide my embarrassment at being caught staring, I shifted my gaze to my friend and inquired, "Does not having a concubine and a wife together cause a problem, Tom? I suspect no English wife would countenance the presence of a concubine!"

"Quite the opposite, Edward. They live together in the same house and even sleep together. And all in perfect harmony!" He smiled at me. "And stop your staring!"

A table had been set up under an awning amidships and Tynah, his wives, and several others who seemed to be lower functionaries, joined Edwards, Larkan, and, for convenience in translating, Hayward. The rest of us stood about watching and listening, as there was little we might offer.

Gifts of iron products including nails, knives, and tomahawk heads, appeared and delighted our guests. A small cask of wine provided some liquid refreshment for the men and multiple toasts were offered to our King, George III (whom Tynah repeatedly made clear was his equal!), Tynah, Captain Edwards, *Pandora*, and to our hoped-for success in the completion of our commission.

This last surprised me somewhat, given that our success would remove from the island Tynah's English subjects and cause grief among his native subjects by taking away "husbands" and lovers.

But maybe Tynah and his people have grown weary of the mutineers and he wants his island returned to 'normal.' Perhaps that is why he is willing to assist us for a few paltry pounds of iron!

Tapping the captain's personal stock, his steward brewed tea for the ladies. Tom explained to them that the English ladies preferred tea and drinking it was a proper English custom when people gathered in a social setting. This so convinced the elder of the queens that she quickly became very fond of it. I was not so sure about the younger one; she seemed less enthralled with the taste of the tea and smiled broadly when Tynah gave her a taste of his wine. Just seeing the way her whole face lit up caused a smile to break out on my own face.

After some time, during which we all exchanged idle pleasantries, Edwards, through Hayward's skills as translator, began to maneuver the conversation around to securing Tynah's help in accomplishing our commission. Abruptly, Tynah stood up, walked to the side of the ship, and shouted to one of the boats below.

"What have I done, Mister Hayward? Created some gaffe, a breach of local custom?" Edwards seemed upset by Tynah's sudden departure.

"No sir. I don't believe so. Tynah is not leaving; indeed, he called for one of his men to bring him something. Perhaps a gift for you, sir. I do not believe he is offended.

"Ah. Here he comes back."

Tynah was indeed coming back from where he had stepped to the rail and was clutching a canvas-wrapped parcel to his chest as though it were a religious icon. With great ceremony and a lengthy speech, he presented it to the captain, who stood to receive it. He had to look up at the chief.

Between Tom's translation and Tynah's mixture of English and Polynesian, we were given to understand that the gift was not a permanent gift, but rather a loan, something we were to hold aboard until we were ready to leave. At that time, as part of the departure formalities, it must be returned to Tynah. Then with great reverence, Tynah carefully removed the raffia twine from around the package and then slowly, almost eloquently, unwrapped the canvas, revealing an oil portrait of our great explorer and navigator, the late Captain James Cook.

Tynah explained in halting English and rapid Polynesian, which Tom struggled a bit with, that his great, good, friend Captain Cook, still living (he said) on the island of Whytutakee, had given the people the painting as a gift when first Cook visited Otaheite. Of course, as chief of the Matavai District (where Cook had indeed spent much of his time), it was up to Tynah to protect and husband the gift and, in a gesture of friendship, he had begun a tradition of lending the painting to visiting English ships. Upon their departure, each captain or first lieutenant had inscribed the back of it with the dates of their visit, the name of their ship, and some pithy brief comment. I craned my neck to see as Edwards turned the painting over.

And there, among others, was *William Bligh, HMAV Bounty*, and the date he sailed away to disaster: four April, seventeen eighty-nine. There were an additional half dozen names and dates as well, including several by Cook himself, HMS *Adventure* under a Captain Furneaux, and *Discovery*, Captain Clerke, but Bligh's, of course, caught my eye at once.

The captain made a suitably eloquent speech, stopping every so often to allow Tom to translate, to which Tynah listened most attentively. At the end of the speech, Edwards got to the point of this entire ceremony, namely, enlisting Tynah's aid in finding our mutineers.

He explained in simple words that the men were lawless villains (Tom struggled a bit with that), and he and his officers and men were commissioned to bring them back to England for trial. Tynah nodded, though I am not sure he quite grasped the finer points of the argument in spite of Tom's abilities. At one point, Tom laughed, said something in the local language, and then translated for us.

"Tynah says 'If they are villains of the worst kind, why not let me take care of them for you? It would save you much time!' I offered that while it was *his* custom to deal with *his* villains quickly and harshly, we did not have that amount of power in our law. He seemed to understand."

Before Tom had finished this translation, Tynah was speaking again and Tom had to ask him to repeat what he had said. Instead, Tynah spoke in his best English. "You carry King meet great good friend George. See law."

I took this to mean that he wished us to take him with us to England so he could meet his counterpart, George III, and see our justice system. The captain apparently understood it as I had and I watched as a smile spread across his face. Tom waited to see how this would play out.

"Oh, my good friend, King Tynah. I would enjoy nothing more than having you and your family as my guests aboard the ship and to introduce you personally to King George. But as you can see, *Pandora* is a small ship and, with the extra souls we will have aboard, there simply would be no room. Further, I am charged with finding *Bounty* and Christian as well, and we will not be sailing directly to England, but casting about in these waters in that quest."

Tynah seemed to understand some of it, but looked to Tom to translate the rest. Upon hearing he was being denied, he scowled and said something sharp to his entourage, each of whom suddenly stood up.

Oh my goodness! Are we going to have a battle right here in the deck? Why couldn't have Edwards just played along until we had his help secured?

Larkan spoke for the first time. "Hayward, tell him he should not have to go and see his friend in England; the next time a ship comes out, they will bring George to him. Lay it on thick; you know, you are a mighty king and other kings should come to you. See if that might calm him; we need his help."

Tom nodded and made a lengthy, albeit halting, speech to Tynah, presumably following Larkan's orders. And then it was over. Our native guests sat down again, Tynah smiled, nodded, and picked up his glass, and drank the remains of his wine in one gulp. I never asked Tom what exactly he had said, but whatever it was, it solved the problem!

After further deliberations, another cask of wine and some small beer for the ladies, followed by a brief tour of the ship, Tynah and his party took their leave. Edwards and the officers saw them off with promises of further visits, both ashore and in *Pandora*, and Tynah's reminder to keep Cook's portrait safe.

As the hour was approaching for spirits up and the evening meal, the officers retired to the wardroom to discuss the events of our stay so far and what likely would happen next. And for Surgeon Hamilton to once again present his case for letting the captured mutineers out of what the crew had now dubbed, Pandora's Box. An apt description, I thought.

"I can tell you why the captain is reluctant to let them roam the decks, George." Hayward offered, enjoying, I think, his new role as something of a celebrity and advisor to the senior officers.

"Oh, Thomas, do tell! I can scarce contain my curiosity!" The doctor's sarcasm was not lost on any, but possibly Tom.

"It's really quite simple: you see, several of the men we have in the Box were married, and one, George Stewart, had fathered at least one child. Out there, paddling 'round the ship, are, among others, their wives and relatives. Should our captive mutineers show themselves at the rail, you can not imagine the hue and cry that would go up from the natives." Hayward sat back, a satisfied smile on his face.

I could see him thinking, "How could these men be so obtuse as to not figure that out?" But I said nothing.

The surgeon, it was, who threw cold water over our smug junior officer. "And why would Cap'n Edwards care whether or not the natives put up, as you say, a hue and cry? Strikes me that any man who would keep human beings in those conditions, prisoner, mutineer, or what-have-you, could not care a fig for some ignorant natives and their feelings!" Clearly Hamilton was still seething at Edwards' actions.

Our evening supper was less than joyful, what with the lament of the natives in their canoes, the troubled feelings of many of us, and the thought that the morrow would bring, at least for some of us, a trip into the mountains . . . on foot.

CHAPTER SEVENTEEN

Otaheite

In the event, it was Robert and Hayward who once again made the trek ashore, gathering a few natives as guides and porters, and, accompanied by a handful of armed Marines, headed inland for the mountains where Tynah had thought the men might be, at least the ones who had not run off in their boat. Robert was the best choice for this assignment as he had, at one time, held a commission in the land service. I did not envy him his task, especially considering the height of the nearer mountains and his ample girth. But Larkan would not be denied and, with his usual cheery smile, Corner climbed down into the boat and directed his crew to pull for the shore.

With Corner and Hayward on the chase early, I thought I might have to spend yet another day biding my time in *Pandora*. Larkan sought me out at mid-morning and instructed me to take a boat in, collect Tynah, should he be willing, and go round the end of the island to see if the mutineers might have landed somewhere other than Matavai Bay. I, too, was to take a party of armed Marines with me.

"Uh, Mister Larkan. Did Hayward or Robert perhaps share with you where I might find Tynah's house? I have yet to be ashore here and . . . "

"Don't be daft, Edward. Tynah lives just there, the big round structure right off the beach." He pointed, and handed me his glass.

I focused the telescope and trained it where I thought the first lieutenant had pointed. All I saw was a black beach and trees. Jungle, sand, a few canoes pulled up above the tide line.

"No, no, Ballantyne. Over *there*." Larkan moved the glass, which I still held to my eye, to larboard.

"Oh yes, sir. I see the building. Quite large it is. Suitable for a king, I should imagine!"

My attempt at humor fell a bit flat, but I did get a smile as Larkan said, "Take the pinnace and a crew. Check with the corporal to see how many Marines he might spare you and shove off.

"Should you get lucky, you might even encounter the rascals at sea. Perhaps one of the swivels and some grape might answer should fortune smile on you."

"Aye, sir. I'll see to it straightaway. Will you be expecting me back by nightfall?"

"I shall expect you back, Mister Ballantyne, when I see you—hopefully with their little schooner under your command and those villains under guard by our Marines. Should your task require more than the hours remaining in the day, take what time you need; perhaps Tynah will put you up over the night." Larkan hurried off on another mission, gesturing at a native canoe in an effort to move it farther away from our side.

Hmmm. Should I stay in Tynah's home over the night, as his guest, he might feel obligated to offer me the company of . . . Stop thinking that way, Edward. It will bring you nothing but grief!

Tom's haughty refusal to answer my questions about *his* night ashore flashed into my mind and I thought that should I be so fortunate as to experience their wonderful custom, I would remain close-mouthed about it, especially to Tom!

In jig-time, the bosun had the pinnace rigged out and the crew rounded up. I shifted to an older uniform, given that I had little idea what I might encounter, brought out, not only my shorter fighting sword, but also a pair of pistols and some ball and powder which I drew from the small arms stores. And off we went, the little boat sailing nicely once we had rowed a distance from *Pandora*, heading through the crystalline waters of Matavai Bay for the point of land where Larkan had shown me Tynah's dwelling. I hoped we would find him at home and, more equally important, willing to be of help. Should he require a "gift," I should have to improvise as I had brought nothing with me that might answer.

As we neared the shore, a stretch of black sand beach just upwind of Tynah's compound, I watched for the bottom to come up. The water was so clear I could easily make out stretches of coral and even brightly colored fish below us, but I had no idea how *far* below us they were. As a result, when I figured we were about to ground the boat, I ordered the bowman over the side to guide us on to the beach.

He jumped over promptly on my command and disappeared from view; the water was well over six feet deep! He sputtered his way to the surface and clung to the side of the boat as our oarsmen shipped their sweeps again and pulled a few strokes toward the beach. Then he laughed, a small boy taking a plunge in a country pond.

"Got the bottom, Mister Ballantyne." The bowman now stood, pushing the bow of the boat away from him as the forefoot scratched its way into the soft sand.

Must shelve pretty sharply, I thought. *A bit obvious, Edward, as the poor sod you sent over the side was over his head only half a length off the beach!*

I stepped forward and jumped into the sand, losing my balance as the softness of it gave way under my boots. I did notice a few giggles and smirks from the men, but, as I regained my composure and my feet, I chose to ignore their rudeness.

"You Marines: two of you stay here and mind the boat. You other two, come with me. Let's pay a visit to King Tynah." I marched off, toward the trees and Tynah's dwelling.

As my little party approached the edge of the jungle, a native appeared, heavily tattooed and brown as a berry. As he held no weapon, I did not perceive him to be a threat and raised my hand in a silent greeting.

"I'd warrant you gents would be off the frigate anchored in the Bay. I'm Brown. John Brown, late of the brig *Mercury*."

"You're English? Took you for a native!" I recovered my composure and then asked him, "You are not of *Bounty*?" I took his hand in greeting.

"Not a bit, I am, sir. Took my leave of the American brig *Mercury* as I mentioned. Must have been two and a half, three years back, it was. Aye, three years. Only white man on the island until the chaps from *Bounty* appeared. Got a special relationship with Otoo here."

"So you are a deserter? And English? From an American vessel?" I was puzzled by the brief history he offered and wondered should I take him into custody as well as our mutineers.

"Well, no, sir, I am surely not a deserter; Cap'n Cox held me in low esteem, especially after I took a razor to one o' me messmates. Clapped me in irons, he done. When the brig set her hook here, I thought I might do better here than in that ship and so asked to remain behind. Ol' Cox was happy as a lark to grant me that, I can tell you. Happy as a lark, he was, and likely as glad as I was to part company. Been here three years, I have, and never a cross word with any. Don't much care for some o' those Bounties, I might add. Right rough some of 'em are, I'd say. But they mostly keep to themselves and their wives and I keep right to leeward of Otoo. Act as his aide, I'd say. Yes," he nodded in agreement with himself, "his aide."

I noticed that my two Marines still held their muskets at the ready and that their firing locks had been drawn back.

"I think you may relax a bit, men. I am certain that Mister Brown means us no ill will." The Marines did as I said. Then I turned back to Brown. "I would imagine you speak the local dialect, Brown? And that you're familiar with the geography here and the customs?"

"Aye, familiar as three years o' livin' here can make me. And I speak their lingo like them. Yes, sir. Three years I been here, and fit into their culture as good as they do themselves. Yes, sir."

"Perhaps you'd be willing to assist us, then, Brown. We're to find the English schooner which we understand sailed off when *Pandora* arrived. Said to carry seven or eight Englishmen in her. Any idea where they might have sailed her?"

"I do. And I would be happy to help you find those rascals. If you're to take them away with you, it'd be better for me. I think they annoy Otoo most of the time. Keep pretty much outta their way, my own self, I do. Got no truck with 'em. Not a bit. Drunk, they are, and killin' each other, on top of it."

"What do you mean, 'killin' each other,' Brown? I was given to believe there were sixteen of them here, left by *Bounty* when Christian sailed off with eight others. Are there fewer?"

"Aye. Fewer there are. Fourteen now, as one of 'em shot his mate, and the natives killed him. Churchill and Thompson, it were. Nasty gents, they were, and good riddance to 'em, I say!

"Now, if you gents want to get after that schooner, I'd say we oughtta get underway. Ain't a moment to lose, there ain't." Brown walked past us and headed for our boat. He said, over his shoulder, "But there surely ain't seven or eight of 'em in the boat. No sir. More like three or four is what I seen. And some women as well."

Hmmm. Only three or four . . . and women. Well, I reckon I'll take what I can and let Robert and Tom have a go at the others!

"Hold on, there, Brown. My orders are to take Tynah—Otoo, as you call him—with us. He offered to help when he came out to the ship."

"Oh, Otoo ain't here, he ain't. Off to the mountains with a pair of English officers and some sailors and locals. Had to laugh, in spite of meself, I done; those officer chaps was dressed in their full uniforms, they was! Just marchin' up the beach had 'em sweatin' like nothing' I ever seen. They'll be sheddin' them woolies sooner than later, I'd warrant! Said they was trying to catch some mutineers and goin' up the mountain after 'em. Reckon that'd be the same ones you're after?"

Robert and Hayward must have found Tynah and persuaded him to accompany them inland. So now what am I to do? Larkan said I was to take Tynah if he'd go. Well, Brown will have to answer!

"Very well, Brown. Since you're here and Tynah is not, you'll have to do. Climb aboard.

"Bowman, push us back and jump in quickly." I remembered the sharp drop from the beach and saw no reason to dunk the poor chap again!

Once we were again under sail, scudding along nicely with a fine quartering breeze; Brown instructed me to steer around the point at the end of the Bay, giving it a wide berth. "Mind the rocks, there, right at the end," he warned. He called it Venus and told me that he was "pretty sure, yes, sir, pretty sure, indeed" that he had seen the schooner pass the other side of Point Venus and anchor in a small bay about four or five miles distant.

"When would that have been, Brown?"

"Mighta been yesterday in the morning, I think." He scratched his head and looked at the shore line, as if the proper answer would be found there. Then, apparently having found the answer, he muttered, "Likely comin' back from a visit across to Mo'orea, be my guess." He pronounced it *Mo-or-aya.*

"So you don't know where they might have gotten to since you saw them?" I countered.

"Be my guess they'da gone inland. That's what I woulda done, my own self. Yes, sir. Go inland. Up to the mountains. Get ol' chief Tamarrah— he'd be headman of the upper district and less than friendly to Otoo, I'd say—to hide 'em or mayhaps, even protect 'em." He paused, looked around a bit, and added, "So you see, Lieutenant, you're better off with me helpin' you than ol' Otoo. He might'a started a war, if he'd asked Tamarrah to do something without he paid handsomely for it."

I took this to mean that "gifts" would be in order should we find this chief of the upper district. I had nothing to offer and briefly considered returning to *Pandora* for a cask of iron nails, coin of the realm in these islands, but, as we were about to turn Point Venus, I decided against losing the time it would take. I'd have to figure something out myself.

Within no more than an hour, we entered the small bay, more of a harbor by all rights, and, after dropping the sails and masts, rowed the boat into the shallows. All the while I had been casting my eyes about, seeking the schooner which Brown was 'pretty sure' he had seen enter the bay. The little bay was completely empty of any vessels, large or small.

Where could they have got to? If Brown was right, I would think to see them in plain sight.

217

There was a small indentation in the shoreline, lined with black, smooth rocks. A prehistoric lava flow, I surmised, proud of myself for forming such an educated opinion. The trees had grown through and around the rocks, almost to the water's edge. I began to steer for it, thinking it a fine place to leave the boat while we traipsed off into the jungle, when one of my sharp-eyed sailors cried out.

"Sir. Mister Ballantyne! There's masts showin' above them trees. Must be that schooner!"

I looked, and, indeed, there were masts. "Quiet now, men. Might be someone aboard. Easy on the oars," I hissed.

We approached the little ship from astern. She was stout and well built. These mutineers had done a fine job of her construction. Sails made from palm mat lay furled on her booms, the only evidence that the vessel had not been built in Deptford or Chatham. And there was not a soul aboard. Empty as a tomb.

"Well, Lieutenant. I'd reckon I was right as right could be. Yes, sir. Right. Seen 'em myself, as I said, come right 'round Point Venus and into this little bay." Brown was wreathed in smiles, practically dancing in his glee at being right!

"Yes, Brown. Fine job." I hated to cut off his somewhat premature celebration, but, now that we knew they had been here, I felt a pressing need to get after them. "Oars: backwater together."

We back away from the schooner and made for a bit of sandy beach a pistol-shot away.

He was right about the schooner; let us hope he guessed right as to their destination. I looked up the mountain, high above us. *Looks to be a bit of a hike up there. Hate to waste the time if they're not there.*

Our now dry bowman peered cautiously over the side, gauging the depth, before he jumped out into water barely to his knees. In no time at all, we were all out, led by former seaman Brown, and, again leaving two armed men to guard the boat, we were quickly heading into the jungle, following the trace of a path as it led us up the hill. As the foliage closed around us, the heat became oppressive; the canopy of the trees protected us from the sun, but it also quite stopped the breeze, leaving us sweating and gasping at the pace Brown maintained.

Finally, I called a halt and sat myself down on a fallen tree. The men, sailors and Marines both, dropped in the path, exhausted from their labors. Brown stood above me, a hard look on his face.

"Thought you wanted to catch these villains," he said. "If we have to stop all the time for you sods to rest, we ain't never gonna get up there.

Who knows where they might get to, with Tamarrah helpin' 'em. Your two officers what went up with Otoo likely got Tamarrah riled up already. Who knows what mighta happened?" Clearly Brown was concerned about what we might find.

"Just a few minutes, Brown. These men have been cooped up on the ship for four months; they're not used to this amount of exercise. Let 'em rest for a few moments. We'll get there quicker if we give them a bit of rest."

"Looks like you're as whipped as them sods, Lieutenant. Can see it in your eyes."

"Aye, and I am, Brown. A bit of rest is all I need. It's the heat. Not used to it at all." I struggled to keep my tone level.

Brown sat down, rested his back against a branch of the tree I used as my seat, and promptly fell sound asleep.

So much for us being tired! Looks like he could use a bit of a rest too, and he's used to the heat!

Just before dusk—well, there's really no dusk here; one moment it's daylight, the next it's dark—we arrived in the clearing where Tamarrah's village was located. Brown, using the native's language, asked after the chief and was told he had gone off with two British officers, some English, and natives from the Matavai District apparently in pursuit of the other English. He directed Brown to the priest and off we went to seek him out.

The priest offered us their hospitality for the night and mentioned that we would be welcome in their village, sharing quarters with several of the locals.

Oh my! Would this hospitality include . . . No, Edward. Don't think that way. Besides, you are taken with Tynah's young concubine and . . . Well, what will happen will happen!

Brown wandered off, his work for the moment done, to find some chums he had up here. The priest made me understand I was to be his guest and the other six men, four sailors and two Marines, would sleep in the common hut, among some of the islanders. The evening meal would be taken in the center of the village, all hands included. Apparently, the arrival of a *second* party of English was cause for something of a small celebration.

The priest, Oripai, motioned me into the house, where he bade me remove my wool coat and hat. I did so, and also removed my sword. I kept a pistol tucked into my waistband, but left the other tucked carefully under my coat along with my sword. Oripai lifted my coat up, exposing the weapons, and picked up my sword. He studied it carefully before withdrawing it from the scabbard.

As he drew the blade, he cast a furtive glance in my direction. I watched his eyes; clearly he was hoping I would offer it to him as a "gift," but before I would do that, I thought it prudent to discover whether he would be of help to us, and how much. Gently, I removed the sword from his hand, sheathed it, and returned it to its hiding place under my coat.

Some hiding place. The man clearly wants it and knows exactly where it is. These people seem to believe it's all right to help themselves to others' possessions . . . maybe I should just take it with me.

Which, likely to Oripai's chagrin, is exactly what I did. I am sure he hoped I would discover it missing later and make a valiant offer to help turn it up, unsuccessfully.

Maybe if you're of some help to me, my friend, we'll see about a gift for your labors!

The general population of the village turned out for supper, as it happened. A great bonfire was blazing in the center of the clearing and quantities of food were in evidence. Many happy faces seemed more interested in a party of sorts than seeing more English, but some, both men and women, tried to communicate with us and, for the most part, were successful in making themselves understood. I think my men and I were also successful. If it got tricky, Brown intervened. He also introduced me to a sprightly young maiden who could not have been more than sixteen years of age.

Sparkling dark eyes, long, dark, brown hair, interwoven with flowers, skin of a lighter hue than many, and the usual tattoos about her ankles and posterior, she seemed to attach herself to me for the evening's festivities. Her entire costume, apart from the flowered wreath encircling her head, consisted of a bit of cloth wound about her waist and between her legs, leaving little to the imagination.

Several of the women, slightly embarrassing to me in their immodesty, performed a rather suggestive dance, later to be joined by the men in an equally ribald display. The music was superbly rhythmic, performed on five drum-like instruments carved from trees in various sizes and shapes; each made a different sound, some high and penetrating, while others offered a throbbing, bass beat. The deeper tones came from drums covered in skins, while the higher pitched instruments, open at both ends, made their distinctive tapping sounds by being struck on their sides with intricately carved sticks. The combination was captivating and, while providing the beat for the dance in which I was only a spectator, I found I was quite caught up in the unique and hypnotic rhythms. During some of the songs, the drummers sang—more like chanted, I'd reckon—and, though completely unintelligible to me, made my new companion smile and laugh as she, from time to time, joined in. I suspected the words were a bit ribald based on the reaction of the audience. But, in spite of my complete lack of comprehension, I could scarcely avoid being swept up in the mystical sounds which provided the dancers with basis for their rather rude gyrations. And then the young girl, my companion, got up and joined the dancers, utterly giving herself over to the music. I watched, rapt.

The women (the majority of the dancers) performed the dance differently from the men; moving their hips from side to side or in a circular motion, they moved their arms in fluid gestures which reminded me of waves on the ocean. Their feet moved in tiny steps, front to back and side to side. All the while, their hips continued to gyrate enticingly. My new friend seemed in a trance as she moved through the steps of the dance, a beatific half-smile on her face.

The men, on the other hand, assumed a squatting position and moved their knees from side to side in opposition to each other. Their arms and feet mimicked the motions of the women. Muscular and glistening with oil and sweat, their movements were not as fluid and graceful as the women's, but made a nice counterpoint to the gentle and erotic actions performed by the women. I preferred to watch the ladies.

In spite of the quantity of strong drink which attended us all, I resolved to restrain myself in the interest of decorum; I would confine myself to watching the dancing and partake of the grog only sparingly. I was an officer, after all, and responsible for the well-being of my men. And it would be most unseemly for me to succumb. I watched the dancers, my friend, and tasted the cup as it passed my way.

But, as the potent liquor continued to flow, the Pandoras became less inhibited, joining in the dancing and, from time to time, quietly and discretely disappearing into the darker shadows, away from the firelight. It would appear that I had quite failed in that aspect of my duties!

My new friend, when she finished her dancing, returned to sit beside me. The dew of her efforts shone in the firelight, coating her youthful body and face with a glistening sheen. She gently stroked my arm and leg while we watched the dance, the flickering light of the fire casting eerie shadows on the performers, exaggerating their movements. And the cups continued to make their rounds of the spectators. It would have been rude of me not to take a swallow as it passed. I wondered, a bit dreamily, if Corner and Hayward had gotten a similar reception, but realized they likely did not, as they must have headed off in their quest soon after arriving. Too bad!

As the night ended, more and more of the natives, my sailors, and Marines drifted off into the dark, presumably to fall into a state of unconsciousness . . . or sleep. For my own self, the scene became a bit fuzzy, as if a strip of gauze had fallen over my eyes, and I had difficulty focusing. I have a dim recollection of returning to Oripai's house—I think the young lady might have followed along—but little more, save for some very disturbing dreams, until I awoke, feeling ill-used, at first light. The beautiful girl was not in sight. Maybe I had dreamed the whole night? Perhaps not!

Seaman Brown, formerly of the brig *Mercury*, arrived on the scene promptly, all of a titter with news.

"Mister Ballantyne. I have news for you. Yes, indeed, I do have some news for you and I think you'll be wantin' to hear what I have to say."

I could barely stand the sound of his voice. Nasal and grating, and loud enough almost to drown out the drum beating a determined tattoo in my head. I looked at him, bleary-eyed, slow witted, and stupid with sleep and the effects of the previous night.

"Yes . . . Brown. What is it?"

"I found some of your English sailors—the Bounties, they are—and not far from here!"

"Bounties? Oh, the mutineers!" I struggled to make my brain focus. "Where away, Brown. And did you find the chief . . . uh . . . " His name had quite escaped me.

"Tamarrah? No, he ain't here. We was told that yesterday, remember? Off he is with them others from your ship. But I reckon we can scoop up some o' your lads quick as ever you please. Didn't give myself away when I seen 'em. Just watched as they laid with their women. Not far from here."

Aye, I'll just bet you watched as they lay with their women! And where did you get yourself off to last night?

My addled brain was slowly, ever so slowly, beginning to function, sorting words, sights, and sounds into some form of reality. I could focus my eyes more easily now, and studied Brown as he shifted impatiently from one foot to the other. What I needed was a strong cup of tea, or even coffee. Not likely here.

"Mister Ballantyne?" Now what?

"Would you care for a cup of coffee, sir?" It was an English voice. I must have fallen back asleep and was dreaming. But it was not my steward, Black. I turned my head slowly toward the voice. No, I was quite awake and the voice was real!

Hargrave, one of my second division men and part of the crew for this mission of recovery, stood behind me, a steaming cup in his hand. The cup, more of a bowl from its shape, was wooden, ornately carved, and, when I turned, he extended his arm toward me.

"Oh, Hargrave. I would, indeed. More than you might imagine. Where on earth did you turn up coffee, here? These folks don't drink it, according to Mister Hayward." I didn't call him an 'angel of mercy', sure that it would embarrass him and make me out to be somewhat weak in his eyes. But that is exactly what he was. I took the cup. And drank, gratefully.

"We brung it with us, sir. Me and Bill Pudney. Hope it's all right to have done that." He looked questioningly at me.

All right? Oh goodness. I'll say it's all right!

"Yes, Hargrave. Well done! A good job, indeed. And I thank you for sharing it with me."

Brown continued in his agitated state, clearly afraid of missing the capture of the mutineers, should I delay too long.

"Hargave, stir up the others and bring them here. We'll see what Brown has discovered. Do not forget to bring weapons." He left as instructed.

To Brown I said, "Might there be a few strong natives willing to assist should we need them? Maybe a half dozen or whatever you can gather quickly."

"Already done, sir. It's them, standing right yonder. Aye, thought you might be wantin' some help, so I picked them ones my own self. Yes sir. Picked 'em myself!" He pointed to a cluster of four men, big strapping fellows they were, near one of the huts. Each carried a large club and what I took to be a sling. Clearly warriors.

"Very good, then. As soon as my men get here and I get my own arms, we will go off and see what we might find."

Once I had secured my fighting sword and pistols, we traipsed single file after Brown into the thick jungle; the canopy overhead quickly cut off the sunlight, allowing only small patches to filter through, making bright spots on the foliage and ground. The wind also, as we found before, was cut off and, within only a few moments, we were all sweating profusely. My men and I suffered; the natives and Brown pressed on without missing a beat. Then Brown, still leading us to God knew where, stopped and held up his hand.

We had marched barely two hours from Tamarrah's village, and through the thick vines and trees, I could make out two rude lean-tos built into the side of a small hill and mostly surrounded by trees. Brown motioned us forward, his finger to his lips in a signal for silence. I noticed the natives

223

had put stones in their slings and seemed poised to whip them about their heads and fire them. I drew a pistol, saw that it was primed and cocked, and crept after Brown.

The occupants of the lean-tos slept, undisturbed by our approach. I counted six large feet and six small ones, their ankles tattooed, all next to each other. The rest of their bodies disappeared into the deep shadow within the hut. I nodded at Brown.

The former British seaman, assisted by one of the warriors, leaned forward and, at Brown's nod, without a sound, they each clapped onto one of the large feet, giving a mighty pull. Out came a darkly tanned, tattooed, and very startled man. And quite naked. He cried out in English.

"Damn it Charlie. I've told you before, that ain't funny! Hello, what have we here. Who in bloody hell are you?"

"It ain't me you need worry about, sailor. No, sir! Not me at all. It's them ones, there." Brown answered with a smile, pointing at me and two armed Marines, each pointing a cocked musket at whoever it was we had caught.

"Just stay where you are, sailor. Brown, stir up those other two." I said, quite unmoved by the startled sailor.

In short order we had the three of them standing in front of us, each tattooed like a native and very nearly as brown. Their women remained under the lean-tos, but had set up a constant and penetrating wail seeing their men—or husbands?—captured.

Their confused expressions incited me to introduce myself. "Good morning, men. I am Lieutenant Ballantyne of His Majesty's Frigate *Pandora*, Edward Edwards commanding. We have come to provide you safe passage to England. There are a number of gentlemen there who would very much enjoy having a chat with you.

"Now, I have told you my name; it's only right for you to do the same."

I waited. They looked from one to another, the dawn finally breaking on them. Behind them, their women, who had apparently perceived the situation more quickly than their men, increased their wailing.

"Brown," I said, raising my voice over the commotion, "would you please ask them to pipe down? Can't hear myself think over that row!"

"Uh . . . sir?" One the mutineers spoke. "Lieutenant Ballantyne? I am John Sumner. Is it finally over?"

"Aye, Sumner. Over it is—at least for you and your mates, here—and I am sure you're much relieved." I studied the man before me. I am sure he missed my sarcasm.

He was quite slender, likely about twenty-seven or eight year heavily browned by the sun and tattooed over much of his bod decorated his left cheek. He spoke with a Manx inflection.

"And who would your colleagues be, Sumner?"

Before he could answer, another spoke. This one bobbed his he spoke, making his eyes roll in a most remarkable fashion. About th age as Sumner, less tanned, but carrying the scars of the pox, he trifle taller than Sumner and several inches taller than his other frie

"It's Norman, sir. Charlie Norman." Head bobbing, eyes rolling a parts were caught in a heavy seaway.

"Well, Norman, a pleasure, I'm sure. Just remain quiet there, a1 not to provoke these Marines. I suspect they might be a trifle touch morning.

"And you? The smaller one? Who might you be?" I studied the thi them, holding my cocked pistol loosely at my side, but careful not to the powder in the priming pan.

"McIntosh, sir. Tom McIntosh. From Galway I am, and pleased tc ya. Been a terrible strain, these past two years. Almost held as captives were. Had nothing to do with Christian and his cutthroats!" He actu smiled at me while the blarney rolled off his tongue.

This one was also slender (Was there insufficient food here in this tr ical paradise? So far, all of the mutineers I had seen were quite thin!), a h a head shorter than his mates, and also bore the scars of small pox on I face. Like the others, he was tattooed about his legs and arms. His che wore an image of a bird, and on his thigh was the emblem of the Emeral Isle, a shamrock. Also, like the others, he was quite naked.

"Well, McIntosh. A pleasure it is, lad, to be makin' yer acquaintance!" offered my best Irish accent. Switching back to the King's English, I spok(to all three. "You men are under arrest for mutiny. If you have a garment of any kind, put it on and then follow this gentleman here back to Tamar-rah's village. You will this same day be enjoying the hospitality of the Royal Navy, once again."

"Sir? What about our wives? What are we to do with 'em? They're not part of Tamarrah's district and I fear for their safety. They belong in Tynah's district, Matavai, you know."

"I suspect they'll just have to make their way down behind us, McIntosh. I'd warrant they know the way!" As two of our captives had disappeared into their lean-tos, to find some clothing, I presumed, I motioned to the two Marines to follow.

Without warning, a shot rang out. One of our native warriors gasped and dropped to his knees before falling face down on front of me. A great bloom of crimson had appeared on his chest. Instantly, I swung around, my pistol raised before me, seeking the source of the shot. A little wisp of smoke rose in the still air from the larboard lean-to.

One of my Marines darted in, his musket before him with the bayonet in place.

"Don't kill him." I shouted.

In short order, the Red Coat was dragging John Sumner out into the opening. His musket was still cocked, but the bayonet showed a smear of crimson, apparently from the fresh wound in Sumner's arm. The other two mutineers came out, loin cloths in place, hands held above their heads.

"Sumner. That was remarkably silly of you. What possibly did you expect to accomplish against two Royal Marines, two seamen, me, not to mention these stout native warriors? And you've gone and shot one of Tamarrah's warriors. I'm not sure that will sit well with the king or his people. It is lucky you weren't shot by this Marine."

"Likely woulda been better for me, if he'd done that. I know the only thing waitin' on me in England is a rope strung from a yardarm on some Royal Navy hundred gunner. And if that king chap wants me first, well, that might not be so bad either. Likely be quicker." Sumner held his arm as the blood oozed from between his fingers.

"Well, Sumner, you wouldn't want to deprive the Admiralty the pleasures of the rope, now would you? Get in line here with your mates."

I told one of my seamen to bind their hands and have a look in the lean-tos for any other weapons. Wouldn't do to have the women surprise us on the march back to the boat. He shortly reappeared with the recently fired musket and an ornately decorated war club, each of which he place over his shoulder for the march back.

"Off you go, then. Brown will guide us back." I stood silently congratulating myself as the group marched past. The remaining warriors had picked up their fallen comrade and two carried his corpse between them.

The women, their wailing now reaching a new crescendo, stood agape and more naked than not in front of the lean-tos watching their men, hands securely tied behind them, vanish into the jungle. I suspected we would see them again.

CHAPTER EIGHTEEN

Otaheite

"Well done, Mister Ballantyne! How many of the rascals did you manage to catch?" Larkan's voice drifted over the calm waters of Matavai Bay.

"Just three of them, sir, but we secured their vessel as well." I shouted back.

The pinnace approached *Pandora*, well ahead of the slower sailing and severely short-handed schooner. In quick order, we had the sail down and the sweeps manned, making our approach to the side of the frigate in a most seamanlike manner. As I climbed up the boarding battens, I glanced back in the direction we had just sailed; the schooner was sailing nicely, her palm-mat sails shining in the late day sun. I saluted, doffing my hat, and stepped aboard to be greeted by the first lieutenant and captain. A notable group of natives, more women than men, congregated aft of the mainmast. I noticed at least two children, one of whom was a babe at the breast.

Our prisoners struggled a bit with the man ropes as they still had their hands bound, now to their fore, but made it to our deck. Manacles and the master at arms awaited.

"Cap'n, Mister Larkan, these are Sumner, McIntosh, and Norman, late of *Bounty*. Found 'em just this morning up on the mountain."

"Did you encounter Corner and Hayward? They and their party have yet to return." Larkan asked me.

"I did not, sir. But they had been in Tamarrah's village, apparently with Otoo and some natives. Oripai, the priest up there, told us they had gone farther afield in their quest. We were assisted by this man, John Brown, late of the American brig *Mercury*." I gave Brown a gentle shove forward and introduced him to Edwards and Larkan.

"Sir. If you should be able to use an extra hand in the ship, sir, I would work my passage. I would dearly love to get back to my native England again. Yes, sir. Been yearning to see old England for nigh on to three years, now. Aye, three years it's been since I landed here. Wonderful place, it is, but I do sorely miss my native England." Brown rambled, even to Edwards and Larkan.

At a nod from Edwards, Larkan said, "Are you not a mutineer, Brown? How did you happen to land yourself here, in Otaheite? A deserter, I'd warrant."

I stepped up to Brown's defense. "Oh no, Mister Larkan. He had a bit of a falling out with the captain of an American vessel, the brig *Mercury*, I believe he said, and they agreed—the cap'n and Seaman Brown—that all parties would be better off without Brown in the vessel. He'd been here nigh onto a year before the Bounties appeared."

Larkan studied me carefully for a moment, then nodded, having determined I had nothing to gain from lying for the sailor.

"Very well, then, Brown. Should you pass muster with the surgeon's inspection, you'll sign the Articles and join the ship's company. You will not be 'working your passage,' you'll be a seaman in the Royal Navy. Have you any dunnage or should I have our purser provide you with slops against your pay?" Brown was as well dressed as the mutineers and natives.

"Haven't nothin' ashore I need, sir. Nothin' at all. No, sir. I am happy to sign the Articles. Just want to get meself back to England, I do." Brown looked most earnest, then broke into a smile.

Grimwood, by now, had manacled our three new prisoners and led them aft. To the Box, I thought. But when I looked aft, I saw all our prisoners outside the Box, and surrounded by natives.

"What's that about, John?" I asked Larkan quietly after the captain had gone below.

"Natives came alongside, just as they've been doing since we set the hook. This bunch apparently includes wives and some children of our captives. Brought fruits and bread, some meat and other vittles for them. Cap'n finally relented and let them come aboard and turned the prisoners out of the Box, as long as they remained manacled and ironed.

"No one was more surprised than I, but I reckon he figured that we'd be needing the cooperation of the locals if we're to be successful in rounding up the others and thought this a good start." Larkan shrugged.

Looking at the assemblage again, I did notice several of Grimwood's men, armed with both cutlass and musket, standing attentively about the quarterdeck and poop.

"Then I'd warrant the next canoe alongside will hold the women of these three. Had to drag the men away and the women followed us all the way down the mountain. They couldn't understand why I wouldn't take them in one of the boats." I looked past the approaching schooner, half expecting to see a native canoe paddling furiously in our direction.

"I wonder how Robert and Tom are getting on. I'd wager they spent an uncomfortable night up there." I looked to the shore, the mountain towering over the sea, marveling that I had just been most of the way up there! And remembering the night *I* had spent—hardly uncomfortable, I thought!

"Well, they'll be back when they catch those villains, I imagine. There are but nine left at large, by my reckoning." Larkan looked at me for confirmation.

"Uh . . . John? We have seven now, I believe?" He nodded in assent. "According to Brown, two of them got killed shortly after they got here, so that would leave fourteen alive. We have seven of them. Corner, if he gets them all, will only have the remaining seven, not nine, to deal with." I paused, then went on.

"Brown, who seems to know these people pretty well, suggested to me on the way down the mountain that some notable gifts would be in order to the head man up there. Especially as one of his men got killed in a minor fracas when we took the three of them. " I looked at the mountain. "And likely wouldn't hurt were we to invite them out to the ship. He said they're generous to a fault and more like children, if they like you."

"Thank you for that, Edward. I shall surely pass it on to the cap'n. I know some of their antics give him cause for worry, but perhaps he'll go along. Thieving villains, as well, I've been warned by Hayward. Best to keep a watch on the ship while they're aboard us." He stepped aft, presumably to speak to Edwards about my suggestion.

I went below to get a change of clothes and rinse off some of the grime from my sojourn ashore.

"Well, one of our intrepid warriors has returned. And with some level of success, I collect." Hamilton sat in the wardroom and saw me through the open door as I entered the passageway.

"Hello, George. Lovely place this! Most scenic, especially up close! I'd recommend a tour up the mountain for your own self; might be quite healthful. Interesting people, too." I stood without the wardroom, hoping to escape to my cabin before he got too caught up in his cleverness.

"Must have been an interesting night, there. You spend it with Otoo in his village?"

"As a matter of fact, I did not. Spent it up on the mountain in the village of a chap named Tamarrah. About three quarters of the way up. Now I must go and change clothes and wash a bit. Please excuse me."

As I stepped into my cabin, I heard him call out, 'That chief on the mountain, Edward. He have a big celebration in your honor? Break out the local grog for all hands? He offer you his daughter or wife as a companion for the night?' I could hear the derision—or was it envy?—in his voice.

The comment conjured up an image of the night previous in my mind; the fire, the lewd dancing, the potent drink, and the girl. Especially the girl. I was still blank on anything past my returning to Oripai's house, the girl in tow. Perhaps I would never know for certain if she had offered her favors or not. And I recalled quite clearly how I had felt at daybreak this morning! And that she was nowhere in sight. For now, however, I thought it best to remain silent, a gentleman. I also recalled my silent promise to keep my own counsel should I have occasion to experience the delights of the local customs. So I pretended I did not hear the surgeon's probing question and went about having a quick wash. I found a clean shirt already laid out on my cot.

Black! You are amazing! How do you manage this sorcery?

By the time I returned to the deck (Hamilton was still sitting in the wardroom, a glass, half empty, before him.), the mutineer's schooner was riding to an anchor fifty yards off our larboard side, its sails neatly furled and sheets and halyards coiled down in true Royal Navy fashion. Several of our sailors stood at the rail, questioning their returned colleagues about the vessel, their adventures ashore, and casting appraising eyes on the little schooner. Idly, I wondered what would become of her. Maybe Edwards would make a present of the ship to the people of Otaheite, or one of the kings. It was built with their wood, presumably.

It was just then that the boson piped spirits up and the evening meal. And four more canoes arrived alongside, the occupants of which, seeing their friends already aboard, wasted no time in scrambling up the main chains, the battens, or, in one case, up our anchor cable. Larkan had ordered the ration of spirits to be issued on the spar deck instead of the gundeck, a concession to the heat, so our crew was mostly topside, mingling with the native visitors, trading personal possessions for personal favors, and enjoying a welcome break from routine. All in all, it was a quite lively throng peopling the deck of one of His Majesty's frigates! And, for some, in a most lively fashion! I continued to be amazed at our captain's uncharacteristic attitude.

I tried to study our visitors, especially the females, to see if I recognized any of the ladies who we had discovered with the mutineers; their faces blurred in my memory until any one of the women aboard *Pandora* might have been them. I simply could not know. Perhaps if they sought out the three I brought back . . .

I made my way through the barely dressed natives and the delighted English sailors crowding our spardeck as I headed for the quarterdeck, where I had espied Larkan keeping an eye on all the goings-on. He had a pistol shoved ostentatiously into the top of his britches.

"Sir? Mister Ballantyne?" I turned about and saw one of the mutineers standing before me with a native man, woman and baby. I recognized him to be one of the first to surrender aboard, but struggled to recall his name.

"Stewart, sir. Midshipman George Stewart." He likely recognized my perplexed expression.

"Oh yes, Stewart. What have you to say now?" I tried to sound as harsh as I suspected Cap'n Edwards might have.

"Sir, if I may, I'd like you to meet my father-in-law, Stewart. And this is my wife Peggy, and my son." He pointed to each in turn.

Stewart? What a strange name for a native man, and quite a coincidence, I'd say! How strange, that and Englishman named Stewart should "marry" the daughter of a man named Stewart!

The native man was taller than I, and heavily tattooed on his legs, arms, and posterior. The bluish-black markings showed up well on skin the color of polished bronze. His face was unmarked, but his neck bore a pattern of lines and dots, not unlike that on his upper arms. His hair, long to his shoulders, was a dark golden brown, streaked with white, an indication of his age. His lips were thin, his eyes dark and alert, and his nose quite long and straight. He was, by any standards, a handsome chap. And his daughter had, at least in a physical sense, taken after him.

"Peggy" was most fetching: dark eyes, shining brown hair to the middle of her back, ripe breasts likely augmented by suckling the child she toted, and a statuesque physique. Her height was within an inch of my own, and she wore the expected tattoos on her ankles, wrists, and posterior. Like her father, her skin was polished bronze and shone in the late-day sun as one might expect the metal to shine. The child, clearly of mixed heritage, was maybe a year or so in age, and quite naked. He wore no tattoos. I guessed they would come later, as he reached some predetermined level of maturity.

I nodded to each in turn—except the infant—and turned back to former Midshipman Stewart.

"How is it, Stewart, that your father-in-law shares your name? Most unusual, I'd reckon."

"A local custom, sir. Father of the girl takes the son-in-law's name as soon as the marriage is done . . . assuming he approves. And Peggy's most assuredly does approve of her role as my wife."

A look of concern darkened his face. "What will become of her, Mister Ballantyne? She is most concerned that we will never see one another again. As am I."

"Well, Stewart. I couldn't say. But I'd warrant she'll find herself another chap to take up with as quick as we're hull down. And soon enough, you'll be enjoying the hospitality of the Admiralty in a prison hulk until you're court-martialed. After that, well . . . that will depend on whether or not the court-martial board is feeling compassionate or not. Touched, you might say, by your unusual family situation. My guess is you'll swing, like most of your mates, Heywood included!" Suddenly I felt quite unmoved by Stewart's tale of romance in the South Seas. I saw him in no different a role than any of the others.

Stewart's small dark eyes flashed angrily at me. He said something in the local dialect to his "wife" which set her to wailing volubly. His father-in-law scowled, bunching his hands into fists, and setting his feet in a belligerent stance.

"Stewart, you are older. You should have known better than to participate in such a heinous crime. Heywood is just a youth and might have been caught up in it; you, on the other hand, should be more experienced and worldly. You deserve whatever sentence you might receive from a court-marital."

"Sir. I wanted no part in the taking of *Bounty*. None. I begged Cap'n Bligh to take both me and Heywood in the boat with him, but with Bligh and eighteen others, there was not a bit of room for even one more, let alone two. They had barely four inches of freeboard as it was. Two more—nay, sir—even one more, would surely have swamped them should they encounter anything but the most placid of seas. Neither Peter nor I had any choice but to remain aboard the ship and take our chances; to do otherwise would not only have imperiled our own lives, but the lives of nineteen other good men." Stewart was nothing if not passionate in his cause.

"Stewart, you are wasting your breath. I can do you not a shred of good. Save your speeches for the Admiralty and the court-martial board. Maybe you can convince them!" I kept my voice hard, though in truth, I was not as sure as I had been that he would be convicted. Maybe he *was* simply caught up in something beyond his control.

Stewart stepped away with his native family. I looked around the deck, seeing only the natives and our prisoners. One of them approached me.

"Mister Ballantyne, isn't it?"

"Aye, it is. As I recall, you are Heywood, are you not? The one with all the unpleasant accusations about Lieutenant Hayward?"

"The truth is often unpleasant, sir, but had he and Hallet not been sleeping when Christian came to relieve the watch, there would most likely have been no mutiny. Christian would have simply taken the raft he had hidden and slipped away, perhaps never to be seen again, or perhaps, to successfully get to an island that was near at hand. But, what's done is done and we'll never be certain of how it might have happened had those two remained awake. Unless, of course, you chance upon Mister Christian and his confederates." Heywood smiled disarmingly at me.

"Well, Heywood, I reckon we'll have to see what a court martial has to say about it. But it would appear that only you mutineers will be on trial, not Hayward or Hallet, or any of the others who chose not remain with the ship . . . and Christian.

"I seem to recall Tom Hayward mentioning that Christian is a Manxman." I raised my eyebrows, then went on. "I collect you are as well, from your accent and the Manx symbol there on your leg. Perchance the Admiralty will find that you were merely supporting your fellow denizen from the Isle of Man. Countrymen should support each other, wouldn't you think? Were I you, I would dwell on that whilst we take you home. I am sure there will be plenty of time to discuss it with your fellow mutineers!" I had purposely referred to him as mutineer in an effort to provoke him, but he was not taking the bait.

I tried another tactic, this time with a smile. "Have you any thoughts on where your mates—the ones here, in Otaheite—might have gotten to? You know we'll find them, eventually, but it would be rather convenient were we to discover their whereabouts sooner than later. You likely have noticed that we captured your lovely little schooner this afternoon, so it might suggest that the rest of the villains are on Otaheite rather than another island." I again raised my eyebrows questioningly at him, hoping for a confirmation.

"Really? We 'villains' have had use of local craft all during our time here. Why would you think that the others might be inconvenienced by the loss of our boat? Mo'orea is but a scant fifteen miles from where we stand right now. A short paddle in a local canoe. And to answer your question, I have not a clue as to where they might have gotten to. But I would wager they'll lead you on a merry chase! Is not my old messmate Tom and another of your officers—the fat one, I think—hunting them as we speak?" I detected a definite sneer in his voice and answered accordingly.

"Aye, they are and I have no doubt whatever that they will be successful in their mission." I strode away, angry with myself that he had provoked me.

Captain Edwards shortly came topside, looked about him, and ordered the prisoners again confined and the natives off the ship. It was almost dark and I suspected he feared mischief from our guests . . . and perhaps the prisoners. Although, with the seven we had, securely ironed hand and foot, that they would cause us any grief seemed unlikely at best!

I watched as some of the natives clambered down the side of the ship while others simply dove over the side into the darkening waters of Matavai Bay, to be picked up by their mates in the canoes. Their lithe forms and grace were captivating and they seemed as at home in the water as on land.

When I returned to the wardroom, our surgeon, still nursing his glass of wine (or perhaps another) had been joined by the sailing master, Mister Passmore, and John Larkan. I took a chair and Black appeared, as if by magic, with a glass for me.

He surely was a good find. I was lucky that he had been assigned to my division early on. My! Those wet, cold days in Portsmouth seem so long ago! And how the men had grown into a crew. Not just mine, but the entire ship's company. Of course, I reasoned to myself, *they had certainly not been tested to any degree. No fighting, save against a few waterspouts, and barely a bit of untoward weather. Time would tell, perhaps. Maybe on the homeward voyage their mettle would be tested.*

"Well, Mister Ballantyne, our friends have been gone some time now. Any thoughts on their whereabouts?" Hamilton looked at me over the rim of his glass, paused in its apparently frequent journey to his lips.

"Like you, George, I haven't seen them since they left the ship. I know they were on the mountain, but beyond that, I haven't any idea where they might have got to!" I thought Hamilton might be a trifle in is cups.

The first lieutenant chimed in, possibly in an effort to soften my somewhat sharp response to the surgeon. "I would expect them back tonight—or at the latest, tomorrow morning. I imagine the remaining mutineers led them a merry chase. Should they come up empty-handed, mayhaps it would answer to have a parlay with one or two of those chiefs. I would think they'd know all the likely hiding spots the villains might have found, would they not?" Larkan shifted his gaze to me, his eyebrows raised.

Suddenly, I had become the expert on the goings on ashore! But then I *had* found a few of them . . . or rather, our new recruit, Brown, had.

"Should Robert and Tom be unlucky in their quest, perhaps it would be beneficial to employ Brown to assist us. He seemed right savvy yesterday and this morning, I must say."

"It would please the captain no end to get those rascals aboard, confined, and *Pandora* under way again. We are still charged with finding the rest of them—those who went off with Christian, that is—and leave us not forget *Bounty*. She's still out there somewhere and there are untold numbers of islands where they might have got to. I suspect should we find the ship, we'll find Christian and his cutthroats."

I nodded in agreement and took a swallow of my wine. Black and the other stewards showed themselves again, this time armed with a table covering and dishes. It must be time for supper. I stood and stepped away from the table to give them room to work, as did my companions. Hamilton, as if to confirm my earlier thoughts, seemed a bit unsteady on his feet.

A knock sounded on the open door. The captain's steward stood without the room awaiting someone to acknowledge him.

"Yes?" I said.

"Sirs, Cap'n Edwards asks that Mister Larkan attend him in the Cabin."

"Very well. Thank you. I shall be there straightaway." Larkan stepped around the table. I assumed he would retrieve his jacket from his cabin en route.

When he had yet to return some time later, I suggested we eat rather than wait for him. "Perhaps Edwards invited him to dine in the Cabin." I offered by way of explanation.

With both Larkan and Corner gone, it fell to me, as senior officer, to sit at the head of the table, which chore I handled easily.

It was full dark—with supper served, eaten, and cleared, I had gone topside for some air—when a sentry cried out.

"Boat approaching from shore!"

I grabbed a night glass and scanned the shoreline, expecting to see a native craft heading our way. It was not; it was our own cutter, and even in the dim starlight, I could make out Robert's ample form seated in the sternsheets.

In short order, the boat was alongside, oars thrown up with expected precision, and Tom grabbing the man ropes to climb up the side. Robert followed him, landing on the deck close on his heels.

"Well, gentlemen! Welcome back! Did you have a nice run ashore? How many of the rascals did you bring with you?"

Once again, Larkan had mysteriously appeared behind me and now, as he spoke, peered through the darkness into the boat below.

"Nary a one, John. Gave us a right jolly chase through the jungle though. Couldn't get close enough even to see 'em, let alone clap the irons on 'em." Robert answered. His usually jolly voice sounded frustrated and tired. His face, in the glow of the lanterns, looked haggard, with a two day growth of beard covering his jowls and chin. I noticed that his shirt was stained with sweat and something dark, and was torn in several places. Tom looked no better, and seemed to have lost his hat during their sojourn in the mountains.

"Well, Cap'n Edwards has a plan that just might work. Tomorrow, Tom, you and Brown will go ashore and invite that chief who was here the other day—Otoo? Aye, Otoo, or was it Tynah?—and his chum up the mountain, for a parlay here aboard. There will, of course, be gifts aplenty and enough grog to float the ship. With all of their attendant family and cohorts, it should be a right lively party. With a bit of luck, it will go a long way in securing their help." Larkan shifted his gaze around the three of us.

"Sir? Who is 'Brown' if I may inquire?" Tom, of course, would have no knowledge of my success or our new seaman.

"An English sailor left in Otaheite by his American cap'n some six and more months before our lads showed up. Been rather helpful to us already." Larkan, with a nod to me, spoke before I could.

"Oh, I see." Said Tom, but of course, he clearly did not. The still perplexed look he gave Larkan and then me, confirmed that he had no idea whatever of what it was Larkan was talking about. "Perhaps, sir, if there's nothing else pressing, I might go below and find a fresh uniform and some vittles. Right sharpset, I am, and smelling like a goat, even to me!"

"By all means, Mister Hayward, by all means. We shall talk after you have attended to yourself. Shall we say the wardroom in half an hour? I am sure that Black or one of the others might organize something for you two to eat, as well."

In the event, it was closer to an hour by the time Larkan returned to find us in the wardroom. Hamilton and Passmore were still there, eager I am sure, to hear the tale of the chase through the mountain jungle. As was I. And our good surgeon had managed to get himself even more inebriated, bringing out his best rancor and sarcasm.

"Empty handed, I collect, lads. Well done! Two and more days chasing through the jungle and nary a thing to show for it! I certainly hope you managed to bring back at least those sailors and Marines who had the good fortune to join your foray ashore! I am sure they must have enjoyed their shore leave!

"Young Ballantyne, here, caught three of the rascals and recruited a new crew member as well! And with a shore party half the size of yours! Is that not so, Edward?" Hamilton looked at me, a bit bleary eyed, but smiling, either at me or his own cleverness.

I simply nodded and, when he pursued his glass again, caught Tom's eye and winked. Corner was tucking into some melted cheese and toast which his steward had managed for him and Tom. He glared at the surgeon.

"You wouldn't have survived half a day up there, George. Beastly hot and those rascals led us through the thickest part of the jungle, they did. Sleeping out at night, eaten alive by voracious bugs, some big enough to carry off a rat, and worried that the villains would come back and attack us while we slept.

"Tamarrah had told us they were armed with both cutlass and musket and had several of Otoo's natives with them. Would have made short work of us, had they wished, I am sure. Even with Otoo himself in our company." Robert's anger came through, even with his mouth full of hot cheese and toast.

"Meant no harm or disrespect, Corner. None at all. Surely would not have been my choice on how to spend some time ashore. Much rather have been with Edward, here. Big party they threw for him, plenty of food, liquor, and a bed in the chief's hut. Even, it seems, a young maiden to comfort him. Yes, sir. That is more to my liking, indeed." Hamilton winked luridly at me, causing me to go crimson.

How he had surmised that there was a young maiden involved was quite beyond me; I wasn't even certain of it my own self! I caught Hayward studying me and recalled our earlier conversation about officers remaining silent on such topics. So much for that! But, still the question burned, made all the more central to me now by the obvious disdain of my messmate.

I kept my own counsel, studying my wine glass to avoid making eye contact with either of my friends. I did catch a raised eyebrow and a quizzical smile from Robert, but he said nothing. The silence hung a bit heavy; finally, I could stand it no longer and, as they seemed to be waiting for some form of response, spoke.

"George, you have no idea what happened up there. For that matter, I'm not too sure my own self! Had a snoot-full of their local brew and barely recall going to bed. If I did have companionship, you couldn't verify it by my reckoning!"

"Oh, I know all too well, young Edward." Hamilton smiled evilly, certain that he was about to further embarrass me. "You see, I was obligated to have a look at our new sailor—couldn't have him sign the Articles without determining he was medically sound, now could we?—and he chatted up a storm. Told me the whole sordid story of the lovely little lady who accompanied you throughout the festivities and well into the night, he said. And no one's blaming you, lad. As I said, I would surely have enjoyed spending the night ashore that way than the way our two colleagues must have!"

"Well, it would appear that Seaman Brown knows more about how *I* spent the night than I do myself! I do recall that *he* wandered off early on during the evening. Can't imagine he had time to watch me, let alone determine how I spent the night!" I retorted hotly.

"Ah well. No harm done, I'd imagine." Hamilton smiled again, certain that he had made his point. Then he continued on a different tack. "Tom, do you think Larkan's plan—or should I say Cap'n Edwards' plan—will produce results? Seems to me, those villains are more likely to get protection from their native friends than we are assistance."

"I have no idea, George. But I will say, the locals are easily swayed by gifts and English generosity. Perhaps it will do the trick. I imagine we'll have to try it and find out." Tom swallowed the last of his wine and stood. "Gentlemen, with your permission, I shall take my leave and retire; I am tired enough to drop in my tracks." He looked around the table, his gaze settling briefly on me.

I made a show of hauling out my watch and looking at it. I, too, stood. "Bit weary my own self; long day, it's been. If you gentlemen will excuse me?"

When we got to our shared quarters, Tom wheeled on me and, fixing me with a hard look, said, "I can not believe you took advantage of your situation while you were on the mountain, Edward. Especially after the conversation we had just the other day. And I can not believe you even mentioned it aboard, especially to Hamilton! Until such time as he has something else to talk about, that will be his subject of choice!"

I angered, resentful of his accusation. "Apparently, Tom, you weren't listening. I said I knew nothing of what he accused me of as I was quite intoxicated at the time and have little recollection of the evening past a certain point. Yes, there was a young lady—a very pretty one, in fact—who sat with me during the meal and dancing. Did she join me in my quarters? I have no idea. If she did, she was not there when I awoke, I assure you. So the simple answer is, I simply don't know."

I determined that should he continue to press the subject, I would bring up Heywood's repeated accusation, which, in my opinion, was a great deal more onerous than whether or not I bedded some native girl. A mutiny may indeed have resulted from Tom's action, while from my own, there were no consequences, whatever!

In the event, my messmate simply shrugged and rolled himself into his cot. I pulled off my boots, hung up my jacket, and, still annoyed, did the same.

CHAPTER NINETEEN

Otaheite

It was the next morning, well before Hayward and Brown could form a plan and take the jolly boat ashore to extend Captain Edwards' invitation, that several of the sentries cried out, almost of one voice.

"Boats approaching from the shore. Canoes they are and big ones!"

Larkan appeared on deck before the sentry's call had completely died away. "Well, *that* looks interesting. Must be one of the chiefs or kings. Brought his whole entourage with him, looks like. May save you a trip, Tom. It would appear that somehow, either Otoo, or Tynah, as you call him, or that chap up the mountain, Tamarrah, must have got wind of what the cap'n was planning. Bloody convenient, I'd say!"

"Aye, sir. That first canoe, the one with the raised poop, that'd be a chief's vessel. Usually fifty and more paddlers, all warriors, and room enough for most of his family. Second or third wives will follow in the next one with the rest of his family, the district priest, and personal guard. No idea who it might be, though, sir. Could be either of them or even another, come out to demand his slice of the pie, so to speak."

"You may inform Cap'n Edwards we are about to have company, if you please, Tom. And do let him know you think it is likely a chief." Larkan spoke without shifting his gaze from the approaching craft.

As we watched, a half dozen more had shoved off from the beach, each one laden with many paddlers, warriors (presumably) and women. I could scarcely tear my eye from the glass as I studied each vessel in turn.

What am I looking for? Is it the one I met on the mountain? I barely recall what she looked like . . .

And then the first was alongside and the captain was striding purposefully toward the break in the bulwark. I looked down into the ornately decorated canoe. Handsome women bedecked in flowers both around their necks and in their hair; tattooed men, glistening with sweat from their efforts at paddling out to the frigate, and wearing garlands of greenery both about their heads and on their arms, stood in the canoe. I marveled at their ability to balance the narrow vessel until I figured out the secret: to larboard, a single outrigger, consisting of two intricately carved and gracefully arched arms, or poles, held a diminutive canoe at its outboard end and was obviously designed to provide stability for the craft. The vessel itself was beautifully carved and painted with all manner of designs, each appearing to be a marvelous work of art. This was certainly a special craft for a notable among the natives.

Within moments of its having reached our side, a huge native stood in the prow and blew a mighty blast on some type of shell. The note echoed across the water and was repeated by another and then yet another, each closer to shore than its predecessor. I was enthralled, but, like my colleagues (including Tom, I thought), had nary a clue as to what was happening, save that one of the chiefs was about to grace us with his presence.

"That'll be Tamarrah, there, in the stern, sitting on the throne." Tom offered, to no one in particular. "Wonder what decided him on all this?"

"No idea, then, have I? But were I to offer a wager, I reckon it was your visit and the chase through the forest with him. Likely looking for some reward for his trouble. But bloody convenient for us, I'd say!" Edwards responded, echoing the first lieutenant's earlier statement. "Likely ought to get the people moving to rig the ship for a party!"

Tom looked confused for a moment. "But sir, we came up empty. We caught not a single one of the rascals!"

"Aye, but Mister Ballantyne did, and in the chief's district. Got one of the locals killed into the bargain, as well. No matter, I'm sure, that the chief was off with you and Corner. He'll want the credit. Or perhaps, payment for the unfortunate who died at the hands of a mutineer." Edwards' sarcasm gave voice to his whole attitude about the locals.

Larkan listened, shrugged his shoulders, and doffed his hat to the captain, without comment. Then he stepped away to find the master at arms, the carpenter, and the bosun.

We would rig a spare t'gallant sail over the spardeck and drape it with flags to add a festive note to the occasion. Food would have to be prepared and brought up, along with grog, wine, and small beer. In the meantime, natives were beginning to climb aboard, much as they had on previous days: up the battens, the main and fore chains, the bow sprit, and even the anchor rode. Tom greeted some by name, showing a familiarity with the natives that seemed to do little to put our Marines at ease; they maintained their grips on their muskets and kept wary eyes moving across the assembly.

With great fanfare, Chief Tamarrah hauled his bulk up the battens, using the manropes. He landed, slightly breathless, on the deck and looked about him.

Clearly, then, this one has not the familiarity with a man o' war enjoyed by his coastal colleague, Otoo. Must not come down from his mountain all that often.

His eyes, indeed, his whole body, turned this way and that, taking in the spar deck, our visible armament, the sailors who stood gawking (mostly at the women who were now appearing on deck), and aloft to our rig with the neatly furled sails adorning each yard. When he cast his gaze back to those of us standing ready to greet him and his party, he identified Captain Edwards immediately and turned to face him.

The captain smiled thinly and extended his hand in greeting. Tamarrah took it and let forth with a rush of words; the only one I could catch in the Otaheitian tongue was his name, which, at each utterance, included a thump on the man's chest. Edwards looked helplessly at our fourth lieutenant and now, official translator, Tom.

When the chief paused, Tom looked from him to the captain and translated his words. "He said that we are welcome to his island and he is glad to help us in our . . . quest. I assume that means finding the remaining Bounties. He also mentioned that he was glad to be of help to Mister Corner and me and stands ready to offer further assistance. He did mention Oripai's hospitality to Mister Ballantyne and made a passing reference to his dead warrior. But I heard no request for any compensation. According to him, Otoo is a useless buffoon who would be strained to find his own backside . . . or words to that effect!

"He also mentioned that since the villains are in his district, we should be happy to have his help as we would never find them without it." Tom spoke a few words to the chief, who nodded in agreement.

Then Edwards stepped forward. He stood erect, but was still nearly a head shorter than Tamarrah, the chief's height exaggerated by the headdress of scarlet feathers and greenery that adorned his head. His bulk and great girth added to the illusion, making our captain appear, by comparison, even smaller than he was.

"King Tamarrah, I welcome you to His Majesty's Frigate *Pandora*. We are most happy to have you visit us and are preparing a splendid celebration to commemorate the occasion and your cooperation in helping us find the rascals who stole Cap'n Bligh's ship." He paused, allowing time for Hayward to translate.

"You and your people have been of great help to us already, and we look forward to your assistance in collecting the remaining villains, should they still be hiding like frightened children in your district." Again, Tom translated, struggling a bit, and, in my opinion, saying more than Edwards had offered.

Tamarrah smiled broadly, again extended his hand to Edwards and then to Hayward, me, and the Marine sentry (who refused to release his grip on his musket to take it).

George Hamilton chose that moment to appear, grinning, and seeing the joviality of the gathering, stepped up to offer his hand to the mountain chieftain along with a hearty greeting.

A silence followed, awkward at best, as Tamarrah looked at the hand, then at Hamilton's face, still covered with his most winning smile. Perhaps the chief was confused by the fact that, as surgeon, Hamilton wore no uniform, but a white shirt with the sleeves rolled to the elbow, a forest green waistcoat, and green knee-britches above white stockings. Hamilton's hand remained extended, expectantly, and finally, after what seemed several minutes, but was in fact, only a second or two, the chief took it and pumped it heartily, uttering a string of words which I took to be friendly.

I could see that Larkan had already begun the process of getting a spare t'gallant unfolded preparatory to hoisting it above the deck to provide some shade. The quartermaster stood waiting, his arms laden with what seemed to be every flag in our inventory, and sailors, under the careful eye of Mister Bentham, the Purser, were stacking casks of wine and small beer around the base of the foremast.

"Mister Hayward, invite the king to my quarters, if you please. We shall pass the time there until the deck is rigged. His people may remain topside. I shall also need your assistance in communicating with him." Edwards nodded at Tamarrah, then touched his shoulder, as if to propel him aft.

Tom passed on the captain's invitation and Tamarrah, who had initially recoiled slightly at being touched, relaxed and stepped off behind Edwards, heading aft. I could not help but notice as his eyes caught the Box on the poopdeck and lingered. Over his shoulder, he said something to Tom, to which Tom offered only the briefest of answers.

It was an hour later, no more, when John Larkan found me chatting with Robert about his adventures ashore.

"Gentlemen," he said without preamble, "we have a bit of a problem: there is some unfriendly weather approaching. I have informed the captain who seems unwilling to call off the festivities he has planned.

"I need you two to collect your men and herd our guests back into their canoes. I have already instructed the bosun to unrig the sail they just spread over the spardeck. I believe we are in for a blow and that sail is the last thing we need. Bloody disastrous, if I am right about the weather."

Corner and I came up from the wardroom and looked seaward. A swell was working into the bay and beyond Point Venus, roiling, dark clouds tumbled over each other, in seeming haste to be first to dump the nasty weather they held. The natives on our deck stared and chatted in hushed voices, their anxiety clear. Some had already taken to their boats and were paddling for shore. Larkan was right; we were in for it. Robert put it to words.

"This isn't likely to be merely a spot of rain, Edward. We're in for it and on a lee shore. Might even want to put out another anchor. Why don't you get the men gathered and see if the bosun might spare you a few from his detail of getting that sail doused to haul up a spare cable. I'm going to have a word with Edwards."

I wished him luck, but thought that all he had to do was convince the captain to take a look for himself. The signs were unmistakable; we were, as Robert had put it, "in for it." I found a clutch of my second division sailors lounging about the foremast, unsure as to what was more fascinating to watch, the weather moving in or the barely-clad maidens still milling about the decks. I instructed them to start those natives, still uncertain as to what to do, into their boats.

The t'gallant now lay in a great heap between the main and fore masts as a dozen and more sailors struggled to fold it and secure it. The bosun, running this way and that, shouted orders, pushed men, and gradually saw the big sail accede to his wishes. I approached him, reluctant to disturb him until his task was nearly done.

"Mister Cunningham. I will need a few of your lads to get the spare cable up from the orlop. Mister Corner and I think the captain might want to set another anchor, in view of the storm. See to it, if you please."

Cunningham glared at me for a moment, shot a look to the northwest, and nodded in silent agreement. He shouted to six of his men, now almost unemployed in their task, and sent them below.

The waters of Matavai Bay were no longer still; a long swell was rolling in, a precursor to the storm. The winds here had yet to change and ruffled the surface of each wave, blowing spray back over the tops of the rollers. In the distance, I could see more spray being blown into the air as the waves landed on the shallow reef surrounding the bay.

Yes, I think Larkan and Robert got it right! We are surely in for it!

Robert reappeared on the quarterdeck, followed by Captain Edwards and Tamarrah. Tom stepped onto the deck last. Each man looked to the northwest for a moment, following Corner's outstretched arm. Words I could not hear were exchanged and then Robert detached himself from the little group. He and Tom hurried forward. Tamarrah followed, but seemed less agitated than I might have expected. I would have thought he had seen many storms like this one approach his island and been alarmed, but then I recalled his district was up on the mountain, well away from the sea. Perhaps the storms weren't as bad up there. As he came into the waist of the ship, he spoke to his people, each of whom stepped to the bulwark and called down to their mates in the boats. Soon most of the natives were off the ship. The chief's big canoe was alongside, fully manned and waiting only for their king to climb down and take his seat on the throne aft. But Tamarrah wasn't ready to leave just yet.

He found Tom and, gesticulating and pointing at the shoreline, held a brief conversation with him in the native dialect. Tom nodded and shook Tamarrah's hand in the native manner, clasping each other's wrist. Then he hurried aft to find Captain Edwards as the chief clambered down the battens to his boat.

"Cap'n, Tamarrah has offered to leave some of his men aboard to assist us and keep watch for any of Tynah's people who might take the opportunity to sneak aboard during the storm. He says they are not to be trusted and will make off with anything they can lift. I have thanked him and accepted his offer." Tom explained to Edwards.

"You what?" The captain boomed, clearly annoyed with Tom's decision. "And what is to prevent these savages from stealing us blind themselves? I can ill afford bad relations at this point, but I am uncomfortable with locals aboard and having run of my ship." The captain's eyes darted about the deck, perhaps seeking those natives left aboard as sentries. "Should I decide to get the ship under weigh, what am I expected to do with our guests? Pitch them into the sea? Take them with us?"

Tom, clearly uncomfortable now in his role, dropped his eyes and mumbled something I could not catch. Edwards strode away, and found the first lieutenant, perhaps to upbraid him for Tom's actions, but I was unable to follow any more of the captain's rantings, as I felt a light tap on my shoulder

I turned to find Midshipman Renouard standing at attention, his hat doffed in salute. I returned it and raised my eyebrows questioningly.

"Uh . . . sir? Mister Ballantyne? I think we have a problem below, sir."

"What Renouard? We have a storm coming in, which, if Larkan and Corner are right, will be a severe one. We will need all hands, officers, and mids alike to prepare the ship for it, and quickly."

"Yes, sir. I know. That's the problem. We don't have *all* hands, sir. Tim Calligan has gone missing. I ordered two of his messmates to search the ship for him, but they found naught. It appears that he has run, sir."

I thought for a moment, trying to place Calligan. He wasn't one of my men; I recalled he worked for Robert. And then I remembered: he was the one Bully Rodgers had heaved over the side in the gauntlet, only to get himself shot for his trouble, just before we crossed the line.

"When did he disappear, Mister Renouard? Who reported his absence? As I recall, he's the one who accused Rodgers of stealing, back before we got to South America, is he not?"

"Aye, sir. That's the one. George Reynolds, it was, who discovered him missing. Mentioned it to Mister Corner within my earshot. Thought you'd want to know. Not sure when he noticed him gone, though."

"Please find Mister Corner and tell him I am looking for him, if you please, Renouard."

Hmmm. Calligan accuses Rodgers of thievery and after getting thrown into the sea, becomes somewhat of a Jonah with his shipmates. Then he runs at the first opportunity. Wonder what he's thinking. He surely knows why we're here and catching one more would not strain us a jot! Every Royal Navy sailor knows the penalty for desertion is the same as for mutiny: hanging. Dreadful risk to take, should he be caught!

I thought about this as I roamed about the gundeck, ensuring the battery was well secured against any seas we might take, whether we headed out to the open ocean or remained at anchor. Over my head, I could hear the stamping of feet as men marched around the capstan to haul the spare anchor cable up from the orlop deck. Shouts and creaking of blocks seemed strangely magnified in the quiet of the gundeck; I could not hear the wind even though I knew it was building and would soon be making its distinctive keening sound as it moved through our rig. The ship was beginning to react to the waves washing into the bay with a gentle rolling and surge as she worked at her anchor.

I found Steward forward on the gundeck, directed him to correct a few loose side tackles I had noted and close all the gun ports securely. Satisfied that my acting gunner's mate would see to my orders competently, I returned topside. Corner and Larkan were in deep in conversation in the bows and I joined them, remaining at first at a respectable distance so as not to intrude, should they be having a private talk.

"Ballantyne. I am just learning that one of your men has gone missing. Calligan, it was." Larkan spoke when he noticed Robert's eyes shift in my direction.

"Aye, sir. Heard it my own self just moments ago. But he's not one of mine; belongs to Robert, in the first division."

Robert raised his eyebrows at me, perhaps embarrassed he had not recognized one of his own, albeit not one with whom he had had much contact.

"Reynolds mentioned that one of Calligan's messmates had offered that Calligan lately recanted his story about Rodgers stealing from him. Thought he might suffer should anyone discover his lie—what with Rodgers getting himself shot and all—at the hands of his chums, or even by the cap'n, and ran. At least that's what Reynolds thinks. Won't know if it's right until we catch the rascal. Just one more to find, I reckon." Larkan shook his head. "Can't worry about that now, though. We've got a bit more weighty matters to deal with first."

A flurry of shouts drifted up from beneath the bow as our cutter came to under the cathead to receive the second anchor. Cunningham was directing the careful lowering of it to be secured alongside the boat which would then row it out at an angle to the ship and our best bower. Hands were lined up in the waist to pay out the heavy cable now attached to the ring on the anchor's stock. Corner peered over the side and, careful not to usurp Cunningham's authority, watched carefully. Lowering nearly a ton of metal into position next to a relatively flimsy boat was tricky business, especially now that the waves were beginning to make and *Pandora* and the cutter—especially the cutter—were both reacting to them.

At length, the anchor was secured safely to the stern of the boat and, as the rode was paid out, the oarsmen pulled mightily for a position directed by Lieutenant Larkan. Finally it was done; the capstan took a strain to set the hook and *Pandora* was now moored with two stout anchors in the event the storm should demand it.

The storm was now close enough to darken the sky and pelt those of us topside with rain. The wind had begun to whine in our rigging and Captain Edwards, his boat cloak drawn about him for protection from the increasing rain, gazed aloft, looking for anything that might come loose and cause a problem, either by falling to the deck or, in the case of a sail, cause the ship to begin to sail on her anchors. Satisfied, he returned his penetrating stare to the deck, wet sailors and officers finishing up stowage of anything loose there. Our Otaheitian guests stood in a cluster near the foremast, rain cascading off their mostly naked bodies without notice, as they talked with raised voices, possibly about the storm and what might happen to the ship. At least that would be my concern had I no experience in a man of war.

Now the full fury of the storm was on us, and the wind, which had been only moments before blowing from the south, abruptly shifted to the northeast. *Pandora* reacted as any ship would: she swung her bows into the new direction and promptly twisted the two anchor cables.

"Mister Reynolds: get a crew and see if you might sort that out." Larkan called to the master's mate currently checking halyards and sheets for the foresails.

"Aye, sir." Reynolds shouted above the storm.

Exactly what Larkan expected him to accomplish was a mystery to me; without hauling in one of the anchors and resetting it, I could discover no way the twist could be removed. Apparently, neither did Reynolds or Bosun Cunningham who accompanied him in the cutter.

When the boat returned, Edwards was waiting in the bow and, immediately took charge.

"You men there. Clap a stopper on the larboard cable, smartly, now."

Cunningham saw at once what the captain was about and, grabbing a handful of sailors, did secure a stopper to the larboard cable and another to the starboard one. Ordering them paid out a trifle, the stoppers took the strain on each, leaving the inboard ends loose. He then directed his men to reverse the cables, the larboard to the starboard post and vice versa. When the stoppers were released, the cables again took the strain of the ship, this time, with no twists.

"Have I to think of everything in this ship? Reynolds, and certainly Cunningham, should have seen that before I ever came forward. Mister Larkan, I think some time to reflect on their seamanship might be of benefit to Reynolds and possibly the bosun. See to it, if you please." Edwards marched off through the downpour, clutching his hat to his head and holding his billowing boat cloak more tightly about him.

And so, Master's Mate George Reynolds, who I had thought quite knowledgeable and agreeable, was confined to his quarters. He was not ironed or shackled, but the ignominy of being placed essentially under house arrest sat heavily on him. But it did have a positive influence—perhaps that was the captain's intent?—on his messmates and the midshipmen. Renouard and John Sival both approached me at different times to question the sentence, but they and their messmates' appearances on deck and involvement in shipboard evolutions seemed to increase. And young

Renouard was frequently spotted reading instructional material to further his knowledge of his employment.

The storm raged in waves for two days; unusual, I was told by Tom Hayward, in these parts, but nonetheless, rage it did. Each time it would appear to blow through, leaving us to catch our breath in peace, more heavy clouds, filled with rain and wind, would make up in the northeast and stir up the seas until the line of huge breakers at the reef seemed ready to quite overcome the protection the coral offered to Matavai Bay. The seas rolled through the bay and crashed upon the shoreline, threatening to wash the canoes, pulled up safely above the reach of the water, out to sea.

And *Pandora* lay between the reef and the shore, rocking and dancing like some maddened beast, tugging on her anchor rodes, but mercifully, unsuccessful in dislodging either. Constant vigilance on deck, chafing gear on the rodes, and tight furls on all our sails, ensured our safety. The captain and first lieutenant seemed constantly to prowl the decks, quick to spot a potential problem and order it remedied immediately. Our local protectors all dove over the side, after reporting their dissatisfaction about the conditions on board to Tom, and swam through the surf to the shore. I watched as two of them actually positioned their bodies to ride the waves rolling in, saving their own efforts and winding up in a sea of foam at the shoreline. It was impressive and even looked like fun to those of us who watched!

"Why do you suppose the captain doesn't want to get us out of here?" Tom asked me during a brief lull in the wind.

"Simple, Tom. Can you see the opening in the reef?" I craned my neck toward where I recalled the opening to be and saw only white foam as the waves crashed and rolled across the protective barrier. Tom was equally unsuccessful and I think my point was made.

"But is not there some place we might get to within the reef that would afford us more protection? This seems awfully exposed. And on a lee shore."

"You know the water here, or at the least, I would imagine you should, having been here for so long with Bligh. If you have a look at the chart we have from Cap'n Cook—the one that Bligh marked up—you'll see there is precious little water in this lagoon, save from where we are here. Fine for canoes, but I fear, insufficient for *Pandora*."

While he pondered this information, I studied the mutineers' schooner, working at her anchor even more violently than did the frigate. Rolling and pitching this way and that, it seemed only a matter of time before she would break loose and smash to bits on the beach. Feeling a sense of ownership in the little vessel, as I had captured her, I went off to find Larkan.

"Glass is rising, now, Edward; likely won't have a problem with it now. But if you really are concerned, you have permission to take the cutter and see what you might do." Larkan seemed less than sympathetic to my concerns.

As the seas in the bay still ran high, I decided that discretion was the better part of valor and stayed in *Pandora*, keeping an eye on the schooner, but not willing to risk a boat and crew—not to mention my own life—to do what little I might for her. And in the end, she rode through the storms brilliantly, a further testament to her construction and sea-worthiness.

On the first fine day following the unseemly weather, calm seas dominated the bay, the breakers on the reef were gone, and cloudless blue skies filled the heavens. A canoe put out from shore manned by only two natives who had wrestled their craft out of the jungle and into the water.

"Boat approaching!" A not-so-eagle-eyed sentry cried out. Most of us on deck had seen it launched.

Midshipman Sival had the watch on deck and joined me in the waist to await the arrival of the vessel. One man, clad in the usual cloth about his midsection, but no garlands of leaves or flowers, clambered up the battens and landed lightly on deck. He looked around a bit, tugged at his waist cloth, and fidgeted nervously, his eyes big and round. Then he spoke to us at some length in his language, which, of course, neither Sival nor I could understand.

"Send your messenger to find Mister Hayward, John. Tell him we need his translation skills." I said when Sival kept looking from the native to me, unsure of how to proceed.

"He carries an invitation to visit with Tamarrah on Mount Taharaa. It's for Cap'n Edwards, the officers, and, I presume, the mids. Send your messenger to tell Larkan and the cap'n, John. My experience with matters of this stripe is that the meeting—or perhaps a party—will commence upon our arrival." Tom had listened to the frustrated native intently.

Before the first lieutenant had stepped onto the deck, the native was back in his canoe and, with his mate, was paddling furiously for shore.

"Sounds as if we would be rude to decline. Obviously, we'll not be taking everyone; someone must remain to keep the watch. But I am sure the cap'n will want most to attend. He mentioned that we must cultivate this chief to curry his favor and assistance in finding those infernal mutineers." Larkan started aft to inform Edwards.

Sival was rapturous. "A party ashore! How lovely! I do hope Mister Larkan will let the midshipmen go. I would enjoy seeing the island from somewhere besides out here!"

CHAPTER TWENTY

Otaheite

In the event, Sival got his wish; all the mids and master's mates went, save for Reynolds who remained in the captain's disfavor and his messmate, William Oliver, a nice chap who, we all knew, would spend the remainder of his days without ever seeing a lieutenant's swab on his shoulder. The first lieutenant had decided that they would be left in charge of the frigate during our absence. Three boats took us ashore to a spot designated by Tom Hayward as the place where Tamarrah's men would meet us to guide us up the mountain.

The men were there, sitting on their heels in the black sand; they rose as the crews jumped from the boats and leaped to help steady the vessels as the officers debarked. Tom greeted them effusively.

In return, the two chattered away in their own tongue. Tom explained. "Seems Tamarrah has decided that making the march up Mount Taharaa would be too strenuous and has moved the party to Point Venus. They were very excited that Otoo and his entourage will be there as well. Apparently, the two kings have buried the hatchet, for the moment anyway, and seem willing to entertain us together. Perhaps even help us find the Bounties."

"Are we to trek up the beach or should we take the boats?" Larkan asked, after a brief consult with Edwards.

"Having been up that bloody mountain, I am most grateful for their consideration! I would think using the boats would save time and our legs." Corner answered before Tom could utter a word.

And so, we all returned to the boats, including the natives who seemed delighted at riding in an English longboat. They guided us unerringly to a gently sloping beach directly below a clearing where already dozens of natives were milling about.

As we marched in tight groups to the clearing, drums started beating a rhythmic tattoo and the islanders all stopped whatever they had been doing to stare at us, each of us in full uniform (in spite of the heat) complete with swords and gloves. I suspected that once the events began to unfold, gloves, jackets, and then swords would be cast off and stowed in a safe place. I had planned to put mine in the boat so that the crew might forestall the likelihood of pilferage by our hosts.

Tamarrah and Otoo sat side by side on what could only be described as thrones: tall, high-backed chairs, intricately carved, and decorated with feathers and bright bits of cloth. Their retinues, wives and concubines stood beside each and smirked behind their hands as each of the officers, beginning with Captain Edwards, made a leg as a suitable gesture of respect.

Otoo spoke first, given that we were in his district and, by all rights, we were his guests, as were Tamarrah and his followers. Tom translated for Edwards and Larkan, and while I was unable to catch all that he said, the words were flowery and welcoming.

When Tamarrah spoke, he offered similar sentiments and, by his gestures in Otoo's direction, thanked his sometimes-rival for his hospitality. Edwards likewise was effusive in his words, grateful for the hospitality and that he hoped the two kings would remain friends even after *Pandora* sailed. He also expressed his thanks for the kings' offers to help us find the mutineers, perhaps a reminder as to our purpose here. From what I had gleaned from Tom's translation, neither had mentioned the Bounties.

And then the party began. Each guest was handed a well carved wooden cup brimming with a dark liquid. As quick taste confirmed it was the same potent potion to which I had succumbed during my night with Oripai. I resolved to be more careful this time, especially with Edwards and Larkan in attendance! It was apparent that the locals had been tasting well before their guests arrived!

As with my welcome in Tamarrah's district, the drums started with a slow beat, and this time, two long flute-type instruments, each made from a perfectly straight tree branch, played a tuneful but simple melody. With the music in full cry, two men stood and stepped into the middle of the clearing. They wore the simple cloth covering wound about their midsections, wreaths of green leaves about their heads, and similar leafy decorations on their arms and legs. They entered the circle, actually a stage of sorts, about which we all sat, and began what could only be described as a series of lascivious gyrations, distorting their mouths, as their legs, torsos, and arms moved in a pantomime of moves one would expect to see only behind the closed doors of a boudoir. While the captain seemed rapt, I found the display unseemly and passed the time watching our companions, native and English alike, as they reacted.

"Have a look at the mids, Edward. They are enthralled with this. Wait until they see the women's dance. It will quite upend them!" Tom laughed in my ear.

I shot a glance at our young gentlemen; titters and giggles, whispers behind protective hands, and wide-eyed stares gave credence to their delight at seeing first hand a native celebration. As Tom had said, "Wait until they see the women!" Indeed!

In due course, the men completed their dance and received applause from us Englishmen. The mids were particularly enthusiastic in their response. Then it was the women's turn to entertain us.

Tom translated their introduction made by Oripai, the priest who had hosted me on the mountain. "These young women," he said, "have been trained in the art"—neither Oripai nor Tom mentioned which "art" it might have been—"and are skilled in entertaining. They performed for Captain Bligh and their mothers performed for Captain Cook. Their dance will mimic a native bird during its mating ritual."

Three stunning young women—they could have barely attained sixteen years of age—strode to the center of the "stage" and posed for a moment. They wore wreaths of flowers in their long hair, and necklaces of white flowers which my untrained eye took as orchids. Around their middles, they wore very short leafy kilts which barely covered their privates. But the kilts did not go all the way 'round them; open in the back to show their well-tattooed rumps, each had affixed a fan-like piece made of brightly colored feathers, which spread about five feet across, not unlike the tail feathers of a peacock. I assumed this, then, was how the 'native bird mating ritual' would be portrayed.

The gasp of delight that emanated from our midshipmen at the sight of these comely ladies—none older than any of the residents of the cockpit—caused a spate of laughter from the officers and the mids' older brethren, the master's mates. And a frown from the captain. So transfixed were they with the scene before them, I doubt any among them noticed the captain's expression or even heard the laughter from the rest of us.

The music began again, five drums beating a slow rhythm in much the same manner as I had heard during my mystical night on the mountain, and again accompanied by the same long flutes that had played for the male dancers. The ladies listened for a moment, then, facing us, began to sway their bodies in a most graceful manner in perfect time to the music. The feathers, which spread well to their sides, made a most interesting addition to the ladies' costumes and their dance. Their dance was performed on their toes, and their legs and arms moved in perfect compliment to the movements of their bodies. This time, it was not just the mids who were captivated; I was rapt. For just a moment, I tore my eyes away to see if my messmates were equally enthralled; they were, indeed. And our surgeon, eyes glued to the stage, fumbled his cup, only to spill a portion of the elixir down his shirt. I am not sure he even noticed.

The dance continued for many minutes, the tempo increasing gradually, as the graceful moves of the dancers kept pace. At several points during the spectacle, the girls turned their be-feathered backsides toward us, and bending over, made their fans of feathers move in a most tantalizing manner. During these moves, we all marveled audibly at the wonderful agility of their loins. And, of course, our less than gentlemanly young gentlemen were quite caught up in the moment, offering, to the captain's disapproving looks, whistles and hoots of approval as the comely maidens displayed their talents!

At the conclusion of their dance—perhaps thirty minutes or more—the maidens, each of whom had worked themselves into a perfect furor, approached the front of the stage and, with a quick tug on some hidden bit of twine, dropped their kilts and feathers to the ground, exposing for all to see that which is better felt than seen. The audience was quite undone! The older among us, smiled and clapped save for a few (Edwards included) who scowled disapprovingly. The youngsters gaped and gasped, taking in what I was sure would be the main topic of cockpit conversation for the duration of the voyage!

Personally, I enjoyed watching the dancers *and* the cream of England's future officer corps. It was particularly entertaining when the ladies left the stage and, quite without a shred of shame, marched straight toward us, stopping before Captain Edwards and Mister Larkan. The English officers overcame whatever emotion they might be feeling to offer deep bows and smiles in compliment of the performance.

Otoo then made another speech which needed no translation; food appeared in plentiful quantity, cups were refilled, and the Pandoras moved as one, with proper regard to rank and privilege, of course, to the cooking area. Here, a vast assortment of meats and vegetables were displayed in a cornucopia of riches. Every imaginable fruit filled another table and the combination of wonderful aromas threatened to overcome the senses. George Hamilton waxed positively poetic.

"What a Garden of Eden is this place," he began. "Not only are the people, especially the women, handsome beyond expectation, but it is apparent that they are all versed in, and passionately fond of, the Eleusinian mysteries. The earth produces an abundance of riches, both for foodstuffs and clothing, without tillage; the trees are loaded with the richest of fruits, there for the plucking. The loveliest and most aromatic of flowers fill the air with their glorious scent. And the fair ones are ever-willing to fill your arms with their love."

"My goodness, Hamilton! What has got into you? Never have I heard you so rapturous in your praise of anything! I suspect you have been overcome with ardent spirits!" Corner's eyes twinkled as he accused our surgeon of being in his cups.

"Uh, sir? I couldn't help but hear your comment. And I quite agree, but could you tell me, sir, what is 'Eleusinian?' I have not before heard the word." Renouard stood respectfully to the side, but obviously had listened carefully to George's speech. Six months ago he would have not asked, but now, with his new-found enthusiasm for learning, he was unafraid.

"You bumble-headed nitwit! Have you no classical education? I am dismayed that a midshipman in His Majesty's Navy should feel moved to ask a question about such a common classical reference. Are you but testing me, or are you really that ignorant?" Hamilton studied the young lad through slightly bleary eyes with such intensity that Renouard actually took a step back.

"Oh George, Don't be so arrogant! Not all of us share your world travels and affinity for the classics. Answer the boy's question; is it not obvious that he wants to learn? Else why would he have asked? I also am lacking in knowledge of your reference." Corner rushed to the defense of the youngster, a move that made me smile.

"Oh, all right, then." The surgeon looked at both Corner and the midshipman with baleful stares, then explained. "There was a city called Eleusis, near to Athens, in classical times, which was known for its rich harvest, particularly of corn, and the worship of the goddess, Demeter. Everyone knows that they held frequent ritualistic saturnalias devoted to the goddess which became legendary throughout the classical world, even as they were happening.

"Now you both have expanded your wisdom!" Hamilton did nothing to hide a haughty look of recrimination at the ignorance of his shipmates.

I had not known the word, either, and was pleased that Renouard had asked and Robert had pressed the issue.

We ate. And then we ate some more. And drank of the plentiful but potent local liquor. I noticed a stupor coming over me, as well as a lack of feeling in my lips and extremities, and had to will myself to rise and walk over to where Tom was in conversation with Otoo. I might have staggered a bit, but had anyone noticed, I would have written it off to the uneven ground underfoot. On the way to see my shipmate, I noticed our beloved surgeon sharing a cup with a plump lady of indeterminate age, but clearly past her prime. No dancer this one! They were laughing and struggling to communicate, each without a shred of knowledge of the other's language. But it seemed not to matter to Hamilton—or the lady, for that matter. They chattered away like two youths who had designs on one another.

"The doctor seems to be quite enthralled with the lady, Mister Ballantyne. Do you think he might need some help with the lingo? I can help him with that. Speak it as good as the locals, you know." Our newest recruit, Seaman Brown, stood to one side, having made his way up from the boats. Perhaps Tom, sensing that he would be overcome with his translation duties, had sent for assistance.

"Oh Brown. I think he's getting right along. Seems not to have a care that neither can speak the other's language. And he might resent the intrusion. Best to offer your services to some of the others!" I realized that I was speaking slowly, struggling to feel my lips and trying not to trip over my words.

"I wonder, does the good sir know who that is? The one he's chatting up so friendly? I wonder if she might have told him, or if one of the others have. Important lady, that. Yes, sir. Important."

"And who would she be, this important lady, Brown?"

"Well, sir. Like I said, she's an important one hereabouts. That ain't none other than the one the English call Peggy, sister to Otoo. Quite unpronounceable local name she has. Aye, the king's own sister, it is, that Mister Hamilton's takin' up with. And married, she is, to that large chap yonder." Brown pointed to tall native some twenty feet distant, who seemed quite disinterested in the tableau only a few strides away.

I studied the woman again, my new found knowledge possibly coloring my impression. She was well seasoned, plump as a ripe mango, her skin the color of coffee and milk, and even the three flower necklaces she wore did little to hide her ample bosom. Her lustrous brown hair was streaked in gray and ran to a point midway down her broad back. Knowing the custom of the men here to offer their family members for the pleasure of their guests, I suspected that Peggy had seen her share of visitors' sleeping mats. And from the way it looked, Hamilton would be her next companion. I wonder if Otoo knew, or indeed, had organized it!

Well, now maybe Mister High-and-Mighty will be less inclined to offer his ready criticism to those others of us who might have experienced the delights of these fair people! It's clearly not my business, but should he again bring up my own possible indiscretion, I will surely mention this sight!

"With child, she is, you know, sir." Brown lowered his voice to a conspiratorial whisper. "Aye, be my guess she's about six months into it by now." He sighed, then repeated, "Aye, carryin' a babe, she is. And no spring chicken, either!"

"Edward, Otoo wants to show us Bligh's cattle and gardens. Some of us ought to go; Cap'n doesn't want to offend him as we still need his help. Seen the mangy beasts my own self right before we weighed in *Bounty*. And helped plant the bloody garden! But I reckon I'll be going along as an interpreter. Brown ought to come along as well. He's better with their tongue than I am, by a long shot." Tom had detached himself from the chief and seemed to have been assigned to gather up some of the officers at Larkan's behest.

So, off we trudged, staggered, and stumbled in Otoo's wake, trying ineffectively to keep up the brisk pace he set. Jackets came off, swords were unhooked from their hangers, and stocks loosened, as the sweat poured down our bodies. I have little recollection of anything save the heat and viewing a few horrible examples of bovines, including one, a bull, with a stunted leg. Then back to the clearing for more food, drink, and, for our young gentlemen, ogling at the maidens.

The next morning dawned brilliantly clear with a delightful cooling breeze which carried along with it the fragrances of the island. Sitting in the wardroom with Robert and Sailing Master Passmore, I was eagerly anticipating my first sip from a glass of coffee that Black had just placed before me, when a Marine private appeared.

Sent by Captain Edwards, he was summoning all officers and mids to the Cabin. Hastily, I took a sip of the healing liquid, shot a look at Corner who seemed not to have heard a word; his head held in his hands, his breakfast untouched, he moved not a muscle.

"Robert, Cap'n Edwards wants us all in the Cabin. Suspect he means now, rather than when we all heal!"

Larkan popped his head in before Robert moved. "Come along, gents. Cap'n's waiting! Edward, stir your friend there. Where's Hayward? Didn't see him in your cabin."

"Aye, sir. Tom's on deck. Has the watch." I answered. Larkan didn't look much better than Robert did. I didn't try to imagine what I might look like, but from how my messmates looked, I couldn't be much better my own self!

"Am I to attend this meeting, Mister Larkan?" Passmore mumbled around a mouthful of biscuit.

"Well, George, I would suspect you are. I've no idea what he wants us for, but as the sailing master, I think it would be to your credit to at least show up."

Passmore had been ashore with us and the other warrant officers, but I had little recollection of seeing him later in the day. Perhaps an early return might explain his untroubled countenance.

I had no recollection of returning to the ship the night before nor did I recall how I might have found my cot. Did I undress myself and hang my clothes neatly on the peg, or did Black? Good old Black! Always there when I needed him! I realized my lips were still numb, but the feeling was returning to my fingers. Hopefully, a good sign.

Up a ladder to the spardeck, squinting into the glaring tropical sun, staggering (in Robert's case) aft, and down another ladder to the Cabin passageway. The Marine stationed there stood ramrod straight and hardly blinked when he saw the four of us approach. He simply reached behind him and opened the door to the cabin, nodding—a slight incline of his head—as we passed.

"Had I dropped my head that suddenly, Edward, I fear it might have come detached! Oh my! I think I might be dying!" Robert whispered as we stepped into the captain's domain. "What *was* that stuff we were drinking, anyway?"

"I think they call it *cava* and it's a favorite, according to Tom. Reckon we're not used to the kick it packs!" I whispered back, grateful for the more subdued light in here.

Tom, apparently relieved by a master's mate for the meeting, sat on the window seat under the quarter gallery. He looked little better than we did. None of the young gentlemen had yet to put in an appearance, but I wasn't sure Edwards had noticed, yet.

He sat at his desk, a sheaf of papers before him which he shuffled through, occasionally making a note on one or another with his quill. He wore no waistcoat or jacket, and his shirtsleeves were rolled to his elbows. He had not yet shaved, I noticed, as *Pandora* swung to her anchor causing the light from the quarter gallery to highlight his whiskers. And the somewhat haggard look he wore told me that he likely felt no better than any of us did!

"Where are the rest, Mister Larkan? The young gentlemen, the other warrants, our illustrious surgeon?" Edwards scowled, spoke his words quietly. He wiped the back of his hand across his mouth, as though the words left a bitter taste behind.

"I have sent the messenger for them, Cap'n. Should be along directly. As to Hamilton, I have yet to see him. Not sure he slept aboard last night, though. His quarters were empty and his cot seemed untouched."

"Hmph. Thought as much. I suppose it would be unnatural were he not to have the same cravings as his mates in the wardroom! Or perhaps he's teaching Otoo the latest technique for opening a skull! Yes, I think that must be it." Edwards' comments seemed directed at no one, merely ruminations about our good surgeon, and mostly made to himself.

I had just taken a seat between Tom and Robert, when the door opened to reveal a trio of midshipmen. A sight to behold!

Sival led the group, his hat tucked under his arm, and while he had most of his uniform on, his jacket hung open to reveal an improperly buttoned waistcoat. His trousers were a sight, appearing as though he had spent the night in them. Renouard was next, looking no better, save that he had managed to secure the front of his jacket. He wore his hat, perched on the back of his head, and visible perspiration ran down his forehead and cheeks. One stocking had fallen well below its proper place, exposing a red, bony knee below his none-too-clean white britches.

I caught his eye, and looked pointedly at his head. He raised his eyebrows at me, clearly not understanding my intent.

"Mister Renouard, you're in the cap'n's quarters; remove your hat, if you please." Larkan spoke sharply to the befuddled young man.

The midshipman snatched his hat off his head, dropped it and, when he bent to retrieve it, staggered and almost fell. The ship was motionless.

"Sorry sir. Lost my balance there for a moment." He offered, hopefully.

He quickly found a chair and, without further mishap, sat down next to Sival. And pulled up his errant stocking. Henry Pyecroft was the final of the three and was fresh-faced, properly dressed, and almost marched into the Cabin. Apparently, he had remained aboard yesterday with George Reynolds, Master's Mate, who had had the watch during the party; Reynolds also made his appearance, fresh and proper.

"And your mates, gentlemen? Where might they be?" Larkan queried.

"Mister Larkan, sir, I tried to rouse them, but failed in turning them out. I fear they are still suffering the effects of their time ashore." Pyecroft spoke clearly and loudly, causing some of us to wince.

"Larkan, I assume you'll take care of that when we're finished here. But I shan't wait any longer for laggards and sluggards.

"To get straight to the point, we still need help from those two chiefs ashore in completing our commission here. Yesterday, with Lieutenant

Hayward's aid, I struck a bargain with them to assure their assistance. We will help them with their agricultural problems, including those pathetic bovines we saw—the ones Bligh left to ensure a future supply of beef for Royal Navy ships calling here—and teach them to cultivate and manage a few vegetable and fruit plants. Obviously, their interest is less than enthusiastic, but I think Bligh had the right idea. I aim to see that we will have done what we might to provide for those who might call here after us.

"I am given to understand that a similar situation exists on Mo'orea as well, but I have neither the time nor the interest to attend to that; we shall focus our energies here.

"Hamilton has some plants—limes and oranges, I think—that he found in Rio and has been cultivating. That is why his absence is a bit troubling. We will take his plants ashore, plant them and teach the natives to grow and harvest them. Or rather, our young gentlemen will, under the direction of Mister Reynolds. Otoo made it clear to me that his people refused to eat the fruits that Bligh planted, and I hope to change that attitude before we weigh.

"At the same time, Mister Corner and Mister Hayward will sally forth in pursuit of the mutineers whose whereabouts we have yet to discover. Otoo has promised to provide men and whatever assistance you might need. And I suggest you take that new chap—what's his name . . . Brown, I think—along with you. He seems quite adept at dealing with our native friends."

I glanced at Corner. Seated behind the captain and thus, out of his line of vision, he simply rolled his eyes heavenward, and coughed delicately into his handkerchief.

It was not until the next day that two boats left *Pandora*; one, the pinnace, was carrying Robert Corner, Tom Hayward, a clutch of Marines, sailors manning the oars, and Seaman Brown. The other, our cutter, ferried the young gentlemen, two master's mates, George Reynolds and Bill Oliver, along with a small party of our sailors and several dozen plants, each of which had been painstakingly tended in a clay pot. I remained in the ship, taking watches several times per day. I also, as instructed by Captain Edwards, kept the native canoes carrying the wives and children of our captives at a distance from the ship. Edwards had hardened his heart now that he seemed to have the cooperation of the two chiefs and refused to let our prisoners walk the deck or their island relatives come aboard—or even approach too closely.

The women kept up their keening and wailing and continued to cut their heads and arms with sharp implements—shells, I assumed—as a sign of their dismay.

We had seen no sign of our single runner, Calligan, but the Master at Arms, Mister Grimwood, had done a bit of digging into the events that had occurred in the Atlantic. It was beginning to appear that Calligan was afraid of Rodgers, mainly because of Rodgers' size and pugnacious manner. In his mind, it was only a matter of time before Bully Rodgers did something to the sailor. In fairness, Rodgers did have a reputation for settling arguments with his fists, and he was good at it. One good blow from his ham-sized fist would have done a great deal of damage to the slightly-built Calligan, a fact not missed by his messmates.

After Rodgers was shot to death, Calligan, at first boasted of his good fortune, not only of being rescued, but in Rodgers death. Several weeks later, he had kept to himself, avoiding contact with any in the crew who claimed Rodgers as a friend and held Calligan responsible for his being shot, notwithstanding that the Marine had shot Rodgers on the direct order of our commander. Grimwood found me on deck one evening and had a young sailor in tow.

"Lieutenant, this is Millar, Seaman. He was one of Calligan's messmates and, from what I have gathered, one of his only friends aboard.

"A heaver he is, on deck, and this morning, told Moulter, the bosun's mate, that Calligan had told him he was going to 'take his leave' of the ship. Ain't that right, Millar? Tell Mister Ballantyne what you told Moulter."

The young seaman looked at his bare feet and fidgeted for several breaths. Then he mumbled something I didn't catch.

"Speak up, Millar. Mister Ballantyne ain't goin' to bite yer. Or clap you in irons. If what you say helps us find Calligan, there might even be an extra ration of grog in it for you." Grimwood looked at me, eyebrows raised.

"Indeed, Millar. Can't have a sailor run, now can we? Be a bad example to his shipmates, were he to be successful, eh? What was it you wanted to say?" I spoke gently, though I did notice a bit of an increase in my heart beat as I thought of catching the rascal who had run.

"Uh, sir? What I said to Moulter, sir, wasn't nothin', but that Calligan told me a few days back that he was gettin' afraid of what might happen to him. Some of Rodgers' messmates was givin' him evil looks and saying bad things to him." Millar twisted his hat into a shapeless mess as he spoke.

"Now why would Rodgers' messmates be doing that, Millar. Especially after so much time has passed since Rodgers . . . uh, died? I would have thought the threats, were there to be any, would have been right after Rodgers pitched Calligan over the side."

"Yes, sir. Well, back then, I don't know if any of 'em knew Rodgers hadn't done nothin' . . . he never stole a thing from Tim . . . uh, Calligan, I mean, sir. But a few weeks back, Calligan let it out that he had made up the whole story just to get Rodgers a few strokes of the lash. Never thought the cap'n would make him run the gauntlet. Guess he felt some bad about that. But he kept his silence, especially after Bully . . . uh, Rodgers, that is, threw him overboard. Thought Rodgers likely deserved to get hisself shot for that. I mean, *throwing someone overboard?*

"But then Calligan started to feel troubled about that . . . I guess, when he thought about it. Thought we was all mad with him on account of Rodgers getting shot. And I guess we was, but figured *he* ain't ordered him shot. So we left him alone. Then when he told Dunnet—he's in Calligan's mess—that ol' Bully . . . uh, I mean, Rodgers, sir . . . ain't stole nothin' from him, and Dunnet told some of us, Calligan got scared some of Rodgers' old mates might go after him. 'At's why he ran, sir. Afraid, he was. Told me them mutineers outta *Bounty* had done right good for theirselves here and why couldn't he. And word below is, we still ain't caught 'em all. Maybe he figures to throw in with them, if he can find 'em."

"Well, Millar. That's an interesting story. You think Calligan's trying to find the mutineers so as to elude capture? You know, we will capture the remaining mutineers and, should your friend be with them, it will go hard for him. And like as not, we'll find and punish your friend whether or not he turns up with the mutineers." I stared hard at Millar who responded by, once again, looking at his feet and twisting his hat. The sweat running down his face was prompted by more than the temperature, I thought.

"Mister Grimwood, thank you for bringing Millar to me. And, if you please, see if you can come up with any more of Calligan's mates who might have heard the same tale."

Grimwood and Millar returned forward and I returned to pacing the quarterdeck, mulling over what I had just learned.

It would be grand indeed were Robert and Tom to catch the elusive Bounties, and were I—or they—to capture our runner, it would be even grander. I suspected, given our captain's harsh manner, that if Calligan is caught, he will be hanged. And purely as an example to the rest of the crew.

But, I suppose it's right. It is *the penalty for desertion, after all. And good riddance to him, I say. Rodgers, for all his tough ways, was a good sailor. Had it not been for Calligan, Rodgers would likely still be alive.*

I shot a glance at the mutineers' schooner, bobbing happily to her anchor a pistol shot to larboard. A fine little vessel, she is, and I still had no idea what Edwards and Larkan had in store for her. Perhaps presenting the vessel to Otoo as a reward for helping Corner capture the mutineers would be nice gesture. Assuming they did, indeed, capture the scoundrels!

CHAPTER TWENTY-ONE

Otaheite

With the passage of a mere two weeks, we had—or rather Robert Corner and Tom Hayward had—captured the remaining mutineers. The other officers and midshipmen, along with dozens of our sailors, planted fruit trees, showed the islanders how to harvest and plant Indian corn, offered advice on animal husbandry, and entertained Otoo and Tamarrah, all their royal entourages, wives, concubines, and several dozen warriors in the frigate. A jolly time, indeed!

Of great amusement to most of us, we had to hoist aboard the women from the canoes, they being unable to make their way up the boarding battens. These normally lithe souls had wound so much cloth material about their mid-sections that they were barely able to move. And certainly were unable to climb the side of the ship! So Mister Cunningham, the Bosun, rigged a sling, not unlike that which we would use to hoist cattle aboard, and, with a gang of heavers manning the tackle, brought the ladies aboard amid shouts of glee and gales of laughter from their men. Also hoisted up were great numbers of coconuts, bananas, some sort of peach, and previously prepared puddings and other vittles, including at least six hogs. The foodstuffs and hogs represented a gift from Otoo to Captain Edwards. Much of it disappeared during the festivities, being consumed in great quantity by native and Englishman alike!

Captain Edwards, at the direction of the natives, unrolled the fathoms of cloth from the midsections of the ladies, in the custom of the island for one receiving a gift of cloth, and gave great mirth to them when he wrapped it about his own middle! I must say, had I not witnessed it with my own eyes, I would have been hard pressed to believe such a tale in the telling! And a slim and most attractive lady, Medua, who, it developed, was Oripai's wife, took a great fancy to the captain's laced coat. He at once, at a nod from Mister Hayward, removed it and, with great ceremony, draped it about her royal personage. I wondered briefly if Medua could have been the mysterious damsel with whom I enjoyed Oripai's hospitality, but quickly gave it up as futile, given my dim recollection of that night! And she seemed not to pay me any special attention. But she surely was greatly joyed to have received such a fine gift, and focused her considerable charms and smile on Edwards.

The party, awash with spirits both locally brewed and courtesy of the Royal Navy, went on well into the dark hours. A band, consisting of drums and long flutes, appeared before dusk and immediately struck up a series of lively tunes. The natives began to dance and were quickly joined by officer and sailor alike, all in various stages of incoherency. Some of our seamen who enjoyed a talent, real or imagined, with fiddle, pipe, and squeezebox, attempted to join in, making an ungodly racket. But no matter the comments, they pressed on to the certain chagrin of our native instrumentalists! I suspect there were also those among us who may have enjoyed some personal entertainment with the ladies of the party in any number of discrete locations about the frigate. It is quite amazing what a single iron nail would buy! But I did not, and, to my knowledge, neither did Tom. The others, I could not say. Perhaps Hamilton did.

The surgeon had returned from his spontaneous shore leave after several days, rapturous in his joy of discovering, as he put it, the "native way of life." He seemed unwilling to share any personal details of his experience, so naturally, Tom and I pressed him at every opportunity.

"I can not, for the life of me, understand you lads' interest in my social experiment ashore. It was purely of a fact-finding nature, and involved little that would be of interest to either of you." He complained one evening, a week or so after returning aboard.

"But, George, you seemed so . . . interested in *our* 'social experiments' that we were sure you would want to share your own, from a purely scientific view, of course!" I responded, using different words than the three other times I had chided the man, but with the same intent. And result.

"Aye, Edward. But you have no basis in science, being an officer of the Royal Navy. Having known you and talked with you about all manner of subjects, I know your knowledge of natural philosophy is quite as lacking as young Renouard's knowledge of the classics. So were I even to consider sharing my observations with you and your friend, it would be akin to casting pearls before swine." Hamilton smiled, sure he had put an end to our constant questioning.

"Oh, George. Not at all. Edward, here, grew up on a farm and is quite well versed in, as you put it, 'natural philosophy,' and I have experienced the way of life here in Otaheite for longer than six months, during the time *Bounty* visited. We would be most interested in your assessment of their culture." Tom countered.

"Have you no shame, Hayward? Was it not you who maintained, quite vocally, I recall, that an officer keeps such matters to himself?" The surgeon, again sure he had trumped Tom's ace, took a long draught from his glass.

"Indeed, sir. And I am . . . an officer. As is Edward. But you, sir, are not an officer of the Royal Navy. You, sir, are merely a *warrant*, and at that, warranted only by Cap'n Edwards, *not* the Admiralty! So you may, without fear of violating any code of officer-like conduct, share out your tales of indolence and excess. And you may be equally assured, that with *our* need to conduct ourselves as officers, we would never *think* of sharing them any further!" Now whose ace got trumped!

"You are, as I said, Hayward, shameless. And you too, Ballantyne for letting your junior officer proceed in such a fashion!" As George worked himself farther into his outrage, Tom and I winked and smiled at each other, adding fuel to the already brightly burning fire in Hamilton's brain.

"Does it not matter to you that I am well senior to you both in age? A modicum of respect would be warranted by that alone! I should have thought your parents might have instructed you in such niceties of behavior. And," he added in a final desperate salvo, "I would surely hope, that with your complete lack of respect for my person or my skills, that I might not ever chance across either of you in the sick bay!

"Now, surely there must be something requiring your attention on deck!" He picked up his glass, rose from the table and stepped to the sideboard for a refill.

Tom laughed. "Surely, Mister Hamilton, you don't take umbrage at our teasing. That's all we were doing, you know. Simply having you on. Your absence created a bit of a stir in the wardroom and we, that is, Edward and I, were merely having a bit of sport with you. Meant no harm, at all. And, should either of us have the misfortune to require your ministrations, I am certain you will not stint in their delivery."

We left to the surgeon's "Harrumph!"

Within a day or so of our final assault on the surgeon, Robert and Tom had returned to the ship in their boat and were accompanied by a dozen and more native vessels. Larkan led the party at the break in the bulwark which included me, George Hamilton, Mister Passmore, several midshipmen, master's mates, and, of course, Jim Grimwood, Master at Arms. Our two stalwart hunters looked surprisingly well and fit for having chased through the mountains of Otaheite for over a week.

"Oh, but John, you see, we were doing nothing of the kind!" Corner responded to the first lieutenant's query. "We spent most of our time being entertained in high fashion by King Tynah and his minions. There was no running through the jungle, up mountains, and across streams for us this time. Once was more than enough of that!

"No, sir! The king saw to it that our every need was provided while *his* men went out and brought to us the rascals late of *Bounty*. While they were not trussed up, they seemed meek as kittens, laying down their arms without a fuss when we asked them. Of course, half a dozen Royal Marines did have muskets leveled at them. But no, sir. Wasn't a hardship this time by any lights!"

"How on earth did Otoo—or Tynah, as you call him—convince them to turn themselves in?" Larkan's tone spoke for all of us.

"Oh, sir, he did not. We took care of that chore. With our Marines." Tom took over the story. "Apparently, Tynah sent several messengers into the forest, each carrying the king's mark and asking the men to come to his home. Seaman Brown, we decided should accompany them.

"As the mutineers had remained together, it was a quite simple task to deliver the message. More difficult, it seems, was finding them in the first place! They were being led by a Bosun named Morrison and one of their number, if you can believe it, is very nearly *blind*! A fiddler he is." Tom pointed behind him, into the native canoe just coming alongside. We could see several white men in the vessel as well as the one behind it. "There. The one with the yellow hair and the spectacles of colored glass. And here is their leader.

"May I present Bosun's Mate James Morrison?" Tom grabbed the tall man by one of his arms as he stepped awkwardly through the bulwark; his hands were securely tied, to his fore, but still it was difficult for him to navigate the boarding battens and man ropes.

We all looked at the mutineer. He appeared little different from the ones we had already confined. Black hair unbound to just below his shoulders, slender, and tattooed about his arms, chest, and leg. He wore no vestige of a Royal Navy uniform, rather the simple cloth about his midsection in the native fashion. He looked sullenly at his captors as Grimwood stepped up to manacle his hands.

"You, Morrison. Why did you run? Did you not think we would find you eventually. Or that trying to evade us might make it harder on you and your men when we did catch you? Your colleagues, including your former midshipmen Stewart and Heywood, have been aboard for some time now. Even they thought it only a matter of time before we discovered your whereabouts." Larkan faced Morrison, eye to eye.

"Not surprisin', it ain't." Morrison mumbled, watching as the irons were affixed to his wrists, but seemed unwilling to offer more.

Three more of the mutineers were struggling up side and soon appeared in our midst.

"Say your names, lads. Wouldn't do at all not to be acquainted!" Grimwood asked as they stood on deck, each looking little different from the other, or from the natives.

"Burkitt, sir. Thomas."

"Ellison, is mine, sir. Also Thomas."

"I am Henry Hillbrant." Though he appeared physically as the others, his accent was decidedly German.

Now the native canoe was under the battens and several strong warriors pushed up two more men.

"And you would be . . . ?" Grimwood asked.

"Muspratt, I am. William."

"I am going to guess that you would be Byrne, the blind fiddler. Would that be correct?" Larkan studied the man who had last arrived on deck. He waved a hand before the man's eyes.

"Aye. I'm Byrne. Ain't you the clever one! And I ain't so blind as to not be able to see you wavin' yer hand about me face. Just not so good with the eyes as to stand as lookout!"

I doubted that the man could actually *see* Larkan's hand; he must have either sensed it or felt the movement of the air on his skin.

"Not likely, Byrne. We have a place for you where you won't need to strain your eyes one bit." Larkan actually smiled at the man's spirit.

Another canoe drifted under the battens and a well-tanned white man, equally as tattooed as his mates and the natives, clapped onto the man ropes and, even with his hands bound before him, scampered up the side nimbly as a monkey.

"And you are?" Grimwood, finished manacling the others, asked the newcomer.

"Millward, I am. And can't say as I am happy one bit to be aboard a frigate of the Royal Navy. Thought those days were gone forever, I done." He held out his bound hands.

Larkan, counting heads, said, "Well, I reckon that's the lot of 'em. Sorry looking bunch, I'd say. Take them aft, Mister Grimwood; they can join their mates in the Box." After a beat, he called out, "Belay that for a moment Grimwood; we must tend to one last bit of business."

The master at arms stopped, as did his prisoners. All turned to face the first lieutenant.

"You men are each charged with mutiny on the high seas. Should you be convicted by the Admiralty, you will hang. That is a mandatory sentence under the Articles of War. I am sure that Cap'n Bligh read them to you many times aboard *Bounty*, so you know well what you risked."

There were nods, snarls, and *soto voce* comments, none of which I heard clearly enough to report, but, clearly, Larkan's words had given them something to think on!

"Now, Mister Grimwood, you may escort our prisoners to their quarters aft. And, if you please, see that they are well secured. It just would not do to have them foment yet another mutiny." Larkan turned to Hayward and Corner.

"Well done, gentlemen. I am sure the cap'n will be pleased when he returns to the ship."

"Thanks, awfully, sir. But I should be remiss were I not to point out that Tynah's men did much of the work. I should think some gifts would be in order for them. Tynah was quite specific in his desire for some muskets." Hayward shot a glance at Robert, seeking his accord, which he readily received with a nod.

"Hmmm." Intoned Larkan. "I'd suppose that would be for Cap'n Edwards to decide. Not sure we want to arm them with guns. They seem quite capable with their spears and slings. And muskets would surely give Tynah's men a decided advantage over his enemies. Disrupts the natural order of things, don't you know?"

Neither Tom nor Robert offered an opinion on that remark.

While the prisoners were being received and confined, more canoes had arrived and, while not coming under the boarding battens, lay to along the side and under the stern, less than a pistol shot distant. Those vessels which had assisted Corner in bringing out the mutineers drifted back to join the others in which the women had set up a dreadful, shrill wailing. Again, as they had when the first mutineers came aboard, they cut their heads and arms with sharpened shells causing great quantities of blood to pour down their bodies. No flowers in their hair, no garlands of leaves about their arms or necks, this was clearly a mourning party. The water around their canoes took on a decidedly crimson tone.

They seemed to know we would be weighing soon and believed that they would never again see their husbands, lovers, and, in some cases, the fathers of their children. Their wail was a frightful lament, heartfelt and sad. Now, with all the Bounties aboard, I was sure that the captain would be unwilling to allow any more natives into the ship. And, save for a shore party to restore our provisions and make our water, I doubted that there would be any of us returning to the island.

Hayward was standing on the poop, contemplating the array of canoes and their sorrowful burden when I approached him sometime later that day.

"Tom. You surely must have enjoyed your visit with Otoo and his family." I started off innocently. "Likely as much as I enjoyed my stay up the mountain with Oripai."

"Are you seeking to discover what may have transpired there, Edward? I assure you, beyond any mundane happenings, you will hear nothing that might titillate you . . . or the surgeon, for that matter, from my lips. Perhaps you recall our earlier conversation on the subject. And again, with Hamilton."

"You misunderstand me, Tom. I am not prying into your personal experiences with Otoo's family members. Simply interested in hearing of your other adventures. You were gone nearly a week, so there must be something to tell. You couldn't have spent *all* that time in debauchery!"

"Well, I will tell you both Corner and I spent quite some time helping Tynah's people understand the care of their new garden."

"But they've had a garden since Cap'n Cook was here. Surely they must understand how to grow crops!" I was surprised at Tom's revelation.

"You see, Edward, their soil is so fertile that they find it unnecessary to tend their crops—crops that others, like Cook, Bligh, and now, we—have planted for them. They simply reap their harvest and if it doesn't grow back, so be it. They simply do without. You saw their cattle. My goodness! The poor beasts had no one looking after them. That bull with the stunted leg? He broke it, I am told, falling into a pit. They could not even be bothered to try to fix it. Just hauled the poor thing out and turned it loose. They were about to butcher it that day when we went to see them. Corner talked them out of it, saying the animal is perfectly capable of standing at stud and if allowed, will populate their remaining herd.

"I did learn, quite by accident, that, not realizing the difference between a horse and a cow, they first killed and tried to eat a horse—one of Cook's gifts. Hated it, they said. Stringy, tough, and not flavorful at bit! As a result, they did not try to eat the beefs they had, but simply let them wander and die as they would. I recall Bligh left them a half dozen at the least,

273

and only three remain! Why they were going to butcher the lame bull is quite beyond my ken, but apparently that was their intent."

"Seems a trifle strange to me, as well, Tom. Maybe on account of it being lame? Or perhaps they thought they might trade it to us, expecting us to be leaving shortly upon catching the remainder of the mutineers." I offered.

"Could be, Edward. But it is in our best interest—and the best interest of any other ships of the Royal Navy which might call here—for them to continue to breed the beasts. Provides a welcome supply of beef for 'em. A damn sight more pleasant than a steady diet of pig! That was Bligh's original intent." Tom stopped, as a sudden increase in the wailing caused us both to study the canoes for the cause.

"Cap'n's coming back. Ought to let whoever has the watch know, in case they haven't noticed yet." I observed, and Tom set off forward to carry out my suggestion.

As his jolly boat passed through the fleet of native vessels, the wail and cry continued to increase. Women, earlier tiring of the effort and, perhaps, becoming less enthusiastic about ripping their scalps with shells, renewed their efforts with even greater intensity. Again, blood flowed down their faces and necks, arms, and torsos, coloring the water around their canoes. Edwards, his face stoically fixed, kept his eyes on the ship and paid the keening natives scant attention.

By the time the boat had reached the battens, Larkan and the watch officer, George Passmore, were standing at the break. Curious as to what had held the captain's attention ashore, I drifted in their direction. Corner, having hauled his bulk up from below, stepped into the group just as Edwards' feet touched the deck.

"Welcome back, Cap'n. I trust your trip was fruitful?" Larkan doffed his hat as the bosun's pipe shrilled.

"It was. Indeed. I will have all officers, midshipmen, warrants, and the master's mates in the cabin directly, if you please, Mister Larkan. No need for full uniforms, just as they are, assuming they're presentable!"

Passmore's messenger scurried off to collect the requested parties as the captain and first lieutenant walked briskly aft, deep in conversation.

The captain began without preamble, immediately we had all assembled. "Gentlemen, we will be weighing in two days. Part of my purpose ashore was to negotiate with Chief Otoo for provisions. I feel that I have struck an equitable arrangement and you may expect native canoes alongside by the morrow." Edwards stopped, his eyes casting about for the form of Mister Bentham, our purser.

"Bentham, make arrangements for storage, if you please. Use whatever men you deem necessary. I expect some livestock in the bargain.

"We will be providing the locals with red cloth, iron implements, and those four geese. Yes, those most annoying of pests. I assured Otoo they were good layers and would provide a ready supply of eggs for his people. Please see that those items are made ready, as well."

The captain paused. After a quick look around his Cabin, he faced Mister Larkan. "Where is the sailing master?"

"Sir, Passmore has the watch. He is on deck."

"I was under the impression I requested *all* officers to this meeting." His eyes narrowed as he studied the first lieutenant.

"Marine!" He shouted at the closed door.

In less than a heartbeat, the door flew open and a red coated Marine sentry barged in, musket at the ready.

"No need for that, Marine. There is no trouble. I need Mister Passmore. Here, in the Cabin. Now."

The sentry's salute was crisp and smart, though hasty. And he was gone as quickly as he had arrived. We could hear him clattering up the ladder and calling for the sailing master, urgency ringing in his voice.

"Mister Passmore." Edwards began at once the man had stepped into the room. "I will have a survey of the Bay, the reef, and the entrances, if you please. And it will be done inside of two days." Edwards paid no attention to the shocked look on Passmore's face as he digested the order.

"Here is Cook's survey. It will give you something to start with. See to it." The captain handed the still surprised sailing master, the one man best qualified to provide the requested survey, a folded and well-worn sheet of heavy paper.

"Aye, sir. Straight away, sir."

"For the rest of you, in order for us to be ready to depart as I stated, you will all be required to bear a hand. I will tolerate no slacking and, it goes without saying, there will be no more shore leave. And Mister Larkan, do something about that infernal racket. I have had a sufficiency of it.

"Dismissed."

We left, not a sound save the shuffle of feet on the deck, and quickly mounted the ladder to the weather deck.

"I must get shore, Edward. Leaving in two days! My God! What is the man thinking! We shan't be close to ready. Provisions to take aboard, trade goods to break out, Passmore's survey, a myriad of tasks and no time. But I must get myself ashore!" Tom's concern was palpable.

"And telling Larkan to make the women cease their lament! Quite impossible, I'd say. That's their way of grieving. Won't stop 'til we're hull-down. Won't make a bit of difference to them what Larkan wants, or Edwards, for that matter. They're going to continue and it will increase as we get closer to sailing. I wonder, has the cap'n told Tynah when we are to weigh?" Tom paced up and down in the waist, shifting his glance from the canoes laying off the quarter, to the shoreline, to me.

"Well, as he has struck a bargain with Otoo for provisions, I would imagine he has told him. Else, Tynah might take his own sweet time to deliver them." It struck me odd that Tom couldn't have gathered that himself, but I wrote it off to his obvious distraction.

In the wardroom later, Larkan held forth on the slovenly appearance of our crew and their lackadaisical attitude.

"Disrespect, it is, and nothing else. You gentlemen will see to straightening them out. I will not have a crew of a similar stripe to the one we had out of Portsmouth. We have many months of sailing before we get home again, and I will tolerate no slackers!

"Mister Hamilton. What is the condition of their health? I have heard talk of the French Pox running through the berth deck. Any truth to it?"

Hamilton looked up from whatever it was he had been studying so intently. "Yes, John. There is some evidence of the pox. Mister Innes has mentioned it to me on several occasions in the past several weeks. This lush paradise of plenty boasts a bounty of everything: all manner of food-stuffs, clear waters, ample fish, and, of course, lovely people and willing women. And it would appear that some of those 'willing women' suffer from what they call the "British Disease"—a form of the French Pox. They call it that as they have only had contact with British ships, hence they assume its origins to be English. I maintain it is not, but I have no earthly idea of its source. Suffice it to say they have it and now, according to Innes, there are more than two dozen of our crew that he has treated. I have heard no complaints from the officers or midshipmen." He looked pointedly at Tom, me, and Robert as he commented dryly on the health of the ship's company.

Tom blushed scarlet, Corner just smiled, and I became enraged.

"Perhaps, Mister Hamilton, the reason you have heard no complaints from the wardroom or cockpit, is the lack of intimate contact between those individuals and the local populace. I, for one, resent such an implication that impugns my moral turpitude." I stormed at him. The surgeon simply looked at me and smiled.

"Well, George. Should it appear, I am quite certain you will treat any afflicted with your usual efficiency and skill. And Mister Ballantyne, you needn't take offense at the surgeon's remark; I am sure he was not referring to you, specifically!" Larkan spoke calmly, an obvious effort to head off further discord in the wardroom.

Hamilton was not ready to leave it alone. He waited patiently until the first lieutenant had finished trying to smooth my ruffled feathers, then looked directly at me with a quite smug expression.

"Did you not spend the night on the mountain with Oripai and that delightful young woman, Edward? Seems to me I recall our newest recruit recounting in some vivid detail your escapades while there. Perhaps you were simply lucky." He shrugged and shifted his gaze.

"And Hayward, you have spent many nights ashore and I would doubt your virtue remained intact. After all, you spent some six months here with Bligh. Surely you must have had old friends to reacquaint yourself with!"

"And what about you, Mister Hamilton? We all watched as you swooned over that plump and, I might add, pregnant, sister to Tynah. Surely you can't hold your own self up as a model of virtue and chastity!" Tom bridled at the surgeon's slight.

"All right, gentlemen. That will do. I have heard quite enough on this subject and we will consider it closed.

"Doctor, should any cases of the pox appear beyond those you have mentioned, I will expect to be informed." Larkan had a hard edge to his voice.

We went off the subject of carnality and disease and on to stowing the ship, provisioning, and making our water. Much to do in a scant two days!

"Mister Larkan. I would be pleased to take the watering party ashore should you wish it. I know of several places where we can refill our water butts with fine water of sufficient purity." Hayward volunteered.

I recalled his comment earlier about *having* to get back ashore and assumed there was a young lady to whom he intended to offer a proper farewell.

"Sir," I had a thought. "What are we to do about Calligan? The seaman who ran? I know his name has already been marked in the Articles with an 'R', but should not we have another go at finding him?"

"Well, Edward, a fine thought, that. Were we to catch the rascal, his hanging might serve as a perfect lesson to any others considering the same thing! But, sadly, we haven't the luxury of time to go chasing off into the wilds looking for one man. It would be akin to seeking a needle in a haystack! And we will require every man-Jack aboard to prepare for getting under weigh. Calligan will simply have to fend for himself and, were one to judge by the joy of Otoo and his people at our relieving them of the Bounties, I might suspect that Calligan might not find such a welcoming reception as he would wish!"

For whatever the reason, our illustrious surgeon did not take the evening meal with us in the wardroom. His absence, an unusual occurrence, save for the several days he spent ashore, drew some comment—lewd, skeptical, and not in the least complimentary—but, at least for Tom and me, it was quite pleasant not having to constantly be defending ourselves. Larkan mentioned, in an offhand way, something about Hamilton collecting some specimens ashore and seeing a couple of locals he had been treating. This, of course, drew another round of ribald and derisive remarks.

Tom did take the watering party ashore, accompanied by Midshipman Renouard and two dozen seamen. And shortly after he left the side of the ship, a veritable fleet of canoes pushed off and made for our side. As they came under the boarding battens, we could see they were loaded with all manner of fruits, produce of an amazing variety, even some livestock, and, of course, coconuts; hundreds of them. Cunningham's men rigged hoists from the mainyard and swung Otoo's gifts aboard faster than the human chain, commanded by the purser, Gregory Bentham, could strike them below. A dozen hogs, squealing in terror, were hoisted in and penned on the weather deck along with some ten goats of both genders, several dozen chickens and other fowls, and a horse, which Bentham graciously declined.

The local women had resumed their lament, seemingly with a bit less enthusiasm than they had shown earlier. And from time to time, a voice would call out from the prison—*Pandora's* Box, as it was now universally known—and the women's wails would swell in response, only to die off again in minutes.

The watering party returned, casks and barrels full and floating behind the boat to be hoisted aboard, and our surgeon returned in a native vessel, loaded down with an enormous variety of plant life, each carefully potted in what appeared to be the same pots as he had grown his plants in from Rio. At the end of this frenzied activity, the royal canoe approached, carrying Otoo and a noticeably smaller retinue than before.

He climbed up the battens alone and greeted Larkan at the bulwark. Looking around, he uttered something in the local dialect which neither Larkan nor the sentry could make sense of. Seeing me loitering nearby, the first lieutenant called out, "Mister Ballantyne. Find Seaman Brown, if you please, and bring him here. We need an interpreter."

Otoo repeated his words to Brown. "Sir. It appears that King Tynah has a final gift for you. Aye, it's a gift he's brought out. It's just down in the boat, if you please, sir."

I could see a package wrapped in matting, held by one of the king's warriors. As it was passed up, we all watched in great curiosity. Our captain chose that moment to arrive and he nodded politely to Otoo, who immediately began speaking quickly. Brown listened carefully.

"Cap'n, Mister Larkan, sir. He says this package belongs to us. It's rightly ours, aye. Something we'll want . . . and he doesn't. Says it don't belong in his island . . . or rather, sir, his *district*. Aye, that's what he says, 'his district.'" Brown nodded at Otoo and the package appeared, to be handed to Edwards.

The matting had come open, revealing a ghastly sight: a head. Clearly, a human head. And, it appeared, not native.

Gasps from all, save, of course, Otoo and his men. Edwards, as he unwrapped the rest of it, shuddered, gasped again, and dropped it. The head, clearly that of a white man with a sailor's queue, rolled across the deck, a macabre sight. Two or three sailors jumped back as it rolled toward them. One cried out. And then another.

"My God! That's Calligan! What . . . how . . . ."

"Serves him right, it does! Reckon he wasn't as welcome as he thought he'd be. Har Har!"

"Looks like ol' Calligan lost 'is 'ead yonder! Pity!"

"I think some explanation might be in order, here." Edwards had recovered his composure and spoke to Brown.

"Aye, sir." Brown spoke quietly to the king, his voice serious. I suspected Brown knew what Otoo's response would be before he heard it.

"Sir, King Tynah says that man is one of ours and had . . . uh . . . imposed himself on a woman in Tynah's district. Turns out, sir, the woman was Tynah's daughter and taboo. These people have more taboos than you might shake a stick at! Aye, they do that! Seems there's taboos about all manner of things."

"Ahem." Larkan cleared his throat and gave Brown a displeased look. "Get on with it, then, Brown."

"Aye, sir. That taboo on Tynah's daughter means, sir, in their parlance, 'hands off' or suffer the punishment. And the king's own daughter. Oh my! Just askin' fer it, sir, were you to ask me. Aye. Seen more 'an my share of these kind of things hereabouts. Mostly was locals, though. Aye, locals. And right tough on 'em they was."

"Brown! Get on with it!"

"Oh, aye, sir. Reckon yer man, there, didn't believe it—or maybe it was on account of he didn't speak the lingo. Hard to learn it is, and I should know; took me most half a year to learn to talk native."

"Yes, Brown, we know of your ability with the language. That's why you're here!" Larkan was past frustrated with Brown's rambling tale, but simply rolled his eyes at the interruption.

"Aye, sir. Anyway, seems as though your chap here," he pointed to the head still laying on the deck some feet away, "gave offense to the king. A very bad thing to do in these parts. Yes, sir. A very bad thing, indeed." Before Larkan could prod him forward again, Brown went on.

"So Tynah took care of the matter in his own way. He had him beheaded and the corpse burned to a crisp, he done, sir. Aye, burned him to a crisp! Brought you the head on account of he didn't want it buried in his district. They sometimes throw 'em into the sea, they do, but he figured, as how this was our man, you'd want it."

Larkan and Edwards' eyes went from horrified to hard and back to horrified in the telling of the tale. Larkan recovered first.

"And what, exactly, does he expect us to do with it?"

"Oh sir. I don't reckon he cares a whit!" Brown said.

"I'll tell you what we'll do with it." Edwards said. "We shall make certain that all hands are aware of this happening and point out that this is what will fall to any who care not to sail with us. I'd warrant there are a few aboard considering just that. Should act to prevent any desertion, I'd imagine.

"Mister Larkan, we'll muster our people if you please. Brown, thank Otoo, and inform him we will manage this now. You are all dismissed." With that, the captain nodded politely to the chief and walked aft. The crew—officers, warrants, mids and master's mates—was called to assemble on the spardeck.

"You men knew that one of your number, Seaman Calligan, deserted some weeks back. While we sent a party ashore to seek him, the search was unsuccessful. Calligan had, it appeared, eluded us.

"But he did not elude the local district chief who took umbrage at his presence among his people. The king has told me he will not give succor to any Englishmen who hold the desire to take up a life here in Otaheite now that he has rid himself of the Bounties." Edwards turned for a moment and pointed aft, at the Box on the poopdeck.

Then he continued. "You have all heard me read the Articles of War in this ship and some of you have heard them many times over the years you have sailed in the Royal Navy. You are well aware of the punishment for desertion, should you be caught. Had we managed to bring Calligan to justice, his fate would have been little different that what he actually suffered. But it might have been less painful."

There was, among the men, some muttered comments, rumblings that were undistinguishable from where we officers stood. Edwards ignored them and nodded at the Master at Arms. Then he stepped back from the quarterdeck railing. Each of the officers also stepped back to give him room. Grimwood, seeing the captain's nod, bent and retrieved a boarding pike from where it had lain at his feet. He raised it above his head.

To a man, every sailor followed the motion and looked at the end of the pike, now held aloft some six feet above their heads. Those in the rear ranks had to crane their necks initially to see, but once it was extended fully, they all could see quite clearly. Some gasped, some shook their heads, and some began to gag. On the end of it was Calligan's severed head, his queue moving slightly in the easy breeze that had cooled us every day. More rumblings from the sailors greeted the display.

"This, then, is what happened to your shipmate. And I learned from the king that his body, following the separation of his head, was burned to ashes. Of course, by then, he was quite dead and felt nothing." Edwards added dryly.

"We will be sailing on the morrow now that we have made our water and, through the generosity of King Otoo, our provisions. There will be no further shore leave.

"Our mission is only half completed; we have yet to find the remaining mutineers and *Bounty*. You, regardless of how you may feel at this moment, are still in the employ of the Royal Navy and will conduct yourselves as such. I will tolerate no slacking, skylarking, or slovenliness. That will apply to all hands." The captain paused for a moment to look about the assembled crew—petty officers to the fore, seamen behind them—and then, turning, he met the eyes of each of the officers and warrants lining the quarterdeck behind him.

"Mister Larkan, after you have read the Articles to them, you may dismiss them. Oh—and get rid of that *thing*." As the captain turned to walk aft, the ranks of officers, warrants, and midshipman parted before him, as if by divine order.

CHAPTER TWENTY-TWO

In Pandora*: 169° 15' E, 10° 18' S*

"I truly doubt we'll ever find *Bounty* or Fletcher Christian. We might search for a year and more and never see hide nor hair of those rascals. Simply too many islands for them to hide in." Larkan had become exasperated with the seemingly mindless ramblings of *Pandora*. "In the six weeks since we sailed from Otaheite, we've not even caught a sniff of them, save for the spars we found in the Palmerston's Islands. And it could even be a fool's errand; they might already be dead, killed by savages who were a bit cool to their making a home on some remote island.

"And already it's cost us the cutter, four seamen, and young Sival. Pity about him; might have made a fine officer one day."

Larkan's comment was greeted with a round of "Aye's." We all agreed that the men in the jolly boat, sent shoreward at Palmerston's, must have experienced an ugly and, most likely, painful death at the hands of the warlike natives of that group of islands.

"You know, I truly thought we had 'em—the remaining Bounties, that is—when we found those spars. Clearly belonged to the ship, marked with both '*Bounty*' and the broad arrow. So what happened to the bloody ship? And where did those scoundrels get off to? Too many questions to answer that we can't. Actually makes my head hurt, just trying to figure the answers!" Corner squeezed the bridge of his nose between his thumb and forefinger, as if his confusion over the myriad facts and unanswerable questions did, indeed, give him pain.

"Aye, Robert. And too bad it was that the surf was so high we couldn't even get the schooner in close. Would have helped to have some extra hands when we did get ashore. I thought for certain Sival would have made it to shore, but when the weather turned nasty so bloody quick, who's to know if he made it or not. It is possible, you know, they were not killed by natives; they might have simply drowned trying to get through that surf." Hayward offered.

I reflected on the events of the past several weeks as the conversation swirled about me, each offering a different opinion of where the Bounties might be or what had happened to the cutter and its occupants. My own thoughts swirled in an opposite direction; all of the events of the cruise and, more importantly, the past weeks.

We had left Otaheite in a blur of wailing women, tearful natives, and dispirited sailors. Edwards had ordered a salute fired as a farewell to Otoo and his people, but the gun crews were out of training and what should have been a smart and impressive volley from our six-pounders was instead, a ragged, amateurish display unworthy of a British man of war. The captain was incensed, justifiably, and a round of floggings followed the inept gunnery, adding further to the misery of all hands, especially those four gun captains responsible for the failures of their crews.

A fine start to the remaining portion of our commission! Hope it doesn't turn out to be a harbinger of things to come! I thought, as I stood the middle watch that first night back at sea. The stars filled the skies, bright in the muted light of a quarter moon just rising from the eastern horizon. An easy sea, driven by a fine tops'l breeze, gave *Pandora* a most comfortable, gentle motion. *But it's surely good to be at sea again. It's where we belong!*

I missed my midshipman, Renouard. He had come along nicely with his studies and his attitude and, as a reward, Larkan had appointed him first lieutenant under Master's Mate William Oliver in the mutineers' schooner, which Edwards had rechristened *Matavia*, in recognition of her origins. I still felt some sense of ownership in her, though, of course, in reality, I had none at all. A smart little ship, she was!

I well recalled how thrilled Renouard had been when Larkan told him the news. Thinking about him that first night out, I remember that I turned to leeward and could easily see the little ship scudding along under my lee, her new canvas sails a ghostly white in the starshine. Renouard had earned his position aboard and I hoped he was doing well. Of course, they had only been at it for a bit less than a full day, so I suspected he still reveled in the novelty of his success and likely was still as nervous over the assignment as he had been when Larkan appointed him. The schooner's role as our tender would add some small measure of esteem to our lonely meanderings through the islands in the South Pacific, at least in Captain Edwards' eyes. Generally, only first and second rate ships were entitled to a tender and here he was, commanding a *sixth* rate, accompanied by a smart little schooner as her tender.

Short stops in Mo'orea and Huahine, one close by Otaheite and the second some distance farther had produced no sign of our quarry, but

did result in additional gifts of fruits and livestock from the local populace, some friends of Otoo and some of Tamarrah. Edwards granted shore
leave to none, but did let the locals come aboard. Cries from the prisoners confined in the Box, their complaints of the heat and discomfort
softened him not a whit and they all, fourteen of them, remained ironed
and locked within the wooden walls. The scuttle in the top of the Box
remained closed and locked, but at least the two ports in the sides where
open, allowing a breath of air to circulate within, were we on the right
tack. Hamilton had complained bitterly to us in the officers' mess about
the inhuman treatment and felt sure none would live to see a court-martial in England unless they were allowed too take the air and get a bit of
exercise. I must say, it seemed to me that his surmise was spot on.

Our wanderings had taken us to a variety of islands, each a possible
haven for the remaining mutineers. At each one, we sent the schooner
Matavia in, armed with a pair of swivels and a clutch of Marines, to have
a look, while *Pandora* made a circuit of the island. Until Robert had spotted the marked spars floating in a lagoon, we had found naught save for
several groups of decidedly hostile natives and several more who, while
not exactly hostile, were surely not welcoming.

At Palmerston's Island, some three weeks following our departure from
the Society Islands, Corner had sailed with Oliver and Renouard, in the
schooner, into the beach. I watched their progress as they found the opening in the surrounding reef and cruised serenely through the lagoon's
placid turquoise waters. I could see some activity forward in the vessel and
picked up a glass to get a better look. One of the men was priming the
swivel gun mounted in the bow. As I watched, it fired. I looked about for
the fall of shot and saw nothing.

Oh dear, I thought, *another hostile reception! I do hope they can defend
themselves as we could never get the frigate into the lagoon, even if there were
sufficient water, in time to help them.*

But I was mistaken; I saw no fall of shot because they had fired the
gun as a signal. Quickly, a series of flags appeared on the foremast and I
needed no code book to decipher that Robert and his men had discovered
something of interest. Sival was assigned to take the jolly boat in and find
out what. At the same time, *Matavia* continued to follow the shoreline in
the calm waters of the lagoon, which I could see plainly, went some long
distance, perhaps all the way 'round the island.

It was several hours later when the midshipman returned aboard and
reported finding the spars, each marked with *Bounty* and the broad arrow
mark of the Royal Navy. He had landed his crew and marched some distance

inland, encountering nothing but jungle. He saw nary a sign of human habitation.

After conferring with Captain Edwards, Larkan sent him and the jolly boat back with the instructions to explore farther afield. If the spars were there, surely *Bounty* and the mutineers must be. How else could have the spars have been drifting in the lagoon?

No sooner had the boat left our side—*Matavia* was now well out of sight, having turned a headland—than the weather took a rather sudden turn for the worse. The seas began to grow, threatening to overpower the boat, and the wind blew fresh. Sival had obviously ordered boat's sail struck, thinking oars to be more manageable and safer. The clouds thickened, and promptly dumped a blinding rain on us. We lost sight of the jolly boat and its crew just as it breached the opening in the reef.

Because of the weather that had sprung up, Corner, unable to safely navigate the opening in the reef, did not return to *Pandora* until the following dawn. He reported that he had discovered little, beyond the spars, of any interest, and that he had seen nothing of the jolly boat nor any of its occupants. He was, indeed, most surprised that it had gone missing. An additional boat, our cutter, under the command of Master's Mate Thomas Rickard, was launched and, together with the schooner returned to the island in the now-moderating weather. Each went in a different direction around the island, hopeful of finding the jolly boat, Bounty, or the mutineers. Or all of them! Again, Robert spent an unexpected night ashore, as did Rickards and the cutter crew. I recalled clearly Robert's tale of the night ashore, searching for our men and the mutineers.

"Hot wasn't for it, Edward." He had said, shaking his head at the memory. "Beastly it was and the air thick with insects of every imaginable stripe. Must have been brought out by the rain we had. Voracious, not a bit selective in their choices, and obviously delighted to have fresh human meat to dine on! Had they appeared a trifle more appetizing, we would have happily dined on *them*! Not a scrap of provisions had we in the schooner and by ten o'clock that night, we were all some sharpset, I can assure you! Fortunately, our lad Renouard and one of his sailors found a clutch of enormous cockles at the tide line. Each one took two men to carry it from the sea. Boiled them up into a disgusting burgoo, but it filled the belly." He laughed and patted his ample girth. "Got to keep my strength up, you know!"

"But what of the men—Sival and the others—and their boat? Were you able to find no trace at all? Nothing that might tell us what happened to them? I can not conceive that they simply vanished! Did you meet up with Rickards and his crew?" I asked yet again.

"As I have mentioned several times, Edward, we had found nary a hint of Sival, and Rickards went 'round the other side of the island. I suppose it is possible we ended up camping within a musket shot of each other, but we never made any contact with them until we returned to the frigate." His patience at my frequent interruptions was wearing a bit thin. But he pressed on. "We had managed to collect some coconuts and their milk was as savory as it had been on Otaheite.

"Of course, it was not good claret or even decent Jamaica, but it was surely better than sea water and we made do. We set a watch and I ordered the rest of them to sleep. And fell into a bit of a doze my own self!

"Now, Edward, as you recall, the ship had been firing signal shots throughout the latter part of the day and into the evening. We were quite used to hearing them, knew they were for Sival and his mates, not us, and became somewhat casual about them. You might imagine our shock, not to mention our dismay, when a resounding shot was fired right in our midst and in the middle of the night! We all, to a man, leaped to our feet and grabbed up our muskets, cutlasses and whatever else might answer as a weapon. We were sure we were being attacked, but had no clue as to by whom. The man on watch had seen or heard nothing until the shot was fired close aboard. We ran about, helter-skelter, seeking our adversary until Johnson, the Marine, shouted out that he had found the 'enemy."

I simply looked at my friend, having been only half listening to his tale. He took a large gulp from his wine glass and followed it with a forkful of fresh fruit duff. He raised his eyebrows at me.

"Are you not a little curious as to who the enemy turned out to be, Edward?" He asked through the mouthful of duff. His disappointment in my lack of interest was clear.

"Oh, aye, Robert. Sorry. Of course. Just wondering about poor Sival and whether he was savaged by some natives or simply drowned and was carried out to sea."

"Well, we saw no natives, should that put your mind to some ease. But to get back to my tale, when we all rushed back to the camp, we found Johnson standing by the fire holding the charred remains of a coconut. One of the men had thrown it on the fire before we went to sleep and, when the milk within boiled, it made the nut explode with a sound like a shot! We all laughed heartily, relieved beyond measure that it was simply a coconut, and went back to sleep.

"Now isn't that a tale worth the time?" Robert, his story done, dug with renewed vigor into his duff.

I returned to my reverie, taking the occasional sip from my wine, but leaving the wonderful duff untouched.

We had sailed round the island bearing Palmerston's name for two days, intermittently firing a gun, but found not a trace of the jolly boat or Sival and his crew. *Matavia*, carrying its regular crew plus, from time to time either Robert, me, or Tom Hayward, also had searched, sticking her bow into little coves and inlets in the vain hope of discovering some sign, some indication, that our men had been here. Nothing.

After three days, Captain Edwards had given up the search. He directed Oliver to take the tender to the beach and leave a message for Sival, which he did. And then we sailed on, the tender, freshly provisioned with food-stuffs and powder and shot, keeping pace, all of us sure that Sival would never read the note his former messmate had left for him.

Over the course of the next week or two, we discovered several islands that were not shown on any of our charts—Edwards named one "Duke of York" and the other "Duke of Clarence" Island. The former showed signs of habitation, but we caught no glimpse of any human beings. George Hamilton postulated that the people used the islands only for fishing dur-ing certain seasons and did not live there regularly. We had seen nets hung in the trees and huts, empty save for a few utensils, just on the shoreline. A ship's wooden anchor buoy gave us a short-lived hope of discovering some sign of *Bounty*, but, of course, we found nothing. Farther inland, we discovered a *morai*, or open-air temple, lending further credence to the fact that someone surely used the island. On the Duke of Clarence Island, we did see natives, rowing their canoes across the lagoon. The ship fired a signal to call the tender alongside and, with Tom in the cutter and me in the schooner, we went cautiously into the lagoon. The ship's guns covered our approach, the water being sufficiently deep as to allow a close proximity.

We made signs of peace to the natives, but either from a lack of curios-ity or a surfeit of fear, they refused to close with us, preferring to run in the opposite direction. With nothing of note to see, we re-boarded *Pandora* and continued our restless wanderings, hopeful of at least finding more signs of our quarries.

Any number of islands passed under our lee, each stirring fresh hope of success. Edwards and Larkan became increasingly testy and the men responded in kind. Tensions ran high in the wardroom, fueled by our frustration, the loss of our shipmates, and Hamilton's constant harping on the condition of the prisoners, sweltering in the close confines of the Box.

On still days, we could actually see their sweat running from the scuppers cut into the corners of the jail, and the stench drifting from the open ventilation ports was enough to turn one's stomach; body waste, unstaunched sweat, and moldering food. The man named Morrison, the bosun's mate late of *Bounty*, frequently called out for consideration, but none was, nor would be, forthcoming. In private conversation, Hayward, whose former shipmates they were, confided that he wished the captain would at least let the men have some time on deck, if for no other reason than to hose themselves down and relieve some of their misery—and ours. Hamilton, of course, had espoused a similar wish, adding to it the need for some exercise. He often stated that "we should lose the whole lot of them before we ever see England."

The men did receive the same rations as our crew, except, of course, for the grog ration, even though the Admiralty only required that, as prisoners, they be given two-thirds rations. They were given some canvas from which they might make more comfortable their surroundings, but the canvas itself was infested with vermin, making it unusable.

We ticked off the days on the calendar, watch after watch, each day blending into yet another of blazing sun, easy or light breezes, islands popping up on the horizon to be searched without success, and tempers both in the wardroom and fo'c'sle becoming as hot as the days.

Knife fights, half-hearted to be sure, fisticuffs, and insubordination to the officers and midshipmen seemed to be the order of the day. Mustering the crew to witness punishment seemed almost a daily occurrence. Even Edwards seemed a bit more testy than usual. Toward the middle of July, we suffered another blow to our well-being.

We had discovered yet another island, this one clearly inhabited, and called by the residents, Otutuelah. It was some forty miles in length, well wooded with trees that spread large, leafy canopies not unlike the large oaks of England. None of the natives wear any clothes, preferring instead, a leafy girdle about their waists. The women wear flowers in their hair similar to the women we knew in Otaheite.

Hoping for information about *Bounty*, the captain invited a group aboard. They all, men and women alike, trembled in fear when they arrived on our deck. They had never seen a European ship nor any firearms and immediately assumed positions of submission. When they realized we meant them no harm, they became most inquisitive and eager to trade all manner of foodstuffs for bits of iron, knives, and looking glasses.

Unlike their cousins in Otaheite, they had little interest in red cloth. In exchange, they gave us huge quantities of foods, live fowls, and local curiosities. Worthy of note was a pudding they had made that was rife with aromatic spices and quite delicious.

Due to the remaining "gifts" some of the men still carried from our stay in Otaheite, Edwards had given orders that none of the women would be permitted below decks, thus ensuring that those in less than perfect health would continue to mend.

The native men, on the other hand, roamed at will, helping themselves to all manner of personal possessions. Hayward had a uniform coat taken from our cabin and Robert discovered a fighting knife he had procured in Otaheite was missing. Iron nails, loose fittings, and the head of a rammer seemed magically to grow feet and walk off the ship.

It had only been a few hours, during the time the locals were visiting, before the weather took a turn for the worse and came on to blow. Edwards gave the order to win our anchor and get the ship under weigh as we now faced a lee shore. Most of the natives were completely unaware of the change in our status until we had made a mile and more into the offing. With excited chatter befitting their alarm, they leaped over the side *en masse* and swam to their, now distant, canoes.

As the weather continued to worsen, we lost sight of our tender, *Matavia*, which had lagged us a bit getting to sea. We set false fires, fired off the great guns, and had our Marines fire volley after volley of musket fire to attract the attention of Master's Mate Oliver and his crew. None of our efforts paid off and, as the weather continued the blow thick as the darkness settled, we lost hope of finding the schooner before the dawn.

The next morning arrived with little improvement in the weather, but we cruised around the island, searching and firing guns with no success. As we had stores for *Matavia* on our weather deck, preparatory to replenishing their supplies, we knew that the provisions they had on board would last no time at all, but Larkan had given Oliver instructions that, should they become separated from *Pandora*, they were to sail to nearby Anamooka and wait for us to rendezvous with them.

"At least they have some trading goods and weapons aboard." Tom mentioned as we lamented the fate of yet another of our boats and its crew.

"Aye, and a seven barreled piece or two that will serve them well, should they get caught up in an unfriendly situation. Was her boarding net still rigged?" Corner asked.

"It was when they were alongside. Hopefully, Oliver and Renouard have the sense to leave it rigged. It would not take a large force to get aboard and overpower them." Larkan said, a bit morosely. "But perhaps we shall discover their whereabouts shortly, or at the rendezvous in Anamooka." He added on a brighter note.

Poor Renouard, I thought. *He studied his lessons, took out the slack, and was rewarded with a position of responsibility in the tender. Now he's lost—or worse—and likely wondering what possessed him to accept the employment! I know I would be! Hopefully, should his lot be unfortunate, it will be quick.*

We were swinging to our best bower in Anamooka four days after our last sight of *Matavia*. The anchorage was devoid of any craft, save native canoes which approached us even before the anchor was set. Larkan, with Hayward translating, negotiated to hire a large sailing canoe in which he sent me and a Marine, along with four sailors, to neighboring islands. We were to inquire as to the mutineers, *Bounty*, and our tender. Captain Cook had named these the Friendly Islands and, though we felt little threatened by the natives, saw to arming ourselves well, before sailing off.

Here I am! Sailing off from Pandora *just like poor Renouard and Oliver did. Except I'm in a native canoe with no idea where they might be taking us, should they wish us malice.*

I stroked my pistols, hoping for some comfort from the smooth texture of the wood and steel. Each of the sailors carried cutlasses and our Marine private, a musket and a blunderbuss.

Well, I ruminated philosophically, *should they attempt to do us evil, we are well enough armed to prevent it.* I hope!

Two days it took for our visits to the other islands in the chain; it was a complete waste of effort as we gained no intelligence of any use whatever in our quest. And no sign of hostility from our native escorts. I reported back to Larkan dejected and frustrated.

"Bloody too bad about your little cruise, Edward. You would have enjoyed more, I think, being ashore with us. Well-civilized these folks are." Robert mentioned casually that evening at supper.

"Oh? I couldn't comment on the islands I visited. Never left the beach. And that only if we landed. In several, the locals came to us on the water and we never set a foot on the shore." I reckon I was still feeling a bit sorry for myself and my failed mission.

"Indeed! I say! Too bad. We had a lovely visit with these islanders. Is that not so, Tom?" Robert wanted none of my self pity.

"They are surely more civilized than the people of Otaheite, by my reckoning. Roads, proper plantations, fences even. Their houses all have paths leading to the opening and are planted with lovely flowering shrubs. Great fields of pineapples, they have, and are very proud of them. Robert showed them how to transplant seedlings to improve their fruit-bearing capability. Most grateful, they were. And we took them some orange plants which we showed them how to cultivate. I would reckon that ships calling here in the future will reap the benefit of our visit."

"And the women, Edward. Magnificent, they are. Many are six feet high and, while not as soft as the ladies of Otaheite, make up for that lack in many creative ways!" Robert was grinning as though there were more to tell, but he remained silent.

"Well, Mister Corner. Sounds as though you and young Tom, here, had a most illuminating experience ashore. Do tell us more." George Hamilton, smelling a hint of the prurient, urged Robert to go on.

"George, I'm afraid you'll have to satisfy your craving for the salacious elsewhere. Neither Tom nor I had any experiences worthy of reporting to you!" Robert's eyes never lost their sparkle and his voice held a smile.

Silently, I applauded his ability to cross tacks with our surgeon and gain the weather gage. Especially, without losing his good humor. I recalled my own encounter which only added to my poor spirits.

We remained, patience waning, for nearly a fortnight in the lagoon at Anamooka. With each passing day, hope of seeing our shipmates and the tender dwindled. The prisoners in their misery, still called out, pleading for water, more ventilation, and, of all things, some compassion. I was certain that, with the ship stationary, the conditions in the Box must truly be miserable, but their entreaties fell on deaf ears. Only Hamilton still made his frequent and futile trips to the Cabin, hoping each time that Captain Edwards would find merit in his medical opinion on the mutineers.

A short trip in *Pandora* to the neighboring island of Tofoa relieved some of the tedium, especially as we carried Tatafee, the king of Anamooka, with us at his request. He sought to collect the tribute due from his subjects on that island and was of the opinion that arriving on such an errand in a frigate of the Royal Navy would add considerably to his image.

"I've been here before, Edward." Tom spoke as we came to the anchorage. "I did not recall the name, but I was most surely here in Bligh's boat. It was our last stop and our last hope for some provisions and water. Sadly, we were chased away by natives of a clearly hostile bent when we tried to barter on the beach. Barely escaped with our lives! I wonder if any here recall that incident."

"Since it's likely Edwards will be in need of your linguistic skills, I'd reckon you'll get the chance to find out, Tom." I answered, glassing the shoreline for signs of life.

My prophesy held true and both Tom and I, along with the captain, Larkan, and a well armed party of Marines, accompanied Tatafee ashore. Edwards wanted to ensure that, should our tender make a landfall here, they would be treated properly, unlike the hostile reception Captain Bligh experienced. Robert stayed aboard the frigate with orders to get under weigh should the situation ashore turn hostile.

It was obvious, even without speaking their language, that some of the natives who greeted us on the beach remembered Tom Hayward. After paying their obligatory respects to their king, many of them shrank away from us, thinking, I am sure, that we were there to extract justice from them. But no. There would be no justice dispensed; Larkan and the captain wanted to create cordial and conciliatory relations here should Oliver and his crew come ashore. So the king collected his tribute and the following day, *Pandora* sailed for Anamooka, our hopes momentarily flaring that we would find *Matavia* bobbing to an anchor in the lagoon. It was not to be, and Captain Edwards determined we should wait no longer.

The evening we sailed from that charming place, our captain, quite out of character, invited the officers and our surgeon to join him for the evening meal in his Cabin. The first lieutenant make it abundantly clear to each of us that proper uniform, regardless of the heat, would be the order of the evening and a return invitation to the wardroom would be appropriate.

"You gentlemen have, for the most part, performed admirably. I am pleased, and pleased to compliment you." Edwards began without preamble once we all we were seated at his table. His words, while indeed complimentary, seemed perfunctory; his countenance showed no hint of pleasure, nor did his voice.

The first lieutenant answered, unnecessarily, for all of us, as we remained mute, acknowledging his words with simple nods. "Thank you, Cap'n. The officers and mids, in my opinion, have done their best in the face of some unusual circumstances. I am pleased you felt moved to comment." Larkan smiled as he spoke.

"Hmmm. Yes, indeed. I'm sure they have. But we will need to continue to do our best for the remainder of the voyage. We have yet to find any trace of Christian and his cutthroats, or of *Bounty*. And now we have lost our jolly boat and our tender." No mention of the men in each vessel.

"I shall expect each of you to achieve even higher levels of performance. We have waters to sail that are only poorly charted and must maintain a constant vigil for the hazards and dangers that are still to be discovered."

We all mumbled agreement, most around mouthfuls of savory fresh meat and vegetables recently procured at Anamooka. I shot a glance at Tom, seated across the table from me. His face remained unchanged, a mask of neutrality concealing his thoughts.

The supper progressed with no undue conflict, save the surgeon's gratuitous report on the health of our men. A further increase in the French Pox, a lingering gift from the natives of Otaheite, but, he mentioned, there was also good news: there was not a single incident of scurvy, thanks to his regimen of citrus, malt of wort, and fresh vegetables. The captain, a gentleman at his own table, cut him short and suggested they might discuss it privately with Lieutenant Larkan on the morrow.

"We will be making a more westerly course now, and a bit south. My sailing orders are quite explicit that we make the Straits of Endeavor before the storm season begins and brings a change in the winds. I prefer to find the passage in the reef Captain Cook wrote of from a southerly direction. By being in the area by late August, I will allow sufficient time to beat the change in weather and find Cook's Passage. As well as have a fair wind through." The captain's tone was conversational.

"When does the weather become . . . uh . . . unseemly, sir?" I ventured.

"We are not assured passage through the Straits after the month of September, though the Admiralty admits it could be accomplished as late as November. They seemed a bit vague about that, but offered that they have no firm knowledge of the weather and winds save for Captain Cook's observations in his various cruises in those waters. I shall not be gambling on their wisdom, and fully expect to find fine weather off New Holland. The Admiralty seemed more concerned about the wind direction being favorable than my having to deal with storms." Edwards looked square at me, then shot a look at Larkan.

What was that about? Had I stepped out of line? Was Larkan being silently told to chastise me later? I only asked a logical question that any officer should be thinking about.

The remainder of the meal was filled with silence, broken by polite requests to pass this or that, a few amusing stories of interaction with the locals at our various ports of call, and a monologue from Hamilton on flora and fauna he discovered in Otaheite, cut off with a look from Larkan. And then we were dismissed.

CHAPTER TWENTY-THREE

In Pandora *15° 43′ S, 146° 23′ E*

The twenty-fifth day of August found *Pandora* and her weary crew on the latitude of the Endeavor Straits, possibly a bit to the south. Our weather of late had been unseemly, the sky overcast day and night, and our position was tentative at best. But Mister Larkan and Captain Edwards both seemed confident that we were at the proper place to begin looking for the opening in the reef that Captain Cook had written of.

The officers, save for Robert Corner who held the quarterdeck, were enjoying their dinner and some fine wine which Larkan had secreted in his cabin, but chose to share out today. The ship sailed in a fresh breeze on the larboard tack, her motion easy and comforting. Conversation was, with the food before us, minimal, as we all tucked into the delightful duck and vegetables, gifts of our friends at Anamooka.

"Breakers! Breakers ahead!" We all heard the cry of the lookout posted in the foretop and, to a man, pushed away and scrambled to the companionway ladder.

"Hands to braces. Stand by to wear ship!" Robert's voice rang out even before most of us had attained the deck.

I ran forward, leapt into the larboard ratlines, and climbed halfway to the top. Before me, I could see a line of white seas breaking on a reef. Below me, men ran to their sail handling positions while topmen started up the ratlines behind me, causing me to ascend the rest of the way to the fighting top. The breakers appeared to be less than a half mile distant, but already, Robert had ordered the helm over and *Pandora*, her jibs billowing out as we turned, began to ease away from the danger. The captain was on the quarterdeck with Robert, and I could see the first lieutenant adding his voice to the cacophony of voices urging the heavers to move smartly. Bosun Cunningham and Sailing Master Passmore moved among the sailors, occasionally glancing aloft to see that the topmen were ready to clew up or ease sails as ordered.

"Ease your sheets and coil down." The command from the quarterdeck drifted up to my position at the maintop as *Pandora* now sailed north along the line of breakers.

After an hour and more of progress, the lookouts, now even more vigilant, spotted more breakers ahead of us and Captain Edwards tacked the ship a full one hundred eighty degrees, seeking an opening to the south. We shortened our spread of canvas to make further maneuvers quicker, should they be necessary.

I took the watch following supper, and Hayward, whom I was relieving, instructed me. "We are simply sailing off and on, Edward. The captain is reasonably certain there is an opening near at hand, but is desirous of waiting until daylight to attempt it. Stay clear of the reef. I was told to approach no closer than one mile, so you'll be keeping the sailing handlers busy throughout your watch.

"For my own self, I am going to get some supper and go to bed. This toying with the reef is a bit stressful. Some fatigued I am!"

I gave him a perfunctory salute and encouraged him to enjoy his evening. Then I made a tour of the ship, while my assistant officer of the watch, Midshipman Pyecroft, stayed on the quarterdeck. The lookouts, now stationed in the bows and amidships larboard and starboard, seemed alert and I cautioned them to keep a weather eye peeled. Each had a night glass and, while I expected no untoward events, I instructed the watch captain to change them at every turn of the glass. A half hour watch at lookout would ensure that the men would not become overly bored or inattentive.

"Having a walk about, are you, Mister Ballantyne?" Passmore emerged from the dark as I rounded the foremast.

"Just making sure the watch is up to snuff, George. Sailing this close to the reef with the breeze up and no moon is a trifle unnerving, I find. Helps me to know the men are actually 'looking out!'"

"No worries, I think. Cap'n Edwards knows what he's about and won't be takin' any chances with his ship." He spoke confidently, but kept his eyes in the direction where we knew the breakers would appear when we got closer.

The next morning, when I returned to the deck, little had changed; we still sailed off and on, each time making a bit more way south and then, on the opposite tack, to the north. Edwards was on the quarterdeck, his glass tucked securely under his arm, pacing back and forth. The sailing master held the watch and stood with his hands clasped behind his back, feet rooted to the deck, and his eyes aloft, scanning the sails for the first hint of a luff.

We spent the day cruising along the reef, searching for a break in the seas and the line of white foam that would indicate a breach in the coral. We found nothing.

Could Cook's charts be wrong or perhaps he was as unsure of his position when he found the opening as we are! I thought ruefully.

When darkness descended, Edwards decided to heave to and, as the wind now had moderated some, allow the ship to drift to leeward rather than try to make headway, sailing off and on as we had done the previous night. Of course, the watches still had a job of work to do, ensuring we did not drift too close to the reef or, should the wind change, make way into danger.

In the wardroom, Larkan, Corner, and Hamilton sat, as did I, each engrossed in our own thoughts. Hamilton hauled out his lovely gold and silver watch, studied it for a moment, then carefully wound it.

"Believe I can stand another wee taste and perhaps a turn about the deck before I bed down for the night." He had spoken to no one in particular, but now looked squarely at the first lieutenant.

"By the bye, John, Mister Innes, my surgical assistant, informed me this afternoon that there have been no more cases of the Pox. In fact, not a soul turned up for sick call this morning. A fine thing, if I do say so myself! Obviously, my preventions are proving proper. I shall write them up for the Admiralty, should another captain in these waters wish to have his surgeon employ them."

"Well, George, your scurvy preventions are certainly not original. Cook and Bligh both used them to great success as well. In fact, is not that from where you derived your own preventions?" Larkan, as all of us were, was becoming weary of Hamilton's self-congratulatory discourse.

"Well, they certainly gave me the direction, but, I think, I am entitled to credit for my improvements on what they began. Try to be grateful, John, that your crew is healthy and allow me some of the credit for it. I assure you, were they not healthy, I would most certainly bear the brunt of your blame!" Hamilton, clearly soured by Larkan's statement, slipped his watch back into his waistcoat pocket and stood up. As he got to the door, he stopped and turned back.

"Should you really wish to do something besides rob me of the credit due me, you might approach the captain in support of my pleas to have the prisoners allowed access to fresh air and exercise! While we have lost none yet, I fear that during the remainder of our voyage we are most likely to, unless they receive some consideration." With that, and without await-ing a response, the surgeon left our midst, presumably heading for the weather deck.

"He does get wearisome, does he not?" Robert asked as soon as the door closed. "His supposedly scientific inquiries into each of our forays ashore are little more than thinly disguised attempts to titillate and he has a remarkably undeveloped sense of propriety, especially for a man of his superior education!"

"Our good surgeon is a most unique individual. We must allow him his peccadilloes and be grateful for his medical skills. I, for one, am glad we have his services. I must remind myself to compliment him in the morning." Larkan helped himself to another glass of claret, tossed it off, and left.

The next morning, however, I doubt that he had the opportunity to carry out his intentions. The lookouts had spotted a place in the line of white foaming water where there appeared to be only the turquoise blue of the sea. Immediately, Captain Edwards was in the foretop with his glass.

"Mister Larkan, prepare a boat to investigate that gap. We will send Lieutenant Corner as the boat officer, if you please." He announced the moment his feet touched the deck. "He is to determine if the opening, should there in fact be one, is sufficiently wide and deep enough to allow passage of the ship."

Robert, immediately upon being assigned the duty, took a glass to the mizzentop and spent some considerable time surveying the area all around the ship. The yawl was swung over the side, equipped with an axe, provisions, water, and a compass—the memory of the schooner and, before that, the jolly boat and Midshipman Sival, were still too fresh in our minds to be ignored—and off they sailed under still-overcast skies, but with a nice breeze and easy seas.

I took a glass and climbed to the maintop to watch my friend's progress. I was pleased that Robert stayed well clear of the waves that could suck the boat into their maw and smash it to kindling on the coral. Up and down he sailed, sometimes steering toward the reef, at others, (perhaps having gotten a bit too close) using both oars and the sails to claw his way back to safer water.

Toward two bells in the first dog watch—about five in the after-noon—we saw a signal from the boat. It was the agreed upon hoist for their having found a suitable passage. With night closing fast upon us and the weather beginning to turn sour, Captain Edwards ordered us to make the signal to recover the boat. The misfortune of our lost boats was still foremost in our minds. Muskets were fired in a pre-determined pattern and answered properly by Corner in the boat. Though we could scarcely hear his shots, we saw plainly the flashes from the muzzles of his muskets. Edwards waited an hour and, when the boat, now laboring under mounting seas and a growing wind, seemed to be making less progress than he had expected, he ordered the signal to make haste. The wind continued to blow hard, driving large swells before it.

In two hours, the boat was close under our stern and experiencing some considerable difficulty from the mounting seas. Breaking seas to our larboard hand indicated shoals and the presence of a reef, but as we were more or less stationary, with topsails backed, their threat presented no immediate concern. We were, as well, in deep water; the leadsman, throwing his heavy leadline repeatedly, had finally found the bottom at fifty fathoms. Bosun Cunningham and his sailors worked the boat around and began to hoist it aboard. The sun had set; a final flare of light shot up from the horizon, momentarily lighting the heavy clouds. And then it was full dark, broken only by the occasional flash of lightning.

Without any warning, save a tremendous *whoomp*, the foretops'l filled and the ship began to make way. Amid shouts and curses, the topmen were quickly dispatched and the heavers on deck clapped onto the sheet and braces in an attempt to spill the wind from the billowing sail. It was too late.

The grinding noise and the lurch of the ship, which shivered her entire rig, told us the worst possible news: we had struck the reef. Now the topmen and heavers were ordered to let the sail fill in the hope of sailing off the pinnacle that held us in its clutches.

Edwards, who had been on deck throughout, ordered more sail set and the carpenter to sound the hold. The sails did nothing; the ship remained pinned to the reef, buffeted by the still-mounting seas which seemed to jam the rocks even farther into our damaged hull. Recognizing the futility of what he was attempting, Edwards ordered the sails furled.

"Sir. Eighteen inches in the hold and rising as we speak." The carpenter's report to Edwards did little to calm our fears. It had only been five minutes. At that rate, the ship would sink in hours! As if to confirm my fears, the carpenter returned just a quarter hour later to report that sounding the hold showed there were now *nine feet* of water in the ship.

"Man the pumps and set bucket brigades in the hatches. All hands to bailing." The captain cried out.

The wind built steadily, fueling the savagery of the seas which now broke in unrelenting ferocity on our starboard side, driving the vessel into a sharp heel to larboard.

A voice cried out from the Box. "Let us out to help. It's our lives at stake too! We can pump."

"Aye, let a few of them out and turn them to on the pumps. Not more than four or five and have a Marine watch them; they're still rascals and, mingling with my crew, they might try to foment a mutiny!" Edwards, even in a moment of dire need, was still concerned about the intentions of his prisoners.

Hamilton, who now stood mute just off the quarterdeck, heard the exchange and muttered to on one in particular, "About time, it is. Those poor sods are likely too weak to do much good, bailing, or on the pumps! Had that stubborn man listened to me, he might have more useful men to help him save his ship!"

I was overseeing a gang on the after pump and was able, through the gloom of the night, to see one of Grimwood's men climb up on the Box and open the hatch, unlocking the bar with his key. He called down into the darkness below him and shortly disappeared within its recesses. As I watched, four pale, naked, and wan looking men struggled out of the little hatch and jumped to the deck. A Marine was there to great them, his musket at half-cock in case they tried to escape. Though where they might escape to was quite beyond me! We were all looking to escape this disaster that had beset us.

With the added strength, albeit slight, the after chain pump continued its clanking as bucket after bucket rose from the hold on its endless chain, driven by the men who turned the wheel as though their very lives depended on it. I saw to the relief of the men on my pump every fifteen minutes and Hamilton watched them closely for signs of excessive fatigue. I could see Pyecroft, my new junior watch officer supervising the forward chain pump and Bosun Cunningham shouting encouragement to the men on the bucket brigade. Edwards stood on the quarterdeck, its surface listing severely to larboard, watching, seemingly without even blinking, as his crew tried to save our ship.

Larkan moved across the deck, holding on to his hat as the wind gained strength.

"You men there," he cried to a knot of sailors waiting to relieve their mates on the chain pumps, "report to Mister Passmore. He's needing hands to rig a fother to slow the water. Lively, now!"

If the rock is through the bottom of the ship, what possible good will it do to try to spread a tops'l underneath the ship? Wouldn't the rock, jammed into our hull, prevent the sail from being passed under our hull?

I dismissed the thought as quickly as I had it. Not my place and, truly, I would welcome every effort to keep us afloat.

"Mister Ballantyne. No more lollygagging about! Find your gunner and see to casting loose our battery. Get every bloody gun over the side! We need to lighten the ship. Move man!" Larkan shouted at me from across the slanting deck.

Lollygagging? How dare he! I am quite occupied with seeing to the pumps. Are they not more important to our survival right now?

Nonetheless, I staggered up the deck, fighting the wind and taking several green seas as I gained the weather side. I found Mister Packer, the gunner, and gave him Larkan's instructions. Then I decided to help him find men and release the heavy guns from their stowed position. They would roll down to leeward once they were free and more than likely, simply smash through the larboard bulwark into the sea.

"Mister Larkan. See to getting the bower anchors into the boats and quickly! Perhaps we can haul her off." Edwards voice rang through the cacophony of the deck; over the men shouting to one another, the cries from the Box for the prisoners' release, the shouted orders of the officers, the howling of the wind, and the waves crashing into our exposed side. And the groaning and grinding of our hull.

The boats were lowered, but because of the seas, were unable to be maneuvered to a position where the anchors might be lowered carefully into them. It was simply too dangerous. In the flashes of the lightning, we could watch as, despite the crew's desperate efforts, the boat smashed repeatedly into the side of the ship.

"Here now, Mister Ballantyne. Mind that one. It's going to get away from you, you're not careful!" Packer realized that I was about to release the breaching tackles on a gun that would have rolled straight into the men on the forward chain pump. I stopped, looked at him stupidly, and then at where the gun would have gone.

"Aye, Packer. Thank you. Get a line about her so we can control her speed." I responded, shouting, even though he was barely six feet away.

By ten that evening, the storm had abated not a jot, but we had all but a few of the battery over the side. In some cases, men had to chop through the bulwark to leeward with axes to allow the beasts to roll through, but at this point, consideration for the appearance of the ship was of the least concern. The livestock and caged fowls had likewise been pitched into the sea to fend for themselves. Anything that might lighten the ship, even a little, and could be gotten off, was thrown into the water; spare spars, cable, hogsheads of salted beef and pork all found their way in to the churning, foam-capped waves. The boats, standing off since our failed attempt to set anchors, dodged the crates and barrels as they fought to stay upright in the raging seas. Recovering them now was simply out of the question and, while they remained near at hand, their officers and crews struggled to keep them from overturning.

And then, with another shudder, bigger than those we had been feeling each time a wave smashed our poor hull onto the rocks, the ship floated free!

"She's off, lads." A lusty cry went up throughout the ship. Men at the pumps stopped cranking, the bucket brigade stopped passing buckets up from the hold, and for a moment, all hands held their respective breath.

The ship was still heeled over from the accumulation of water in her bowels, the waves pressing hard on our starboard side, and the wind still blowing hard on her top hamper. But she was most assuredly afloat! She felt suddenly alive, logy and slow, but definitely alive.

"Leadsman to the chains. Get me a sounding, quickly now." Edwards voice again rang out, this time with no competition; the ship was still silent.

"Fifteen fathoms, sir." Came the shouted reply from the starboard forechains.

"Mister Larkan, get an anchor down, if you please." The captain's voice was quieter, but still audible the length of the ship.

"Mister Cunningham. Drop the best bower, if you please. Quickly." Larkan's order was unnecessary. We had all heard the captain and the bosun was already moving with his men to the bow.

I stepped aft in an effort the see where the boats had gotten to. I peered through the gloom of the night; the lack of a star, moon, or any heavenly lights made the visibility difficult. I could not distinguish where the heaving sea ended and the pitch black sky began. And then I heard a shout and made out the dim form of our yawl as she crested a wave about a pistol shot from our larboard quarter. Where the other boat was I had no idea. But I recalled that Tom Hayward had been in the yawl when she was launched and breathed a sigh of relief.

"Sir? Cap'n?" The carpenter, Mister Montgomery, stood just off the quarterdeck, clutching the rail to maintain his balance.

"Yes, Montgomery, what is it? Are the pumps keeping ahead of the water?"

"Uh, sir. No sir. Comin' in faster than ever now we're off the rock. Just sounded the hold; twenty feet it's showin', sir, and gainin' on us."

"Very well. Put more men on the buckets. We must keep her afloat 'til the dawn, at least."

The carpenter left to find more men as instructed. Having heard the exchange, I thought it unlikely the ship would remain afloat for another six or eight hours, but then I had never been in this position before.

"Chain pump's gone! Busted the bloody chain!" The cry from the men working the forward pump might as well have been our death knell. Without the pump working throughout the night, we were surely doomed.

"Mister Ballantyne, step forward, if you please, and have a look at the pump. See if a little creativity might be employed to restore it." Edwards spoke so calmly I was startled. My own heart was racing and I seemed to be sweating profusely, and not from the heat of the night.

"Aye, sir. I'll see what I can do." I ran forward, noticing as I made my way through the dark that *Pandora* seemed to be riding with her bow down a bit.

"WATCH OUT, THERE. STAND CLEAR!" A disembodied voice rang out of the darkness from the starboard side.

I stopped and heard the rumble of one of our guns rolling down the canted deck. There would be no stopping it until it hit the larboard bulwark and either stopped there or crashed through into the sea. The sound of it was coming from behind me and now, more from the larboard side. It had grown in intensity and I knew it would smash into the bulwark in seconds.

The sound of splintering wood did little to cover the scream of some poor soul who had not heard or heeded the warning to stand clear. I later found that he was crushed between the gun carriage and the bulwark as the gun struck and, when it kept going, he was carried by the force of it into the sea. No time for sorrow now; try to save the ship.

More sailors, midshipmen, warrants, and petty officers now passed sloshing buckets up the from below decks. Due to the increasing height of the water, the lower end of the line had shifted up an entire deck, shortening the line of passers. At every hatchway, grim-faced men took buckets from their mates, poured them onto the deck, and threw the empty bucket back in the void below them.

Hamilton had seen to refreshment of some type for them. They were all suffering from weakness and fatigue bordering on total exhaustion. They were becoming faint from their monumental exertions. A cask of strong ale, brewed at Anamooka, had been brought topside and was being dispensed to the men as they were relieved on the pumps or bucket brigade. It would provide sustenance without intoxication, though, privately, I thought a little intoxication might help!

"Just a bit longer, lads. Daylight's coming soon. Just a short while now. Be strong." Hamilton and his assistance, Mister Innes, doled out good cheer, both liquid and spiritual. I think the brew had a more positive effect on the men than his cajoling them into believing that sunrise was only a short time away. By my reckoning, it would be another five or six hours before we saw the first rays of the sun rise from the eastern horizon.

There was nothing to be done about the broken chain pump. The men who had been working it steadily since shortly after seven o'clock got no respite; they were given buckets, pans from the galley, and canvas bags and told to form a new bucket brigade at the companionway just forward of the now defunct pump.

A spare topmast, its lashings gone, rolled off the booms and crashed to the deck, killing another man. Without ceremony, his body was heaved over the side, along with the topmast.

The ship continued to heel, more sharply now, and I could feel the bow dip farther into the sea with each passing wave. As each hour we survived brought us closer to the dawn, I began to think we might actually see the sunrise from our own decks. The night dragged on; men relieved of bucket or pump duty caught a quick nap, sleeping where they collapsed until roused again for their shift. The officers and midshipmen were exempt from neither the strenuous work nor the exhaustion; only Captain Edwards and Mister Larkan seemed unaffected, moving about the decks, encouraging the men, and assessing the situation. It was only a matter of time . . .

We struggled on, working the remaining pump, manning the buckets, and hoping. Still the ship settled lower and lower in the water, her deck now canted at an even steeper angle; one had to hold on to something to climb from the larboard side to the starboard. On the positive side, the wind had abated and the seas seemed to be settling down. No longer were they crashing into our exposed hull, but that might have been due to the fact that we were now inside the reef and enjoying the protection of the very rocks that had put us in this position.

About a half hour before the sun was due to rise—and it appeared that we would actually *have* a sunrise—Captain Edwards called all the officers, except for Tom Hayward, who was still in the yawl, laying to off our larboard quarter, aft to the quarterdeck.

"Gentlemen, I needn't tell you our situation is most grave. I fear we can not save the ship. Your men have behaved exceptionally well, working to exhaustion, as I know you each have as well. It has been reported to me that the larboard anchor is now under water, and, as you can see, even our stern is settling farther and farther into the sea. The water is pouring in through the gunports to larboard and there is little to do now, save protect the lives of ourselves and our men.

"Mister Larkan, have the armorer release the prisoners from their irons, if you please. I have not come all this way to drown them, though I would shed not a tear at the loss of any!"

Larkan waved at Grimwood and called out the instructions to him. The master at arms sent Hodges, the Armorer, to release the shackles and leg irons from the prisoners. We stood and watched as the man climbed atop the Box, unlocked the hatch, and dropped inside. The captain returned his attention to us.

"Should any of you have anything to say or offer that differs from my feeling, now is the time to speak up." And then he was silent.

No one said a word. Each of us was lost within himself, turning this way and that, looking at the sad condition of *Pandora* and wondering where we might wind up, should we take to the sea. George Passmore, our Sailing Master, stepped forward and looked the captain square in the eye.

"Sir. I quite agree with your assessment of our situation. In my own opinion, the ship is only moments away from sinking and we should abandon her. Which is what I intend to do. I bid you farewell, sir." He turned away, walked calmly to the larboard quarter, and flung himself into the ocean.

Edwards looked after him, momentarily stunned. Then he gathered up his logbook, sextant, and a roll of charts, all wrapped in tarred canvas, and followed his sailing master over the railing.

Well! I'd reckon that would be the right thing to do! Cap'n ought to know what's best! I thought.

And I thought, just for a moment, of the possessions I would be leaving behind in my cabin. It only took an instant to realize that, should I survive this disaster, all of them could easily be replaced. If I did not survive, then I surely would not miss them! The Admiralty might even reimburse me for their loss. I suspect each of us shared similar thoughts and we all stood, for a moment or two, motionless on the quarterdeck. A sudden shout brought us out of our individual reveries and called our attention back to Pandora's Box.

The hatch on the top was again closed. No one had seen Hodges climb out, so it was natural to assume he was still inside with the prisoners. They may indeed be free of their irons, but they were securely locked inside. All of them.

"Robert, the prisoners. They'll not get out!

"THERE SHE GOES!" A cry went up from forward.

From the Box, we all heard Hodges quite clearly cry out, "Don't worry lads; we'll all go to Hell together!"

I could see in the first glim of dawn all the men on the weather deck scrambling up to the windward side as the ship took a sharper heel to larboard, leaving the bulwark on that side in the water.

"The prisoners! Turn them loose! They'll drown, should we leave them locked in the Box!" Grimwood bellowed. And one of Cunningham's bosun's mates, Moulter, leaped onto the top of the box.

Clapping ahold of the closed hatch built into the top, he ripped it from its hinges and sent it sailing out to the sea. Then, he knelt down and extend his arm into the Box.

Slowly, and with Moulter helping them, the mutineers and Hodges dragged themselves up to the top of the Box, looked about them at the condition of the ship, and flung themselves into the sea. It was plain to me that a few still wore wrist manacles.

Those men will drown for certain with those irons on. But there's nothing for it. I can not help them.

Larkan, still on the quarterdeck, stepped to the rail and hailed the boat, which had just plucked Edwards and Passmore from the sea.

"Mister Hayward. You will pick up our prisoners, if you please. They will be overboard on the starboard side."

With that, the ship took a mighty lurch and settled deeper into the water on her larboard side. We all, with a mighty yell driven as much by fear as by any other thought, leaped into the sea, fully expecting to have no deck beneath our feet in only a moment.

The cries of the men drowning in the sea was dreadful; those who could not swim tried to find bits of jetsam to cling to: a spar, a chicken coop, a barrel, anything. The unsuccessful floundered in the water, crying out for rescue even as they sank beneath the surface. Gradually, the cries grew fainter, as more of the men perished. Soon the sea was silent, save for the occasional shouts of the men in the boats and those swimming as they were rescued.

Of course, I too, was in the water. I had only the clothes on my back, and while I was not a strong swimmer, I was fortunate in finding a spare tops'l yard near enough that I could paddle to it. Several others already had wrapped their arms about it and together, we kicked our legs and gradually moved the spar toward the yawl, busy with picking up others. It took us some time to accomplish the swim and, I must say, Tom Hayward looking down at me, haggard, sleep-deprived, and wet, was a most welcome sight. Never was I so glad to see someone!

I looked back at my ship; she was gone. Only her topmasts showed above the water, leaning at a frightful angle. The sun was now well up, casting a reddish glow on the sea which reflected off the masts, giving the whole area a devilish, fiery cast.

We made our way to a sandy, low-lying cay some four miles from the wreck. Most of us, officers, midshipmen, and sailors alike, collapsed at once on the sand. The four boats, employed in the rescue of our shipmates, finally accomplished their task and were pulled up into the shallows. Once we had all rested a bit, Edwards ordered a muster to by division.

When the tally was done, we determined that we had lost thirty-five of our own men including the purser's steward, one of our Marine corporals, and the master at arms, Mister Grimwood. Four of the prisoners had drowned as well. I could not help but think of the ones I had seen jumping into the sea still wearing their manacles.

Edwards then set Mister Larkan to discovering what, if any, provisions we might find. It was immediately apparent we would find nothing on this island, really little more than a sand bar. Not a tree, shrub, or single sign of life could we find. Barely thirty paces long, it and we would soon be at the mercy of the sun, now mid-morning high.

The first lieutenant found that we had, besides some spare sails for the boats, a small barrel of water, a cask of wine, some biscuit, and a few muskets and cartouche boxes which had providently been thrown into the boat as the ship sank. Larkan also had his sextant and, for some reason, his sword. For my part, I had nothing save the clothes I wore. Of course, neither Tom nor Robert had any more; indeed, Robert had shed his jacket during the night and now did not even have that.

Edwards ordered the prisoners, each naked as the day they came into the world, put under guard. He also saw to making use of a sail as a shelter from the sun, whose rays, reflecting off the sand and the sea, were excruciating to our eyes. In spite of our travail in the sea and the considerable amount of salt water we had swallowed during our long time floating— and floundering—about before being picked up, there would be no fresh water issued today. The captain had determined that if we limited each man to two small wine glasses of water each day, we could make it last for sixteen days.

Sixteen days! There is nothing, absolutely nothing, near at hand. Where could we go that we might reach in just sixteen days? I wondered. And what would we eat? There is nothing here and nothing survived the wreck.

I resolved to do what I was told and not complain; we were all going to suffer equally. Except the prisoners.

CHAPTER TWENTY-FOUR

In the boats

"Sir? Cap'n? Might we have use of a spare sail to make us a shelter? The sun is scorching our skins raw, sir." Morrison, Bosun's Mate late of *Bounty*, approached the captain with some trepidation.

"You may not. You may burn in Hell for all I care and be damned!" Edwards' response was startling.

The prisoners, though freed of their manacles, were quite naked and, having been confined in the Box for near four months, had lost the toughness of skin they had enjoyed while living in Otaheite.

Larkan called to one of our surviving Marines. "Corporal, see to the prisoners, if you please. They will remain separate from the ship's company and together. Put them there," he pointed to a patch of sand to windward of where we all had settled. "and see that they talk to no one save each other."

I watched, horrified, as the ten *Bounty* men who survived the wreck were shuffled off to a spot about fifteen paces from us. The Marine, armed only with a boat's cutlass, directed them to sit on the sand and be still. But former Midshipman Heywood refused.

"We will burn to a crisp, sitting out in the open. We should be provided some cover, as Morrison requested. This treatment we are receiving is even more inhuman than what we got in *Pandora*. We are without any kind of garment. Your shipmates are clothed *and* have a shelter rigged. Are we less deserving?"

"Aye, you're prisoners. And mutineers. You heard what Cap'n Edwards said. 'No shelter for you.'" The Marine brandished his cutlass for emphasis. "You are all scoundrels and infamous wretches and deserve nothing, save being kept alive for the noose in Portsmouth." He then turned his back on the helpless, pale men.

"I daresay, men, we will be roasted alive. Bury each other to the neck in the sand. It will provide at least some protection from the sun, and might keep us warm during the night." Heywood directed. He then turned to the Marine again.

"Might we have a bit of water or something to swallow?"

"Aye, when Mister Larkan or the cap'n says you will. Ain't my responsibility to see to your comfort. You are prisoners."

Their voices carried quite clearly and all but a few of the officers, now huddled together under the boat sail and out of the sun, heard the exchange.

Tom stuck his head out and, indeed, the prisoners were burying themselves in the sand. "Reckon that ought to help 'em some. Wouldn't want to be out there naked as they are."

We all agreed. The captain's order that no water would be issued this day remained firm, but we, the men, and even the prisoners, received a small glass of wine and a mouthful of bread. Hardly enough to sustain us, it seemed only to serve to sharpen our appetites and make us more acutely aware of our deprivations.

The Carpenter, Mister Montgomery, and several of his mates were ordered to see to the boats. We would be making an open-sea voyage in them to somewhere, and Larkan instructed him to use what he could find to make them more seaworthy. One in particular had been badly damaged while alongside the sinking frigate and had gotten her side partially stove in. How she had remained afloat to rescue the swimmers from the sea was truly a miracle, but the sea had been quite calm by then, as opposed to how it had been earlier in the night.

Montgomery and his men ripped out the floorboards and cut them into strips which they affixed vertically to the sides of each boat. The stove-in side of the red yawl was patched with the floorboards from that boat. By stretching canvas cut from another spare sail around the newly affixed uprights, the men raised the freeboard of each boat by a foot and more. With a bit of luck, the raised "sides" would keep out all but the worst of the seas. A sorry looking lot they made, but, hopefully, with a smile from the heavens, they might carry us *somewhere*.

"Tom," I said, when he had awoken from a well deserved nap under the shelter, "you were with Bligh in the open boat for . . . what, a month and more, right? You think we have any chance with so many of us to sail to civilization? I am not even sure where we are!"

"I reckon we're somewhere to the south of the Endeavor Straits. Much closer, we are, than Bligh was when cast adrift, to Timor. We were in that blessed little boat for some forty-eight days, Edward. I would guess, that should the weather and the seas be merciful to us, we might make Timor in less than a month. And as to our 'sixteen days of provisions,' I would wager that Edwards will make them actually last longer.

"We caught precious few fish and an occasional bird when we were lucky, but, with Bligh's careful rationing, we actually had *eleven days* worth of rations left when we landed. I would think Edwards would be no less frugal."

What a stroke of bad luck! Tom set adrift with Bligh just a few years ago and sailed half way across the Pacific in an open boat. Now he's going to do it again! How does he not . . .

"Edward, I know what you're likely thinking. But as I have done this before, I think I can face it again; I know well the hardships and rigors of what we endured with Bligh and console myself with the fact that Edwards is every bit the seaman that Bligh is and we have a shorter distance to sail. We'll make it, my friend, with a bit of luck." He turned to look squarely at me. "And, consider that none in Bligh's boat died of our privations; one, a big Irish chap, was stoned to death by natives, but he was the only loss on the voyage."

I could only shake my head. I admired his confidence and wondered how I would manage over the course of the next month. But a sailor does what he has to and there's an end to it! I resolved, once again, to face my troubles and get on with it! Be more like Tom; aye, that's it.

When the sun lost its will to broil us alive and finally dropped below the watery horizon, we set a watch and went to sleep. During the night, we heard cries of distress from where the sailors were camped. I awoke with a start, sure that I was having yet another nightmare.

As I lay there, close by to Robert and Tom, I realized that I had not been dreaming; some one was acting rather irregularly, indeed. I nudged Robert awake.

"Do you hear that? Sounds like one of the crew is drunk. He must have gotten in to the wine cask. We should have a look."

"The watch will deal with it, Edward. Go back to sleep." Robert rolled over, slung his arm under his head, and promptly did just that.

I got up. When I crawled outside the makeshift tent, I could see our watch standing resolutely nearby.

"What's the noise from the other camp, Sentry?" I inquired.

"Haven't a clue, sir. Likely one of the boys making a bad time of it. Wouldn't worry meself about it, sir." He seemed unwilling to investigate.

"You might go and have a look, sailor. Sounds to me as if someone of your mates might have gotten into the wine cask. Those cries sound like a man laboring under a surfeit of spirits. Should he not have drunk it all, you might be able to save some; we'll likely be needing it."

"Aye, sir. I'll have a look." He shook his head and wandered off, perhaps not sure whether or not *I* was in my right mind.

"Connell, it was, sir. A landsman." The sentry reported upon his return. "Didn't get into the wine cask, just drunk his fill of sea water. Terrible thirsty, he was, and complaining to his mates. Made him crazy. They got him secured so he don't do it again, but he surely won't be gainin' his senses anytime soon, I'd reckon."

I knew the dreadful thirst he had experienced; we all did. But most seafaring men are well aware that drinking sea water is the worst antidote for the plight. And should you drink enough, it will kill you surely as a musket ball through the head. Just not as quickly.

When the sun rose the next day, Edwards dispatched Mister Passmore, Sailing Master of His Majesty's late Frigate, *Pandora*, out to the wreck. He took one of the boats and a crew with the intent of discovering what, if anything, he might salvage from the remains. Almost any item he could find would likely be useful to us, considering our distressed state.

He found little of use. As the boat beached, Mister Passmore stepped into the shallow water, cradling something in his arms. I could not make out what it was. I strolled the ten steps to the water's edge as he walked up the beach. The bundle in his arms moved and, carefully, he bent down and released a decidedly happier ship's cat to run up the sand.

"Found her clinging to the t'gallant masthead, Mister Ballantyne. Couldn't rightly leave her there, now could I?" He smiled weakly.

"Did you manage to secure anything *useful*, George?" Larkan had come up behind me, something I still had not gotten used to.

"Not much, sir. He turned to the boat as the crew began unloading it. "A piece of the t'gallant mast, which I hacked off with the boat's hatchet, and about fifteen feet of the lightning chain. Thought as how it's copper, might be of some use. Precious little, though. Wasn't much to be had. Nothing floating around her, either. Reckon the seas or the tide carried away whatever might have been there. Sorry, Mister Larkan. Bit disappointing, it is, sir."

"Aye, disappointing indeed. We'll have to manage on what we have." He turned and walked back up the beach to report the paltry success to Captain Edwards. "We'll need to be resourceful." He muttered as he drew away.

The captain and Larkan remained closeted under the captain's tent for much of the day. I could see they had a chart spread out on a cask. Robert and I wandered off to see what, if anything, we might discover on our sandy little island. We returned quickly. There was nothing to see and no ground higher than a foot or two above sea level from which to gain a vantage point. We retreated to the officers' tent and collapsed into a fitful sleep.

That evening, the promised wine glass of water was distributed to each man, including the prisoners, who remained, by their own choice, buried to their necks in the sand. Some of our sailors had found some giant cockles, cut them up, and boiled them in sea water. They offered to share them with all, but most of us were too thirsty to attempt anything which, having been boiled in sea water, would only serve to increase our thirst.

Our surgeon, George Hamilton, had discovered a paper of tea, which some thoughtful soul had thrown into the boat just before we abandoned, and suggested that, should we all combine our water allowance, we might boil it up for a refreshing taste each.

This we did, in the captain's tent. After the tea boiled, each man took a salt-cellar spoonful and passed it to the man to his left until the tea was gone. This way, every one of us got an equal share which we savored and found quite refreshing.

"Gentlemen, get a good night's sleep. It may well be the last one you enjoy for a while. We will leave here on the morrow, and voyage to Timor." Edwards stated.

I shot a look at Tom. He raised his eyebrows at me, and winked. Edwards continued.

"I make it about eleven hundred miles from our present position. Each boat will carry at least one officer, two or three prisoners, who will remain bound, and an even distribution of seamen and midshipmen. I personally will see to the initial distribution of rations to each boat, however, most will remain with me, under my control.

"The boats will remain together, at least within hailing distance, and at night, or should the weather get up, we will rig lines between them to ensure we do not get separated. Are there any questions?"

I hesitated. He had not said how long he expected the voyage to take and all I could think of was the 'sixteen days of nourishment' we had. And we had already used up two days worth. Finally, I spoke up.

"Cap'n, how long do you anticipate it will take us to reach Timor, sir?"

Edwards looked at me, then moved his gaze in the dwindling light to the others. "Mister Larkan and I estimate that, with a shred of luck and good fortune, we should reach Coupang in sixteen to seventeen days." He offered nothing to alleviate our concerns.

Needless to say, few of us followed the captain's earlier order to 'get a good night's sleep.' During my frequent bouts of wakefulness, I could sense the others equally restive and wakeful. Mister Larkan prowled the campsite most of the night.

After a morning taste of water and mouthful of bread, we prepared the boats. Each was supplied with the latitude and longitude of Timor and a rude chart. As he had promised, our stores of food and drink remained in the captain's boat. Each also was given a musket and cartridge box and a cutlass. We pushed off into the shallows and began to climb aboard.

Into the pinnace went Captain Edwards and Tom Hayward, followed by the captain's clerk, Midshipman Rickard, the gunner, three prisoners, including Bosun's Mate Morrison, and sixteen sailors and Marines. As they pulled out into the sea, I heard Morrison (I think it was he) say to his mates, "Lads, we have jumped from the frying pan straight into the fire. *Bounty* seems like a paradise to rival Otaheite compared to our present state!"

Another voice hushed him.

The men rowed the boat a short distance from the shore and rested on their oars while the mast was stood up and the sail rigged.

The red yawl carried Lieutenant Larkan, our surgeon, two midshipmen, two prisoners, and eighteen sailors. They too pulled out and lay to alongside the captain's boat.

Robert was in command of the longboat, accompanied by our Purser, Mister Bentham, the carpenter, two mids, two prisoners, and twenty-four sailors. A well laden vessel. I hoped we would not encounter any rough water!

I received the responsibility of the blue yawl, but I had both our Bosun, Mister Cunningham, and George Passmore to assist me. In addition, we carried the Surgeon's Mate, Mister Innes, two midshipmen, including Mister Pyecroft, who had stood as my junior watch officer after poor Renouard had disappeared in the schooner. I also boarded three prisoners and fifteen sailors. All I could think of when I surveyed our little flotilla was Tom's remark about Bligh's boat having only four inches of freeboard when they left *Bounty*. I doubted that any of the four of us had more! One hundred three souls setting off on an open-sea voyage of eleven hundred miles! Oh my!

Following Edwards' example, as quickly as each boat reached deep water and rigged a mast, we laid our oars athwart the gun'ls of the boat.

This provided, in effect, a second tier by which the men in each boat might experience a bit less crowding, as well as find, for those laying in the bottom of the boat, some shade from time to time. At Edwards' order, we also made a makeshift scale in each boat, using a musket ball as the balance, which would be used to share out our meager rations. And then, sails raised to the wind, and with a *huzzah* more lusty than most of us felt, left our little sand bar astern, sailed past the forlorn wreck of our ship—her topmasts still showed above the water, canted to a rakish angle—and headed northwest, inside the reef, following the captain's pinnace toward the Endeavor Straits. We all agreed that rigging tow lines at night would be prudent.

The first night was quiet. I doubt that many of us slept, but there were no untoward incidents and the weather remained placid. We did, in fact, rig tow lines between the boats and kept sailing, standing watches as lookouts and helmsman, sail handlers and bailers, throughout. The prisoners, bound by their wrists, simply lay in the bottom of the boat, forward under the "oar" deck and muttered to each other. I imagine some actually did sleep.

Upon the dawning of the new day, Edwards ordered my boat and Larkan's to sail closer to the shore and investigate the coastline. We were still inside the reef—we would have to find an opening to the sea before we could make for the Endeavor Straits—and Larkan commented that, according to his recollection of the captain's chart, there was precious little to be found here. And likely no fresh water.

But Providence smiled on us; a beautiful bay opened up off our larboard bow and we eased our sheets and steered for it. As we pulled into the shallows, the bow man jumped out and, instead of guiding the boat into the beach, ran away a short distance where upon he fell on his face, dropping as if he had been shot. We knew not what had happened to the poor chap.

Once the boats were properly secured, we followed to find him splashing in a little river than ran from the forest lining the beach.

"It's fresh, sweet!" He exclaimed when he lifted his head for a breath.

We all followed his lead and drank our fill. Then we filled every container we could find in both boats. It wasn't much: a tea kettle and two quart bottles.

"We must try to signal the others." Larkan stated, looking out to where we could make out two specks, the longboat and the pinnace. "Fire a gun, if you please, Mister Ballantyne, and see if they respond."

"John, with the wind against us and them as far off as they appear, I doubt they will hear. Besides, the cap'n won't like us wasting the powder." I suggested we not fire a gun, especially as all we had was one musket and a few drams of powder which, according the Edwards' instructions, were for emergencies only. "We have filled our containers and our selves. Perhaps we should simply sail after them."

"Very well, then. I reckon that's sage advice. Get your boat underway."

In two hours, we had caught up—they had hove to when they saw us heading their way—and started back to the spring. Upon again entering the bay, we spied two canoes, each carrying three very black men, putting off from the beach. They stood in their boats and waved, beckoning us closer. They appeared very savage to all of us.

"We'll not be getting that water. I think it prudent to head back out. Those chaps have a look about them that might be troublesome.

"Make sail and continue northwest." Edwards had glassed the canoes, standing in his pinnace, and determined to avoid contact with the locals.

Off we went, sailing in a line about two miles off the coast. The remainder of the day passed in perfect boredom, but at ten o'clock that night, those who were asleep were rudely awakened with the cry of "Breakers ahead!"

Bleary eyed—I had fallen into a deep sleep, driven, no doubt, by exhaustion—I stood and looked about. White water, lit by a half-moon, seemed to be all around us! It thundered hollowly, like one of the bass drums we had heard in Otaheite. Somehow, we had blundered into another reef. The pale moonlight reflected off glistening, wet rocks and made the whiteness of the broken water even starker in contrast against the black of the rocks. And, not only were they ahead of us, they were also to our starboard hand and our larboard. The boats were still connected by the tow line and, I think, all of us were befuddled by the spectacle of the breakers almost all around.

I have no idea how we managed to get away; it appeared that should we stand clear of one line of rocks, we would be driven into another. But, somehow through Captain Edwards' leadership, we escaped the horrifying situation, and continued at a peaceful pace again to the northwest. And I doubt that any aboard any of the boats slept a wink for the remainder of the night!

At the meridian of the following day, we approached an island, which, by all appearances, was inhabited. We surely should be able to find water here!

The natives, each black as night and quite as naked as newborn babes, flocked to the beach as we approached. We dared not land yet, but several men in each boat stood and made signs of distress and our need for water. They seemed to understand and presently a few of them waded out to the boats.

We offered them some trifling presents, knives and some buttons cut from our coats, and made more signs of being thirsty. The men smiled and waded back to the shore, presently to reappear with a small cask of water. Passed around boat to boat, it was emptied in a flash and we signaled for more.

This time, however, the natives would not bring it out to the boats; they set it upon the beach and made signs for us to come and fetch it.

"Look there, Mister Ballantyne. The women and wee ones seem to be passing out bows and arrows!" One of my seamen pointed at the shoreline.

"Pull back. They're going to attack us!" Edwards' cry rang out before I could utter a sound.

Suddenly, the air was filled with a shower of arrows landing all around the boats. The men, while they weren't ducking the onslaught, worked feverishly to haul out the sails and get us away. Though none of us were hit, one arrow did hit a thwart in the captain's boat and actually went through the one-inch oak plank! We fired a single volley of muskets at them, which ended the attack and put them to flight. None that I could see were hit, however. We would be getting no water here! We pressed on, again to the northwest.

"Damn his eyes! We could have had our fill there, were he to let us land and shoot the bloody bastards!" Larkan spoke, perhaps, a bit louder than necessary, as Edwards heard him, quite clearly.

"You will be silent, Mister Larkan, and obey my orders. I will hear no more about this matter!" Even with his voice raised to be heard, the menace in it could not be missed.

And it was his first lieutenant he addressed that way! We can thank our lucky stars it was none of us who had made the comment; we'd have been keel-hauled!

For several more days, we pressed on. Our weather had remained calm and a good thing it was. The boats had barely a hand's breadth of wood above the sea; any kind of rising weather would have caused us problems. Occasional splashes were, for the most part, prevented from boarding us by the canvas Mister Montgomery had rigged, but nonetheless, we still had to bail frequently, a result of leaks and the odd sea which chose to baptize us. We followed the land, hopeful of finding sanctuary, should the weather take a turn for the worse, and equally hopeful of finding a source of sustenance and water.

Just before we would enter the Endeavor Straits, after which we would be unable to stop, we came upon an island, clearly inhabited. As it was coming on night, we anchored the boats off the shore and waited for daylight. And listened to something—it sounded like wolves—howling in the dark.

In the morning, Robert and an armed party went ashore to forage and find water. About an hour after he landed and disappeared into the trees, I could see his lumbering form again on the beach. He waved his arms and we approached cautiously to within earshot. Each boat had stationed a man with a loaded and cocked musket near the bows.

"Found a spring and some kind of berries," he shouted through his cupped hands. "No natives that I've encountered."

"We'll land the boats, Mister Larkan. Post sentries and a guard for the prisoners."

As we made our way inland, following Robert and one of his seamen, we discovered a *morai*, similar to the ones in Otaheite, but covered in bones, animal and human, according to our surgeon's expert judgment, and two human skulls.

"There have been sacrifices here," he stated, a bit obviously (I thought) as he held aloft a human skull. "And look at this." He pointed to a long paddle, supported by two forked branches. "This is a grave of some sort— someone important, I'd wager."

We looked around the makeshift temple and found signs of a recent fire as well as many footprints leading to and from the site. There were many paths leading into the forest, each showing signs of being in regular use. Silently, we pressed on to the spring Robert had found and began to gorge ourselves on the lovely, cool, sweet water the rushed up from the bottom of the hole one of the men had dug. We drank ourselves into a state of perfect, waterlogged joy!

And then realized how hungry we were. Water—or rather the lack of it—had been our primary concern, taking our minds off our empty bellies. Now, with our fill of water, the emptiness hit us hard.

I found some berries that seemed to bear the signs of being picked at by birds. Hamilton studied my find and declared them safe. "If the birds eat them, we should surely be able to as well." He later confirmed his scientific prognostication by discovering undigested berries of the same type in the droppings of larger animals.

Of which there appeared to be a plentiful supply. But we dared not shoot any, or even a bird, as it would signal our presence to the natives which could only be a short distance away, to judge by the paths and occasional sounds we had heard, human in nature. We placed armed sentries around the area as we filled every container we could find, including the carpenter's boots.

The weather continued unbearably hot. Despite of our good fortune at the spring, Edwards had increased our water allowance only a jot. So, following our debauchery, we once again returned to our survival ration, and would remain in a constant state of desperate thirst. I noticed that two of my prisoners, Muspratt and Coleman, I recalled their names, were actually drinking their own urine, surely not a good thing.

"Mister Innes. Should we prevent them from doing that? It can't be salubrious to their health." I pointed.

"Little of this is salubrious to any of us, Mister Ballantyne. However, body fluids will likely not be overly harmful to them. Surely is better than should they partake of seawater." He went silent for a moment, as if thinking.

"You may have learned from Mister Hamilton when we were ashore last, that the sailor who filled his belly with seawater directly after the wreck had found his way to Fiddler's Green?" He asked, perhaps reminded of the fact by his own comment.

"Excuse me?" I queried him.

"He's died Mister Ballantyne. And not a pleasant death it was. Out of his head and ranting like the madman the salt made him. A landsman, to be sure, he was, but one of his mates ought to have stopped him from drinkin' the sea. By my lights! What a dreadful way to go. Give me a ball in the head anytime over that! But at least he ain't suffering like us."

I agreed, most heartily, but thought privately that death was surely the last choice I would make, as long as we had the chance to make it to Coupang, no matter the privations!

"We'll be in the Torres Straits soon, Mister Ballantyne. I think we might be well served by securing things about the boat and bein' ready for some less pleasant sailing." Passmore had made his way to the stern of the boat where I had parked myself.

"Uh, George? I thought we were heading for the *Endeavor* Straits. Have I lost my head?"

He laughed. "Not a bit, sir. Same place, mostly. Cap'n Cook called 'em Endeavor after his ship, but most call 'em Torres. Just a habit, I reckon."

I took his advice as sound and gave the order to make our little vessel shipshape, though I freely admit there was precious little we could do with the number of people we had jammed into her. The other boats, perhaps on seeing my actions, followed suit. But the Torres Straits, when we passed through, proved as docile as a millpond and our passage was uneventful.

The Indian Ocean was a different story, however. We had accomplished only a few hundred miles of our journey, with the bulk of the remainder in the open ocean. I feared for our survival.

But Bligh and Hayward made over three thousand miles, mostly in the open ocean. Their boat wasn't any lighter than ours and they lived to tell the tale; why should we not?

I argued with myself, quite unable to be at peace with what might lay ahead.

Well, there's nothing for it but to do it! Perhaps the sea will calm and we will sail unscathed into Coupang. I tried to convince myself.

And the weather tried to convince us otherwise. The seas rose to alarming heights, towering over the small boats. Edwards ordered us to rig the tow lines even though there were still a few hours of daylight remaining.

With the boats riding the waves—perhaps their smallness assisted them in climbing up and over the waves, rather than crashing through them—we bailed between life and death. Two men, relieved every fifteen minutes, used the canvas bags, now empty, we had earlier filled with fresh water and, working as fast as they might, tried to stay ahead of the seas that had no respect for our canvas boat cloths. The waves were large enough that when we dropped into a trough, the sails slatted, quite devoid of the half gale we found when cresting a wave. It made managing the boat most challenging. And the tow lines gave us problems.

We were towing very hard, the line tightening and going slack with every sea. It was apparent to all but perhaps the landsmen, that the towline would part sooner or later. And it chose sooner. In the dark.

Afraid of smashing into to each other as we rigged new lines, orders flew about, some heard, others carried away by the wind. And the boats did collide, but with little beyond superficial damage. We finally, after working for nearly two hours, managed to secure new tow lines between each of the boats.

But history has a way of repeating itself and, with the weather still up, these lines also parted and we were obliged to make our way separately. The captain ordered each boat officer to stay close by so would we not become separated in the dark. And dark it was; the moon was obscured behind the heavy clouds, making it difficult to see the others or the waves rolling at us.

By five the next morning, with the sky lightening a bit as the sun tried to show itself, we were still afloat. Three of us had maintained contact by shouting across the water to each other throughout the remainder of the night, but we could not see the captain's pinnace.

Oh dear I thought. *What has become of them? Could they have upset during the night? Where do we even begin to look for them?*

My thoughts were confused, jumbled like a handful of twigs thrown willy-nilly onto a table.

"George," I called out to the sailing master. "Where do you reckon we might find the cap'n's boat? It appears that the other two are as confused as I."

Mercifully, the wind had eased a bit during the night, but the seas, in the aftermath of the storm—if that's what it was—remained uncomfortably high. Passmore stood up, balancing himself on the oars and the shoulder of one of our sailors.

"I'd think back the way we come, sir. And I'd add that we ought to stay together. Be hell, indeed, to lose another while we rush off to find the pinnace!" He peered through the early morning light, waiting until the boat crested a wave, and shielded his eyes with a hastily thrown up hand, which quickly returned to hold onto the sailor's shoulder.

"Mister Larkan. Passmore thinks we might sail back a ways and see if we can't find Cap'n Edwards." I shouted across the hundred or so feet to the first lieutenant's boat.

"Aye, John, seems like the right thing to do." Corner chimed in, cupping his hands around his mouth.

Larkan waved an acknowledgment and tacked his boat carefully, timing the movement to avert capsizing. And ran off, downwind, back the way we had sailed in the night. Corner and I followed suit, and soon, all three of us, spread across a hundred yards of ocean, were sailing east, hoping to find the pinnace still afloat.

And, to our joy, barely two hours later, Larkan's men espied it, not only still afloat, but sailing toward us. When Edwards saw the three of us, he made the signal to join up. It was exactly what we were doing! I wondered why he felt it necessary to signal us to that effect.

When we were close enough, I called to Hayward. "We were concerned about you. Did something untoward happen in the night?"

Immediately, I realized that Edwards would plainly hear what I said and wondered if he might take exception to my asking.

"I ordered us hove to for the night, Mister Larkan. Thank you for thinking to come back. But I reckon, as I have the provisions, you had little choice!" Edwards appeared unmoved by our concern.

Larkan, for his part, simply waved his acknowledgment, tacked around again, and headed back to the west. We all followed along, keeping a safe distance between the boats. As the sun continued its steady climb, the seas eased considerably, and we baked in the unrelenting glare and heat.

For another several days—I had lost track now of what day it was or even how long we had been embarked on this voyage—we sailed our course through the Indian Ocean to the west. Larkan and Edwards took sun sights every clear day at noon and compared their findings. We were on the right track, and making reasonable time, Edwards reported to all of us, after they had compared their findings. We continued to tow each other at night so as to avoid another separation. And then, having given us three or four days of scorching sun, pleasant winds, and reasonably calm seas, Mother Nature once again decided to test us.

We rigged the tow lines as darkness fell and the winds increased. Shortly before midnight, we enjoyed the same parting of the lines as we had before. This time, we did not re-rig them. In fact, Edwards made the decision we would use the tow lines no more. I later discovered in talking with Tom, that he feared pulling the boats asunder with the strain and jerking of the line when the seas were up.

Two days later, we watched as the crew of the pinnace caught a booby, a bird common the that part of the world, according to Mister Hamilton. While it was not terribly large, it was food, but the captain shared it out with the men in his own boat, not the whole of us. Of course, had he parceled it into over one hundred pieces, there would have been barely enough for each of us to smell, let alone actually eat. We hoped we would have the same good fortune as we pressed on, mouths drooling with envy and hunger.

The sun, when it shone on us, was relentless. Our skin had burned red and blistered painfully. Our eyes stung and itched, crusted with salt both from the sea and our own sweat. Headaches were the order of the day and, while they would often go away in the dark, we knew they would return quickly after the sun rose again to bake our minds into merciful insensibility. Some of the men took to soaking their shirts in the sea, then draping them over their heads. The relief this provided was transient at best, and the longer lasting effects of the practice proved unpleasant.

According to the surgeon's mate in my boat, Mister Innes, our skin had absorbed the salt from the water after several days of constant exposure to the wet shirts. The heat of the day speeded the process and, within three or four days, our body fluids were tainted with salt. Saliva became intolerable, but there was nothing for it save to stop the practice. We spat when we could, but even the fresh water ration tasted a bit salty causing some of us to question the sanctity of the containers.

But it wasn't the containers; it was us. Food, even the sparse rations we were allowed, lost any appeal and some of the men even rejected their allowance, complaining that their mouths were too parched to eat. Their rations were returned to the general stock of food.

Tempers flared, men became irrational at the slightest provocation and suffered delusions even when left alone. It was only our severely weakened state that prevented fights among all of us. No one was exempt from the strain, parched mouths, sunburned skin, and hunger. Had it not taken more effort than any of us were capable of expending, I am certain that even minor disagreements would have quickly erupted into shear mayhem.

We happened to be alongside the captain's boat one day when Edwards called out to a prisoner, Morrison it was, who had been lying on the oars forward.

"Come here, you rascal, and lay down here, where I might keep an eye on you." Edwards shouted in unexpected wrath.

"Sir, What is my crime. I have done nothing." Morrison complained, even as he dragged himself aft.

I watched and wondered, with the mutineer, what indeed he had done; I had noticed nothing save the man resting. The captain ordered another man forward to fetch aft another prisoner in the boat, who had been lying in the bilge under the oars. I thought I recognized Ellison. Edwards had both men bound hand and foot and ordered them to silence.

"Sir," cried Morrison, "what have I done to be so cruelly treated? It is not right, sir, and a disgrace to the commander of a British man of war to treat a prisoner in such an inhuman manner!"

"Silence, you piratical dog! What better treatment do you expect? You are nothing but a murdering villain and, should you say another word, I'll heave you overboard myself!" The captain was in a rage unlike any I had ever seen, shouting at the mutineer to the extent that many of us even began to feel sympathy for him. As I was taking my turn at the tiller of my boat, I steered away a bit, putting some distance between us.

On we sailed, grateful for the easy weather, but at the same time, wishing for the relief of overcast skies and rain. I had lost all sense of time, save for the constant cycle of day to night to scorching hot day. Our clothes seemed to have more holes than cloth, so sun and salt rotted were they. We stood our watches, bailed, managed the sails, and steered. I knew the men in the other boats were in exactly the same state; the same glassy-eyed looks, red and blistered skin, lethargic movement—and then only when necessary—and occasional voices raised in argument. Would we ever find a safe haven where there was plenty of water, fresh food, and dry clothes? Would we find Timor? Would I ever see England again? Just thinking about these things took more energy than I was prepared to spend. I dozed when off watch, and dreamed uneasy dreams.

One day, I dreamed of seeing birds flying overhead. They were not sea birds and seemed to be heading in the same direction as we were: toward land. In the dream, my spirits lifted and I woke my boat-mates to point them out. They all responded, "Mister Ballantyne, you're just dreaming. We're not close enough to land to see shore birds. Go back to sleep and let us do the same."

But I was not dreaming, and the very next day, one of the men in Captain Edwards' boat saw a smudge on the horizon and cried out "Land. I see land."

But in his parched and weakened state, his voice, hardly a croak, carried barely to the men in his own boat. Those of us in the other boats noticed movement and activity in the pinnace and, more particularly, the captain standing amidships, his glass to his eye. Then they all cried out and we, too, saw the same dark smudge in the distance. Excitement reigned and we all trimmed our sails to make for the land. It could only be Timor. I think we were more excited about getting water and possibly, some food, than the fact that the voyage might be at an end. And then the wind died completely.

The men retrieved their oars from where they had lain for most of the trip and began weakly to pull toward the shore. We became separated as some crews seemed to find more strength than the others of us. As we drew nigh to the beach, we could see a huge line of breakers. There would be no landing here.

A bit farther down the beach, two of Corner's men slung bottles around their necks and jumped into the water, swam through the surf, and walked for several hours along the shore. They finally signaled there was no water to be had and swam back through the breakers back to rejoin the boat. They had quite exhausted themselves in the process.

In the meantime, Larkan's boat, an English Jack hoisted to her top to help us follow her progress, cruised along the shoreline and disappeared into a creek that ran into the sea. We all made sail and hastened after her.

The men under the first lieutenant's care waded into the sea to help us beach our boats. I have to acknowledge the skill of Master's Mate Reynolds who guided each boat in over the reef and, apparently, also brought Larkan's boat in safely. We staggered—our legs were stiff with lack of use, and, at first refused to follow our orders—up the beach to where a spring of cool, fresh water fed the creek and collapsed around it, drinking and laughing like children. It was immediate relief and after we had drunk our fill, somebody remembered to take several casks of the water to our prisoners, who had remained tied in the boats and under guard. Then we slept.

I awakened to find a stranger in our rude camp. He was an old man, and had come upon our bedraggled party while fishing in his canoe. He had several men with him. I was immediately alarmed, given the nature of our previous encounters with the natives and then I noticed several of the officers and midshipmen clustered about him, trying to communicate. I had thought our appearance would be quite effective in communicating our plight.

He spoke for quite some time in his own language, bowed, and climbed back into his canoe.

"Did he speak Otaheitian, Tom?" I queried my friend.

"Not a word. Nor did he speak French or English."

"Then how on earth did you manage to get across to him that we were in distress?" I pressed.

"Edward. Look about you. If ever there was distress displayed, this is clearly it! He made us to understand that he would return with food and his friends. I think he was some kind of chief, though I have no certain knowledge of that." Hayward watched the canoe paddle swiftly away.

With hope rekindled and help at hand, we all became more animated and conversations, recounting our travail, the future, and where we thought we might be, flew about. And we watched the sea in the direction our new friend had gone.

"Well, by my lights! That was quick!" Hamilton spoke and reached out of habit for his watch.

He shook his head and tried to cover his embarrassment by putting his hand in his pocket. He had lost his watch in the shipwreck. No one noticed as all eyes were focused on the small flotilla of canoes rounding a point and heading for the spot we occupied on the beach.

As they landed, we could see a cornucopia of fowls, pigs, milk, bread, vegetables and fruits in each canoe. The men and women, under our new friend's direction, began to unload everything onto the beach. The starved English sailors—and officers—quickly began to pick them up, but our savior stopped us with a torrent of his words and gestures.

He wanted to trade. Mister Innes, the surgeon's mate who had spent so much time in my boat, found some silver in pocket and offered it to the chief. He wouldn't take it, but motioned to Larkan that he would like

325

some buttons off his uniform jacket. We ate. And ate. And that night, roasted fowls and boiled a pig.

"Gentlemen: I have no doubt but what we are in Timor. I believe Coupang to be some seventy miles 'round the end of the island. We will have a look up the creek to see if we might shorten our sail on the morrow.

"Mister Larkan, post sentries at the boats, if you please, not only to guard our captives, but to protect our boats in the event these local chaps might visit us again with less kindness. Set watches around our camp as well." Edwards strode off a few paces, removed his coat—which now had precious few buttons—and, spreading it out on the sand, lay upon it and went quickly to sleep.

We all followed suit.

There was no shortcut in using the creek; it dwindled to a trickle some four miles from the coast and shortly after the meridian, we loaded the boats with our new provisions and water, and set sail for Coupang. As our destination was now within reach and our provisions and water plentiful, we enjoyed them to the fullest. As night fell, we put into a small bay, anchored the boats, and ate some more. Edwards was certain Coupang was within one more day's sailing, and rather than overshoot the harbor in the dark, had us lay up during the night.

I sat in the sand next to Robert. "You look a bit better than you did yesterday, my friend. Amazing what a bit of food will do for you!" I joked to him.

"It's clear you have no looking glass, Edward. You have improved, but only a trifle, since we landed yesterday. And I am sure that when I have new uniforms made, they will be a good measure smaller than what I lost!"

"And your disposition seems slightly better, as well!" I retorted to his insult. "I think that had any had the strength, there might have been a bit of unpleasantness in the past few days at sea."

"Aye, likely unpleasant enough to make the Bounties look like choirboys! I know Edwards was thinking all the time they might rise up and try to reprise their earlier mischief. Likely why he had them bound hand and foot in his boat. Of course, when you are too weak to stand up, it's more difficult to foment a mutiny!" Corner had not lost his sense of humor in spite of our depredations.

"Gentlemen: I would caution you not to overindulge yourselves in light of our previous limited diets. I assure you, were you to eat your fill, you will retain little of it. Better to begin slowly and not gorge yourselves!" Our surgeon, ever mindful of keeping us in good health, was going around the camps and offering his sage advice, albeit a trifle late.

"George, I could eat an entire pig myself! And what I wouldn't give for a cask of good wine!" Robert smiled at the doctor.

"And were you to give in to that imbecilic notion, Mister Corner, you would regret the after-effects no end!" Hamilton, not seeing Corner's humor, retorted and left us.

We both laughed and went to sleep, dreaming, I'm sure, of our return to civilization and all the luxuries it held.

Underway in the boats at dawn the next day, we sailed until nearly five in the afternoon. We had a fine breeze, calm seas, and all manner of birds flying overhead and fishes showing themselves beneath us. It was almost as if Mother Nature was saying, "You have won, my friend, and now you shall see my benevolent side!"

"There! There it is!" We all clearly heard the cry from Larkan's boat as the harbor at Coupang opened before us. British flags flew to the mastheads and, in a ragged line, we sailed in, Edwards in the van as would befit his position.

He's done it! He's gotten us to Coupang and with almost no one heaved over the side. A hard man he might be, but perhaps a more gentle soul might not have seen us through!

I recalled the poor landsman who drank sea water the first day after the wreck and succumbed to his stupidity several days later.

Sails came down, and oars were shipped. With strength born of our deliverance, the men rowed smartly to the quay and tossed their oars aloft with the precision expected from a frigate's boat crew. I am sure, to the townsfolk who saw us, we made an impressive sight! Rags, beards, and barefoot we were, but at least we conducted ourselves like proper English seamen!

Having left a guard for the prisoners, we were led by Captain Edwards and climbed up the steps to the pier with straight backs and heads held high.

"You know, Edward, those are the self-same steps we climbed when I landed here with Cap'n Bligh. And we looked only slightly the worse than today!" Tom Hayward mentioned to me as we found our way to the governor's house where we were received with the utmost civility and kindness.

CHAPTER TWENTY-FIVE

In Timor

"It's a wonder we found Timor, what with having the date wrong by a day!" Hamilton, while a skilled surgeon, was not a seaman and did not understand the workings of navigation.

"Wouldn't have made a difference either way, George. We were sailing almost due west, down a line of latitude, so the date had no bearing on our position, north to south." Larkan responded, accompanied by nods of agreement from Robert and the rest of us.

We sat in the parlor of the Governor's house, taking some tea and biscuits. As we had arrived on sixteen September, a Saturday, we assumed the next day to be Sunday and marched off to the local church to give thanks to the Almighty for our deliverance. We were disappointed to discover that, having made our passage east to west, we had gained a day and in fact, it was not Sunday, but Monday!

Edwards had made arrangements, on the strength of the Admiralty's credit, to book passage for all the survivors and prisoners to Batavia where we could expect to find another Dutch East Indiaman on which we could book further passage to Cape Town and home. Goodness, did that sound wonderful!

And so, with hearts and minds eager to begin this first leg of our homeward journey, we boarded the Dutchman *Rembang*, sailing for the island of Java on the sixth of October. Our prisoners, having been issued slop clothing in Coupang, again using the credit of the Admiralty, were released from their confinement in that city's gaol and were manacled and confined in the Dutchman.

This would be a short voyage, barely of three weeks duration and most of us saw it as chance to regain our health which, while surely improving, was still far from robust. The Dutch crew and officers would work the ship and we would make every effort to fulfill our roles of passengers to the best of our abilities. But it was not to be.

Our winds were light and fickle, the weather sultry at best, and the Dutch crew, almost to a man, took ill. As the ship turned the island of Flores, the weather worsened and we found ourselves in a frightful storm. With a sick crew, mostly unable to get aloft quickly, our sails were torn to ribbons in no time and, to compound the situation, the ship's pumps became choked and useless to the point where the multiple leaks that had opened up were filling our holds with alarming speed. Thunder and lightning ripped the sky and rain, driven by the tempest, lashed at every soul who dared to appear on deck. And we were blowing onto a lee shore, some seven miles distant.

Edwards, on deck as was his habit regardless of the weather, saw the Dutch seamen scurry below and, at once, took command of the situation and the ship. Our English tars, roused from below, hastened to the deck and, with ardor fueled by their past experiences, scrambled aloft, worked the sheets and braces, and saved the ship. God bless the British sailors!

We saw the island of Java several days after passing through the straits of Alice and, four days later, dropped our best bower in Samarang.

"Sir. Is not that our tender?" I pointed at a small schooner anchored near at hand.

"Why, by my lights, I do believe it is." Larkan studied the little ship with his glass.

Rarely in my life have I experienced such joy! It was akin to seeing a dear friend, thought dead, appear on your doorstep in perfect health. I could scarcely contain my joy and determined to get ashore quickly and discover what had happened to Master's Mate Oliver and my midshipman, Renouard.

Corner and Tom were equally delirious with joy and accompanied me as I sought them out.

"What a joy it is to see you, lads. We thought you were long dead and gone. Where have you been; tell us, pray, what has happened." Tom spotted Oliver enjoying a glass of wine at a grog shop on the quay.

"Where is *Pandora*? How did you get here? It's a fortnight we've been idling here, hoping to find a way home." Oliver stated, quite ignoring our own queries.

"Where is Renouard?" I asked, ignoring his questions. There would be time enough for all the tales we each had to tell, but I wanted to be sure that the young man in my charge was still among the living.

"Oh, David is quite well. Indeed, I expect him directly." He answered me, perhaps seeing my concern.

A round of drinks appeared, followed at once by Renouard and the stories began. Corner and Hayward gave the account of our travail, searching fruitlessly for *Bounty* and the other mutineers after our long wait for the tender in Anamooka, the wreck, and our voyage in the ship's boats to Timor. By the time they had finished, we found ourselves suffering from a mite of overindulgence and determined that the story our long lost shipmates would tell would be best told over some vittles.

"The night we parted with the frigate—you may recall, Mister Corner, the weather turned squally—and we lost sight of her. All at once, whilst we were casting about in our search, we came under attack by some of the most savage natives in canoes. We had barely a scrap of sail up and they had quite quickly surrounded us, firing arrows and slinging rocks at us." Bill Oliver began, once food had been placed before us. He shook his head at the memory.

"One of the men fired the swivel gun at them and, while he killed a great number with one shot—it was loaded with grape—and upset their canoe, it did nothing to stop the others. Apparently, they had never seen a European gun and had no understanding of what had happened to their brethren and so, continued the attack. Mister Renouard, here, then opened up with one of the seven barreled pieces and created absolute havoc among them." He winked at Renouard who beamed.

And took up the story. "One of the rascals actually managed to get over our boarding net and brandished his war club—a huge thing it was—at Bill . . . uh, Cap'n Oliver." He smiled broadly at his mate. "And with complete nonchalance, the cap'n shot the man square in the face with his pistol. Dropped like a stone he did!"

A round of well-dones, handshakes, and congratulations followed from all of us. Their travail not yet done, they had searched at some length for *Pandora*, but then decided they would sail to the rendezvous at Anamooka.

"You can not imagine the distress we experienced from our lack of provisions, and, more importantly, water. It was dreadful, I think the most dreadful experience I had ever had to that point." Renouard shivered at the memory.

"And he took dreadful sick from it, as well." Oliver added. "Spent much of the following month—even after we had gotten some water—quite out of his head. Delirious, ranting, and raving like some wild-eyed maniac. Hardly in keeping with the best traditions of the Royal Navy!" Oliver winked at Renouard, who blushed.

"When we arrived at Anamooka—we did not discover until nearly a week had passed that we were actually at Tofoa—we bartered with the locals for provisions and, of course, water." Oliver went on. "The same natives who had been so helpful now tried to take the schooner. By force. Again, we beat them off with our firearms. I reckon they thought because our vessel was small, they would have no trouble overpowering us and winning her. Likely, they learned a lesson!"

"Aye, and now having heard your story, I collect that by the time we actually made Anamooka, *Pandora* had sailed, presuming us lost." Renouard added. "So Bill decided to sail for the Dutch settlement he had heard of in Batavia."

"A smart choice, I'd warrant. And here you are! Well done, chaps! A magnificent feat of seamanship and navigation, I'd say!" Robert chimed in, thinking their story told.

"But that wasn't the end of it. We must have found the same reef off New Holland that you did and very nearly wrecked ourselves. Of course, had we, we likely would have all gone to our great reward. But Mister Oliver navigated us *over* the reef with such aplomb as you would not believe!

"Once we passed Endeavor Straits, we thought we would only have to sail west and we would stumble across the island of Java. And fortunately, we fell in with a Dutch trader who provided us provisions, water, and sailing directions to a small Dutch settlement, where we were placed under guard by the governor!"

"Under guard! My stars! Whatever for?" Hayward asked, as incredulous as the rest of us.

Oliver continued. "He had gotten a description of the schooner the mutineers built—the very same one we now sailed—and assumed we were they. Of course, we had no way of proving who we were, no warrants, commissions, or anything save our word. While he withheld nothing for our comfort and succor, we were under constant scrutiny. Even so, our situation was quite agreeable."

"After a fortnight, Bill convinced the governor we were not the mutineers, but rather were part of the crew who had been sent to fetch them, and yes, we had their boat. But that was *because* we had succeeded in our commission. He let us leave, fully provisioned and watered, to sail to Batavia. It was only by chance that we stopped here in Samarang for some provisions. We've been here barely a week, now." Renouard concluded their tale on a somewhat grim note. "And even in that short period, one of our men has gone over. Barker, it was, and the physician who attended him determined that the privations and strain of our adventure were just too much for his constitution. Died just yesterday; our only casualty."

"Well, a shame indeed that is. But your's is a tale to rival our own, gentlemen. I commend you on your abilities and instincts! You must tell Larkan and the cap'n of your travails. I'm quite sure they will be as fascinated as we.

"Perhaps you would prefer to move your quarters to *Rembang*? A bit more comfortable than the schooner, I'd warrant!" Corner offered.

"Actually, sir, while your offer is very kind, we have all found quarters ashore. But of course, we will sail with you to Batavia, when you depart." Oliver responded.

But Captain Edwards had other plans for the schooner he had renamed *Matavia*. He determined that the little ship would be only a hindrance to the remainder of our voyage and sent her, with a local crew, back to Timor as a gift to the governor. Out of gratitude for the kindness the governor had shown the Pandoras, said Mister Larkan, and, in a further gesture of his goodwill, Edwards distributed shares of her value to his crew.

We languished in Samarang for another fortnight during which time, the number of prisoners for whom we were responsible increased by ten: seven men, a woman, and two children.

I happened to be standing at the bulwark of the Indiaman that would be carrying us to Batavia when they appeared under guard and escorted by Mister Larkan. Even the children were bound.

"And who are these?" I queried, once the first lieutenant had turned them over to the Dutch equivalent of the master at arms.

"Escaped convicts, Edward. Almost had the governor convinced they were cast away sailors from a British ship. When we arrived, it only added credence to their tale. But, as you know, we had left no one behind, certainly not women and children, and when they were brought to the cap'n, who quite denied them, their true story came out.

"They had escaped from the prison colony at Botany Bay on New Holland in a boat in which they had planned to rendezvous with a sympathetic ship at sea. Sadly for them, the ship did not meet them and they determined to sail, much in the same manner as we had, to Java. Only they got lost and landed here, on Samarang. The governor has requested we see them back to England for whatever the authorities might have in mind for escaped convicts."

"A decision surely based on the fact that we were already seeing to the welfare of our own prisoners, I'll wager." put in Robert, who had joined the conversation shortly after Larkan had begun his narrative.

"Indeed. But we will see them safely confined below, most probably in the 'tween decks, with our own rascals, and their 'welfare' will be seen to as well." Larkan responded.

And so, with twice the number of prisoners in our care, we sailed the next day for Batavia, where we went through all the formalities expected of Englishmen in a foreign country. As with his predecessors, the governor was exceedingly kind to us and arranged for us transport on two vessels, one bound for Capetown and the other, to Europe.

Mister Larkan, George Hamilton, and some forty of our sailors sailed from Java for Europe on the first of these. The remainder of the Pandoras, including Captain Edwards, Robert Corner, myself, and Tom Hayward, accompanied our prisoners and the Botany Bay convicts aboard the East Indiaman, *Vreedenbergh*, bound for South Africa.

The trip was uneventful, save for the demise of two of our Pandoras, who, having become so hampered by their travail that they never regained robust health, finally gave up the ghost about a fortnight out of Java. The mutineers, as well as the convicts, were allowed on two occasions, to walk the decks, at the insistence of the Dutch doctor aboard. Hamilton would have been pleased!

We arrived in the roads of Table Bay, Capetown, on eighteen March, 1792, having made the Cape three days previously. We were overjoyed to discover an English man of war, *Gorgon*, a third rate ship, rated at forty-four guns, anchored under the Dutch fort, taking on provisions and water for an imminent departure for Portsmouth. She was returning to England from the penal colony at Botany Bay (how ironic for some of our prisoners!) and Edwards was quick to secure us all, prisoners, convicts, officers, and seamen, transport in her.

We sailed on four April and, following stops at St. Helena and Ascencion, set our best bower in the mud at Spithead on nineteen June, seventeen hundred ninety-two, our voyage of circumnavigation completed, at long last.

EPILOGUE

England

With the mutineers transferred to His Majesty's Ship *Hector* to await their court-martial, little remained for most of us to do. We had no ship, few possessions, and, while the war with France was escalating, we were not assigned to any King's vessel sailing to that theatre.

Instead, we would testify at Captain Edwards' court-martial—it was proper in the minds of the Admiralty to hold a court when a ship has been lost—and appear at our own. In the event, the two were combined, as both courts-martial would deal with the same subject and testimony.

Having never been part of a court-martial, either as a witness or defendant, I was understandably nervous at the prospect. Robert and Tom, who, of course, had been a witness at Captain Bligh's court-martial, assuaged my concerns.

"Edward, in your opinion, could Cap'n Edwards—or for that matter, you—have done anything to prevent *Pandora* from finding the reef and foundering?" Robert asked me one evening.

"I have no idea, Robert. We were lying to and when the wind shifted a mite and that tops'l filled, we simply blew onto the reef. I doubt there was little anyone might have done to prevent it."

"Did Cap'n Edwards, and you, and John Larkan, for that matter, do everything you might to get her off? And when she came off of her own accord, did you try to keep her afloat?" He pressed.

"You know we did. You were there, too." I was beginning to get a bit hot at his questioning.

"Then you have nothing to worry about. Those are the questions the court will ask you, should they ask you anything. Edwards will be the one being asked most of the questions and all you will have to do is support him." Robert smiled at my own visible relief.

The trial was held aboard HMS *Hector* in Portsmouth Harbor and lasted only two days. And it went exactly as Robert had predicted: the court-martial board found that "everything was done for the preservation of His Majesty's ship *Pandora* and for the good of His Majesty's Service and the said Captain Edward Edwards and the other officers and company of His Majesty's Ship *Pandora* are hereby honorably acquitted."

Tom Hayward and I sat in the gallery for the mutineers' court-martial, which began two days later and lasted only six days. Lord Hood presided over twelve captains in the Great Cabin of HMS *Duke*, also in Portsmouth Harbor. They were charged with the most heinous of crimes against the Royal Navy, mutiny in His Majesty's Armed Vessel *Bounty*.

All had lawyers of varying degrees of expertise, and all professed their innocence, claiming the absent Fletcher Christian and the eight men who sailed *Bounty* off from Otaheite were the *real* mutineers. But they were not present in the court and could not be tried.

"Did you see the letters stacked on the table in front of Lord Hood, Tom? What do you suppose they were?" I asked after the first day of trial.

"I'm sure they were requests for clemency and casting the blame for the entire mutiny on poor Cap' n Bligh." Tom said churlishly. He had been chafing at his lines to see these men convicted and hanged.

Well, I can not blame him for wanting these men punished. After all, he enjoyed the pleasures of two open boat voyages across vast stretches of open ocean, and all on account of their actions. Aye, he deserves to feel as he does!

"Hallet's testimony surely wasn't much help to my old messmate, Peter Heywood." Tom observed. "He actually said that Peter had laughed as Bligh was put in the boat and turned away. A far cry, I'd say, from what he said to me about imploring Bligh to take Peter and George Stewart with him . . . and there not being any room for more."

"Hallet is clearly a wretch. I reckon getting himself out of harm's way was all he cared about and the devil take the rest." Hayward was working himself into a rage.

"But, Tom. You said yourself, back when Heywood first came aboard *Pandora* that he was in league with Christian and his cutthroats."

"From what I've heard so far, it's possible I was mistaken about that. Peter and I were friends—as was Hallet—and I felt betrayed by his remaining in *Bounty*. It's a pity, indeed, that George Stewart drowned in the shipwreck; he might have refuted Hallet."

"No one else mentioned that they saw him laugh at Bligh, so maybe it's just Hallet making it up. And he surely offered some damaging comments about Morrison." I thought to move my friend off the subject of Heyward.

"He did that! When he quoted Morrison as jeering at Bligh *and* holding a cutlass, I could see members of the court react. Morrison's likely to be hanged, unless someone else comes forward and gives him a fair breeze off the lee shore he's headed for! And I surely did not witness that. That day remains as clear in my mind as if it were yesterday!"

The following days of the court-martial brought more testimony against the mutineers, but, sadly, the main witness was not present; Captain Bligh was back at sea, with two ships and full complements of officers, men, and Marines, to retrieve the breadfruit plants for which he had originally been sent, and take them to Jamaica.

With the pressing need to put the matter behind them, the Admiralty elected not to wait for his return to England. It was up to those who remained loyal to him to testify on his behalf. But the mutineers and their families did inestimable damage to Bligh's reputation, jigging the events and words spoken to suit their own story and, as Bligh was not there to defend himself, their slanders carried some weight. For some reason, his published journal, which I had attempted to find before we had sailed back in November of 1790, remained unmentioned and was not presented as Bligh's voice during the court-martial.

At the conclusion, the court pronounced their findings of guilt or innocence. Among the mutineers acquitted of their crime were Coleman, Michael Byrne (the blind fiddler), Norman, and McIntosh. Muspratt was convicted, but his clever lawyer found a technicality—an error committed by the court in his case—and he was reprieved.

Midshipman Peter Heywood and the bosun's mate, James Morrison were found guilty, but in a curious turn of events, the court of captains recommended them both to the mercy of the King. By doing so, the court's gesture was a complete reversal of their findings of guilty and tantamount to a full pardon. The King, of course, granted it.

Seamen Burkitt, Millward, and Ellison were found guilty of mutiny and sentenced to hang. Which they did, at twenty-six minutes past eleven in the forenoon, from the foreyard of HMS *Brunswick*, on twenty-nine October, 1792, putting an end to the story, which quickly faded into obscurity in the light of more pressing events. And no one ever saw Fletcher Christian again.

END

AUTHOR'S NOTES

While this book is technically a work of fiction due to the addition of several fictional characters and dialogue from real ones, it is, nonetheless, historically accurate except as noted in these notes. Of course, our narrator, Edward Ballantyne, is a creation of the author; Tom Hayward was, in fact, third lieutenant in *Pandora*. The other officers, warrants, and petty officers were real people.

The *Bounty* story has been written, filmed, and discussed many times over the course of the two-hundred-plus years since the mutiny, but very few of the writers, including those who wrote contemporary accounts of it, got it completely right; the men who experienced it—William Bligh, James Morrison, and Peter Heywood—all had their own "spin" on it, while historians have routinely credited them with "getting it right." Caroline Alexander, author of *The* Bounty: *The True Story of the Mutiny on the* Bounty, actually did the research, using the testimony at the trial of the mutineers along with other primary sources, to tell the real story. But rarely has anyone paid attention to the tale of *Pandora* and the recovery of the mutineers. When I stumbled across it, courtesy of Ms. Alexander, I decided this amazing tale needed telling. I hope you have enjoyed reading it.

One of the events that makes this story more compelling and current is the discovery of the wreck of *Pandora* off Cape York, Australia in 1979. Archaeological surveys and multiple dives were carried out over the ensuing several years and many artifacts were recovered, including the captain's stove and Surgeon Hamilton's watch. Both were in remarkable condition for having been under water for nearly two hundred years! China from the wardroom, cannon, small arms, and an enormous variety of important relics have been brought up and carefully preserved.

In addition, three skeletons were found, one of which was identified as Purser's Steward Robert Bowler, and following a consecration of the wreck site, were reburied, closing the site to any future exploration. The artifacts are brilliantly displayed in the Museum of Tropical Queensland, Townsville, Australia, in a large section dedicated to *Pandora*. As a matter of interest, the wreck was found in very close proximity to Edwards' calculated site, about four miles from Sandy Cay, and in ninety feet of water, just as his leadsman said. Tom Hayward had drawn a map of the site which proved remarkably accurate.

The reader should be aware that most of the characters peopling Ballantyne's Second Division are fictional. Of course, this would include Bully Rodgers who was falsely accused of thievery. The punishment for that crime was the gauntlet, though of course, the events that transpired during the execution of the punishment are entirely from the author's imagination.

Hamilton's ongoing battle against scurvy was factual; his research of those who had written theories about its cause led him to take the protective measures he did, and to his credit, there were no incidents of the dread disease during *Pandora's* voyage.

The mutineers of *Bounty* are, of course, real people. Their activities were chronicled carefully by Bosun's Mate James Morrison during their time on *Bounty*, the mutiny itself, and, for those who chose to remain, on Tahiti. He also described in some detail their capture and the conditions in Pandora's Box, as well as during the voyage from Australia to Java. Captain Bligh had left careful descriptions of each of the mutineers with the Admiralty to assist Edwards in identifying them. The physical descriptions I used were taken from Bligh's notes.

A comment regarding the names of the natives of "Otaheite"—Tahiti, now: the use of primary source material for research can be fraught with problems of spelling (contemporary versus modern) and an Englishman's interpretation of the complex and often confusing names they encountered. Both Hamilton and Morrison, as well as Bligh and Edwards, not only had different spellings of native names, but often different names for the same person! I settled on one spelling for consistency, but offered the more commonly used alternate names for the same person in an effort to remain true to the history. Otoo (Tynah) was indeed a real king; he became known as POMARE I (1743-1803) after he had assumed leadership of the entire island. What the English did not understand was the use of "O" as a sign of respect. Starting with Captain Cook, the name of the island was misunderstood to be "Otaheite," not O Taheite.

Midshipman David Renouard's story is true. To my knowledge, he was not a whiner or complainer, but did secure his warrant to midshipman, having been Edwards' steward, without serving time before the mast. In fact, his warrant is dated just three days after his enlisted discharge papers! While, in an effort to "humanize" his youthful inexperience and vulnerability, I gave him the name of "Willy," there is nowhere any indication of him having any other name save David. Interestingly, there are even conflicting spellings of *his* surname!

The loss of the cutter, skippered by Midshipman Sival, was a true accounting, as was the story of the captured schooner, *Matavia*. The latter was described by David Renouard in a published journal, subsequent to his return to England.

Shooting to destroy waterspouts did occur and, according to Hamilton's journal, *Pandora* did, indeed, fire at several in the South Atlantic. Neither I, nor, apparently, the good doctor, can attest to the efficacy of the practice.

A note on Seaman Brown, the English sailor found on Tahiti: his story is true as well, and he did, with the consent of the captain of the brig *Mercury*, leave that ship for the reasons he stated to Edward Ballantyne. He survived the ship wreck, but chose, for unknown reasons, to remain in Indonesia when the other survivors sailed for England in the Dutch East Indiaman. At least, there is no record of his returning to England.

The tale of the escaped convicts from Botany Bay is a story in itself, but suffice it to say, they did escape from the penal colony in New Holland (Australia), and made it to Indonesia where they almost convinced the governor they were shipwrecked sailors. And Edwards did see to their passage back to England. They received sentences varying from death to transport back to Botany Bay, with most being incarcerated in Newgate Prison. One, the woman, a Mary Bryant, was given her freedom.

Also worthy of note is the story of Tim Calligan, an actual member of *Pandora's* crew, rated Able Seaman. Of course, he was not involved with Bully Rodgers (a fictional character) and further, did not "run" in Tahiti. Therefore, he was not captured by the natives and beheaded as depicted in the story; I used that vehicle to "close out" the fictional account of his interaction with others in the crew.

Edwards did not order the "Box" constructed until the first of the mutineers had been captured; he held them in the 'tween decks, fully ironed and shackled, until it was finished. I took liberty with the timeline of its construction to show his absolute commitment to the completion of his commission; there was never a doubt in his mind that he would be successful in capturing the mutineers.

The description of the native "show" put on for the crew and officers of *Pandora* in Tahiti was reported in detail in Hamilton's journal, and quite apropos of the surgeon's aplomb, he handled a potentially delicate matter in a most genteel manner.

It might be of interest to the reader that Peter Heywood and James Morrison, both granted pardons by King George III, went on to illustrious careers in the Royal Navy.

Heywood attained the rank of post captain and enjoyed a successful career as a respected commander in the Navy. In 1818, he declined the position of commodore on the Great Lakes of Canada, citing poor health, and would have been named admiral, had he not finally succumbed to his ill health at age fifty-eight in 1831.

Bosun's Mate Morrison went back to sea, petitioning the Navy for a position in 1793. With the war with France gathering headway, the Navy had great needs for skilled hands; a man with his experience found no difficulty securing a position. But there was a *quid pro quo*: the Admiralty did not want him to publish his "tell-all" journal and so they traded sending him back to sea for his agreement not to publish the journal until all the participants were dead. He lived until 1807 when his last ship, HMS *Blenheim*, foundered and sank in a frightful storm off the Madagascar coast on 1 February; Morrison, survivor of mutiny, captivity in appalling conditions, shipwreck, and court-martial, finally went to Fiddler's Green and a watery grave.

Edward Edwards, following the events depicted in this book, never returned to sea, though he did achieve the rank of admiral. He rose to the honorary title of Admiral of the White Squadron (by title, the third most senior officer of the Royal Navy) in 1814, and died ten months later, in April 1815.

Robert Corner, second lieutenant in *Pandora*, returned to the sea as first lieutenant in HMS *Terrible* following the court-martial of the mutineers. His career ended as superintendent of marine police in Malta, and he died in February, 1819 at the age of sixty-six.

George Hamilton, *Pandora*'s surgeon and chronicler, also went back to sea, again as surgeon. He was invalided out of the service after losing an arm in battle aboard HMS *Lowestoft*.

The ironies and parallels of the *Pandora* story and its players to that of Bligh and *Bounty* are quite amazing. I am sure the reader has drawn some of his or her own, so I will mention only a few here.

Of course, most obvious is the dichotomy between Bligh and Edwards: Bligh was painted a tyrant, though he was not, and Edwards indeed was a tyrant though no one ever mentioned it! When Bligh returned to England with the horrific story of his travails, he was a sensation; when Edwards brought the mutineers back, few, save the Admiralty even noticed. The new American president and a looming war with France had quite over-shadowed the story of a nearly four year old mutiny.

Both men made arduous open boat journeys with barely a loss, suffering unspeakable hardship. Both men were superb seamen and able commanders. And while both were exonerated by their courts-martial, Bligh's reputation was forever besmirched by the trial of the mutineers (indeed, his name survives in the modern lexicon as synonymous with tyrant), while Edward Edwards, even though he was never given another command, made it through the trials without a scratch!

William H. White
Rumson, New Jersey
September, 2008

For more great historically accurate fiction from William H. White, read the books on the following pages. You can order them online at www.tillerbooks.com if your local bookseller doesn't have them.

The War of 1812 Trilogy

"Read the trials and tribulations of Isaac Biggs and enjoyed them immensely. Haven't read anything like this since Forester. You write better sea stories than I do."

Clive Cussler
Best-selling author of *Arctic Drift, The Chase, Plague Ship*, and many more....

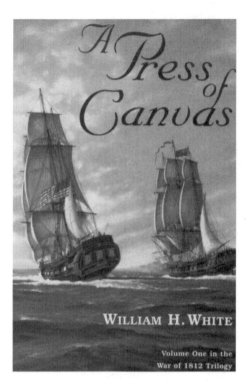

A Press of Canvas

Volume 1 in the War of 1812 Trilogy

"The Age of Fighting Sail has been well portrayed by C. S. Forester, Patrick O'Brian and their followers. But all of these writers saw the world from the quarterdeck. Now comes William H. White with A Press Of Canvas *to present the same conflicts on the same ships from the viewpoint of a fo'c'sle hand. It is a worthy effort, well executed, and thoroughly engaging, and all of us who love the subject matter are in his debt."*
  Donald Petrie, Author
  The Prize Game, Lawful Looting on the High Seas in the Days of Fighting Sail.
  Naval Institute Press 1999

"A great read . . . a very engaging story with believable, honest characters . . . taught me a lot about this period of history . . . just fabulous!"
  John Wooldridge, Managing Editor
  MotorBoating and Sailing

"Sailors everywhere will rejoice in the salt spray, slanting decks and high adventure of this lively yarn of the young American republic battling for its rights at sea."
  Peter Stanford, President
  National Maritime Historical Society

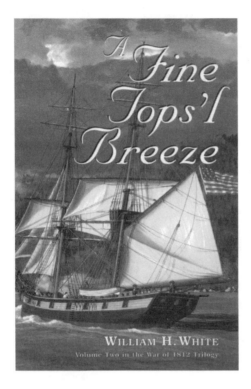

A Fine Tops'l Breeze

Volume 2 in the War of 1812 Trilogy

"By the publication of A Fine Tops'l Breeze, *the second in his War of 1812 Trilogy, William H. White had taken his place in the charmed circle of writers of really good fiction about the days of fighting sail: Melville, Forester, O'Brian, Nelson, and Kent. Like them, his attention to the detail of ships and their hulls, spars, and rigging and sails is meticulous. And, like them, his characters are not only credible, but memorable. He is a thoroughly welcome writer to this genre, which has brought so much pleasure to so many."*

Donald A. Petrie
Author of *The Prize Game: Lawful Looting on the High seas in the Days of Fighting Sail,* 1999

"Through Bill White's evocative prose, one smells the salt breeze and feels the pulse of life at sea during the War of 1812."

John B. Hattendorf
Ernest J. King Professor of Maritime History, U.S. Naval War College

The Evening Gun

Volume 3 in the War of 1812 Trilogy

"*The War of 1812 truly is the forgotten war. Few Americans recall much except there were some naval engagements and we won the Battle of New Orleans. Many don't realize that Washington D.C. was burned, let alone know about the battles on the Patuxent. The reason for this, I believe, is that there are few novels or films about the war, as compared to the American Revolution and the Civil War.*

"*Bill White has tried to rectify this and has brought this neglected period of our history alive.* The Evening Gun *concludes his War of 1812 Trilogy, with all the drama, panic and confusion that griped Washington, D.C., Baltimore and the Chesapeake region as a whole in 1814. Seen from the viewpoint of the ordinary sailors, the war was not glamorous and all pitched battles. The description of the attack on Baltimore and the writing of the 'Star Spangled Banner' humanize an event that we don't think about, when we sing our National Anthem. The War of 1812 and the sacrifices that were made to preserve our liberty will be better understood, after reading* The Evening Gun. *An enjoyable way to learn history.*"

Doug Alves
Director, Calvert Marine Museum, Solomons, MD

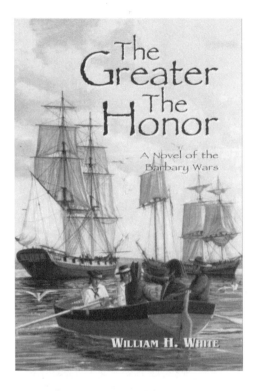

The Greater the Honor

A Novel of the Barbary Wars

"This is a rollicking sea story of the American naval officers who proudly called themselves 'Preble's Boys.' They took their ships to a distant station to defend the new Republic. They cowed the Tripolitans and impressed the British. Finally, Stephen Decatur and the rest of Preble's Boys get their due. Their adventures and courageous acts challenge Jack Aubrey and Horatio Hornblower and they are all the more impressive because their story is true. White's skill as a novelist and his passion for historical accuracy put him on a course with Patrick O'Brian."

William Fowler, Ph.D.
Director, Massachusetts Historical Society

"A fine, fine book. While reading it, I felt like I was carried back in time and witnessed the events with my own eyes."

Clive Cussler
Best-selling author of *Arctic Drift, The Chase, Plague Ship,* and many more. . . .

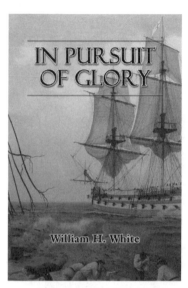

In Pursuit of Glory

"*William White's newest seafaring novel deals with the U.S. Navy as it emerged from the Barbary Wars and enters the difficult period leading into the War of 1812. We see the action through the eyes of Midshipman Oliver Baldwin who had entered the Navy in 1803 and was serving on the ill-starred USS* Chesapeake *as she put to sea from Norfolk. He is eyewitness to HMS* Leopard's *bombardment of* Chesapeake *and its aftermath in the court martial of Commodore James Barron and others in the immediate chain of command. Through his observations and those of his shipmates we are privy to the turbulent emotions wrought by that event and the desire for revenge on the British felt generally throughout the Navy. The protagonist gains further seasoning serving with and under a variety of officers over the next few years. Under the command of Captain Stephen Decatur, Jr., in USS* United States, *Baldwin participates in the battle with HMS* Macedonian *and brings her safely back to Newport as a member of the prize crew. White cleverly recreates the language and manners of days long past while sticking closely to the basic historical facts. He weaves his fictional and historic personages seamlessly into the context of the times and vividly brings to life a time when the U.S. Navy was emerging from infancy to adolescence.*"

   William Dudley, PhD
   Chairman Emeritus Navy Historical Center

"*If you yearn to smell the salt air, hear the wind sing through the rigging, and feel the roll of the sea beneath your feet, but you don't have a ship of your own, step aboard* In Pursuit of Glory. *If you want to duck British cannonballs and ride out storms at sea, all from the safety of your favorite armchair, set sail with William White. If you do, he'll take you on a fascinating voyage into American naval history, and you'll make port edified and entertained.*"

   William Martin
   NY Times Best-selling Author of *The Lost Constitution, Cape Cod, Back Bay, Harvard Yard, Citizen Washington, Annapolis*

For seven years, marine artist Paul Garnett was the shipwright on the "*Bounty*" for MGM, built for their 1962 production "*Mutiny on the Bounty*." The artist's originals can be found at the J. Russell Jinishian Gallery in Fairfield, CT, the Kensington-Stobart Gallery in Salem, MA, and the Art of the Sea in Thomaston, ME. He resides in Newtonville, MA, and is a member of the International Society of Marine Painters. More of his work can be seen at his website, **http://paulgarnett.com/**.

ABOUT THE AUTHOR

Mr. White is a former United States Naval officer with combat service. He is also an avid, life-long sailor. As a maritime historian, he specializes in Age of Sail events in which the United States was a key player and lectures frequently on the impact of these events on our history. He lives in New Jersey. More information can be found on his website, www.seafiction.net.